New

Jorx

# SECOND TIME
# AROUND

WITHDRAWN

This Large Print edition is published by Thorndike Press, USA.

Published in 1998 in the U.S. by arrangement with Dinah Wiener, Ltd.

U.S. Softcover ISBN 0–7862–1486–4 (General Series Edition)

The text of this Large Print edition is unabridged.
Other aspects of the book may vary from the original edition.

Set in 16 pt. New Times Roman.

Printed in Great Britain on acid-free paper.

**Library of Congress Cataloging-in-Publication Data**

Willett, Marcia.
    Second time around / Marcia Willett.
       p.    cm.
    ISBN 0–7862–1486–4 (lg. print : sc : alk. paper)
    †. Large type books.   I. Title.
    [PR6073.I4235S43    1998]
    823'.914—dc21                    98–6683

*To Sue*

# CHAPTER ONE

Market day. The town was busy although there were far fewer visitors about now that the school holidays were over and September was more than halfway through. Tourists jostled to examine the contents of the stalls set up on the quay whilst others made for the café with its tables placed beneath bright umbrellas. It was quite warm enough to sit outside and enjoy a cup of coffee in the sunshine.

Isobel Stangate shifted her weight from one foot to the other and held her collecting tin a little higher. She had positioned herself outside Boots the chemist in a cunning attempt to intercept shoppers as they crossed the road from the car park opposite—and she had not been unsuccessful. She glanced at her watch and fixed her eye meaningly upon a young man who stood on the pavement, waiting to cross. He looked quickly away from her purposeful gaze and, in an attempt to avoid her altogether, sheered off hastily across the road, nearly falling beneath the wheels of a passing car. The driver shouted imprecations and Isobel grinned maliciously as the young man fled, his ears burning with embarrassment.

Years of being dragooned into helping on flag days had given Isobel a cynical outlook. She knew that ladies of a certain age who dressed in navy blue would always put something into the tin. They had stood too often themselves, smiling hopefully and shaking collecting boxes encouragingly, to ignore a fellow sufferer. Young mothers generally allowed their offspring to put a few pennies into the slot and smiled tolerantly as the sticker was placed somewhere upon the child's person. Expensively dressed visitors stared at her brazenly, either passing by without a qualm—or an offering—or pausing to tell her that they wished someone would start up a charity on *their* behalf. The locals would sigh and say, 'What is it *this* time?' as they felt in a pocket or scrabbled for a purse, whilst the lonely ones seized the opportunity for a chat. There were those who would ostentatiously peer at the charity's name on the box and then shake their heads, frowning a little, as if to say, 'Oh, no. I couldn't contribute to *that*.'

Isobel, who was a soft touch and could be relied upon to respond to a cry for help from a busy organiser or committee member, knew them all. She smiled down at a tiny elderly lady, wrinkled and wizened as a nut, who had stopped at her elbow and was peering at the tin whilst struggling to extricate her purse.

'Always someone 'ere,' she said complainingly. 'Ev'ry week. Must think us old age pensioners be made o' money. 'Tis us what should 'ave a collection.'

'Couldn't agree with you more,' agreed Isobel cheerfully. 'You get it organised and I'll come and hold a tin.'

The old woman put ten pence into the box whilst Isobel stuck the paper disc to her ancient jacket.

'Don't forget to take it off when you wash your cardigan,' she said, 'otherwise the glue will make it go all gungy.'

'"Devon against Drugs".' The old woman snorted, squinting down at her newly adorned chest. ''Ow do they afford 'em in the first place? That's what I want to know! I can't 'ardly afford a packet o' tea. 'Ow come these kids can afford drugs?'

'By banging you on the head and stealing your pension,' said Isobel promptly. She smiled at the woman who unexpectedly grinned back at her.

'If you're still 'ere when I come back I'll bring you out a cuppa,' she said.

Isobel laughed. 'I'll hold you to that,' she promised. She watched her pass through the swing door into the chemist and suddenly felt depressed. The poor old thing probably couldn't afford that ten pence. She held the heavy tin invitingly towards a smartly dressed couple who, having parked their brand-new BMW in the car park, had been having coffee at the café on the quay. The woman pretended not to see but her companion smiled patronisingly.

3

'There's too much giving done in this country,' he told Isobel. 'Make people stand on their own two feet, that's what I say. Charity begins at home.'

His wife pulled at his arm, muttering through thin blood-red lips, whilst Isobel suppressed a desire to swing the collecting tin at his smug head. Her depression increased and she looked again at her watch; her two hours were nearly up. She'd promised to stand in for someone at the last moment, agreeing to take the nine-to-eleven stint, and then had woken late and only just made it into Kingsbridge in time to fetch her tin and sheaf of stickers. Having missed breakfast she longed for a cup of coffee and had every intention of stopping off at the Harbour Bookshop when her stint was over. She knew that Pat Abrehart would probably have the kettle boiling. Pat had offered her a part-time job at the bookshop when Isobel's lover had left her and her husband had refused to take her back.

Isobel knew how lucky she was to have even a part-time job in these difficult times and looked forward to her two days each week at the bookshop.

She bent down to allow a small boy to put some pennies into her tin, smiled at his mother and decided that she'd had enough. She folded up the remaining sheets of stickers, tucked the collecting tin under her arm and headed for Mill Street.

Later, feeling refreshed after some coffee and a chat with Pat, she drove out of Kingsbridge and away towards the coast. When Mike had left her, quite callously and suddenly after nearly a year, it had not been the shock that her friends imagined. For several months Isobel had known that she'd made a terrible mistake in leaving Simon; but how to admit it? Everyone—her daughter, her parents, most of her friends—had condemned her for leaving the gentle, loving, caring Simon for the irresponsible rogue that Mike so obviously was. Even now, knowing her mistake, living continually with the results of that mistake, she did not ask herself *why* she had been such a fool. She knew exactly why. After twenty years in a relationship of the utmost security she had been overwhelmed by utter madness. She was bored with kindness, consideration and safety—and the glitter in Mike's eyes and his reckless pursuit had swept away her habitual feelings of loyalty and love.

As she turned on to the lane that led out to Start Point she remembered those exciting days. She had become a stranger, not only to her family and friends, but to herself; a different woman whose only desire was for fun and laughter. The sensible Isobel who organised dinner parties and drove Helen to dancing classes vanished as though she had never been. The passion she felt for Mike reduced the love she had for Simon to a pale cold emotion and she was dazzled by the power of her feelings. The world about her and everything in it seemed larger, brighter, louder, happier; to resist was quite impossible.

Isobel, driving now between tall hedges of dusty fading foliage, sighed for the fool she had been. She had thrown away love, respect, contentment, security; she had mistaken the shadow for the substance and now must live with the consequences. Helen, just sixteen, had been mortified by her mother's behaviour.

'How can you?' she'd cried, resisting Isobel's attempt to draw her close to her, deaf to her explanations. 'Don't touch me! It's disgusting. A woman of your age! How can you do this to Daddy?' She'd refused to see Isobel, despite even Simon's attempts to reason with her.

At what point, wondered Isobel, had she realised that, all through those heady days, Simon's love for her had been like a safety net swinging beneath her as she cavorted on the high wire? Impossible to say. The fever had passed and she had woken one morning thinking of Simon, missing him, wanting him. The game was over but her pride made her hold out a little longer. She went to meet Simon, as she had at intervals, to talk about Helen who still steadfastly refused to see her. Her secret knowledge made the meeting

6

somehow exciting. His continuing love flattered her and she flirted with him just a little, knowing that soon—very soon now— she would make it all up to him. He had watched her, smiling a little, his affection for her still apparent in his eyes. She'd hugged him when they parted and felt his unguarded response with a kind of triumph. Soon, very soon now . . .

When Mike left it had been almost a relief and she prepared for her return with all the confidence of the Prodigal Son but with none of his humility. Simon had been gentle but adamant. Yes, he loved her; yes, he missed her but he would never be able to trust her again. He was not prepared to risk himself. He listened to her explanations and her pleas but refused to be moved. Knowing that stubbornness was one of his less attractive traits, Isobel withdrew and went to see her mother with whom Helen was spending a few days of half term. Her mother received the news of her proposed return coolly. Her sympathy had been completely with Simon, whom she loved, and her adored granddaughter. Presently Isobel found herself alone with Helen.

'What did you expect?' asked her daughter. 'Did you expect him to fall on his knees and kiss your feet?'

'No,' said Isobel wearily—but she knew that she had expected just that. 'Please, Helen, try

7

to understand. I made a terrible mistake. Can't you forgive me?'

'No,' said Helen baldly. 'I just feel shame for you. Poor Daddy . . .'

'Look!' cried Isobel. 'Look! I fell in love with Mike. It was like a kind of madness. An illness. You're seventeen, Helen. Haven't you felt like that about a boy? Mad about him one day, gone right off him the next . . .?'

She stopped and shook her head hopelessly. Helen was regarding her with scorn.

'Surely at your age you know the difference between real love and infatuation, don't you?' she asked contemptuously.

'Obviously not.' Isobel tried to smile. She knew how badly she had hurt her daughter and that Helen's cruelty was the measure of that hurt. 'I know now that it was Daddy I loved all along.'

'That's your problem,' said Helen.

Now, two years on, nothing had altered. Isobel changed down into second gear and swung into the track that twisted off from the road and bumped its way down towards the sea. She negotiated the sharp bend to the right, worrying as usual about the car's suspension, remembering her first visit to this remote, hidden-away cove. She'd seen the advertisement in the *Western Morning News* when she was wondering where she should go and what she should do. The offer of a small cottage and use of a car in return for cleaning and shopping was too good to refuse and Isobel accepted the conditions and settled in with relief. Simon, it seemed, was prepared to support her but Isobel's pride rebelled against it. She needed to be independent of him but wanted to stay near Plymouth in case Simon underwent a change of heart. Perhaps his pride needed time to recover. When Helen went off to university Simon sold the Plymouth town house and moved to Modbury. Now he was barely twenty minutes away from Isobel.

The beach opened out fanwise before her. Here the track divided. The left-hand fork ended in an open area behind an old stone house. She drove the Morris Traveller into a dilapidated building built into the rock behind this odd-looking house, which was constructed on three levels and faced out to sea, and, having collected her shopping from the back seat, she followed the track along the back of the beach. Across the small cove from the stone house a tiny cottage perched above a boathouse, backed into the cliff on its small plateau of rock. This had been her home for nearly two years; her wage from her job at the bookshop plus a minute income from the legacy her father had left her just enabled her to survive.

Isobel climbed the rocky steps to her door and went inside. This door, set in the side of the cottage, opened into a small lobby. Opposite the front door was the door into the kitchen, behind which was the bathroom and lavatory. A second door led from the kitchen into the sitting room. The cottage was both cramped and damp but the view from all four windows was more than enough to compensate for these inconveniences. She recalled how she had run up the stairs which rose from the sitting room to the two bedrooms above and how she had gone from room to room, gazing out on to the sea and the cliffs, her worries forgotten, her heartache soothed. She refused to be alarmed by the spectres of damp and cold, of sea mists and gales. This was where she wanted to be. The owner smiled sceptically at Isobel's delighted ravings and suggested a three-month trial.

As she packed away her shopping Isobel chuckled to herself as she remembered Mathilda Rainbird's expression. It was, she'd pointed out in her precise old voice, an exceptionally mild and sunny November day. Perhaps Isobel should restrain her excitement until she'd experienced a few weeks of wet weather? Isobel had insisted that she loved the rain. Mathilda inclined her head politely and suggested that Isobel should look over the house which it would be her duty to clean. It was one of the strangest houses she'd ever seen. Each seaward-facing room on all three floors had its own balcony and the views were just as spectacular as those from the cottage. The kitchen-living room and the dining room—

now relegated to a storeroom—took up most of the ground floor along with a walk-in larder, a scullery and a lavatory. A solid-fuel Rayburn which, thought Isobel with dismay, must have been with Mrs Noah in the ark, kept this floor warm and dry and helped to heat Mathilda's bedroom which was directly above it. There was a second big bedroom on the first floor and a bathroom. Above again were the drawing room and a study.

As they toiled from floor to floor, Mathilda gave Isobel a brief history of the place. Her father had bought the three buildings at the end of the nineteenth century. At that time they had belonged to an estate which was being broken up; the cottage had been derelict and the boathouse unused. Her father was an Oxford professor, a botanist who studied the plant communities indigenous to the sea-cliffs of the South-West, and he bought the house for a retreat to be used during the long vacation and as a base from which to pursue his studies. He and Mathilda's mother had come to love the place and, after Mathilda was born in 1910, the three of them spent as many weeks together as could be spared each year in happy isolation.

Her mother had died of Spanish influenza in the year following the Great War. As soon as she was old enough Mathilda was sent away to school but, each holiday, she and her father returned to the house in the cove. At the end of the Second World War her father suffered a stroke. Mathilda who had worked with him, collating his notes, writing them up and cataloguing his collections, continued to do so and after his death, and with his College's permission, went on with the great mass of work left to her. Often she undertook similar work for his colleagues and newer research students of the college and so the years passed, calmly and uneventfully.

Now, at eighty-four, she spent a good deal of time reading but, when the weather allowed, she still took out the launch which was kept in the boathouse. Isobel had been alarmed to see her setting off alone for a day's fishing but she grew accustomed to the sight and to hearing the boat puttering out on those clear moonlit nights when Mathilda was unable to sleep. She was undemanding, self-sufficient and undoubtedly odd but Isobel had grown tremendously fond of her. She seemed indifferent to comfort and, should the fire burn low or go out whilst she was immersed in her book, she would merely wrap herself in the old blanket which was thrown across her chair and go on reading.

Isobel cleaned the house, did the washing and the shopping and kept the Rayburn alight. The coke occupied a shed beside the back door and each morning and evening, whatever the weather, Isobel was to be seen lugging in the scuttle and carrying out the ashes. She could understand that gas or oil might be impracticable, so far as they were from other habitations, but she did tentatively mention that an electric stove might be more convenient.

Mathilda raised her eyebrows and Isobel could almost see the words, 'For whom?' forming themselves upon her lips; she began to laugh.

'Apart from which,' pointed out Mathilda, exactly as if the exchange had taken place aloud, 'what should we do when we have a power cut? We have a great many in the winter, you know.'

This was true. When the great south-westerly gales brought the seas thundering into the cove—almost to their very doors—and the ground seemed to shake beneath her feet Isobel was glad to huddle in the big kitchen beside the Rayburn, whilst Mathilda continued to read by the light of one of the many oil lamps which were placed in handy positions around the house. Sometimes, on these occasions, Mathilda would suggest that Isobel stay the night and, tucked up in the second bedroom clutching a hot-water bottle, Isobel would wonder at life's vagaries that through one foolish action, one terrible mistake, she should be in this undreamed of situation; cut off from her husband and child, with only an old woman for company, listening to the noise of the gale battering against her window.

# CHAPTER TWO

The cove lay at the edge of a rocky combe which ran inland between the cliffs and opened out into a wide valley, rich in pasture and deep woods. A small brook had cut a bed through the combe, running down beside the track and issuing forth on to the beach. In high summer it was little more than a damp patch that barely wet Isobel's shoes as she passed across the sand between house and cottage: but in the winter it gushed out from between the rocks and dug such a deep channel across the beach that a granite slab had been placed so as to make a bridge where it issued forth from the combe.

Overnight the weather had changed from summer to autumn. Late in the afternoon clouds massed in the west and, as the sky darkened, so the sea turned a dull lightless grey. During the evening the wind increased in strength and the waves rode in, high and white-flecked, to crash against the rocks. Towards dawn rain fell in torrents, drumming on the roof, filling the rutted holes along the track and flattening the sea. With the first light the storm passed away to the east but the wind was still high and the water poured down from the moors in a thousand streams and issues.

Mathilda Rainbird paused to watch the

brook bubbling over the beach, stepped across the slab and continued her early morning walk. As usual she carried an old plastic bag over her arm and, as she strolled, she kept an eye open for driftwood. It was neither parsimony nor poverty which prompted Mathilda; merely that she liked to watch the blue and orange flames that flickered over the bleached and salty wood. It was a habit formed in childhood. She bent to pick up a piece which was whiter and smoother than her own old fingers and put it into the bag which already had a very satisfactory bulge. The fruits of the storm; that was what her father had called their gleanings. Sometimes the previous eighty years merged together for Mathilda and she was both child and middle-aged woman at one and the same time. She remembered running along the beach, shouting for the sheer pleasure of the feel of gritty sand beneath her bare feet and the wind tugging at her hair; and, too, she was the older woman who had walked more sedately beside her father's research assistant and protégé, discussing his work as they watched the fishing boats heading out to sea.

She missed Nigel. She had loved him, not with passion but as she might have loved a brother. Their minds chimed together; their habits were similar; each was completely at ease in the other's company. He was in love with a married woman and was content to admire and languish from afar and, after

15

Mathilda's father died, he had continued to spend all his vacations with her at the house in the cove. She had known the fulfilment of hard work and the contentment of a quiet mind. Inexperienced as she was, she knew that no man could ever replace Nigel. She had not the temperament for passion or jealous scenes nor was she disturbed by sexual urges. She enjoyed the companionship of a man who thought as she did but she neither desired him physically nor did she have any tendencies to mother him. She more often than not left him to fend for himself; debating and discussing with him as they prepared their separate meals in the big warm kitchen; reading aloud to him to underline some point as he washed his clothes at the deep ironstone sink. When he died of a brain tumour she felt truly alone for the first time in her life.

It was he who had suggested that the cottage should be renovated so that she could offer accommodation to someone in return for some care and attention. He had worried about her as she grew older; concerned that she seemed unaware of damp or cold and was liable to forget to eat. Often she had nothing in the larder even had she remembered. She had shrugged at the suggestion, prevaricating about cost. Knowing that Professor Rainbird had left her with sufficient income to put the house in order, and seeing this as the only method of protecting her, he bullied her until the job was done and a woman installed. To his relief the system worked. The young woman, a widow, was hard-working and grateful for a roof for herself and her small child. She and Mathilda rubbed along well enough although in almost all respects each might have belonged to a different planet. Then the young widow met a man and was lured away.

By now, Nigel was gravely ill. Mathilda left the cove for the first time for twenty years to travel to Oxford. She was with him at his end and, at the wishes of Nigel and his sister, brought his ashes back with her. On the first clear night following her return she took the boat out of the boathouse, chugged quietly into deep waters, switched off the engine and cast what remained of Nigel upon the smooth silky bosom of the sea. For some while she sat quite still, the boat drifting on the gentle swell, and made her final farewell to her oldest, dearest friend. He had been the last link with her past and now there was no one with whom she could share the mild jokes that had grown up over the years; no one who had known her parents or remembered her as a girl. For the first time Mathilda felt truly old.

When the young woman went away with her lover, Mathilda advertised again. She accepted, now, that it was sensible to have another human being close at hand. To begin with she was unlucky. The first tenant had three noisy children and an estranged husband who would appear from time to time, the worse for drink, and create scenes on the beach or in the cottage—if he could gain access. One day an inspector from the social services arrived in the cove to make certain enquiries; there was a matter of payments for five children and a claim for rent allowance on the cottage. A puzzled Mathilda explained that there were only three children, not five, and that the woman worked in lieu of rent. She pointed out, however, that the three children *seemed* like five. The inspector, who lacked a sense of humour, made notes and went away. A week later, mother and children had disappeared and the cove was restored to its erstwhile serenity. The next occupant was a pale, thin, earnest woman in her thirties who had a passion for practising the Alexander Technique stark naked on the beach each morning. This predilection came as rather a shock for Mathilda, taking her first early morning walk after her new tenant's arrival, but she decided that a polite 'Good morning' was all that was required and passed on her way merely hoping that the woman might not take a chill.

She took more than a chill. It seemed that she had eschewed what she referred to as 'death-dealing' foods—with which, she claimed, the supermarket shelves were packed—and had taken to feeding on the fruits of the hedgerows and the beach. Mathilda found her collapsed on the kitchen floor, vomiting, and silently blessed Nigel, who had insisted that a telephone should be installed. The ambulance carried the woman away and she, too, was seen no more.

Cautiously Mathilda advertised yet again. When Isobel arrived, Mathilda was relieved to note that she looked reassuringly normal and appeared to have no dependants or strange habits; no children to be drowned if not watched; no husband waving cans of beer and bellowing drunkenly; no tendencies to dance unclothed upon the sand. It was apparent from the shopping which she brought home in the elderly Morris that she believed in good old-fashioned death-dealing food and what was more—and this was a tremendous bonus—she could hold an intelligent conversation and play a mean game of Scrabble. Mathilda relaxed and began to enjoy life once more. During the ensuing months life in the cove settled down and the two women became easy in their companionship.

During the winter evenings a closer relationship developed. This was because Isobel was lonely and had a need to talk to someone rather than because Mathilda was a natural confidante. The fact that she had been so much alone meant that she had lived through few of the experiences which Isobel described and she listened with surprise as Isobel explained how she had felt and the recent dramas she had undergone. Mathilda,

19

who was used to a more cerebral approach to life, began to be interested in these emotional outpourings. It was impossible for her to enter into Isobel's feelings but she listened to her intelligently and reserved her conclusions until Isobel demanded them.

This was a whole new procedure for Isobel. Her friends were only too ready to join in, cite their own similar cases, offer advice. Her mother argued, but not necessarily constructively, and Simon gently but firmly stonewalled any discussion which became too personal. Mathilda took these outpourings on to a completely different level which forced Isobel to think more carefully than usual.

'Surely you can see,' Isobel would cry, banging pans about upon the Rayburn—she had taken to cooking for Mathilda, fearful that she would fade away entirely if left to fend for herself—'surely *anyone* can see why I left Simon! Isn't it natural to seize happiness when it's offered?'

At this point her mother would have talked about duties and responsibilities and her divorced friends would have muttered sympathetically. Mathilda, huddled in the Windsor chair beside the Rayburn with the inevitable book upon her lap, would remain silent until Isobel looked at her.

'Honestly, Mathilda,' she would say pleadingly, 'don't you think that happiness is the only thing that matters in the end?'

Confronted, Mathilda would raise her still beautiful slate-blue eyes from the pages of her book.

'It all depends on what you mean—' Mathilda was a disciple of Professor Joad—'it really all depends on what you mean by "happiness".'

'Oh, for heaven's sake!' Isobel would groan, bashing about with a spoon in the soup. 'Not that "it all depends what you mean" stuff, Mathilda.'

'But how do you define happiness? Do you mean joy? Or do you mean contentment? If you mean some kind of ephemeral excitement bound up with physical gratification, then I must reject your values. It certainly is not all that matters in the end.'

Sighing deeply and rolling her eyes in frustration, Isobel would ladle the soup into bowls.

'How would you know?' she'd grumble. 'Stuck down here for most of your life.'

'Why ask me then?' asked Mathilda serenely, standing up and moving to the table.

Seated opposite—it had been agreed that, since Isobel had taken over the cooking, she should feed with Mathilda and at her expense—Isobel wondered why. She recognised that there was something tough in Mathilda, some unchanging point of reference, against which she could measure her own ideals. It was rather odd, and she would never

21

admit it, but she felt as if she were growing; developing in some vital manner. She'd grinned at the old woman across the table—a misused and mistreated mahogany Georgian breakfast table on a carved pedestal leg—and sighed with a curious contentment.

'I don't know why,' she'd answered.

Remembering this conversation on the quiet grey morning after the storm, Mathilda glanced up at the windows of the small cottage perched on its rocky plateau. The curtains were still tightly drawn. Isobel was not an early riser and it was a while yet until she needed to be off to the bookshop. Mathilda reached the furthest point of the cove and stood for a moment staring out to sea, thinking about Nigel. She was beginning to realise how lucky she'd been to have shared such a satisfying relationship with him; lucky that he'd been content to adore his beloved from afar. To one of Mathilda's temperament, Isobel's life sounded too fraught to contemplate.

She turned back across the firm wet gleaming sand at the water's edge, her bag bumping gently against her leg. It had been in her mind to suggest that Isobel should move into the house for the winter but something prevented her; some inner conviction that it was wise to preserve that small measure of independence and privacy that existed between them. Privacy had always been a necessary part of Mathilda's existence and she was never lonely. It was fortunate that the cove could only be reached by the track from the landward side and although boats occasionally anchored off the beach during the summer and people swam from them and picnicked, few ever ventured ashore.

She entered the house by the side door and, dropping the bag of firewood at the bottom of the stairs, went on into the kitchen to prepare some breakfast. This was the one meal of the day which the two women rarely shared, both agreeing that early morning was a time for silence. Even when Isobel stopped overnight with Mathilda they still breakfasted separately simply because Mathilda rose so much earlier. Now she took some bread from the crock and, dusting off the green mould which adhered to its crust, she placed it on the bread board and proceeded to hack two uneven slices from the parent loaf. She was too indifferent to food to make any effort to make a meal attractive or appetising. Pushing the slices with difficulty into the toaster she rooted around for the butter and found a plate and a knife. She shoved aside the usual muddle of letters and papers and books, which lived permanently on the once beautiful table, assembled her breakfast and sat herself down.

However hard she tried, Isobel was quite incapable of keeping Mathilda's living areas tidy but at least everything was clean. The old cream-coloured Rayburn had cost her some despairing moments but the kitchen looked welcoming, even if it was not the modern idea of a work station. She had realised that Mathilda liked to live in the kitchen as well as to cook and eat in it and that the shelves of books, the aged sofa by the French windows which led on to the balcony and the ability to use the table as a desk were far more important to Mathilda than dishwashers, microwaves and high-speed mixers.

Mathilda finished her breakfast, put the plate and knife in the deep old sink and, collecting her bag of wood, began the climb upstairs to the study. Here she was working on an idea which had occurred to her very recently and she went at once to the large kneehole desk, with its scratched green leather inlay, which resided opposite the fireplace. She stood for a while, looking at papers, studying her notes, frowning a little. It was a large room with glass-fronted bookcases in each of the alcoves on either side of the fireplace whilst the remaining areas of faded wallpaper were almost hidden by the paintings which covered the walls; some originals, some prints. Above the fireplace hung a tapestry which Mathilda's mother had worked nearly eighty years before. The floor was carpeted by a thick Turkey rug whilst several sagging but still comfortable armchairs were placed strategically about the room. Here Mathilda was happiest.

Presently she crossed to the French windows

and, pushing them open, went out on to the balcony. There was a brightness now to the morning and she saw that Isobel's curtains had been drawn back. Even as she watched, Isobel came hurrying out, almost running, the long skirt flapping round her bare ankles, a silk scarf floating at her throat. Mathilda watched her leap across the brook and disappear behind the house. She heard the sound of the Morris's engine start up and gradually fade as it bumped its way up the track. As it did so, Mathilda remembered the rest of the conversation she'd been thinking of earlier.

'And did you find happiness?' she'd asked Isobel at length. There had been a long silence.

'No,' said Isobel at last. 'But it was worth trying for, surely?'

'That rather depends,' replied Mathilda, 'on what you lost in the attempt.'

There had been a longer, deeper silence and finally Isobel had risen to fetch the cheese and had begun to talk about something entirely different.

Mathilda stood for some time on the balcony, lost in thought. The golden glow behind the cloud brightened and the sun's warmth began to shred the mist, drawing it up, dissolving it. The small wavelets broke decorously against the sand and the brook gurgled cheerfully in the combe behind the house. Mathilda went back into the study and settled herself at the desk.

# CHAPTER THREE

A week later the autumn made its presence known with a more determined ferocity. The equinoctial gales roared in from the west bringing heavy rain. The trees bowed beneath their passing and the last plums and apples were shaken from the boughs. Sailors hurried to secure their boats or take them off the rivers and estuaries for the winter and the locals put away their espadrilles and placed gumboots in readiness by back doors. The swallows had left for the south and only the martins were still to be seen, swooping and diving for insects, their second brood still in the nest.

The pub car park was nearly empty. Isobel halted the Morris beside Simon's hatchback and switched off the engine. She felt the usual uprush of excitement at the thought of seeing him and she altered the angle of the driving mirror so as to peer at herself in the gloomy light of early evening. She'd dragged her dark hair back, securing it with a clip at the nape of her neck, and she still could not decide whether this made her look sophisticated and distinguished or merely older and rather severe. Perhaps her face was too thin, too bony to take such a style? She grimaced at her reflection to give herself courage, collected her bag and slid out of the car with her coat round her shoulders to protect her from the rain. As she locked the door she bent to peer through Simon's window. His car was both clean and tidy, inside and out, and she sighed as she remembered how she'd teased him about his habit of cleaning it every weekend.

He was sitting in a corner, well away from the bar, but got to his feet the moment he saw her. She experienced the familiar shock of seeing as a stranger he who had been her lover, husband, father of her child. This knowledge lent an underlying excitement to all her dealings with him and sometimes she felt almost breathless with longing for him. He bent his head to receive her kiss and she was seized with a desire to hold him and shout at him. 'Let's stop all this politeness and pretence!' she wanted to cry. 'It was a silly mistake. It's all over and I'll never do anything like it again. It's cost too much! Please let's go back to how we were.' Instead she sat down and smiled at him.

'Spritzer, please. Everything OK?'

'Everything's fine.'

He turned away to the bar and she watched him order the drinks. He looked easy and relaxed in his jeans and sweatshirt, his greying hair a little longer than when they had been together. He was head of the English department at one of Plymouth's comprehensive schools and he was both popular and effective. Isobel mentally

27

prepared the questions she would ask about Helen—the supposed reason for this meeting—and wondered why he had never invited her to his new home at Modbury. It had been a tremendous shock when he'd told her that he wanted to sell the house in Plymouth. Still in thrall to Mike she'd made no protest and had signed the forms obligingly but it had come as an unwelcome surprise to see Simon make such a decision without her advice. That was when she'd realised that, although she was happy with Mike, she was still counting on Simon being there.

I wanted to have my cake and eat it, she thought, watching Simon pocketing his change and picking up the two glasses.

It had hurt when he had chosen the house in Modbury without consulting her, although he had asked her which pieces of furniture or ornaments she would like to take. She knew then that she'd wanted her erstwhile home to stay exactly as it was and, after some reflection, she'd taken only one or two small special things of her own and suggested that he kept the rest himself. Since the Modbury house was smaller than the town house certain items were now superfluous and, having decided between them what was no longer required, it was agreed that these things should be sold or taken to the dump. Later, Isobel decided that she was glad that Simon had made the move. It might be easier to start again in a new place . . . except that there was no suggestion that a new start was desirable to him.

Isobel took her glass and sipped at her spritzer. Simon sat opposite, took a pull at his beer and raised his eyebrows.

'So . . .' He let it hang in the air; not quite a question.

'I just wanted to ask about Helen,' Isobel said quickly. 'How the holidays went, whether there's any sign of relenting. That sort of thing. Has she gone back to Durham?'

'Yes, I drove her up at the weekend.' Simon moved a little in his chair, rather as if he found the subject an awkward one. 'Term doesn't start for a week or two but she's moving out of hall and going into a house with a group of friends. Very nice it is too. A little Victorian crescent near the cathedral.'

Isobel was silent. The pain made it impossible for her to speak. That she was not allowed to take part in her daughter's life was unbearable and she quite suddenly remembered Mathilda's words. *'That rather depends on what you lost in the attempt . . .'* Oh, far too much, she cried silently.

'She's fine,' said Simon gently. 'Honestly. She's got some really nice friends and she's doing well.'

Isobel nodded, swallowing hard and trying to smile. 'I'm so pleased,' she said. 'I just wish that I could see her. You know . . .'

'I know,' he agreed. 'I'm really sorry, love.

29

But now that she's over eighteen it's up to her. I do my best to make her see it all rationally.'

'I know you do.' She smiled more easily; the endearment had been absurdly comforting. 'I know. It's just the years are going by.' She looked at him. 'And how are you?'

'Oh.' He seemed taken aback by the direct question. 'Oh, OK. Much the same.' He looked away from her intense stare, made uncomfortable by it.

'Oh, Simon,' she sighed. 'It all seems so silly. Such a waste.'

'Yes. Well . . .' He hesitated, unwilling to point out that it was her doing.

'I know,' she said quickly. 'It's my fault. Do you think I don't tell myself that?'

'Please, Isobel.' He looked extremely distressed. 'Please don't go on. I'm sure that Helen will come round. She's growing up. You must be patient.'

'It's not just Helen,' she said—and stopped.

'I know it isn't,' Simon said, so bleakly that she looked at him quickly, hopefully. 'Oh, Izzy . . .'

There was something almost despairing in his tone and, at the sound of the nickname he had used so often in the past, she found the courage to reach out and touch his hand.

'Honestly, Simon,' she said, 'I never really loved Mike. I know that now. It was like I was ill or something. Mad. You know? Couldn't we . . .?'

'Look.' He took her hand and held it tightly, biting his lip, searching for words. 'The thing is . . .' He sighed and released her. 'It's no good,' he said flatly. 'There's someone else, Isobel. Sorry, but it's best to say it straight out.'

She sat back quickly, clasping her hands together. 'I . . . see.'

'I should have said something before,' he continued wretchedly. 'I knew how your mind was working but I couldn't bring myself to hurt you.'

'That's generous of you, in the circumstances,' she said. She picked up her glass and took a long swallow. Simon stared at the table. 'Do . . . do I know her?'

He hesitated so long that she knew that she must and her shocked mind ranged briefly over their friends.

'It's Sally Curtis,' he said at last.

Sally Curtis. Sally of the long brown hair and green eyes who taught History; Sally who had lost husband and child in a car crash and had bravely started a new life; Sally whom she had invited to a barbecue at the town house and with whom she had sympathised; Sally who had encouraged Helen with her history; Sally . . . He was watching her compassionately.

'She's been a good friend,' he said.

'Yes,' said Isobel. 'I'm sure she has. And Helen adores her.'

'That is a bonus,' he agreed. 'I'm sorry, Isobel—'

'No, no,' she interrupted him quickly, 'I should have guessed there was someone. After all, why shouldn't you and . . . and Sally . . .'

'Shall I get you another drink?' he asked anxiously.

'No,' she said abruptly. 'No. Just go, would you, Simon? Sorry. It's just . . . Please go.'

He finished his beer and stood up, his eyes genuinely worried. 'Will you be OK?'

'Of course I will. I just want to sit quiet.' Go, she begged silently. Just go before I burst into tears or do something bloody humiliating. For God's sake *go*!

'I'll be in touch.' She felt his hand briefly on her shoulder. 'Take care.'

She didn't look up until she heard the door close behind him. She stared straight ahead, seeing nothing. So that was that. What a fool she'd been! Humiliation swept over her, staining her cheeks. Simon and Sally Curtis . . . Sally who was only thirty-something; Sally whom Helen adored and now Simon adored also. The pain was so acute that she could barely breathe and she sat for some moments making an attempt to calm herself. The young barman—probably a student—came to collect Simon's empty glass. He glanced at her curiously and Isobel attempted to smile at him. It was a failure. Her lips shook and she picked up her bag and went out into the windy car park. A gust of wind drove the rain horizontally and she held her coat over her head as she

32

hurried to the car. Once inside she fumbled with her keys and realised that her hands were trembling. Suddenly she wanted to be back at the cove, tucked away inside her little cottage or—better still—with Mathilda in her tall grey house. Just being with Mathilda would calm and strengthen her.

Isobel started the engine and switched on the windscreen wipers. They wiped away the rain but not her tears and she dragged her hand angrily across her eyes before she pulled out on to the road and headed for the cove.

\*    \*    \*

The kitchen was empty. Out of habit Isobel went round tidying up, locking the French windows and drawing the curtains before going upstairs. Having reached the landing she paused to listen at Mathilda's bedroom door before climbing on again, up to the top floor. The study was empty so she opened the drawing room door and looked inside. Mathilda sat reading beside a fire which had burned down to little more than ashes, undisturbed by the rain which streamed down the darkened window panes or the wind which rattled at the catches.

'Honestly, Mathilda.' Isobel shut the door behind her and crossed the room to the French windows. 'You could at least keep the fire going. Aren't you cold?'

33

Mathilda raised her eyes from her book and watched Isobel drag the curtains together. Even she detected a brittle note in the younger woman's voice.

'I didn't notice,' she said. 'Is it dark already?'

Isobel sighed and began to rake the ashes together, putting on small pieces of wood until the fire blazed up. 'You're hopeless,' she said.

'So you keep telling me,' said Mathilda without rancour.

Isobel laughed. 'Hopeless and impossible. Have you had any supper?'

Mathilda's brow wrinkled thoughtfully. 'Soup?' she suggested cautiously.

'That was lunch,' sighed Isobel. 'I left you a casserole in the bottom oven. I *did* tell you.'

'Well, now we can share it.' Mathilda put a marker between the pages of her book and prepared to rise. 'Are you hungry?'

No, thought Isobel. It would choke me to swallow even a spoonful. She remembered that she had planned that she and Simon would be eating together this evening, so sure had she been that he was weakening.

'I've had some supper,' she said aloud. 'But I'll come and watch you eat yours.'

'Good idea. And then we'll have a game of Scrabble.'

Isobel piled some more logs on the fire and put the discarded book on the table beside Mathilda's chair. She was not surprised to see that it was Alain-Fournier's *Le Grand*

*Meaulnes* in the French. It might easily have been *The Hunting of the Snark*. Months ago she'd asked Mathilda how she was able to read Lewis Carroll one day and Descartes the next. Mathilda pondered. 'They were both mathematicians, you know,' she'd said at last.

*       *       *

Later they sat together, a low table drawn up between them before the fire. After the crowded, active atmosphere of the study the drawing room was almost stark in its austerity; one or two large paintings on the otherwise empty walls; a long sofa against the wall opposite the fireplace; two armchairs pulled up to the fire; a bureau in an alcove. There were the usual bookshelves in the second alcove but it seemed to Isobel that all of Mathilda's taste and personality had been crammed into the study.

Isobel rearranged the Scrabble tiles on her rack and wrenched her mind away from Simon and Sally. Instead she thought of an article she'd read only that morning.

'Do you believe in euthanasia?' she asked abruptly.

Mathilda began to place her tiles on the board. 'Of course I do,' she said.

Isobel stared at her, surprised at such a swift and unqualified reply. Mathilda met her gaze and raised her eyebrows.

35

'I must believe in it,' she said reasonably. 'After all, it exists. It happens. How could I not believe in it?'

'Oh, honestly!' said Isobel impatiently. 'You're so pedantic, Mathilda. You know what I mean.'

'If you are asking if I *approve* of it then you should say so,' replied the old woman. 'If I am pedantic, you are sloppy. You were a teacher. You should know better.'

'I taught very young children,' said Isobel, as though that excused it.

'All the more reason for accuracy,' observed Mathilda.

'But do you?' persisted Isobel. 'Do you approve?'

'It all depends,' began Mathilda—and smiled at Isobel's groan. 'It depends on the state of the person at the time. If he is terminally ill and in his right mind I think that he should have as much right to choose the manner of his death just as he has chosen the manner in which he has lived.'

'I notice you say "he"?'

'A manner of speech,' murmured Mathilda, who had been thinking about Nigel.

She had visited him in hospital after his chemotherapy treatment. Even now the remembrance had the power to shock her. 'That's right, love. Come to see your dad?' the man in the next bed had asked. Mathilda, who was several years older than Nigel, had looked

36

down on the yellow, bald, mummified head, too horrified to explain that they were not related. Nigel had been unable to communicate and she had sat clutching the claw that had been his hand, staring into the open lashless eyes, her heart pierced with pain.

'But is it right for someone to kill another person? Even if it is a mercy killing?'

I would have killed Nigel, thought Mathilda. I would have released him from the terrible indignity of those final weeks.

'And don't say "it all depends",' warned Isobel.

'But it does, you see. It depends whether the killer is able to bear the responsibility. Whether the sufferer actually desires release or whether the killer merely thinks he—or she—does . . . It is all extremely complicated.'

'People cling to life,' mused Isobel. 'They say, "Oh, knock me on the head if I get like that," but when the time comes they decide they've changed their minds.'

'This life is all we know,' said Mathilda putting her last tile in place. 'It is the human condition to cling to what we know.'

'Even if it's pretty awful. Mathilda! You can't have that! *Pribble*? I've never heard of it.'

'Look it up.' Mathilda pushed the dictionary towards her. 'It's a perfectly good word meaning "pointless chattering". Go on. Look it up.'

'If you will use a pre-war dictionary,'

grumbled Isobel. 'Pre-Boer War . . .'

'Are you going to stay the night?' asked Mathilda, taking more tiles from the bag.

'I think I will,' said Isobel, listening to the sea pounding against the rocks, the windows rattling beneath the assault of the wind. 'If that's OK?'

'Of course.' Mathilda felt relieved, although she was not quite certain why. It would never have occurred to her to question Isobel but she was aware of a tension in the younger woman.

'Thanks.' Suddenly Isobel dreaded the moment when she would be alone in bed, unable then to postpone any longer the pictures of Simon and Sally together. She gave thanks that, because she slept so badly, Mathilda generally went to bed late. 'I'll make us a hot drink when we've finished this game,' she promised. 'OK. My turn. Wait till you see this one!'

Mathilda jotted down her score carefully. Her thoughts of Nigel had disturbed her and she was in some measure glad of Isobel's company. The fire burned cheerfully, the casserole had been delicious, and she was grateful for the younger woman's care which went far beyond her duties. She wished that she could help Isobel but did not know how. At least they could bear each other's company through this wild night and maybe in the morning the storm would have passed.

# CHAPTER FOUR

It was a few days after her meeting with Simon before Isobel took in the whole meaning of what he had told her. Just as she had—albeit subconsciously—used the knowledge of his love as a safety net during her affair with Mike, so had she regarded their eventually coming back together as a certainty. Simon had loved her so much, with such care and consideration and loyalty, that she could not seriously contemplate his love ever dying. She had even rather enjoyed their meetings, seeing them almost as a prelude to a new, more exciting relationship. Although she had been taken aback when he did not immediately 'kiss her feet', as Helen had put it, deep down she had been sure that she would win him back.

The shock of realising that there had been someone else numbed her and occupied her every waking thought. She recalled each single meeting and conversation she had ever had with Sally, even morbidly wondering if Simon had been attracted to her before Mike had appeared on the scene. She pictured them together and made herself miserable by contemplating Sally's happy, easy relationship with Helen. It was at this point that Isobel began to think about her own future. With Sally around it seemed unlikely that Helen would ever need her own mother again.

Isobel knew now how much she had counted on resuming her marriage with Simon as a route back to her daughter. When she and Simon were living together once more Helen would be confronted with the necessity of seeing and communicating with her. It would be unavoidable, unless Helen gave up coming home altogether. Isobel had been confident that this would be the last hurdle. Now she saw her hopes and plans crumbling to nothing. She was the outsider with no rights to either Simon or Helen. She tried to deal with this as she went about her work, looking after Mathilda, shopping, cleaning and working at the bookshop.

She was grateful for those two days a week in Mill Street. She and Pat often laughed—sometimes rather bitterly—when customers or friends observed what fun it must be to work in a bookshop. They seemed to imagine that the days passed in a leisurely manner, poring over this book or that and drinking coffee. These people had no notion of the business of unpacking boxes of books, ordering new ones, talking to suppliers, tracking down books for customers who had very few details apart from the titles, answering the telephone, wrestling with the computer; nor how much one's feet ached at the end of the day. Most lunchtimes Isobel sat out in the back office with a sandwich but generally the telephone would ring or a customer would appear and her sandwich would have to be abandoned, bites snatched at odd moments during the afternoon. Occasionally she would escape next door to The Hermitage and in the warmer months would sit out in the garden with her drink, gratefully breathing in the fresh air.

It was Pat who made her think about her future. When Isobel told her what had happened, Pat's concern was for how Isobel would survive. She pointed out that she could offer her no more than her two days at the bookshop; perhaps she should think of going back to teaching? Isobel, who had not yet considered this aspect of her troubles, had remarked that she had Mathilda.

'But for how long?' asked Pat.

During the next few days Isobel brooded on this. Until Simon had shattered her hopes she had seen the future somewhat hazily. She could manage on what she was earning but she had never looked upon her work, either at the bookshop or with Mathilda, as a long-term arrangement. At some point she and Simon would be back together in the house at Modbury and all would be well. She had applied for teaching posts, which were very few and far between, but the competition was fierce and she had not been lucky. Then her job with Pat had turned up, along with Mathilda's advertisement, and she had put the idea of teaching on the back burner, so to speak. Now

Pat's question haunted her. Mathilda was old and frail. What would happen if she should die? Isobel began to scour the papers in the hope of seeing teaching posts advertised and wondered who would inherit the house in the cove.

This question was answered almost immediately. The storms subsided and gentler, warmer weather set in. Isobel wandered on the cliffs above the beach but even the breathtaking beauty of the scene failed to raise her spirits. The sea appeared to be resting peacefully against the land, a world away from the recent storms. Beneath the cliffs the water was a pure translucent turquoise fading away, as far as the eye could see, to a softer blue which reflected the cloudless sky until both sea and sky seemed to merge into infinity. Isobel followed the tracks through heather and gorse, which had flowered together in a blaze of colour, and turned inland across the stunted grass towards the fields. A chiffchaff sung his two notes from a hazel bush and the hedges were full of blackberries. She untied the cotton scarf she wore at her throat and began to pick the berries. Mathilda might enjoy a blackberry and apple pie.

Her heart was heavy, however, and even this task seemed pointless and exhausting. Everything tired her and her natural vitality and enthusiasm had deserted her. She sat down upon a boulder, turning her face to the sun, her fingers picking idly at the crumbly dry lichen on the rough pitted stone. At the sudden beating of wings and the raucous cry of a gull she opened her eyes and stared out across to Start Point; at the jagged bony spine of the cliff as it descended towards the sea and at the white column of the lighthouse. The tranquillity of the scene, the sheer timelessness of sea and rock, soothed her and presently she picked up her handkerchief and its contents, strolled back across the cliff and descended the steps which led down to the back of her cottage. Soon the cove would be in shadow and she shivered a little as she thought of the winter drawing on. She knew that she simply must not allow despair to swamp her nor self-pity deaden her will to survive. She let herself into the kitchen which was still warm from a day of sunshine and put the blackberries on the table, determined to make a pie for supper.

Her kitchen was hardly less basic than Mathilda's but at least she had a microwave and an electric mixer. The room was filled with the light from the sea; a white shaking light which continually formed, dissolved and re-formed into watery patterns on the whitewashed walls. On certain days Isobel felt that she was living underwater. She loved it and she loved the sound of the sea shushing across the sand; hissing and sucking at the land as if it were loath to leave it behind as it retreated; whispering secretly across it as it returned.

43

At first she had been fascinated by the changing scene; the colour of the water as it reflected a cloudy sky; the dark outline of the Mew stone; the tall day beacon above Kingswear shining white in the evening sunshine. She had sat late at her bedroom window watching the moon rise clear from a skein of cloud and ride high above the black silk of the sea, its silver path running almost to her very door; and had woken early to see the sun rolling up out of the cliffs to the east to set the water blazing with orange and gold. After a while she had learned to close her curtains against these temptations lest she be too tired to work; but she never grew indifferent to her surroundings. Even now she was aware of the glory all about her and, even if it did not set her spirits leaping with joy, it brought a measure of comfort to her unhappy heart.

Isobel took off her jacket and concentrated on the pie. Now that she did so much cooking for Mathilda she was always finding that certain items were no longer to hand. This afternoon it was her pie dish which was missing; no doubt languishing in Mathilda's kitchen where it had been washed up after they had eaten their last pie together. Isobel debated with herself. Should she run over to fetch the dish or take the ingredients and make the pie in Mathilda's kitchen? She knew that the pie would taste better if cooked in the Rayburn—apart from which she needed company. Gathering up the things she required, she piled them into a basket and went out across the cove. The shadow of the cliff stretched nearly to the water's edge and she was glad to reach the warmth of Mathilda's kitchen. She set the basket on the table, checked the Rayburn and glanced at her watch. Whilst the Rayburn pulled up a little to the necessary temperature she would make Mathilda a cup of tea.

Mathilda was in the study, working at the big desk. Isobel set the tray on the fender and paused to throw a log on the fire.

'Tea,' she announced. 'I'm making a blackberry and apple pie for supper but the blackberries taste a bit funny. Sort of mushy. I hope it'll be OK. Isn't the Devil supposed to spit on them at Michaelmas or something?'

'I think,' said Mathilda, without turning round, 'that the blame should be laid at the door of the flesh fly. He dribbles saliva on them so as to be able to suck up the juice.'

'Eeuch!' Isobel made a face. 'Honestly, Mathilda, I wish you hadn't told me. That's disgusting, isn't it?'

'That depends on whether you are a flesh fly,' replied Mathilda. 'Thank you. I should like some tea. I'm trying to work out my family tree.'

'Heavens!' Isobel kneeled down by the fender and began to pour the tea, attempting meanwhile to expel the taste of flesh fly saliva from her mouth. She scraped at her tongue with her teeth, quite certain now that it was coated with it. 'Whyever?'

'I'm looking for a beneficiary,' replied the old woman. 'I've decided to change my will.'

Isobel's hands were arrested in the act of adding milk; the flesh fly was utterly expunged from her mind—and mouth. 'Your will?'

'Mmm.' Mathilda swivelled round in her chair to look at her. 'I had decided to endow a studentship at my father's old college but I disapprove of their new policy of giving the highest proportion of places to foreign students who can afford to pay huge fees. And now I hear that they are intending to discontinue his field of study in favour of the peat bog. Apparently, with all this fuss about preserving peat it is hoped that it will attract more funding.'

'I see,' said Isobel. She carried the cup across and placed it on the desk. 'So how far have you got?' Her heart was hurrying a little as she tried to frame the words as carelessly as possible. 'I hope you're not planning to pop off just yet, Mathilda?'

'Not just yet,' said Mathilda comfortably, 'but I do want to get this sorted out.'

Isobel stared down at the papers upon which Mathilda's neat writing was quite clear. Names stared up at her. 'Who are Maria and Albert Holmes?' she asked.

'Maria was my father's sister.' Mathilda

sipped her tea. 'She married Albert Holmes and had three children. Ruth died young and Peter and John were both killed in the Great War but John had already married a woman called Ada and had a son by her.'

'It's fascinating.' Isobel peered at the names and the dates. 'What about your mother's family?'

Mathilda shook her head. 'I never knew my mother's family. I can very vaguely remember an old woman who might have been my grandmother but I think she must have died whilst I was still very young. My mother died when I was ten and my father was not good at keeping in touch with relatives. Even with his own family.'

'I can believe that,' murmured Isobel, who guessed that Mathilda was much like her father. 'And who are William and Edith Rainbird?'

'William was my second cousin and died at Dunkirk.' Mathilda frowned. 'It's all rather complicated.'

'And how have you tracked down these people?'

'Some of it was in the family bible and I found a few notes amongst my father's papers but a friend of mine in London is putting in the real work,' admitted Mathilda. She replaced her cup in its saucer and looked at Isobel. She noticed that she was looking thinner, sharper around the nose and cheekbones, and the old

47

woman studied her for a moment. 'Perhaps you should have a holiday?' she suggested.

Isobel, surprised both at the sudden change of subject and that Mathilda should make such a personal remark, looked at her quickly. 'Do I look as if I need one?'

'You do rather,' said Mathilda bluntly. 'Are you losing weight?'

'I'm worried in case you're thinking of turning me out,' replied Isobel lightly. 'In favour of all these relations.'

'Oh, I shan't do that.' Mathilda shook her head. 'You will have all the rights of a sitting tenant. No one shall turn you out.'

'That's a comfort.' Isobel tried to maintain her lightness of tone, wondering whether the beneficiary would require a housekeeper and, if not, how she, Isobel, would afford the rent of her little cottage. 'So which one have you decided on?'

'There appear to be three possible contenders,' said Mathilda. 'Edward Holmes married the year after I was born so, though it's unlikely he's still alive, he might have offspring. Then William married in 1914. He was the one who died at Dunkirk. Apparently he had a son but we have been unable to find him as yet. We *have* traced the third possibility down to the last decade at which point the entire family appear to have vanished without trace.'

'But what will you do if you find them all?' Isobel's question had a certain self-interest behind it. 'How would you decide? Would you interview them?'

Mathilda finished her tea and passed the cup to Isobel. 'Yes, please. I should like another if there's any in the pot. It's a rather difficult decision. There might be an obvious candidate, you see. On the other hand I might decide to leave it to several of my father's descendants.'

'That sounds fraught with difficulties,' said Isobel, pouring the tea and feeling more nervous by the minute. 'They could hardly be expected to live here all together. Surely they'd simply sell it all up and divide the spoils?'

'You may well be right.' Mathilda looked at her papers thoughtfully. 'We are not a particularly *fruitful* family,' she observed. 'Perhaps there will be no one left to inherit after all.'

\*     \*     \*

Isobel carried the tray down the two flights of stairs and set it on the wooden draining board. She felt frightened and lonely; what would happen to her with Mathilda gone? She stared at the blackberries and suddenly remembered the flesh fly. With an exclamation of disgust she heaved the whole lot into the pedal bin and, sitting down at the table, put her head in her hands. She tried to imagine Mathilda's descendants arriving at the cove; going all over the house with an eye to its value, laughing at its old-fashioned kitchen and deciding to turn the house and cottage—not to mention the boathouse—into a kind of holiday park. In her mind's eye she could see it; the house split up into letting units; the cottage frizzed and powdered into the kind of twee 'fisherman's cott' one saw in the glossy brochures. The boathouse with its huge attic room where Professor Rainbird had once worked would be ideal for keeping sailing dinghies and sailboards, as well as a launch—but not Mathilda's old boat—for trips along the coast. She could imagine children on the small stone pier and the cove resounding to their shouts. Even the long winding drive would no doubt be laid down to tarmac and proper garages built into the cliffs behind the house where the Morris now lived in solitary splendour.

Isobel wiped away a tear or two and sighed. Whatever happened would have to be faced. Perhaps she could raise the money to buy the cottage ... Perhaps Mathilda might be right when she said that, after all, there might be no one left to inherit.

## CHAPTER FIVE

Tessa Rainbird sat at the small table in the little back bedroom of a house in Shepherd's

Bush. This had been her home almost ever since her parents and small brother had been gassed to death when a volcano erupted in the Cameroons where her father was working as a petrochemical consultant. At the time Tessa had been at her school in England but even now, eleven years on, she suffered nightmares in which she was desperately trying to save her adored baby brother. Sometimes the nightmare took the form of wreckage, amongst which she crawled whilst explosions and screams reverberated about her. At other times the nightmare had that well-known quality of helplessness: her legs refused to run, her voice died in her throat, and she was unable to warn her brother or her parents or rescue them from their terrible fate.

Her mother's second cousin had stepped into the breach when Tessa's paternal grandmother died two years after the accident. Tessa's father was an only child but her mother, whose parents were dead, had a sister in New Zealand who had offered to care for Tessa. Tessa could barely remember her aunt and dreaded leaving England and the friends she had made at school who had been so kind to her during these years. At last it was decided that she should stay on at her boarding school and go to Cousin Pauline in the holidays. She was already elderly; a quiet, gentle woman who watched a great deal of television and was no companion for a thirteen-year-old. Gradually

Tessa began to accept more of the invitations to stay for the holidays which issued from her friends, and spent very little time at the terraced house in Cobbold Road. She knew that Cousin Pauline had taken her out of duty rather than love and, though she was grateful, Tessa knew that her presence was not an advantage except as a pair of young legs and hands to help with the household tasks.

When Rachel Anderson arrived at the school on the south coast the two girls took to each other at once. Rachel, a warm-hearted, eager girl, was horrified at Tessa's tragic history whilst Tessa was immediately drawn to the family to whom Rachel belonged. Her father was a naval officer, her mother a natural homemaker—wherever she was posted with her husband—and the small twins were the same age that Tessa's brother, Timmy, would have been had he lived. As for Sebastian . . . At seventeen he was the most handsome young man she had ever seen. Tall, fair-haired, hazel-eyed, he treated her just as he did his younger siblings; he teased them, hugged them and for the most part ignored them. Tessa, who had so desperately missed family life, was enchanted by the Andersons and never refused an invitation to stay.

By the time she was seventeen she was wondering what she should do with her life. She could see that a university degree was not the passport to a career that it had once been and she knew that she was not brilliant enough to be one of the lucky few who, in these difficult times, found jobs easily. Once again it was through the Andersons, who gave her help and encouragement, that she discovered, quite out of the blue, what it was she really wanted to do. At the end of the spring term Rachel received a letter from home.

'Doom and gloom,' she announced to Tessa, with whom she shared a study. 'The dog lady can't come, apparently. She's broken her ankle and granny's down with flu. Looks like our holiday's up the spout.'

'Dog lady?' Tessa knew that the Andersons were going skiing as soon as school broke up for Easter.

'You know,' said Rachel. 'The woman who dog-sits when we go away. Mummie's quite desperate. It's the first leave that Daddy's had for ages that fits in with school holidays.'

There was a silence whilst Rachel read her letter and Tessa was visited by an exciting answer to the Andersons' problem. She thought it through carefully.

'I've had a thought,' she said at last. 'Is there any reason why I couldn't do it? After all, Baggins and I are old friends. I'd be quite happy to look after him.'

Rachel had stared at her for a few moments, letting the idea sink in. 'Brilliant!' she'd said. 'Fantastic! Are you sure? It's a great idea. I'll phone Mummie.'

That was how it had started. During those quiet weeks in the Andersons' house Tessa began to see how she could earn her living. She adored dogs, preferred the country to the town and never minded her own company. She still missed her parents and her brother quite dreadfully but she had already learned that it is better to be alone than to be with the wrong people.

Sebastian and Rachel approached the suggestion of her new career with their usual enthusiasm. Sebastian immediately drew up a list of naval families who might require her services and Mrs Anderson recommended Tessa to these friends and wrote a glowing reference. In the following year—her last at school—she had four jobs during the holidays and a growing clientele.

Now, at twenty-two, she worked almost two-thirds of the year. Between jobs she came back to London but she longed for a little place of her own. Her work took her all over the south and west so it was difficult to decide where she might base herself and whatever she chose to rent would be empty for the greater part of each year. The money from her father's estate would come to her when she was twenty-five but it was by no means a large sum. It had paid for her education—which included driving lessons—and her trustees had advanced enough for her to buy an estate car so that the dogs could be taken for walks or to the vet in an emergency—owners did not always leave transport available—but meanwhile she lived on the interest which was paid quarterly. It amounted in all to approximately two thousand pounds a year, which came in very useful.

Tessa bent thoughtfully over her diary. The weeks were filling up very satisfactorily and tomorrow she was off to Devon; a week on Dartmoor. She sighed with pleasure. Kate and David Porteous were probably her favourite clients. David was an artist—an RA—who often went to London whilst Kate tried to juggle their lives between their town house and the country. Kate, who once had been married to a naval officer, knew the Andersons very well and had been quite willing to give Tessa a try. It had been one of Tessa's earliest jobs and she was desperate to do well. She took at once to Kate's large golden retriever, Felix, fell in love with the moor, and now Kate was a regular client.

Tessa shut her diary, picked up her bag and ran downstairs. She had promised to go to the Spar shop in the Uxbridge Road and it was very nearly lunchtime. She put her head into the sitting room, where Cousin Pauline was watching *Neighbours*, told her where she was going and went out into Cobbold Road. As she hurried along, crossing by the library and turning right by the Askew Arms, she was barely aware of her surroundings. Only one thought sustained her; tomorrow she would be in Devon.

\*　　　\*　　　\*

As she drove out through Ashburton and headed for the moor, Tessa was thinking of Sebastian. This was not unusual; Tessa spent most of her time thinking or dreaming about Sebastian. From those earliest days she had been in love with him and she had plenty of hours in which to weave fantasies about him. Yet it was fairly clear that, fond of her though he was, Tessa was little more to him than Rachel's friend. At one time, when he was at university, Tessa believed that their friendship had blossomed into love. He had invited her to a party in London and they had both drunk too much. She had told her love and he had very kindly and considerately relieved her of her virginity. Afterwards she wished that she could remember more about it but the act alone convinced her that he must love her, too.

This sadly had not proved to be the case. He was still as affectionate as he had always been but nothing, it seemed, had changed. Tessa had been shocked and then desperate. Had she thrown herself at him? Had he been just using her? She could hardly ask Rachel, frightened that she might confront Sebastian, and there was no one else in whom she could really confide. Sebastian put things right himself.

'Are you OK, kiddo?' he'd asked, next time

they'd met. 'I hope you're not angry with me. It just seemed the natural thing to do at the time. The first time is rather important for a girl, isn't it? And I wouldn't like you to be hurt or anything like that by some insensitive lout.'

She'd swallowed and nodded; her experience did not allow for this kind of conversation.

'Well then.' He bent and kissed her lightly and instinctively her arms went out to hold him. 'That's all right. But don't drink too much at parties.'

So that was that; but Tessa had not stopped loving him. One day, she was quite convinced of it, he would suddenly realise that he'd loved her all along. Meanwhile she dreamed about him.

She passed Ausewell Cross and a few minutes later was pulling in at the Roundhouse at Buckland-in-the-Moor. She always got up on to the moor as quickly as she could and the Roundhouse was always her first stop. She climbed out of the car and stretched, sniffing at the wind that blew across the hills. The Roundhouse, with its little shop and gallery of artists' studios, was attached to the farm and three generations of Perrymans—if you included young Colin who helped out in emergencies—ran it all. She wondered if Mrs Perryman would be around or whether one of her twin daughters—or perhaps both—would be working today. She looked forward to seeing

57

their friendly smiles and hearing their soft Devon voices just as much as she longed for the delicious coffee. Tessa smiled to herself with anticipation; she felt exactly as though she were coming home.

*    *    *

'The usual dramas!' announced Kate when Tessa had settled into the big Victorian house on the edge of Whitchurch Down. 'Felix has cut his pad and David has left half his belongings behind. Oh, and I think I've found you a new customer.'

'Oh great!' Tessa sat at the kitchen table stroking Felix, who had come to lean against her. 'Who is it?'

'Hang on, I've written it down somewhere.' Kate leafed distractedly through the muddle on the table. 'They're over towards Ivybridge way. Two labradors. Here we are. Carrington. She's a widow, rather elderly, who likes to visit her daughter in the Midlands. Dear old thing she is and the dogs are very well trained and far too fat and idle to do anything antisocial like running away. I'm sure you'll get on very well.'

'Thanks, Kate.' Tessa inspected the piece of paper which Kate pushed across to her. 'I need all the help I can get.'

Kate looked down at the feathery blonde hair cut short and the neat little face with the wonderfully expressive golden eyes; lion's eyes.

58

She admired Tessa who was making such an effort to create a decent career for herself, despite a lack of family to support and encourage her. Sue Anderson had told Kate all about Tessa's past.

'She's an absolute sweetie,' Sue had said. 'We all love her. She longs for a family. It's quite heart-rending, really. Nothing but some old aunt who watches the box all day long. We met her at the school once. Poor Tessa.'

'I've heard that you're doing splendidly,' Kate said now, giving Tessa's shoulder a little squeeze. 'Give Mrs Carrington a buzz while you're here and then go over and see her. You'll love Romulus and Remus.'

Tessa burst out laughing. 'Really?' she asked. 'Romulus and Remus? Good grief!'

'The breeder was having a Roman period, apparently,' said Kate. 'At least Mrs Carrington didn't choose Ptolemy or Nero. One must be grateful for small mercies.'

Tessa grinned up at her. 'It's nice to be back,' she said.

\*       \*       \*

Later, after she'd driven Kate into Plymouth to catch the train, Tessa took the limping Felix for a little stroll. The late October sunshine was warm on her shoulders and she restrained an urge to run and shout. These huge spaces filled her with a sense of freedom and she took great lungfuls of air, still hardly able to believe her good fortune. She might have been stuck in an office somewhere—or in a shop. What luck to have fallen into this job and to have such good friends to help her! Tessa paused to pat Felix, who hobbled beside her, and then turned to the car: she mustn't let him overdo it.

Back at the house, she unpacked and began to settle herself in properly. She always had the little spare room which she had almost come to look upon as her own and, having put her things away, she made her usual tour of the house. Everything was in order and with a sigh of contentment she went into the kitchen and pushed the kettle on to the Rayburn. Felix, stretched on his rug in the corner, watched her, his tail beating a tattoo on the floor. She went to him, crouching beside him and stroking him.

'She'll be back soon,' Tessa told him. 'Don't worry.'

He stretched himself out contentedly and she got up and wandered round the kitchen, peering into the fridge, checking the larder—Kate was always very generous—and pausing before her favourite painting; a moorland scene done by David himself. It was of a bridge over the River Dart and a part of the bank with a group of foxgloves glowing against the sun-warmed stone. The light danced on the water and, in the corner of the picture some words were scrawled, partly obscured by the mounting: 'Bless you for everything. It's been perfect.' The rest of the writing was too hidden to read. The painting never ceased to hold her attention and engage her emotions. Presently a new frame on the dresser caught her eye and she picked it up curiously. It was a photograph of two young men. Tessa had often seen photographs of Kate's twins from her first marriage. They were dotted about the house; in Kate's bedroom on her chest of drawers; in a montage of family photographs in a frame in the downstairs loo; in the bedroom—which was obviously kept ready for them—standing on the bedside table. There were the twins as babies at either end of a huge pram; the twins as toddlers, each clasping the other's hand on a beach; the twins as small boys in uniform, going off to school. This, however, was a very recent one. Tessa stared at it. They were very alike—both tall and dark—but one looked more serious, almost forbidding, frowning a little; the other smiled, his eyes crinkled against the sun, his hands dug deep in his pockets.

Tessa replaced the photograph and sighed a little. Families: everyone seemed to belong to someone.

'Everyone except me,' she said aloud sadly, and Felix opened an eye and sat up.

She smiled ruefully at her self-pity and pulled herself together.

'You wait,' she said to him. 'One day I'm going to have lots of children and at least two dogs. And I shall live here on the moor. You wait and see!'

Felix sighed deeply and lay down again, putting his head on his paws and watching Tessa whilst she moved to and fro making herself some tea. The kitchen was warm and presently he dozed. Tessa sat on at the table, drinking her tea, listening to the slow ticking of the clock, staring across at David's painting on the opposite wall. It comforted her to be in such surroundings; in a family home with an old dog lying asleep in the corner. For this moment in time it was her home, her dog, her kitchen. She sighed, looked again at the piece of paper lying on the table and, slipping quietly from her chair, went to telephone Mrs Carrington.

## CHAPTER SIX

In the end the Christmas holiday turned out to be very different from all that Isobel had imagined. Out of the unhappiness that had dogged her through the autumn a desperate hope had been born. She became convinced that when Helen came home for Christmas she would have relented a little, become mature enough at least to be prepared to communicate with her mother. The few telephone conversations Isobel had with Simon confirmed that Helen was growing up and

Isobel allowed herself to believe that the season of goodwill might extend its promise of happiness to her. Simon agreed to have a serious talk with Helen and, when they had discussed the best approach and Isobel had made her points as much for Simon's ears as Helen's—as to her regrets and guilt, she suggested tentatively that he might meet her for a Christmas drink for old times' sake.

He hesitated so long that her pride almost made her say, 'Forget it! Don't bother! Another time, perhaps?' but her need kept her silent and he reluctantly agreed. As she went about her work she buoyed herself up with the knowledge that, as yet, Sally had not moved in with Simon. Their relationship might still come to nothing. As she shopped and cooked and spent her two days a week at the bookshop she allowed herself little fantasies in which Simon realised that he still loved her and that Sally had merely been a kind of sop to his injured pride; a consolation. She imagined Helen coming home at the end of a busy, happy term with a sense of fulfilment and contentment which might blossom into a generosity towards her mother. All these things were possible and Isobel clung to them.

The blow fell two weeks before Christmas when Isobel and Simon met for their drink. She was at the Crabshell before him and her heart described its usual upward leap as she saw him come in. She stood up and waved to him across the crowd and he smiled in recognition and grimaced comically at the noise and the quantity of people crammed into the bar. Her spirits soared; it was going to be all right, she just knew it. He pushed his way to her table and gave her the usual kiss on the cheek. His face was cold against hers and he wore a thick jersey over his jeans.

'What a row!' he said. 'Is the whole of Kingsbridge here?'

'I think so.' She felt so happy she could only smile and smile at him. She was still clutching his arm and he made no move to shake her off.

'You were very lucky to get a table,' he told her.

'Aren't I clever?' She grinned at him and his expression softened as he looked down at her. There was that strange feeling of familiarity accompanied by the knowledge that they were, somehow, strangers which excited Isobel and made her heart bump.

'Very clever,' he acknowledged. He moved a little away from her and she was obliged to release him. 'Are we eating?'

'I thought so.' Isobel sat down again, glowing with this new happiness. 'I've just come from the shop. It's been hell today. Everyone ordering books. We're really busy.'

'Well, that's good, surely?' Simon sat down and picked up the menu. 'It would be worrying if you weren't busy two weeks before Christmas. What are you eating?'

Isobel shrugged. The food was of secondary importance. 'I think I'll have some pasta. The seafood tagliatelle is good. What about you?'

'Steak and kidney pie.' Simon shut the menu and looked towards the bar. 'I'd better order if we want it this side of Christmas.' He glanced at her glass. 'More wine?'

Isobel shook her head. 'Not just yet.'

She watched him as he fought his way to the bar and then stretched herself with a kind of nervous excitement. She'd been into Rainbow and treated herself to a new outfit she couldn't afford: a long skirt in soft lambswool and angora with a matching wrapover cardigan which belted tightly round her narrow waist and was worn over a cotton poloneck jersey in the same earthy shade. The tweedy terracotta colours lent a glow to her paleness and she had been so delighted with the result that she had bought a pair of dark brown leather ankle boots to finish off the ensemble. Her dark hair was loose, held in place with a twisted silk scarf and she felt a delicious sense of luxury and confidence. She sipped her spritzer and saw that her hand trembled a little.

When Simon returned he was carrying a glass of wine as well as his pint. 'I decided I would,' he said, putting it beside her. 'I'm not sure I can face that again in a hurry.'

'Very sensible,' she agreed. 'So how are you? How's the play coming on?'

Simon always produced the sixth-form play

at the end of the Christmas term and he was perfectly happy to discuss it at length. They were still talking about it when the food came. Simon unwrapped his knife and fork from their paper napkin and said, *'Bon appetit'* and Isobel raised her glass to him and finished her spritzer, revelling in their new-found intimacy. She realised that she had missed lunch and that she was very hungry, and she forked up her pasta with relish. Simon asked after Mathilda and she made light, as she always did, of the strange relationship she had with the old woman in her isolated cove. She told him about Mathilda's plans to divide her property between her unknown relations and Simon frowned a little.

'But where would that leave you?' he asked her. 'After all, she's getting on a bit, isn't she?'

Isobel felt her nervousness returning. She put down her fork and swallowed back some wine. 'She says I'll have the right to stay put,' she said, trying to sound unconcerned, 'but it was a bit of a shock. I've got to think about it, of course. Have you . . .? What are your plans? Any news? When's Helen home?'

Simon finished his pie and pushed his plate aside. 'That's one of the things I wanted to talk about,' he said.

He looked so serious that Isobel took another gulp at her wine and picked up her fork again. 'I'm longing to see her,' she said, spearing a shrimp. 'Have you mentioned anything to her yet? About ... you know. Me longing to see her.'

'The thing is,' he said slowly, 'the thing is— she isn't coming home.'

'Isn't ...? But why not?' Isobel felt a jolt of disappointment but, underneath the disappointment, a tiny hope flared up that she and Simon would spend Christmas together.

'A girl she shares with has parents who have a house in Italy,' he was explaining, 'and she's invited a group of them to go home with her. There's skiing, apparently and goodness knows what and naturally Helen can't resist.'

'Well, I can't say that I blame her.' Isobel's hope was expanding. 'I can send her present to Durham. With luck she'll get it before she goes.'

'I'm sure she will.' He smiled at her, relieved by her philosophical reaction. 'Anyway, she'll be back after the New Year. She's coming home then for a week or two.'

'Well then,' Isobel grinned at him, warmed by his smile, confident that all was going to be well. 'That just leaves you and me.'

His face was suddenly suffused with colour. He looked so distressed that Isobel put down her fork, a sudden anxiety seizing her.

'I shan't be here either,' he said abruptly. 'Sally and I are going to the Lakes. When I heard that Helen wasn't coming down we decided to have a little holiday. Her parents live near Kendal.'

67

They stared at each other. Her disappointment was so great that Isobel was silenced. She had been so sure . . . This is the second time, she told herself. The second time I've made a fool of myself in a pub. Pride made her pull herself together and she nodded, trying to smile.

'I'm really sorry about Helen,' he told her. 'Maybe when she comes down later on . . .'

She knew that he was offering her a way out; that she could pretend that it was only Helen she cared about.

'It would be wonderful,' she said quickly. 'It means so much to me, as you know.'

'Of course.'

She couldn't bear the pity in his eyes. 'Well, I'll send her present on, then.' She racked her brain for something to say and smiled at him quickly. 'Look, I really ought to be getting back. I must make supper for Mathilda and . . .'

She was on her feet gathering her belongings together and he stood up awkwardly, unable to help her. Politely, like strangers, they wished each other 'Happy Christmas', uttered meaningless inanities, kissed briefly and then Isobel found herself on the quay, the cold frosty air cooling her hot cheeks. She hitched the long strap of her bag over her shoulder and stared down into the inky water which reflected the fairy lights strung along the embankment. The pub door swung open and a gust of noise and laughter spilled out, light shafting across the quay towards her. Hastily, lest Simon should come out and see her with the tears wet on her cheeks, she turned aside and hurried away to the car.

*      *      *

Mathilda was sitting at the kitchen table, eating rice pudding directly from the dish, a book propped against the sugar bowl. She glanced up as Isobel came in, brows raised questioningly.

'I thought you were dining out,' she said. 'Oh dear. Have I got it wrong? I'm afraid I've nearly finished this delicious pudding.'

Desperate though Isobel was she gave a short laugh at the sight of Mathilda's comically rueful expression. 'You might have put it on to a plate,' she said, 'but at least you remembered to eat it. It's too much to hope that you had some macaroni cheese first?'

'Much too much,' agreed Mathilda cheerfully. 'Was there some? Never mind. This is extremely filling.'

Isobel shook her head at her and sat down at the table. She knew quite well that everything was now finished between herself and Simon and the overwhelming misery that had engulfed her when he had first told her about Sally was flooding back. She had been a fool to allow herself to hope; to persuade herself that the affair with Sally was a passing one . . .

69

'Is something wrong?'

Mathilda's voice broke in upon her thoughts and Isobel pressed her lips firmly together lest she should burst into tears. She shook her head, trying to smile, and Mathilda stood up and went across to the Rayburn.

'Tea, I think,' she said reflectively.

She pottered to and fro, giving Isobel time to regain her control, and presently the younger woman laughed. It was a rather desperate sound, which almost immediately turned into a sigh, but Mathilda turned to look at her enquiringly.

'I was just thinking,' said Isobel. 'The song is quite wrong. All that business about love being lovelier the second time around. Remember it? Something about it being much more comfortable with both feet on the ground? Quite the reverse, in my case.'

Mathilda was silent. 'I don't think I know it,' she said at last.

This time Isobel's laugh held a note of genuine amusement. 'No, you wouldn't,' she said. 'Now if it had been by Hugo Wolf or Benjamin Britten . . .'

'Possibly,' agreed Mathilda, placing a mug of tea at Isobel's elbow. 'I suspect, however, that each composer tends to write about his own experience. Love is a subject which is far too general to pin down to one person's view of it. It's as foolish as saying that the Italians are wonderful lovers or that the French are

70

marvellous cooks. It is hardly realistic to generalise about the entire population of any country. I imagine that it is the same with love. We each have a different experience.'

Isobel sipped her tea gratefully and wondered what Mathilda's experience had been. Was it some betrayal that had led to her solitary existence in the cove? She knew she could not ask.

'At least you didn't say, "It all depends what you mean by love",' she said rather bitterly.

Mathilda chuckled a little. 'I didn't feel that you were quite in the mood,' she admitted as she sat down again at the table.

'I'm not,' said Isobel miserably. 'Mathilda, what shall we do for Christmas?'

Hearing the desperation behind the question, Mathilda brought her mind to bear on it. She guessed that it was very important that Isobel should be distracted from whatever was making her so unhappy and given some sort of work or responsibility. She needed, thought Mathilda, to be made use of, to be kept busy. With a tiny inward sigh she prepared to make her own sacrifice.

'If you are going to be free,' she said, 'I should like to ask a favour of you. It would be foolish, at my age, to think that I shall live for much longer,' she held up a thin hand at Isobel's protest, 'and I should very much like to see an old friend before I die. Delia is really too elderly to travel to Devon and if you would be

71

prepared to take on the responsibility—and if you think the car can cope—I should very much like to go to Oxford to see her.'

'Really?' Isobel was staring at her in amazement. 'You mean you'd leave the cove? Good heavens, Mathilda, I never thought to hear such a thing!'

'Oh, I've been known to go visiting occasionally.' Mathilda watched Isobel thoughtfully, noticing the new interest in her eyes and the colour returning to the pale cheeks. 'So. Could you manage it, d'you think? It will take some organisation. I'm afraid that my friend is just as hopeless as I am so there will be the travelling to arrange and itineraries and so on. She asks me every year but I have never had the courage to go alone.'

'We'll go together,' announced Isobel, 'that is . . . will she mind . . .?' Her thoughts ranged anxiously over the cost of hotel rooms. 'It's just that . . .?'

'You will be her guest,' said Mathilda firmly. 'She has always suggested that I bring a companion. You will incur no costs and seats for the Christmas Eve service at the chapel in St John's are part of the inducement.'

'It sounds like heaven,' said Isobel. 'But aren't we a bit late? It's only two weeks to go . . .'

'Shall we go upstairs and make some telephone calls?' suggested Mathilda. 'It's certainly not too late, but now that we are agreed on it perhaps we should start the ball rolling?'

Isobel followed Mathilda up the stairs, her heart full of gratitude. It would be such a relief to have something to plan, something to take her mind off her unhappiness and the thought of the empty frightening future. She was suddenly filled with determination that Mathilda should thoroughly enjoy her Christmas and, as she made up the fire in the study whilst Mathilda searched for her address book, she was already considering which route they should take and what presents should be bought. If this friend were anything like Mathilda it might be wise to do a big bake before they set out. She'd need to know all about her before she made any final decisions, of course . . .

She piled more logs on to the flames, preparing for a busy evening, her mind turned resolutely away from pictures of Simon and Sally enjoying themselves in the northern hills. Love *isn't* lovelier the second time around, she told herself fiercely, though it might be for Sally and Simon . . .

'I've got a strange tone.' Mathilda's voice interrupted her thoughts. 'I must have misdialled. Could you . . .?'

Isobel jumped to her feet and hurried across to the desk. 'Shall I dial for you?'

Mathilda passed the receiver over meekly. She could read Delia's number perfectly clearly but her ploy had proved a useful distraction. She had not cared to see such an expression of despair on Isobel's face. Mathilda looked about her study sadly. She would hate to leave it but some instinct warned her that the sacrifice was a necessary one—and it would be good to see Nigel's sister again . . .

'I've got Delia Burrows on the line.' Isobel's hand was over the mouthpiece, her eyebrows raised hopefully. 'Is she . . .?'

Mathilda nodded and took the receiver; the die was cast.

## CHAPTER SEVEN

Tessa spent Christmas in a rather ugly little bungalow on the edge of Dartmoor. Her client, Freddie Spenlow, had been introduced to her through Kate. He, too, liked to spend regular periods with a friend in London and was deeply relieved when Kate assured him that his large Newfoundland, Charlie Custard, would be quite safe with Tessa. Kate had warned Tessa, however, that she might find Freddie's place rather basic.

'I've been over and sorted him out,' she told Tessa on the telephone a few weeks before she left London for Devon. 'If you have a problem we're only fifteen minutes away. Give me a buzz when you've settled in.'

Tessa approached the bungalow with a certain amount of trepidation. She parked the car in the track, noticing that the small garden had a gate leading into an adjoining paddock. At least there should be no problem in exercising this great dog. Kate's description had prepared her for something between a bear and an elephant and her heart beat a little faster as she rang the doorbell. There was no answering bark but presently the door was opened by a broadly built man in his middle thirties whose smile was so eager and welcoming that Tessa's nervousness began to fade.

'Hello,' she said. 'Mr Spenlow? I'm Tessa Rainbird.'

'Hello. Come in. This is wonderful.' He was attempting to shake hands, lead her in and shut the door all at once and she laughed as they stood together in the narrow hallway. He laughed, too, rumpling his thick brown hair and grimacing at himself. 'It's just such a relief,' he said, taking her coat. 'I wasn't planning to go away and then something blew up and poor old Custard . . . Well, he doesn't really care for the bright lights and he's not an easy dog to farm out. I can't tell you how pleased I am to see you.'

Tessa followed him into the kitchen. It had nothing of the charm of Kate's kitchen or the cosiness of the Andersons', nor did it have the streamlined efficiency she had become used to

75

in the homes of some of her richer clients. It was a simple ordinary room but any detail, for the moment, escaped her. Her whole attention was taken by a huge black dog who was sitting sideways on a shabby old sofa under the window. He leaned heavily against the back of the seat, his back legs stretched forward to their full length, his head resting wearily on a grubby cushion. His eye rolled towards Tessa but he made no move.

'Is that Charlie Custard?' she asked. She realised that she had lowered her voice, as though she might be in the presence of some great personage. 'Is he OK?'

'He's exhausted,' said Freddie, bustling to fill the kettle. 'Aren't you, Custard old chap? He's been to two Christmas parties and he's absolutely worn out.'

The dog sighed heavily and shut his eyes. Tessa watched, spellbound.

'*Two* parties?' she asked, rather awed by Charlie Custard's social commitments. 'Gosh!'

'You know the Lampeters?' asked Freddie. 'Well, their Jessie is one of my dogs. Did Kate tell you I bred them? Not any more but there are still a few of mine about. The Barrett-Thompsons? Yes? Know them? Well, Ozzy is Jessie's litter brother. Custard is their father. We have a get-together every now and again.'

Tessa advanced cautiously upon the sofa. 'Hello,' she said, stroking the big black head. 'Who's a beautiful boy?'

76

Charlie Custard was unmoved by this show of adulation. He sighed again but opened an eye to look at her. Tessa laughed. 'You're an old fraud,' she said. 'Worn out, indeed. I suspect you've been coming the heavy parent with your offspring.'

Custard's tail moved languidly once or twice and Freddie chuckled. 'You're right,' he said. 'Don't be alarmed at his size. He's very obedient.'

'I do hope so,' murmured Tessa, gazing at the dog's huge bulk and hoping that a clash of wills would not occur.

'You'll be fine,' declared Freddie confidently. 'And you don't need to take him beyond the paddock if you're not happy about it.'

It had needed only a day or two with Charlie Custard to give her confidence, however. She was used to the Lampeters' Jessie—although she saw now that Jessie was quite a small bitch compared with this male of the species—but Custard was a gentleman and, more importantly, a very lazy gentleman. He strolled peaceably at her side and even should a sheep break cover at his very paws or a rabbit hop into his path, he would merely prick up his ears and stare in amazement at such effrontery. In the evening, as she sat before the wood fire in the ugly tiled fireplace in Freddie's little sitting room, Charlie Custard would come to lean against her legs and the chair would slowly but

77

steadily run backwards under his weight until it came to rest against the wall or some other obstruction.

She had been deeply touched to find a tiny Christmas tree standing on a table beside the fireplace. It was a small plastic thing, with fairy lights attached to its tinselly branches, and beside it were several gaily wrapped parcels— two for Tessa and two for Custard. The labels bore Freddie's good wishes and Tessa stared at them, a lump rising in her throat. She had been surprised to find that she was always much in demand over Christmas and the New Year. The elderly went away to visit their families and many couples went skiing. She was relieved not to be spending a quiet Christmas with Cousin Pauline, who spent the festive season watching the James Bond reruns on television and eating chocolates, but it was nevertheless a very lonely time for Tessa.

However hard she tried she could not help but remember those wonderful holidays with her own parents and her brother and, as she sat alone in some stranger's house, she would feel all the force of her loneliness. It was while she was fingering the presents beside the little tree and swallowing back her tears that the telephone rang.

'Everything OK?' asked Kate. 'Custard behaving himself? Good. So what time shall we expect you on Christmas morning?'

Tessa was quite silent. 'Christmas morning?'

she asked at last.

'Of course.' Kate sounded surprised. 'I hope you weren't thinking of leaving David and me in solitary splendour. Guy got himself married last week and he and Gemma are off on honeymoon to some romantic place abroad and Giles is on a photographic job in America and won't be home till the New Year, so we're counting on you.'

'Oh, Kate.' Tessa bit her lip and blinked away her tears. 'I should love to come. If you're sure?'

'Don't be a twit,' said Kate.

*     *     *

Mathilda was glad to be back in the cove; glad, too, that she'd made the effort to see Delia. She knew that they would never meet again, in this life, and it had been a comfort to take such a gentle satisfying farewell of Nigel's sister, who was her oldest friend. After Christmas Isobel had driven them both to visit a mutual friend, now in a nursing home. This was a mistake. The old lady was beyond recognising them or holding any kind of conversation. She sat smiling vacantly, slipping in and out of sleep, waking to make disconnected remarks. Her hair was greyish-white and tufty, like sheep's wool caught on barbed wire, and there were gravy stains on her cardigan. A television, large as a young film screen, blared in the

79

corner, and relatives and friends sat with desperate smiles attempting to communicate with their unheeding loved ones.

Mathilda and Delia were silent during the journey home whilst Isobel railed against the system and deplored the loss of the extended family.

'Poor old thing,' she said indignantly. 'It's so undignified. What a way to finish, amongst strangers. Hasn't she any children who could look after her?'

'I've always thought that it must be so humiliating to be "looked after" by one's children,' mused Delia. 'One comes full circle. As if one's life and achievements have gone for nothing. Perhaps it is better to disintegrate in the privacy of a nursing home without inconveniencing one's family. At least there would be no guilt.'

'Why should there be guilt?' demanded Isobel, changing gear noisily—the Morris did not take kindly to dramatics—and pulling in outside Delia's house. 'The elderly should be treated with love and dignity by their families.'

'Invariably?' asked Mathilda. 'As a right? Even if they have been cruel or tyrannical or selfish to their children?'

'Yes,' said Isobel. 'Well ... How d'you mean?'

'I was merely testing your theory.' Mathilda prepared to alight. 'If you believe that old age

80

confers such rights automatically then at least your own mother need have no fear for her future.'

Isobel climbed out thoughtfully, trying to imagine her mother aged and infirm, toothless and incontinent. She saw herself dealing with criticism and chilly silent disapproval, not as she did now with argument and defensive rudeness, but with unstinting, generous, unquestioning love. Mathilda was smiling sweetly at her. Isobel glared back and slammed the car door with more force than was usual—or necessary.

'I am very lucky,' said Mathilda to Delia as they went up the path together. 'I have my independence but I also have care and protection. I don't quite know how I'd manage without Isobel.'

'You are very lucky indeed,' agreed Delia, fumbling for her key. 'Long may it last. Just in time for tea, I think. Come along in out of the cold . . .'

Isobel locked the car broodingly. Mathilda had taught her that arguing from the particular to the general was fraught with danger; that an argument was worthless if it could not be taken to a logical conclusion. Sometimes Isobel wondered whether, before Mathilda, she'd ever *really* thought at all. She realised that she found it easier to be with Mathilda than with her own mother; that in some ways she was fonder of her, too. Confused and feeling guilty and rather cross, she followed them into the house.

\*       \*       \*

It was early spring before Tessa went back to
Devon. This time it was to look after Romulus
and Remus whilst Mrs Carrington went to see
her family in the Midlands. She was a kindly
gentle woman whose thoughts centred on her
daughter and her new grandchild. Whilst she
showed Tessa round the cottage and gave her
lists and instructions Mrs Carrington talked
about her only child with tremendous pride.
Tessa listened eagerly and looked at
photographs of the young family with genuine
interest. Family life never ceased to fascinate
her. It was clear that Mrs Carrington was
making sacrifices to help them as much as she
could and this included the sale of a delightful
little bureau.

'The young man is coming to collect it in a
day or two,' she told Tessa. 'Here is his card
and his leaflet. Please let him do what is
necessary but please remain with him at all
times. You simply can't tell . . .' She looked at
Tessa anxiously. 'Perhaps I should wait until
I'm back. It's just that the money would be so
useful and these people take so long . . .'

'Don't worry a bit,' said Tessa reassuringly.
'Have you telephoned this number? You know,
just to check it out?'

'Oh yes.' Mrs Carrington nodded. 'I did it as

soon as he'd left. It's all quite above board. Such a nice girl answered and suggested I visited the office if I felt the least bit anxious. Quite out of the question, since it's in London but I was reassured by her attitude.'

'That's OK then. Don't worry, I shan't leave him alone with all your lovely things. If there's any trouble I'll set the boys on him.'

Mrs Carrington looked at the two dogs wheezing asthmatically on their beds and laughed. It was a rather sad laugh. 'They're getting old, poor darlings,' she said. 'And they miss my husband. We all do.'

'I'm so sorry.' Tessa cast around for a happier topic. 'I see you've been knitting for the baby.'

The older woman's face cleared and she picked up the soft mass of apricot-coloured wool from the table. 'Isn't it pretty?' she asked. 'I was so glad that Julie had a little girl. I'm used to girls and you can make them such lovely things. I'm keeping it out so that I can get some done on the train.'

'And if the young man comes to take the desk away shall I telephone you?' asked Tessa.

Mrs Carrington's cheeks flushed and she looked embarrassed. 'Perhaps not . . .' She hesitated. 'Oh dear. It's just I don't want Julie knowing . . . You see, I haven't told her that I'm not *quite* so well off as she thinks I am. The thing is that the young man tells me he can squeeze as much as three hundred pounds for the bureau and I don't want to give him time to change his mind. He says there are one or two around at the moment so I can't afford to dilly-dally. But he must leave cash and some sort of documentation. No cheques, mind!'

She looked very severe and rather anxious all at once and Tessa longed to hug her.

'Not a penny less than three hundred pounds! And a receipt for the bureau,' she said. 'Don't worry. I shall deal with it.'

It was not the antiques dealer who arrived on the doorstep the following morning, however. It was Sebastian. He hugged her, dealt graciously with her cries of delight and followed her into the cottage.

'You're doing very well, I hear,' he said, pausing to pat Romulus—or Remus—who had waddled over to greet him. 'Loadsa clients. Loadsa money.'

Tessa laughed, digging her hands into her jeans pocket lest she should go on hugging and hugging him. 'Not quite. But it's building up. Did Rachel tell you I was here?'

'No. I telephoned Ma to say that the ship is in Devonport for a few days. Engine problems. She told me that you were down here, too, and I thought you might like to come out for a drink. I couldn't get a reply when I phoned so I drove over.'

From the beginning, Tessa had left her current telephone number and address with Mrs Anderson in case of emergencies but this was the first time that Sebastian had ever taken advantage of it. Tessa felt quite weak with excitement and love but she attempted to keep her voice under control.

'Sounds great,' she said. 'So have you hired a car or what?'

'I thought I might as well get about while we're here.' Sebastian, a lieutenant on a naval destroyer, was based in Portsmouth. 'I've got to be back on board at six. Can you leave the dogs?'

'Oh yes. They've had a long walk up to Wrangaton Beacon.' Tessa was wishing that she wasn't in her old jeans and faded sweatshirt. 'I'll just go and change, shall I?'

He glanced indifferently at her clothes. 'You look fine to me. Tell you what, we'll drive over to Dartmouth and look up one or two of the old haunts. Have some lunch. How about that?'

'Terrific,' she said fervently. She didn't care what they did as long as she could be near him. 'I'll bed Romulus and Remus down in the kitchen . . .'

'Romulus and Remus?' He burst out laughing. 'No kidding? Rommy and Remy.'

'I know. But they're dear old things. You mustn't laugh at them. It's not their fault, is it, boys? Come on. On your beds and you shall have a biscuit.'

He watched her as she stroked their golden heads and gave them each a biscuit. 'Be nice to her,' his mother had said, when she'd given him

85

the address. 'She gets very lonely, you know. And she's so fond of you.'

He'd puzzled a little over those words as he drove out from Plymouth and now, as Tessa rose to her feet and beamed rather shyly at him, he wondered if his mother might be warning him. He remembered how he'd made love to Tessa and suddenly felt ashamed of himself. He'd drunk too much and taken advantage of her affection for him and she'd accepted his explanation—which had been partly true—and made no demands on him. He took in her slender figure and mop of bright hair, the small face and golden eyes, and smiled at her.

'OK, kiddo?' he asked gently—as he'd been asking for the last eight years—and she grinned at him, unable to hide her excitement.

'OK,' she said.

'Let's go, then,' he said—and Tessa grabbed her bag and followed him out, locking the door behind her.


## CHAPTER EIGHT

Mathilda finished the letter to her lawyer and leaned back in her chair. The day was mild for early April and sunshine streamed in through the window, which was open on to the balcony. Without moving she knew the exact state of the tide. It was on the turn, the heavy swell

86

crashing against the wall of sand where it shelved sharply and dangerously, far out at the edge of the cove. Presently, the waves would flatten, rolling above the shelf, surging over the rocks, to run in across the beach, creaming up to the high-water mark. It was the time of the full moon and the springs were at their highest, leaving a line of seaweed and other gleanings way up on the sand.

Mathilda pushed back her chair and wandered out on to the balcony. Behind the house, high on the cliffs, seagulls screamed as they swooped above the nesting colonies and the scent of flowering gorse was sharp on the salty breeze. Beyond the mouth of the bay a fishing boat had hove to, and two men were busy hauling up the lobster pots, bracing themselves against the heavy seas. Mathilda watched them, leaning her elbows on the railings, shivering a little despite the warmth of the sun. The doctor's diagnosis was always with her now; the knowledge at the back of her mind whilst she read or walked, or played Scrabble with Isobel. The lump in her breast had become too big to ignore and she had no intention of allowing matters to be taken out of her own hands.

She had summoned her GP whilst Isobel was at the bookshop and he had examined her in silence and then told her what she'd guessed already. They both realised that it was too late to hope that there was time to save her but, nevertheless, he wanted her to have an operation, treatment . . .

'What is the point?' she'd asked him. 'If my life cannot be saved, what is the point of such a waste of resources on an old woman? What you have described would cost thousands of pounds. Why? So that I can die in six months' time instead of three? Less.'

He was silent, staring out of the window, across to Start Point lighthouse gleaming white in the sunshine that shone out between scudding thunder clouds. Stabs of light pierced the dark green seas which pounded on to the beach and the wind howled and shuddered against the old house.

'Why did you wait so long?' he'd asked. 'We could have done something if you'd come to me earlier.'

She'd shrugged. 'I didn't notice it until recently,' she told him honestly, 'and when I did I suspected that it would have spread. Secondaries, d'you call them?'

'It's worth having a try,' he'd said—but she detected a lack of conviction in his voice and shook her head.

'Surely,' he'd said gently, 'you don't want to just give up. Look at this place. Your view! Isn't it worth fighting for? Life is very precious . . .'

'Ah, no,' she contradicted him. 'Not at any price. It's the quality of life that is important. I've had eighty-four years. It's enough.'

He'd shrugged then, his expression

88

changing, frowning a little. 'There may be no choice, you know. I can't give you a shot in the arm to put you out of your misery.'

She'd smiled at him. 'I realise that. I need time to think.'

He'd looked at her, taking in her frailty, the yellowish tinge to her skin, the strained lines on her face.

'The pain won't get any better,' he said brutally, hoping to shock her into compliance. 'Please be sensible. Let me help you. You have no family?'

Common sense warned her not to arouse his suspicions. 'No,' she admitted. 'You're right, of course. I can't just ignore it. Please allow me some time to adjust . . .'

He'd nodded, taking advantage of her more rational approach. 'Of course. But not *too* long. I'll give you a prescription but I want to see you soon.'

'I quite understand,' she said quickly. 'Of course. Just a few days to come to terms with it.'

After he'd gone the storm had broken; hail clattered on the roof whilst out at sea the lightning sizzled and the thunder rolled round the bay and resounded back from the cliffs. Presently Mathilda had turned away and sat down by the fire, huddling into her rug, remembering Nigel . . .

The fishermen had emptied the pots and the boat was heading back towards Dartmouth, seagulls wheeling in its wake. Mathilda was visited by a moment of utter loss and despair. She knew now why people cling to life; its joys and simple pleasures and all the dear familiar things. How difficult to relinquish them of one's own free will; how much easier to allow oneself to be deprived of them. There would be, she knew, a sense of relief in giving in, in letting some other person take control of her life, of being officially terminally ill.

The sound of the Morris bumping down the track had the effect of stiffening her spine. Her hands clenched for a moment on the balustrade and then she turned back into the room, slipping her letter into the drawer to be put in the post box by the back door later on. She heard the kitchen door bang and went out on to the landing.

'Hi. Mathilda?' Isobel's voice echoed up the stairwell.

'Coming,' she called back, and began to descend the stairs.

'It's cold out there.' Isobel was unpacking bags, putting the shopping away. 'Don't be deceived by the sun.'

Mathilda smiled at her, her heart warmed by affection. 'I shan't be. But I'm thinking of going out fishing tonight. Don't be surprised if you hear the boat.'

'Fishing?' Isobel paused in her labours to stare at her almost indignantly. 'Well, of course you're quite mad. Fishing! Honestly,

90

Mathilda . . .'

'You know I'm more than capable,' said Mathilda calmly. 'You've seen me going out often enough to know that now.'

'You're not getting any younger,' grumbled Isobel. 'Supposing you couldn't get the engine started or something? Sitting there in the freezing cold . . .'

'It will be a beautifully clear night,' Mathilda told her peaceably as she sat down beside the Rayburn. 'Full moon and a gentle swell. The forecast's good. Please don't fuss.'

'Wouldn't make any difference if I did!' Isobel pushed the pan of soup on to the hotplate and put some rolls in the oven. Go and drown yourself and see if I care!'

'Of course I know that you're longing to meet these relations of mine.' Mathilda watched her as she laid the table for lunch.

'Well, I must say that I think you're mean not to invite them down so that we can give them the once-over,' said Isobel, stirring furiously as she brought up this old grievance. 'I almost feel as if I know them. I've got a picture in my mind.'

'We don't know yet that they are alive,' Mathilda pointed out.

'Don't be a spoilsport.' Isobel filled two bowls. 'Come and have some soup. And for heaven's sake wrap up tonight and don't forget to take a flask . . .'

The boat rocked gently alongside the small stone quay. Mathilda stood at her window, watching it. She wondered if she had the courage to do what was needed and whether it would work. Even if it did not, she reasoned to herself, she would be no worse off. She was aware of the house all around her, silent, washed in moonlight; her refuge for so many years. She allowed the happy memories to filter in to her mind, dwelling on each and then letting it go. Finally she thought of her father after his stroke and Nigel in the hospital in Oxford . . .

Abruptly she turned from the window and went downstairs. On the table stood the flask which Isobel, fearing that Mathilda might not bother, had filled for her earlier. She picked it up and put it in the duffel bag that stood by the door and, with one last look round, went out into the dark. She crossed the beach as quietly as she could, her plimsolls scrunching on the sand, and, with a glance at Isobel's curtained window, dropped the bag into the boat and untied the painter.

Mathilda had neglected to take the launch round to Salcombe for its winter overhaul and the engine started reluctantly at the second try. She pushed the gear lever forward and headed out to sea. As she had forecast the moon was full and the water fractured into a thousand splinters of silver as a capricious breeze shivered across its surface. The beam from the lighthouse which swept the sky was pale and insignificant beside the brilliant glory of the night.

Mathilda set course for Start Point but her chin was on her shoulder and she stared back at the cove until the cliffs hid it from her view. She was conscious of the engine puttering gently, the only sound except for the restless sea, and she huddled herself more deeply into her jacket as the boat moved out of the shelter of the land. When she was some way out, over the place where she had flung Nigel's ashes on to the surface of the deep waters, she switched off the engine. She sat for some while watching the moonlight and listening to the slap of the waves against the hull; thinking about her life, trying to decide about her future.

Her intention—to slip over the side and let the sea take her—needed more courage than she had imagined. Here, in the cold empty indifferent spaces, her resolve wavered; her desire to cling to warm, vital life strengthened. Sunk in her thoughts she had not realised that the tide had turned and that the wind was rising. The water was choppy now, and broke unevenly in little wavelets, rocking the boat. The breeze was cold. Mathilda, disturbed from her reverie, glanced around her and saw that she was being carried further round the Point. Suddenly she was frightened. She saw the rocks beneath the cliffs and, getting to her feet, reached to start the engine. There was no response. Terror in her heart, her hand shaking, she turned the key again. The engine puttered into life only to die again almost immediately. The tide was running strongly now but the wind was backing round behind it, driving the little boat closer and closer to the shore.

Mathilda struggled for'ard to find the starting handle. The boat lurched and she stumbled, bruising her shoulder on the thwart before she regained her balance. Trembling, she managed to fit the handle into its bed and, summoning all her energy, she swung it. The engine's flicker of life was extinguished almost immediately and, with a superhuman strength, Mathilda swung the handle again; nothing. Dropping it she crawled into the well beside the engine. The boat was now in shallower waters and the waves broke over the gunwales, soaking her with their spray. She opened the duffel bag with shaking fingers and pulled out her heavy waterproof. Her only hope was that the boat might lodge itself between the rocks where she could wait until help arrived. She dared not look. The thundering of the sea against land warned her that she was close under the cliffs and she lay down, wrapping herself in the coat, wedging herself firmly between the engine housing and the thwart.

A wave lifted the boat and flung it amongst

the rocks, jarring Mathilda where she lay. The boat twisted and caught between two boulders as the tide continued to recede. Shivering, Mathilda raised herself a little; the boat rocked ominously. The moonlight showed her that she was held fast under the cliffs and would soon be left high and dry by the falling tide. Cautiously she stretched her hand towards the bag and felt for the flask. The movement caused the boat to settle itself lower on to the rocks and Mathilda lay motionless, hand still outstretched. Presently she caught the bag in her fingers and dragged it slowly closer. The smooth rounded body of the flask evaded her cold, damp grip but she found the handle of its plastic cup and drew it carefully out of the bag. Barely moving she unscrewed the cup and then the top of the flask, blessing Isobel's thoughtfulness. The smell of hot coffee brought tears to her eyes and she began to cry weakly as she dribbled the liquid into the cup.

The pain, which was always with her now, threatened to overwhelm her and she felt inside her jersey for the little bag of painkillers which she had put on a leather thong around her neck. She managed to insinuate three tablets into her mouth and washed them down with a gulp. A last wave surged up against the rocks, jolting the boat and spilling the coffee, and Mathilda grasped at the flask, feeling for the lid. She gulped back another mouthful but resisted the urge to finish it, knowing that she would need some later. Weakness engulfed her as she pushed the flask into the bag and tried to make herself comfortable. The boat seemed to be firmly held and she prayed that an early fisherman out of Salcombe would spot her; or perhaps the incoming tide would lift the boat free. She burrowed into the waterproof, pulling it across her face and felt the nagging pain begin to recede. Consciously willing her muscles to relax she felt exhaustion overtake her. She seemed to be sinking into a cold dampness which received her kindly, numbing her gently into insensibility . . .

The moon sank into the west and the chill light of dawn showed bright fingers of light along the horizon. The sun rose. A fishing boat motored out of Salcombe harbour and headed for the fishing grounds. Others followed but no one noticed the small boat half hidden amongst the rocks. A walker, taking her early morning constitutional on the cliffs above, was the first to spot it. She shouted down to the bundle curled on the bottom boards and, receiving no reply, began to run as fast as she could back to Hope Cove.

\*      \*      \*

'I told her,' wept Isobel. 'I told her that she shouldn't go. That she was too old.' She stretched her arms across the kitchen table to the young coastguard who watched her sympathetically. 'I said—I actually said—"Go and drown yourself and see if I care!"' Isobel put her head in her hands and cried in earnest.

'We got the boat off,' he told her. 'The engine wasn't working. Our guess is that she was carried round the Point by the tide and swept into the rocks.'

He pushed the mug of tea closer to her elbow. He was a local boy and he'd recognised Mathilda's boat at once. As soon as he was able, he'd driven down to the cove and found Isobel frantically telephoning the coastguard. He told her that Mathilda had died of hypothermia and exhaustion and that the doctor had also noticed advanced stages of cancer. Shocked and silent, Isobel had sat staring at nothing while he made tea and attempted to comfort her. All at once she had begun to cry, the tears spurting from between her fingers, and he'd wondered if he should call her doctor or take her to the surgery.

'She did it on purpose.' Isobel sounded a little calmer, although sobs burst from her uncontrollably. 'She wouldn't have wanted operations and things. If only I'd known. Oh God . . .'

'You can't know that,' he said uncomfortably. 'She was always going out on her own, wasn't she? My dad said she'd done it all her life. No reason why she shouldn't go last night. Lovely clear night, it was.'

Isobel looked at him. 'Yes,' she said dully.

'Yes, I'm sure you're right. Sorry.'

'Nothing to be sorry about. Look, I've got to go. I'm a bit late for work. Only I don't like to leave you. Is there somebody you could phone up? I could give you a lift.'

'No.' Isobel shook her head and attempted to control her trembling lips. 'I'm OK. You've been great. Honestly, I'll be all right.'

'Well, if you're sure . . .'

He tucked his chair under the table and she followed him out on to the beach, raising a hand to him as he climbed into his car and disappeared up the track. Keeping her eyes resolutely away from the empty house, Isobel wandered down to the sea. The sun shone in her eyes and a gull cried mournfully as it drifted above her, white wings outstretched. She thought of Mathilda, of the fear that she must have known during the long cold night, and the tears streamed unchecked down her face. She tried to imagine her own life without Mathilda; without her dry humour or her companionship; without the refuge she had given her against the storms. Now she had no one. Isobel sat down on a rock and, bending her head towards her knees, gave herself up to grief.

# CHAPTER NINE

Sunday morning. The June sunshine slanted through the arched windows of the chapel, touching the heads of the smaller boys in the front rows and lingering on the bowl of yellow roses placed at the altar. The drowsy peace was briefly disturbed by the frantic fluttering of a butterfly as it beat its tortoiseshell wings against the glass. Abruptly it abandoned its struggle for freedom, dropping down to rest on the stone sill. The scent of the roses drifted faintly on the warm air and the headmaster's scholarly voice was soothing—almost soporific—as he read the gentle words of St John . . .

'Behold what manner of love the Father hath bestowed upon us, that we should be called the sons of God . . . Little children let no man deceive you . . . He that committeth sin is of the devil . . . For this is the message that ye heard from the beginning, that we should love one another . . .'

Matron, ever vigilant from her vantage point in the choir, watched the small boy opposite. His face was dreamy and peaceful as he unobtrusively slid his fingers under the thigh of his even smaller neighbour and pinched the bare flesh. The cry of anguish was frozen on his victim's lips as she leaned forward to look sternly at both of them. They stared back at her with innocent guileless expressions—but she saw the sharp jab of an elbow in retaliation and smiled to herself.

'. . . My little children, let us not love in word, neither in tongue; but in deed and truth . . .'

Matron sighed deeply; thirty-five years in the company of boys between the ages of eight to thirteen had given her a rather cynical outlook. The first twenty years of her career had been at a boys' preparatory school in Dorset. When the headmaster retired she decided that she, too, should make a change and she had come here to this small school on the edge of the New Forest. It was the right decision and she had been very happy. A succession of little boys had passed through her capable, caring hands and, after they left, she continued to learn of their achievements through the pages of the school magazine and their occasional visits. How she would miss them! She looked down into the body of the chapel and wondered how she would cope with retirement. Her glance picked out the familiar head of the History master.

She knew without looking how he would be sitting; hands in his pockets, legs crossed at the ankles and thrust out into the aisle, chin on chest. He was unconventional, sometimes outrageous, an inspired teacher—and the boys adored him. She had regulated her love for Tony Priest so that only she knew of it. It was so humiliating to have such feelings when one was over fifty; especially if the object of one's desire was a married man. Yet the thought of leaving him, the school, the boys, was a terrible one. Her closest friend, a widow, assumed that they would enter into old age together at her little house in Winchester; or there was the option of buying a small flat, here in the town, not far from the school. She pursed her lips thoughtfully as she mentally reviewed its advantages. The most prominent of these was its cheapness but also important was the comfort in the knowledge that she would be able to keep in touch with the school; to see Tony Priest from time to time. She thought of the letter she had received yesterday from a lawyer in Plymouth; some distant relative had left her a share in a house. She had never heard of this distant cousin and was surprised that she should have been mentioned in her will. It had been suggested that she travel to Devon to see the house but really there was no point. On the other hand the money would be very useful indeed . . .

The rustle of hymn books brought her to her

feet with the other members of the choir and she felt for the reading spectacles that swung from a chain around her neck. The small boy sitting directly in front of her sniffed juicily and wiped his nose with the back of his hand. Matron poked him sharply in the back and he turned to stare up at her, aggrieved. 'Handkerchief!' she hissed and he fumbled obediently in the pocket of the grey shorts of his Sunday suit.

Tomorrow, she thought, as he blew with exaggerated ardour into the grubby square of linen, tomorrow I shall write and see what it's all about . . .

*　　　*　　　*

Isobel dragged the sheet from her bed and the cover from the quilt and bundled them into a pile on the floor. She carried the quilt to the window so as to hang it out in the warm sunshine and stood transfixed, one hand outstretched to open the window wider. Below her, on the beach, was a girl. She was standing quite still, with her back to the sea, staring up at the house. The sun glinted on the short blonde hair and her whole attitude was one of tense expectation. Suddenly she swung round and extended her arms, fists clenched in a gesture of triumph, head flung back, eyes tight shut.

Isobel realised that she was still clutching the

quilt to her breast; her hand gripping the window latch. She had the strangest feeling that she was spying but, before she could turn away, she saw a man emerge from the house and stroll down the beach. The girl had heard his approach and stood easily now, her hands thrust into the back pockets of her jeans. Nevertheless, Isobel was aware of a kind of joy emanating from the slight figure. Her own heart beat quickly as their voices mingled with the shushing of the tide upon the sand and she saw the man—whom she now recognised—gesture towards her own cottage.

Isobel dropped the quilt and went downstairs and out into the sunshine. James Barrington—Mathilda's lawyer—raised a hand to her and she was aware of the girl looking at her keenly as she went to meet them.

'Good morning, Isobel.' James smiled and held out his hand. 'How are things with you?'

'I'm fine.'

Isobel liked James. He had recently moved back to the West Country from Oxford and had inherited Mathilda from a retiring partner of the Plymouth law firm where, as a law student nearly fifteen years before, James had worked during his holiday placements. He lived somewhere near Dartmouth and had been very willing to come out to the cove and talk to Mathilda about her quest for her unknown relatives. She had been very taken with him and the three of them had spent several immensely enjoyable evenings together. On one occasion, at Mathilda's request, he had brought his wife, Daisy, and their small boy for Sunday tea.

'This is Tessa Rainbird,' he was saying. 'She is Miss Rainbird's cousin, several times removed. This is Isobel Stangate.'

The two women looked at each other.

'So he found you,' said Isobel lightly. 'Hello.' Tessa's hand was warm in hers and the golden eyes looked anxious.

'I never knew her,' she said. 'Isn't it terrible? I didn't know about her, you see. And I've been down in Devon so much in the last couple of years. Oh, it's such a waste!'

'Never mind.' Isobel was taken aback at her intensity. 'She didn't know about you, either.'

'But she was *family*,' said Tessa sadly. 'I wish I'd known her. And now it's too late.'

'Yes.' Isobel winced at the stab of pain which reminded her of her own loss. 'I'm afraid it is.'

'Mrs Stangate will be able to tell you all about her.' James's voice was comforting. 'She looked after her, you know.'

'Well, up to a point.' Isobel looked at Tessa and felt curious. 'Do you like the house?'

'I love it,' said Tessa simply. 'All of it. The house and the cove. It's ... Well, it's magic, isn't it?'

'It's rather special,' agreed Isobel. She was feeling confused. She had been prepared to dislike on sight these relatives who were to supplant Mathilda and turn the cove into a kind of holiday camp—but this girl wasn't quite what she had envisaged.

'I want to live here,' Tessa was telling her, 'but I have to wait to see what the other beneficiaries want to do.'

Isobel looked at James who shrugged. 'Perfectly true, I'm afraid. If they want to sell it'll be two against one.'

'I can't bear it.' Tessa screwed up her eyes as though she might burst into tears but laughed instead. 'Silly, isn't it?'

'Love at first sight,' said James sympathetically. 'Often painful. Want another look round before we go?'

'Yes, please,' said Tessa at once. She hesitated but James knew what was in her mind.

'I'll leave you to go round alone,' he said. 'I'll have a chat with Mrs Stangate, if she can spare the time.'

Tessa's face lit up. 'Great!' she said. 'Shan't be long.'

'Take as long as you like,' said Isobel, who had every intention of pumping James for information. 'Come in for some coffee when you've finished.'

*       *       *

Tessa went slowly from room to room, touching the furniture and ornaments with gentle fingers and reading the titles of the

105

books in the bookcases. Her plan to buy a cottage and live on the moor had been abandoned instantly as soon as she had entered the house. The rooms were full of trembling pearly light and the sound of the sea was like distant music. All was just as Mathilda had left it. Isobel had tidied the rooms and went in daily to dust and air the house but there was an atmosphere of friendly welcome, as though the owner had just popped out and would be returning at any moment. Tessa opened the windows in the study and went out on to the balcony. It had shocked her to learn that she had had a relative of whom she knew nothing; a woman with the same name as her own, with whom she shared a common ancestor, someone of her own flesh and blood who had lived in this magic place.

She leaned on the balustrade and watched the great white sails of a yacht filling with the gentle breeze that ruffled the turquoise sea. On the horizon a tanker appeared to be stationary, painted against the shimmering sky, its great length rendered toy size by distance. The tide washed gently in, hardly seeming to encroach upon the shore, and the sun shone on the stone of the old house and warmed Tessa where she stood in desperate longing.

I want it! she told herself silently. I want it.

She remembered James explaining the terms of the will. There were two other relatives involved so that even if they loved the place as much as she did there must inevitably be certain complications.

'It might be difficult,' James had said thoughtfully, 'all mucking in together, if you see what I mean.'

'Maybe,' she said hopefully, 'maybe they'll just want to come for holidays or weekends or something.'

James was silent. Tracking Tessa down had not been easy and her reaction—in light of her own losses—was not particularly surprising. He forbore to point out that almost invariably his instructions in these cases were to get the property sold as quickly as possible and split up the proceeds. After all, there was no question of Tessa buying out her fellow legatees. Despite the fairly primitive conditions in the house, its position alone ensured a high asking price. Properties of this nature were rare and it would be snapped up quickly. He realised that she was watching him, willing him to agree.

'We must wait and see,' he'd told her gently.

Tessa thought about Isobel. She had the right to stay on in the cottage as a sitting tenant. James had explained that sitting tenants sometimes made a place difficult to sell ... A cormorant skimmed the water, flying south with steady wingbeats. The tanker had disappeared below the horizon and the yacht had sailed round the headland towards Salcombe. Tessa went downstairs, locked the door carefully behind her and crossed the beach to the cottage.

*     *     *

'I always thought it was a crazy idea,' Isobel was saying. 'Leaving it to three people. I mean, why not just one? It's bound to cause trouble.'

She thrust the sugar bowl at him, glaring at James as he maintained a judicious silence. His brief description of Tessa's background had filled her with a maternal concern and she felt cross that the two other as yet unknown relatives would destroy the girl's prospects before she could enter into them.

'Honestly!' she exclaimed. 'It's cruel, isn't it? To see this place and fall in love with it and then be unable to hang on to it! Poor Tessa. I really feel for her.'

James sipped his coffee. He was aware that it must be just as hard for Isobel to have lost her own security and, more importantly, her friend. He suspected that Isobel's anger at Mathilda's will was indirectly aimed at Mathilda. She couldn't forgive Mathilda for dying, for leaving her. James knew how close the two women had become and how important it was for Isobel to have someone to look after, to love, to worry about. It seemed that she was about to transfer her allegiance to Tessa.

'Don't sit there looking so smug!' cried Isobel. 'Sorry.' She caught herself up and sat down at the table. 'I have this terror, you know, of these relations turning the cove into a kind of up-market Butlins.' She folded her arms on the table and shook her head. 'I miss her so much,' she admitted.

Her mouth turned down at the corners and James thought briefly of his own small son when he was hurt or frightened. Just so did he look—although a comparison between a two-year-old boy and a forty-something woman was faintly ridiculous.

'Mathilda had some strange ideas,' he said evasively. 'I don't know quite what was in her mind but she seemed very set on having her way.'

Isobel snorted. 'Nothing surprising about that,' she said tartly. 'But I still don't see . . .'

There was a knock on the door and Tessa put her head in. 'Hi,' she said rather shyly. 'Am I interrupting anything, Mrs Stangate?'

'Of course not.' Isobel jumped up and fetched another mug. 'And call me Isobel. We were just discussing these tiresome relatives of yours.'

James looked at her warningly but she made a face at him. Tessa laughed a little.

'I've longed for a family ever since . . . well, since I've been on my own. But I must admit that I could do without these two.'

'Of course you could.' Isobel put the mug beside Tessa's elbow and pushed the milk and sugar towards her. 'So come on, James. Tell us

109

all about them. Don't put on your lawyer's face. We shall know sooner or later.'

James remembered that Mathilda had taken Isobel into her confidence over her will, how she had always been quite frank before her at their meetings, and gave in. He explained that Beatrice Holmes worked in a boys' school in Hampshire and that Clarence Rainbird had recently retired from his administrative post with the United Nations and had been widowed three years previously. He lived in Geneva. Both had been informed of their inheritance but, as yet, he had received no acknowledgement from either of them.

'Geneva,' said Isobel thoughtfully. 'Listen. Perhaps he'll let Tessa rent his bit of the house from him and he can use it for holidays. How about that?'

James sighed. 'It's no use speculating. We must wait. No good getting hopes up only to be dashed.'

Isobel looked at him. 'Do you ever have the urge to be wildly indiscreet?' she asked. 'To make unconsidered remarks? Commit yourself irrevocably?'

'Not to two women at once,' answered James, shocked. 'Although I have been known to have a haircut on the spur of the moment, without taking advice or making an appointment.'

Tessa laughed. 'It's up to you, Isobel,' she said. 'When they turn up I rely on you to persuade them. Convince them that it would be criminal to sell. I simply can't bear the thought of losing it now I've seen it.'

## CHAPTER TEN

Will Rainbird—he had adopted his second name, preferring it to Clarence, on his first day at school—parked his hired car at the top of the track, tucking it well in beside the hedge, and climbed out. He stood for a moment, looking about him, aware of the drone of bees in the honeysuckle that grew in the hedge beside him, smiling with pleasure at the trailing tangle of fragile dog roses. He sniffed, luxuriating in the salty scented air and patted his pockets absently as he craned about for signs of habitation. The jolly lady at the little bakery in the village up on the main road had been very helpful in describing his route to the cove. He had made no secret of who he was, although he had not yet advised the lawyers that he was in the country, and there had been a mild if discreet sensation when he had told the bakery people his name.

Well, here was a track, precisely where the lady had said there would be a track, but there was no sign board to indicate that it led to the cove. Will located his pipe and his matches and strolled slowly down the dusty path. Cow parsley leaned out at him, its creamy crumbly flowers brushing his arms. Red valerian and sulphurous yellow stonecrop clung in the crevices of the stone wall which bordered a field of grazing sheep. The afternoon was hot and still, with a hint of thunder in the air, and the great spaces of sky, now a purplish bruised blue, hinted at the proximity of the sea. Will packed tobacco into his pipe, his eyes fixed on the blue horizon, and listened to the sea birds screaming on the cliffs.

The track dropped downwards and, as he came round the sharp right-hand bend, Will caught his breath at the view of the sea which appeared briefly before him. He found that he was hurrying, his feet slipping on the small stones, and as he came out on to the small fanshaped beach he gave an inarticulate cry of delight. He stared up at the house, swung round to look about the cove and smothered another exclamation as he saw the figure stretched out on the beach. She lay on her face, head on arms, and he studied the long tanned slender limbs and the dark shining hair that fell across her wrists.

Will stood still. He guessed that this was the tenant of the cottage and he glanced quickly at it perched on its rocky plateau before taking a cautious step forward, clearing his throat noisily. Isobel raised her head, rolled over and sat up swiftly. He took another step towards her, his hands raised in a kind of supplication.

'I'm sorry,' he said, 'so sorry to disturb you.'

He saw that she was older than he had first imagined but he found her tremendously attractive and smiled apologetically as she pulled a T-shirt over her head and fastened a long cotton skirt around her waist. Her brown eyes were angry but there was a touching vulnerability about her mouth.

'I'm so sorry—' he began again—but she interrupted him.

'This is a private beach,' she said as she slid her feet into espadrilles. 'You're trespassing.'

'You've been crying,' he said distressfully, seeing the marks on her cheeks and swollen eyelids, and coloured as he saw her look of outrage. 'Forgive me. It's just . . .' He shrugged at his tactless ineptitude. 'I'm Will Rainbird,' he said simply.

Isobel came closer. It was true that she had been crying. Earlier that morning, on an impulse, she had rung the cottage in Modbury and had been both terrified and delighted when Helen answered. She had countered Isobel's eager questions with monosyllabic replies, refused her invitation to lunch and blocked further conversation by saying that she must go but she would fetch her father to the telephone. Simon had been kind but firm in his refusals to meet 'just to talk things over' and had hung up at the earliest opportunity. Isobel wandered out on to the beach, hurt and unhappy, and had lain down hoping that the heat of the sun would relax her so that she might sleep. Instead, she had wept bitterly then drifted into a brief uneasy doze—and now here was this stranger walking across the beach, catching her at a disadvantage, acting as if he owned the place . . . as indeed he did.

Will held out his hand and, as she took it, Isobel found herself looking into Mathilda's eyes. The shock was so great that she clutched convulsively at his hand. The slate-blue eyes smiled at her as though they quite understood but she pulled herself together and hastily withdrew her hand.

'I do apologise,' she said rapidly. 'I didn't realise who you were. Just for a moment . . . I was asleep, you see.'

'I shouldn't have come unannounced,' said Will, trying hard not to stare at her. 'To tell the truth I wanted to have a look around on my own, d'you see? Just to get the feel of things without lawyers breathing down my neck.'

'I quite understand.' Isobel, too, was trying not to stare. He could have been Mathilda's much younger brother, so strong was the likeness, and, after her initial irritation, she felt strongly drawn to him. 'I'm Isobel Stangate. I live in the cottage.'

'Thought as much,' said Will, though whether his obvious pleasure was the satisfaction of his successful methods of deduction or from knowing that she was his tenant she could not quite decide. 'Not too

114

much to hope then that you've got a key to the house?'

Isobel began to laugh. 'I certainly have,' she agreed. 'Though whether James would approve of what you have in mind I can't imagine.'

'James?'

'James Barrington. Mathilda's lawyer. Never mind. What the eye doesn't see . . . and all that.'

'My view exactly,' he beamed at her. 'You looked after my cousin, I understand.'

As they walked across the beach together, Isobel explained her role. Suddenly she thought of Tessa. 'I'm hoping that you'll all agree to keep the house,' she told him. 'Then I can stay here and look after you. Rent-free, of course. That was the arrangement with Mathilda. I've met your cousin Tessa. She's all for it.'

She gave him a quick guided tour of the house and then left him to it, hurrying back across the beach and feeling strangely excited and apprehensive.

Will, standing at Mathilda's bedroom window, watched her go. Presently he turned his gaze seawards.

He saw the clouds massing on the horizon and looked westward at the spiny huddle of rock on which the lighthouse stood. He felt a strange sense of belonging; a crazy desire to accept this unexpected inheritance and start a whole new life. After all, what was there to

115

keep him in Switzerland now that Bierta was dead and he had retired? His life had been a quiet one, his administrative work unexciting— rather like his marriage. His Swiss wife had been older than he but he had been attracted by her calm blonde beauty, her smiling good-natured charm. Later—too late—he had discovered that her calm good nature masked an unthinking indifference to life but Will was a loyal man and no one, least of all Bierta, guessed at his disappointment. Their only child was stillborn and with it his last hopes of real happiness died but Will was by nature a positive man and had learned to look for those small precious moments of joy which are vouchsafed at unexpected moments.

Now, it seemed, life might take an exciting turn. His trip to England had been quite impulsive. He had been visited with a desire to have a little holiday; to take a look at this house in its cove, although he had fully expected that, having instructed the lawyers to sell it, he would return to Switzerland leaving the whole business in their hands. His gaze wandered back to the cottage. What if he should decide to keep the house? Of course there were the wishes of the other beneficiaries to be considered but if he sold the flat in Geneva he could probably buy them out. He remembered that Isobel had mentioned his cousin, Tessa Rainbird. Tessa, she had said, wanted to keep the house. Will's hands went automatically to

116

his pockets, feeling for his pipe as he made another tour of the house. There was no reason why it should not be divided into two flats. It would need a bit of thinking out, of course . . .

As Will left the house fat warm drops of rain were beginning to fall, splashing on the rocks and pocking the gleaming surface of the water. Far out at sea a fork of lightning stabbed across the darkening sky and thunder growled in the distance. Without warning the rain fell in vertical shining rods and Will raced across the sand to the cottage where Isobel waited with the door held wide.

\*    \*    \*

Tessa sat in her favourite corner of the Roundhouse, pouring a second cup of coffee from the pot which Marie, one of the Perryman twins, had brought twenty minutes earlier. For once she was not thinking of Sebastian—from whom she had not heard since that sudden appearance more than three months before—but was brooding on Mathilda and her house in the cove. She felt that she might die of frustration if her other relatives did not soon appear and make their decisions known to her. For the thousandth time she racked her brains for a solution should they both wish to sell. The small trust set aside for her would hardly be enough for a deposit and, even if it were, how on earth would she manage a mortgage? She had been shocked when James had mentioned the sum the house and cottage might reasonably be expected to fetch and now she knew the desperation of helplessness; the frustration of being powerless.

She glanced up as the door opened and her face lost its anxious look. Kate, accompanied by a tall young man, came in, glanced around and waved as she saw Tessa in her corner.

'What are you doing here?' Kate smiled down at her. 'I didn't know you were around. This is Tessa, Giles. My life-saver. Have you met Giles?'

Tessa recognised him at once. It was the young man she'd seen smiling out of the photograph of the twins, on Kate's dresser. She shook hands with him and he slid on to the bench opposite whilst Kate wandered away to order some coffee.

'I feel I know you,' Tessa told Giles mischievously. 'All those photographs.'

'Oh God!' Giles grimaced. 'That's an unfair advantage.'

'But they're very good photographs.' She grinned at him. 'Especially the one of you on the beach.'

He laughed. 'No point in trying to make an impression if you've seen that one.'

Kate appeared beside them. 'What's the joke?' she asked. 'How are you, Tessa? Are you on your way back home or have you just arrived?'

118

'I'm on my way to Honiton.' Tessa moved along so that Kate could sit beside her. 'A new client. I said I'd be there about teatime so I could have time to settle in properly. They're off tomorrow morning. I've been at the Lampeters' all week.'

'Ah,' said Kate thoughtfully, studying Giles's face as he watched Tessa. He looked as though he'd just discovered something rather special. She decided that a certain amount of encouragement was in order. 'In that case why don't you join us for lunch? We're going to the Church House at Rattery. It's not far off the A38. On your way, more or less.'

Giles glanced at his mother quickly, eyebrows raised. Kate smiled blandly back at him and he gave a little shrug. This by-play was not lost on Tessa.

'Well . . .' She hesitated, longing to accept but wondering what that glance had meant.

'Take no notice of Giles,' said Kate, knowing that Tess had intercepted their little signal. 'We're meeting my other son and his wife. Gemma will love to meet you.'

'Which implies,' said Giles, making room as Marie arrived with their coffee, 'that Guy won't. It's only fair to warn you that Guy takes a little time to relax with people he doesn't know.'

Tessa remembered the uncompromising stare of Giles's twin as they stood together in the photograph.

119

'Perhaps he won't like me butting in,' she began, understanding the exchange between Kate and Giles. 'I don't want to be—'

'Rubbish,' interrupted Kate roundly. 'It's my party. Anyway Guy is old enough now to cope with strangers. Gemma has helped no end with that side of his character. She's such an outgoing girl. Thanks, Marie. How's the family?'

While Kate and Marie talked, Tessa was suddenly seized with a fit of shyness. She stared at Giles's hands as he poured coffee and found herself absolutely tongue-tied. At the same time she felt an odd sense of familiarity; as though she had known him for ever.

'It must be great fun working with dogs,' he was saying. 'Mum says that you've been to Freddie's. How's Charlie Custard? I remember . . .'

He talked easily and amusingly and presently she found herself recounting stories of her own whilst Kate sat by, smiling to herself. Presently she glanced at her watch.

'Mr Perryman's made some new bowls,' she told them. Mr Perryman, as well as being a farmer and carver-in-chief on Sundays at the Roundhouse, produced beautifully crafted wood-turned work. 'Marie says he's around somewhere so I'm going to have a word with him. Back in a minute.'

She disappeared through the door that led to the artists' studios and there was another

120

silence.

'So you live in London,' mused Giles. 'I've got a studio flat in Chelsea. It's tiny but rather nice. Where do you live?'

'Shepherd's Bush,' said Tessa so glumly that he burst out laughing.

'Come on,' he said. 'It's not that bad.'

Tessa wrinkled her nose, shrugged and then quite suddenly found herself telling him about Mathilda's legacy, Cousin Pauline and the tragic loss of her parents and her brother. She told him about her nightmares, how she'd started dog-sitting and how she thought she might die if she couldn't live in the house in the cove. Giles listened in silence, his eyes on her face. Kate had already told him something about her and he felt an old-fashioned urge to be allowed to look after her; to protect her. Whilst she talked he restrained these out-of-date feelings and poured himself more coffee.

'So you see,' said Tessa, sighing heavily, 'I just can't see how it can possibly work. I telephoned James Barrington—he's the lawyer—yesterday, and he says that he's had a letter from one of the others instructing him to sell. She doesn't even want to see the house. I begged him to ask her at least to look at it and he's agreed to give it a try.'

'It's a bit odd, isn't it?' he asked. 'Leaving it to three people. I agree with you. How *could* it possibly work, apart from selling it?'

'I wish I could buy them out,' said Tessa

121

wistfully, 'but it seems to be worth rather a lot. I'm hoping that the other two might like to use it for holidays and I could live there between jobs.'

'Could it be divided into three?' asked Giles. 'And what about this cottage?'

Kate, looking through the glass panel in the door, saw the two heads close together and gave a sigh of satisfaction. She decided that she might have a browse in the little shop; perhaps buy a card or two or some mugs. No need to disturb them yet; there was at least another ten minutes before they had to leave.

## CHAPTER ELEVEN

Beatrice Holmes—who had ceased to be Matron for two whole months—sat listening to the rain drumming on the conservatory roof whilst Norah's voice drummed just as relentlessly in her ears.

'. . . and so I told him that I thought it was quite disgraceful. A whole three pence overnight! Of course, he cheeked me. "Everything goes up," he said. "I have to cover my costs." Well, you can imagine. "Cover your costs!" I said . . .'

Bea fiddled restlessly with the letter in her lap and wondered at what point Norah had become so penny-pinching. She had arrived to teach English at the preparatory school in Dorset when Bea had been Matron for five years or so. In the heavily male-dominated society they had automatically drawn together and, when Norah married and moved into Hampshire, they had remained good friends. Each summer Bea had spent some part of the holidays with her and Bernard, and they had always joked about how they would be tiresome old ladies together. She had sympathised with Norah's irritations at Bernard's feckless ways; his extravagance, his generosity to the undeserving, his tendency to pop round to the pub. He had always effaced himself, leaving the two of them to their own devices, but in the last two months Bea had begun to realise that it must have been no self-sacrifice on Bernard's part.

'. . . of course, the man's a saint but how on earth he puts up with it I can't imagine. She never leaves him alone for a minute and when I found her there fiddling with the flowers although she knows *quite* well it's *my* week . . .'

Norah had passed along from the supermarket to the church with its long-suffering vicar and her arch-enemy, Miss Knowles. Bea thought regretfully of the little flat near the school. It had been snapped up two days before she—rendered brave by the thought of her inheritance—put in her own offer. There was nothing else that appealed to her that she could afford and she had given in to Norah's pleas for company. Bea had insisted on a trial run. Now, she gave thanks that she'd had the foresight.

'. . . The standard's dropped quite shockingly. "Tea bags," I said. "I never thought to see that here." Oh, they trotted out the usual excuses . . .'

Norah had come to rest in the tearoom and Bea decided that she should stay there for the present. She smoothed out the letter and got to her feet.

'Where are you off to?' Norah eyed the letter. 'Something wrong?'

'No, no,' answered Bea soothingly. 'It's the lawyers again. Asking me to go to see them. They're suggesting that I might like to look at the house.'

'But you've told them to get on and sell it,' protested Norah. 'Surely they don't expect you to go all the way to the West Country to look at a house that's going to be sold?'

Bea racked her brain for inspiration. 'The thing is,' she said mendaciously, 'that there might be one or two of my cousin's things that I should like to have as keepsakes. He's suggesting that I have a look before the sale.'

'But you didn't know her,' objected Norah. 'How can you have a keepsake of someone you don't know?'

Bea was visited by an urge to see how Norah would look wearing a potful of geraniums but resisted this unworthy impulse and smiled

124

instead.

'Well, you know what I mean. There might be one or two valuable things that I should like . . .'

'I should have thought the money would be more useful. I've been thinking. Supposing we build a small extension on at the side beyond the kitchen? You know you were saying that we should have a sitting room each . . .'

'Let's wait and see what happens,' said Bea quickly. 'That's why I thought I'd go down and see the place. It's really not that far and it will give us a better idea of what I can afford.'

'I suppose so,' said Norah grudgingly. 'Look.' She brightened a little. 'Why don't I come with you? Make a holiday of it. I haven't been to Devon for years. Bernard always liked decent weather and it does rain so down there. Why not, Bea? You can go any time, can't you? Let's go together.'

'It sounds a wonderful idea . . . but it has to be next week,' lied Bea with an ease born of desperation. 'This whoever-he-is,' she waved the letter, 'is going on holiday.' Lie followed lie. 'Next week's a busy one for you, isn't it? You've got Townswomen's Guild and meals-on-wheels. And haven't you invited Andrew Owen to lunch after decorating the church for Harvest Festival?' Andrew was the vicar and Norah was silent. Bea, scenting victory, shrugged a little. 'Of course, Miss Knowles could take your turn at the WVS and I'm sure she'll be more than happy to feed Andrew. Still . . .'

Norah bridled a little in her chair. 'Do you have to see this particular chap?' she asked peevishly. 'Surely there are other members of the firm who can take you round the house?'

Bea breathed heavily through her nose and resorted to further untruths. 'It seems my two cousins will be there, too,' she said, wondering if it was thirty-odd years in the close proximity to little boys which enabled the lies to roll so convincingly from her lips. 'He's suggested that it's sensible for us to be there together so as to ensure fair play.'

'Oh well.' Norah looked annoyed. 'Then I suppose there's nothing to be done. I can't leave poor Andrew to Miss Knowles's tender mercies . . .'

Bea made her escape, feeling as though she had been let off detention.

'Oh, Bernard,' she muttered into the ether as she went to her room to find her writing pad, 'I'm sorry I said those things about you.'

\*     \*     \*

As she sat in the train travelling west, Bea thought about Tony Priest and wondered how soon she might find another suitable flat in the town near the school. She knew now that she could not possibly consider spending the rest of her life with Norah. She began to think that she

126

had never really known her at all. In those early days they'd been on several holidays together as well as seeing each other daily at school but Bea wondered if the friendship would have survived if it had been formed in any other environment. It was only to be expected that, over the years, they should have grown apart and to imagine they could live together had probably been madness. A few weeks together each year was one thing; the rest of their lives together was quite another.

Bea gazed out over the Exe estuary. The September day was misty and the silvery sea, creeping in over the mud flats, merged with the soft grey sky. She leaned forward to watch a group of dunlin running before the tide; to smile at the sight of a heron hunched in solitary contemplation. A sense of peace stole into her soul and she settled back contentedly, deciding to enjoy her little holiday. The lawyer had written to her offering to meet her at the station in Plymouth but she had refused, saying that she would take a taxi to his office. There was no earthly reason why she should go to see the house but there might very well be a few items of furniture that would be useful if she were going to be setting up in her own flat. Her thoughts drifted back to Tony Priest but she forgot him when the train pulled in at Dawlish and she saw seagulls perched on the breakwaters and the sea breaking against the great sandstone rocks. It was years since she had made this journey and she gave herself up to the pleasure of recognising certain landmarks.

As the train approached Plymouth, Bea put on the jacket of her grey flannel suit, checked the contents of her handbag for the lawyer's letter and lifted her small case from the rack. She was one of the first off the train and the first into a taxi. The offices of Murchison, Marriott were situated in one of the city's Georgian crescents and Bea looked at the tall house approvingly as she paid the driver. Inside, at the reception desk, a young woman telephoned the news of her arrival and led her upstairs. She opened the door and smilingly bade Bea enter.

'Good afternoon,' James leaped up to greet her and then paused as Bea turned from thanking the receptionist and fixed him with a piercing, assessing stare. The years swung back and he found that he was hastily smoothing down his hair and surreptitiously wiping the toes of his shoes down the backs of his trouser legs. 'Good grief,' said James involuntarily. 'It's Matron!'

\*　　\*　　\*

Isobel bumped down the track towards the cove feeling tired and irritable. The day at the bookshop had started badly when she found the brewer's lorry parked outside The

128

Hermitage, blocking Mill Street whilst the driver sat enjoying a cup of coffee in the bar. This amiable young man nodded cheerfully at her and said that he would call her when he had finished unloading. Cursing, Isobel left the Morris—Mathilda's bequest to her—parked behind the lorry and hastened into the shop. The day had gone from bad to worse. She had been driven to curtness by a customer who wanted a book on gardening without knowing its title, the author, or its publisher but was convinced that Isobel *must* know which book it was because it had been so well reviewed. At lunchtime she lost her purse—although it was found and dropped into the shop just before closing time—and later in the afternoon she was ticked off by a mother for reproving her child who was pulling books off the shelves and dropping them on the floor. The door banged behind mother and child and, with a sneaking glance at Pat and Laura, one of the two regular assistants, Isobel went through to the back of the shop to make coffee. The return of her purse cheered her a little but she was glad to get out into the fresh air of the early autumn evening.

She knew that it was tension that was making her so crotchety. Will, who was staying at the Royal Castle in Dartmouth, had made it clear that he was unwilling to sell the house and James had written to Tessa to tell her so. Unfortunately, having no other point of contact, he wrote to the house in Cobbold Road where the letter sat with her other post until she should return. Meanwhile Tessa was in Wales, dog-sitting two Weimaraners, longing to telephone James but afraid of being a nuisance or of hearing unpalatable news. Isobel also knew that, as a result of Tessa's pleadings, James had agreed to write to Beatrice Holmes again with the suggestion that she might like to choose some keepsake from amongst Mathilda's belongings, and in the hope that she might fall in love with the house whilst she was so engaged.

As she turned the Morris into its usual parking place she saw that James's car was already parked at the bottom of the track. She climbed out and stood undecidedly near the door into the kitchen remembering how she would once have gone in, shouting cheerfully to Mathilda, drawing curtains, checking that Mathilda had eaten her lunch. Swallowing hard she stared out to sea, watching the breakers crash against the shelf of sand and thinking of past evenings by the study fire playing Scrabble. The sound of a car's engine made itself heard above the sound of the surf and she turned to see Will's hired car pulling in beside James's Peugeot.

Her heart lifted at the sight of his cheerful countenance and raised hand, and she went to meet him, her loneliness abating a little.

'Have you met her?' he called with a

conspiratorial glance towards the house. 'What's she like?'

'Met who?' Isobel began to feel excited. 'Is she here? The schoolteacher?'

'James phoned to say she arrived yesterday,' he told her. 'She's come down to see if there's anything she wants. Clever ruse, that.'

'But even if she likes the place,' argued Isobel, 'what then? Could you all squash in together?'

'Well, I can't afford to buy her out,' said Will gloomily. 'I had no idea it would be so valuable. It's fifty years behind the times inside.'

'It's the position,' said Isobel, equally gloomily. 'If you sell it the developers will move in. Oh, I can't bear it!'

Will smiled at her encouragingly. The whole affair had made him feel years younger. He had spent the last two weeks exploring the area and he was becoming more and more attached to the beautiful South Hams. One day he and Isobel had taken a picnic up on to Dartmoor. She had navigated, showing him the thickly wooded river valleys and the high bleak uplands with their outcrops of granite. There were still a great many holiday-makers about and, unable to find a quiet place to park, they had abandoned the idea of the picnic and Isobel had directed him to the small grey moorland town of Chagford where they had lunched in the Ring O'Bells, looking out over the market square. Afterwards they drove down to Fernworthy Reservoir, a tiny shining lake hidden amongst tall encircling pines, and had walked at the edge of the water and watched the mallard paddling idly in the reeds. Later, Will fetched the hamper and they drank their coffee at one of the picnic tables, nibbling the buns that Isobel had made. The sun was hot, dazzling from the surface of the reservoir where a rowing boat rocked quietly as its occupant bent over his rod.

Isobel talked non-stop about Mathilda until Will gradually built up a shadowy picture of his cousin and had become even more determined to hold on to her house in the cove. They discussed ways and means of dividing the house so that he and Tessa could share it and had almost discounted the third beneficiary until they learned the value of the house and cottage.

Now, as they stood together on the beach, Isobel smiled back at him. His silvery grey hair, like Mathilda's, was always ruffled and slightly untidy and he had an eager look which gave her confidence and hope. The door opened and James appeared, followed by a tall well-built woman in a grey suit. Her glance at them was keen and Will instinctively dropped his arm lightly round Isobel's shoulders as they moved forward to meet her. James was looking surprisingly cheerful and Isobel's spirits rose as she shook the woman's hand.

'Isn't it amazing?' James was saying. 'This is

Matron. From my prep school. I simply couldn't believe it. She hasn't changed a bit.'

'Which only goes to show,' said Bea, shaking Will's hand, 'what an awful old bat I must have been in my forties.'

'To an eight-year-old anyone over twenty is decrepit,' said Will consolingly. 'I'm your cousin, Will Rainbird. But I can't call you Matron . . .'

'Sorry,' said James hastily. 'This is Miss Holmes.'

'Bea,' she told Isobel, smiling at her. 'How d'you do?'

'I never thought of it being you,' said James. 'I didn't recognise the name. We always called you . . . Matron.'

She smiled at his hesitation. 'Or Busy Bea?' she suggested. 'And other less complimentary things with an emphasis on the B?'

Isobel burst out laughing at James's discomfited expression. 'I'll leave you to discuss in peace,' she said. 'You know where I am if anyone wants anything. Come in for a cup of tea if you feel like it.'

Bea, puzzled, watched her walk away and turned to James. 'Is she not my other cousin?'

'Sorry.' James looked even more confused. 'I should have introduced you properly. That's Isobel Stangate. She rents the cottage. I haven't been able to contact Tessa yet.'

'I see.' Bea looked thoughtful.

'So,' said Will, more heartily than he had

133

intended. 'So what's your verdict?'

She raised her eyebrows. 'Verdict?'

'Now that you've seen the place,' he said, 'what d'you think of it?'

'The position is excellent,' she said slowly, 'if you like deserted coves. I'm sure it will fetch a good price.'

He stared at her in disappointment. 'You still want to sell then?'

She looked at him in surprise. 'What else do you suggest we do with it?'

'I hoped we might keep it,' he said slowly.

'*Keep* it?' She looked at him as though he were mad. 'For what purpose?'

'To live in,' mumbled Will, embarrassed by her penetrating stare. 'I'd like to hang on to it. So would Tessa. We hoped you might feel the same.'

Bea looked at James as though waiting for him to enlighten her. 'They both love the house, you see,' he explained rapidly, rather feeling that he was excusing a particularly muddy rugby shirt or a lost sock. 'They were wondering if the place couldn't be kept and used by the three of you.'

Bea frowned a little, as though she were doing a particularly difficult mental calculation. 'You seriously imagine that the three of us could live here together?' she asked. 'But why? There's nothing here.'

She glanced around her. The tide was swirling in across the sand, bursting in white foam against the rocks, filling the pools; above the cliffs away to the east a new moon hung, just visible in the deepening blue of the night sky.

'I suppose,' said Will slowly, 'it all depends on what you mean by nothing.'

Bea looked sharply at him but James intervened. 'Shall we take advantage of Isobel's offer of a cup of tea?' he asked diplomatically. 'And then I'll drive you back to Plymouth.'

Bea hesitated and then nodded. Will stood for a moment, watching the sky change colour as the darkness gathered and the stars appeared, and then followed them across the beach to the cottage.

## CHAPTER TWELVE

The farm gate stood open. Tessa applied the brakes and the two dogs in the back of the car were caught off balance, claws scrabbling. She reversed back along the lane and sat for a moment looking in at the close-cropped turf. She had found that farmers rarely objected to people walking their dogs in fields where there were neither crops nor stock but she always felt safer where the gates were open and the grass very short. She had once been surprised by a flock of sheep being driven into an empty field whilst she and her somewhat excitable charge

135

were at the furthest corner from the gate. It had been an interesting moment.

Here, however, it seemed that the field had been well and truly cropped and Tessa reversed back to a wider part of the lane where she could park safely. She had also learned never to block gateways with the car. The farmer might arrive on a tractor at any moment to feed the field with some kind of fertiliser and be justly annoyed at being denied entry. The clumber spaniel—who bore the unlikely name of Sidney—looked anxiously from the rear window. He hated travelling backwards; it gave him a feeling of insecurity to see objects hastening towards him. He moaned briefly.

'Shut up, Sid!' muttered Tessa, as she negotiated the verge and the thorn hedge. 'Don't be such a baby. Harry doesn't make a fuss.'

Hearing his name, the Jack Russell who had been standing on his hind legs—forepaws on the wheel arch as he peered eagerly from the side window—let forth a series of staccato barks. Tessa, clad in jeans, gumboots and a warm padded jacket, climbed out and released them and then stood for a moment to breathe in the sharp early morning air. Sidney, happy to be free of the confined space, padded to and fro along the verge, sniffing amongst the brambles and the faded willow-herb. Harry, scenting rabbit, vanished into the field, his excited barks echoing in the quiet spaces of the

Wiltshire uplands.

'Come on, Sid.' Tessa slung their leads round her neck, pushed her hands into her pockets and followed Harry into the field.

Sidney, his noble mien managing to convey a wounded expression at being called Sid, lifted his leg against a large dock and ambled slowly in her wake. Inside the field Tessa felt a familiar sensation as she gazed across a rolling expanse of chalky fields and gentle dun-coloured slopes. Small cottages, slate grey, nestled in the folds of the hills and mist clung in the valleys. A charm of goldfinches, feeding on thistle seed, swirled up into the cool air and a robin in the branches of an alder sang a stave or two before dipping over the hedge and out of sight. The welling up of joy in Tessa's heart reached the point where she knew it must be expressed in some action lest she burst with gratitude at the beauty spread out before her.

She began to run down the field, calling to the dogs, arms outstretched. Harry joined in, skittering round her feet, barking madly whilst Sidney watched from his refuge under the hedge, pained at such unrestrained and plebeian behaviour. The field descended to a small stream, trickling between nut and alder trees, and Harry paused to drink copiously, stumpy tail wagging furiously, short legs planted foursquare. Sidney approached cautiously and Tessa bent to stroke his silky white coat and large domed head.

'It's not right, is it, old boy?' she murmured. 'Leaving you with a ratbag like Harry. Poor old chap.'

Sensing sympathy and a proper awareness of his dignity, Sidney sighed deeply. He consented to drink a little, one drooping eye on his regenerate companion. Tessa watched, smiling to herself. The decision that Harry's owner, a newly divorced woman with two small children, should join Sidney's mistress—also divorced with two children—on a holiday in France had been made at the last moment. It seemed that the two women could share the driving and the expense of the villa which could accommodate them all at a pinch; but what about Harry? Rather reluctantly, Tessa agreed that she would look after both dogs and hoped that Harry would be able to adapt to his new surroundings. Fortunately there was an outhouse where he could sleep, so leaving Sidney in possession of the kitchen and his rather smart beanbag. Harry, unused to such niceties, sniffed about and settled down happily on his torn old blanket to the marrow bone with which Tessa had the foresight to supply him. Sidney had observed these proceedings somewhat dolefully from the safety of the kitchen door but Tessa had been firm with him.

'It's no good, Sid,' she said, shutting the outhouse door firmly and going with Sidney into the kitchen. 'Your missus said, "no bones." That's what comes of being so

138

aristocratic, see? Your digestion's too delicate. Can't have you throwing up on this nice carpet.'

Sidney watched anxiously from his beanbag, fearful that this strange young woman who addressed him so disrespectfully might also forget his night-time Bonio. Tessa pottered, unaware of the distress in Sidney's breast, but talking to him all the time. Finally, however, she opened the cupboard and took out the familiar box. Sidney heaved a relieved sigh as Tessa placed the biscuit beside him, tugged his long ears gently and wished him good night.

Now, as they climbed the grassy slopes to the gate, Tessa was feeling more confident that she could cope with them both and her thoughts slid back inevitably to the house in the cove. She had not been able to meet Beatrice Holmes but Tessa knew now that Bea had no desire to keep the house although James had asked her to think about it, which she had agreed to do but with no real hope of changing her mind. Meanwhile, Will and James were trying to think of some way of buying her out. Between jobs, Tessa had fled down to Devon to meet them. The meeting was held at James's office.

'I know you wanted to meet at the cove,' he told Tessa when she and Will had been introduced. 'But I felt it best that Isobel should be left out of this discussion.'

The two Rainbirds looked at him and he felt an almost hostile reaction. Part of him was pleased that Isobel had made such a favourable impression on them but it did not give him confidence in what he was about to suggest.

'I like Isobel,' Tessa said. 'She's like one of the family, isn't she? She's told me so many things about Mathilda I feel I knew her, too.'

'Exactly!' Will beamed at her, liking this girl who seemed barely more than a child but who had carved her niche with such determination and courage. 'Must have been quite a girl, Mathilda!'

'Yes.' James leaned his elbows on his desk. 'Yes, she was. And Isobel is a very nice woman but we have to consider this from all angles. The point I wish to make is this. If we could sell the cottage it would probably raise a significant sum towards buying Matron out. Sorry.' He shut his eyes and shook his head. 'She'll always be Matron to me.'

Tessa, who had heard the story from Isobel, grinned but almost immediately looked serious. 'But Isobel has the right to stay on in the cottage,' she pointed out. 'And even if she hadn't, where would she go?'

James stared at his desk top, hating himself. 'I think that if she knew that the sale of the cottage would make it possible for you to hang on to the house then she would look elsewhere for accommodation. There are other houses for rent, you know.'

'We *couldn't* ask her to go,' cried Tessa—to Will's relief. 'How could we? She cared for

Mathilda and she loved her, too. She misses her dreadfully. She loves the cove as much as we do. It's her home.'

Will watched her gratefully, glad that it had not been left to him to defend Isobel's position. 'There's another point, too,' he said. 'Would we want strangers living in the cove? In such close proximity the whole atmosphere of the place could be ruined.'

Tessa was staring at him in horror, remembering Isobel's story of Mathilda's tenant with the drunken husband. James raised his hands and shoulders in a helpless gesture.

'I agree it's a risk. But it *is* a way of keeping the house.'

'And where would Isobel go?' asked Tessa somewhat belligerently.

'Well, you might offer her accommodation in the house,' suggested James, 'although I think it's unlikely that she'd accept. No doubt she'd find another cottage. I take your point about undesirable neighbours at very close quarters but every avenue has to be explored.'

'I've had another idea,' said Tessa. 'It just occurred to me that if Mr . . . if Will—' she spoke his name rather shyly and he nodded at her encouragingly—'is prepared to sell his property in Switzerland and we put the proceeds together with my trust we might just raise the money for Matron. We'd probably have to take out a small mortgage but I don't mind paying that if I can.'

The men looked at her in surprise. 'I thought your trust didn't materialise for several years,' said James.

'Two years,' said Tessa. 'But do you think Matron might be prepared to wait if we asked her? She could use the house, of course, and perhaps we could pay her interest or something.' She shook her head. 'I don't know the details but perhaps we might persuade her just to hang on. What d'you think?'

'It's not a bad idea,' said Will slowly. 'Of course, she wants to buy her own place, doesn't she? She might not want to wait.'

'I'll talk to her,' said James. 'It might work. Certainly worth a try. But first I need all the details about this trust, Tessa.'

Will sat back in his chair whilst the other two talked, watching Tessa. It was interesting that neither he nor she had questioned for a single moment their compatibility to share the house. It would be fun, he thought, to have such a bright, cheerful girl around and he could look after the house during her absences; make sure that it was a warm welcoming place to which she could come home. Home; that was the word, thought Will. Perhaps that was the link between them. They had both instinctively looked upon the cove as home; something neither of them had truly experienced. We must make it work, he thought. He was not yet prepared to admit to himself how important Isobel was to his plans but he was glad that

Tessa had reacted as she had. Isobel belonged to the cove, too. She was part of the family . . .

Tessa had been unaware of Will's thoughts; she only knew that they were of the same mind and had been pleased to think that this man was her cousin, if a rather distant one. Now, as she lifted the tailgate so that Sidney and Harry could jump in, she thought about Will. She could see no reason why they shouldn't share the house. After all, it was a very big place for one girl who spent most of the time in other people's houses. To Tessa's young eyes Will, the wrong side of sixty, was much too old to be considering any romantic entanglements and she could imagine them settling down well together. He would have Isobel for company when she, Tessa, was dog-sitting and he had already professed himself willing to undertake much of the work which was needed to restore the house and bring it up to date.

The whole thing turned on Matron. Tessa, with boarding school not far behind her, had adopted James's name for Bea with no difficulty at all. Tessa imagined a severe, starched, difficult individual who would have no compunction in overturning her hopes and dreams. She drove the car into the ramshackle wooden garage which clung to the side of the small cottage, released the dogs and went inside to make herself some breakfast. Sidney followed her, collapsing on to his beanbag as though he had walked miles. He watched, nose on paws, as she fetched muesli and toasted bread and, unable to resist the hope in his eyes, she gave him another Bonio which he crunched with great gusto.

She heard the soft plop of letters on the mat and went out to fetch the post. Harry was barking at the postman and she opened the door to reprimand him, smiling an apology as she hauled Harry inside and slammed the door. Harry trotted into the kitchen and went at once to Sidney's beanbag to investigate the crumbs. Because of his soft mouth, Sidney was a messy eater and Harry obligingly cleaned up after him, even licking round Sidney's jaws, much to the clumber's indignation. He looked to Tessa for support but she was opening an envelope. She had asked Cousin Pauline to forward her letters and, amongst them, was a postcard of Edinburgh Castle. She turned it over, puzzled. 'Stuck up here in the frozen north,' ran Sebastian's scrawl. 'How are things? Thanks for last time. See you soon.'

Tessa waited for the surge of excitement with which she had greeted Sebastian's missives over the years but it was not forthcoming. She felt a small glow of pleasure but it was oddly muted and she read the card again so as to work herself up to it. It was no use. Frowning, she looked through the rest of her post which consisted mainly of circulars, apart from a request from Mrs Carrington for a booking for Christmas and the New Year, and a letter from

144

James. This was mainly to confirm all that she told him at their meeting in Plymouth, nevertheless she noted that her heart bumped much faster as she opened this envelope than it had when she'd read Sebastian's card.

As she sat down to her breakfast she castigated herself for putting the anxiety about the house above her love for Sebastian. Mentally she redesigned the house so that it could contain a married couple as well as Will. With Sebastian at sea and herself away so much, she was sure that it could be achieved without too much difficulty . . . Pushing her plates aside she folded her arms on the table and shook her head sadly. Marriage with Sebastian was as distant a dream as it had been when she was fourteen. Their day out together had been lovely but she was aware that, to him, she was still just a little sister. There was none of the excitement that should be there—well, certainly not on his part. It seemed that he needed to be partly drunk to feel that sort of thing.

She found herself thinking about Giles and how differently he had treated her. The expression in his eyes had been flattering and oddly disturbing, giving her flutters in her abdomen. The lunch at the Church House Inn at Rattery had been great fun. True, Guy had been rather distant to begin with but, after a pint or two, he had soon thawed and Gemma was so friendly and funny. Giles had made sure that Tessa was never left out and for those few hours she had felt part of a family group.

Family; she had an obsession about it. Despairingly Tessa began to clear away her breakfast things. She knew that it was this sense of family and deep affection that she saw and loved at the Roundhouse at Buckland-in-the-Moor where the Perrymans worked so happily together; the cheerful banter of the twins, Clare and Marie; the warm motherliness of Mrs Perryman; Sunday lunchtimes when Mr Perryman came in to chat to his regulars; young Colin old enough now to wait at table . . . these were the things that drew her back and gave her a feeling of safety.

Tessa pulled herself together, propped Sebastian's card on the windowsill and began to do the washing-up.

## CHAPTER THIRTEEN

It was at James's suggestion—and with the permission of the other beneficiaries—that Will moved into the house in the cove. Will gratefully accepted the offer. He had enjoyed staying at the Royal Castle and exploring the busy town of Dartmouth but, as the autumn drew on, he found himself more at one with the countryside than with the urban scene. He drove home on a windy cold afternoon, through the coastal villages of Stoke Fleming and Strete, his eyes drawn again and again to the great sweep of coastline which embraced Blackpool Sands and Torcross beach and stretched away to Start Point, misty and ethereal in the autumn sunshine. He swung left, down the hill and on to Torcross Line where the sea crashed in against the long stretch of shingle to his left and the chilly breeze ruffled the calm waters of Slapton Ley on his right.

He slowed to watch a flock of starlings sweep low over the Ley where two swans sailed, calm and indifferent to these noisy visitors, and ducks swam amongst the reedy edges and huddled together on the tiny beach. The flock of starlings, like a ragged cloud overhead, broke and re-formed and swept away inland. Will sighed with deep pleasure and drove on. The low sun sent long sharp shadows across fields whose red soil glowed richly in its rays, touching the dying bracken in the hedgerows with its fiery glance so that the whole countryside was bathed in brilliant colour.

The entrance to the track was familiar to him but he remembered when he had first seen it in the hot August afternoon. There was no honeysuckle now; the red and gold berries of the black bryony trailed across bare branches which shivered and creaked in the cold rush of the wind and bramble leaves burned darkly in the ditch. Will drove gently down the track

147

wishing that some conclusion could be reached. He had a very adequate pension—and some savings tucked away—but living in a hotel and using a hired car was expensive. Of course, if the house were to be sold then he need not worry about money ever again but if he and Tessa were able to keep it they would need every penny.

As he negotiated the sharp bend to the right and saw that first tantalising glimpse of the sea his heart knocked fast in his breast. He parked the car beside the Morris and climbed out, hearing the boom of the surf as it thudded against the sand shelf out at the mouth of the cove. The beach was deep in shadow but the sea reflected back the blue of the overarching sky above it and, as he walked out on to the beach and looked up at the house, he saw that lights were shining out from the kitchen and the study.

Isobel; at the thought of her his heart became even more unruly and he pushed open the kitchen door eagerly. The room was empty but the smell of casserole assailed his nostrils and he saw an apple pie placed in the middle of the Georgian table. He looked about him; at the scratched but polished table, at the delicate china newly dusted on the dresser shelves, at the battered Rayburn and the beautiful glass bowl of the old paraffin lamp which stood on an oak trolley. On the lower shelf of the trolley was a pile of books. Curiously, Will bent to

148

read the titles. He took the top book out in disbelief.

'*The Hunting of the Snark*,' he murmured with amusement and sank into Mathilda's chair beside the Rayburn . . .

Isobel found him some moments later. The shock of seeing him there, looking so like Mathilda as he gazed up at her with a book in his hand, rendered her momentarily inarticulate. She wavered between delight, at seeing him here where she felt he belonged and at the easing of her own loneliness, and rage at giving her a fright and making her think—for one brief wonderful moment—that Mathilda had returned to her. Delight won.

'Oh, Will,' she said, stretching out her hands to him. 'Welcome home.'

\*         ⋎         \*

Bea swept the iron rhythmically to and fro across the board, carefully but insistently pressing out the creases of her best white shirt. Norah sat behind her at the kitchen table, her voice pressing just as insistently at Bea's mind, forcing itself into the corners of her thoughts, exactly as the iron pushed relentlessly into the stiff cotton of Bea's shirt.

'Never go back, Bea. It's always disastrous. These old sayings may be clichés but there's a lot of truth in them. I was saying as much to Andrew. He feels that you'll be making a mistake . . .'

Bea clenched her teeth on a spasm of irritation as she thought about Norah discussing her private affairs with Andrew Owen, priest or not.

'. . . and we agreed that this is exactly the trouble with Miss Knowles. Because she lived here as a girl she feels she has the absolute right to come back, now that she's retired, and behave as though she's been here all her life. She has a most unpleasant air of complacency . . .'

Bea peeled her shirt from the ironing board and hung it on a coat hanger. She selected a nightgown from the pile of laundry on the table beside her and stretched it out across the ironing board.

'. . . of course, the man's a saint. He'd never noticed that smug look on her face but I was able to point out that I've come up against a *very* stubborn streak in her character. Absolutely *determined* to read one of the lessons at the carol service. I know that one member of the congregation is always asked but I flatter myself that I have a better reading voice than most . . .'

Once again, Bea found herself thinking about Bernard; understanding those smiling silences, the disappearances to the pub. Why had she allowed herself to be drawn in to this trap? When she told Norah how much she was missing her friends at school and in the nearby

150

town she had brought a deluge round her ears. This was their third conversation on this subject and Bea, though exhausted and sorry for Norah, was standing firm.

'. . . simply because her father was curate forty years ago she feels that the church is her property. Unless I'm mistaken it will lead to a great deal of heartache. She should have remained where she was, among her own friends. She simply doesn't belong here any more. And that's what *you'll* find, Bea. You simply don't belong there any more.'

'If that's true,' said Bea, speaking for the first time, 'then at least I shall have discovered it for myself. I did tell you at the beginning that we must have a trial run. I'm very fond of you, my dear, but I had no idea how much I would miss the school . . . and the town. You must let me make this experiment.'

Norah exhaled noisily. Without looking round, Bea envisaged her face; chin drawn in, mouth turned down, a self-pitying expression in her eyes.

'Well, if you insist.' She emitted a short mirthless laugh. 'I don't have much choice, do I?'

'Try to understand,' said Bea gently. 'Retirement has come as a bit of a shock. I need time to adjust. The lease on this little flat I've found is for six months. By then I should know one way or the other.'

Norah shrugged—but her reply was lost in

151

the ringing of the telephone. Bea sighed as she folded the nightgown. She had acquiesced to James's request that Will should reside in the house whilst he waited for the outcome to this new suggestion. Bea selected a Viyella skirt from the pile and turned the iron's dial to a lower heat. It was true that she was not desperate for the money from the sale of the house and cottage; nevertheless two years was rather a long time to wait. Thoughtfully Bea smoothed the soft folds. One thing was certain: that she could not live with Norah. It was odd, almost prescient, that Mathilda had left her house to the three of her relatives who had no homes. Of course, that was not strictly true, Will had his flat in Geneva and Tessa had her base in London, as for herself . . . Bea shook out the skirt and slipped it on to its hanger, remembering that James had told her that they were the only three surviving relatives; all three single or alone. For a moment she pictured the cove and heard Will's voice saying, 'It all depends on what you mean by nothing.'

Surely it would be quite impossible for them all to live there together? Perhaps if the cottage were to be vacated . . . She recalled Isobel's anxious face and Will's eager one and laughed aloud as she thought of James's cry of, 'Good grief! It's Matron!' He had been an earnest and very endearing little boy and it was plain that he was just as keen as these others that their hare-brained scheme should come to fruition.

James, in his letter, had suggested that she might like to use the house for weekends and holidays during those two years and, meanwhile, Will and Tess had felt that she should be recompensed for being deprived of her share whilst they waited for Tessa's trust to mature.

Norah was back, clucking with a kind of delighted impatience over some poor soul's inadequacy concerning the preparations for the Townswomen's Guild's Remembrance Sunday's buffet lunch. Bea hardened her heart, grateful that she'd had the sense to leave the bulk of her belongings in the headmaster's attic. She could probably slip away under cover of the new burdens which Norah, with so much joy, was preparing to shoulder. She would write to James, agreeing to his proposal, and settle into the little flat near the school. Bea took her pyjama jacket from the pile. She smiled at Norah, her thoughts elsewhere. Soon she would see Tony Priest and all her boys . . .

*     *     *

Isobel lay in bed staring at the ceiling. Her pleasure at Will's arrival in the cove had been overshadowed by a letter from Simon asking for a divorce. He and Sally wanted to get married, he wrote, and he felt that would be no difficulty now that he and Isobel had been living apart for nearly four years. Isobel had sat for some time, staring at the letter where it lay on the table: nearly four years. She tried to remember that year with Mike—to recapture the madness, the excitement, the fun—but it eluded her, remaining just beyond her mental grasp. Was it really she, Isobel, who had danced and laughed and made love with the energy of a twenty-year-old? She shook her head. The affair seemed to belong to some other person's remote and distant past but the reality was that, because of it, she had lost Simon—and Helen.

Now, the next morning, she rolled over in bed, huddling into the quilt, thinking of her daughter who was a stranger to her and of her husband who now belonged with Sally. Isobel lay quite still, her eyes shut. Mathilda's death and the arrival of her descendants in the cove had enabled Isobel to keep her own heartache and loneliness in abeyance. It closed in again as soon as she was alone but, though she tried to talk herself out of it, she knew beyond doubt that it was Simon whom she still loved, and the idea of him married to Sally was a dreadful one. Just as she had relied on his unchanging love all through her affair with Mike, so she had hoped that one day he would come back to her. Despite her head's certainty that he was irrevocably lost to her, her heart insisted that he still loved her.

The letter had come as a blow to her hopes. Isobel wrapped her arms about herself, squeezing her eyes closed against the morning light. She knew, with heart and head alike, that once he married Sally he was lost to her for ever. And what of Helen? Why should Helen ever bother with her again? Simon had not succeeded in changing his daughter's mind, although she had received a prim little birthday card with her daughter's signature scrawled across the bottom; no message of love, no best wishes, but Isobel had seen the card as a breakthrough and had carried it with her for weeks and, even now, used it as a bookmark. She had comforted herself with the thought that perhaps Sally wasn't quite so wonderful as everyone thought she was. Perhaps Simon was tiring of her and Helen was realising that she was not a substitute for her own mother . . .

Now, Isobel wondered if it had been Sally who had persuaded Helen to send the card. The humiliating thought made her clench her fists and bury her face in the quilt. She would rather not see Helen at all than to know that it was at Sally's prompting. Such knowledge filled her with shame and tears forced themselves out of her eyes. After all, it was she who had wrecked her marriage; she who had abandoned her husband and child in a wild grab at happiness. What right had she to dictate terms now? In her head she heard Mathilda's voice: *'And did you find happiness?'* How many people, wondered Isobel drearily, refused to recognise the happiness at their own doorsteps and spent their lives searching for some mythical bluebird?

Mathilda had injected a kind of strength into her, making it possible to both face the knowledge and bear the result of her mistake. Without her, Isobel felt as though she were drifting off course. She was not yet aware that she was beginning to look towards Will, as she had looked to Mathilda, for courage; but his coming had given her renewed hope which the letter had destroyed. She lay, listening to the continual music of the sea, watching the changing, trembling shift of light on the walls and ceiling, unable to summon the will or energy to get up. The sound of the telephone bell impinged upon her misery and, at length, she swung her legs over the side of the bed and went downstairs.

'Yes?' she said curtly into the receiver. 'Who is it?'

'Hello, Isobel.' It was Tessa. 'Did I get you up? I'm awfully sorry.'

'It's OK,' said Isobel, peering at her watch and seeing that it was twenty past eleven. 'I wasn't asleep. What's the problem?'

'No problem really. I just wondered if Will had moved in.' She sounded hopeful and excited, and Isobel felt her own troubles receding a little. 'I had an idea, you see.'

'Will's in,' said Isobel as cheerfully as she could. 'He's enjoying himself no end. What's the idea?'

'Well, I'm leaving here tomorrow morning

156

and I've got a week's gap. I was just wondering if I could come down to the cove instead of going back to London. What d'you think?'

'Of course you can come,' said Isobel warmly, as though she were the owner of the cove. 'Why not? You have just as much right as Will, and I know he'd be delighted to see you. So would I. When will you be arriving . . .?'

Isobel replaced the receiver feeling perceptibly happier. She must air sheets, make up a bed and prepare a special supper. It was important that Tessa should feel at home in the house in the cove—and, anyway, it was good to have someone to plan for and to look after. She belted her dressing gown more tightly round her waist and went into the kitchen. Through the window she could see Will walking on the beach, and she paused in her act of filling the kettle to watch him. He pottered, as Mathilda used to; picking up shells or stones so as to examine them; collecting driftwood; stopping to watch the waves. He made no attempt to disturb her privacy or encroach upon her time, always waiting for her to approach him. Her heart warmed towards him and it was with a lighter spirit that, having switched on the kettle, she went running upstairs to dress. She must tell Will of Tessa's imminent arrival and maybe they would go into Kingsbridge together to buy in some supplies, stopping off at Frogmore Bakery to buy some bread from Mary . . .

Isobel pulled on leggings and a warm jersey, thrust her feet into thick socks and hurried back downstairs. The day that had stretched so emptily before her was filled with new purpose.

## CHAPTER FOURTEEN

Tessa's week with Will at the cove was an unqualified success. At first he had been anxious lest there might be some awkwardness about sharing the bathroom or appearing unexpectedly in his dressing gown but these fears were swiftly dispelled by Tessa's own attitude. She had spent most of her life either at school or in other people's homes and she was perfectly natural with him. This allowed him, in turn, to be easy and relaxed and soon it was as though they had known each other for years. They prowled about the house together, exploring, investigating, poking into cupboards and generally making themselves at home.

Tactfully, Isobel left them alone as much as possible and it was Will who showed Tessa the countryside, took her in to introduce her to Mary who made such delicious bread at Frogmore Bakery and drove her to Kingsbridge to shop. She exclaimed with pleasure as they passed over Bowcombe Bridge, where the river ran out from between its thickly wooded banks into the wider shining waters of the estuary.

The small grey town which clung to the side of the hill, with its slatehung houses and old cottages and the estuary at its feet, made her think of other small Devonshire towns. She was aware of a sense of timelessness—despite the bustle and the traffic—and a sense of belonging. The weather was cold and bright, with frosty mornings and starlit nights, and Tessa was happier than she had been for many years.

As the week passed an idea was maturing at the back of Will's mind. He was reminded of it by something Tessa was telling him as they sat by the sitting-room fire one early evening, making toast. She had told him many stories of her dog-sitting adventures and described her employers and their houses so graphically that he began to feel that he knew them almost as well as she did. At the moment she was embarked upon a description of Mrs Carrington and her daughter in the Midlands. When she reached the part about the sale of the bureau, Will let out an exclamation. Tessa paused and looked at him enquiringly.

'Sorry. Didn't mean to interrupt. Just reminded me of something. Carry on. So did the young man come and fetch it?'

Whilst she buttered toast Tessa finished her story and, putting the plate in the grate to keep warm, she began to pour the tea. 'Poor old thing,' she said. 'It's really a squeeze to make ends meet and that daughter of her knows she's a soft touch. You can tell.'

Will shook his head sympathetically but his mind was already busy with his new idea. 'It made me think of something,' he told her, pushing the logs back together so that they could begin to burn again. 'You know, there are an awful lot of valuable pieces in this house.'

'Pieces?' Tessa looked puzzled.

'Furniture.' Will accepted his cup. 'Some of it's terrifically old. Now, it occurred to me that if we sold some of it and split the money three ways you and I could put ours towards buying Matron out.'

'But they're Mathilda's things,' said Tessa slowly. 'Family things.'

Will smiled a little. He wondered if it had ever occurred to Tessa just how well off she'd be if they were to sell up. 'I appreciate that,' he said gently. 'But they're our things now, too, d'you see? If it were a choice between selling some of the furniture or selling the house . . .?'

He let the remark hang in the air whilst he ate his toast, watching her. She sat staring into the fire, deep in thought: presently she looked about the room.

'It wouldn't be the same without her things,' she observed wistfully.

He bit back his impatience, realising that it was the sense of continuity that was important to her. He had seen her, touching the furniture, picking up ornaments, taking down a book, and had known that she was identifying with

160

Mathilda and feeling part of the pattern. Here Mathilda had stood to watch the sea; here she had sat to write and work; here she had slept. Some of the furniture must have belonged to Mathilda's parents, possibly even to her grandparents. There had been Rainbirds here for more than ninety years . . .

'We might only need to sell two or three pieces,' he said. 'Don't think I want to but I'd rather lose a few pieces of furniture than the house.'

'Two or three pieces?' She shook her head. 'Mrs Carrington only got three hundred pounds for her bureau.'

'Perhaps Mrs Carrington's bureau wasn't very valuable,' suggested Will, who was interested in antiques and had a very good idea of just how valuable some of Mathilda's things were. 'It's only a thought. To keep as an emergency. James is hoping that Matron will be prepared to wait.'

Tessa drank her tea. 'Perhaps as an emergency,' she agreed at last.

Will heaved a sigh of relief. 'It will all have to be valued. Perhaps James has had it done already. I'll talk to him. Let's hope it won't be necessary.'

'I hope not but it would be silly to lose the house if we had the means to save it. Oh, I can't tell you what it means to know that I've got this to come back to.' She took a deep breath and nodded. 'We simply must hold on.'

'I'll have a word with James.' He cast about for something to distract her and his eye fell on Mathilda's Scrabble board. 'Ever played Scrabble?'

She began to laugh. 'Not for years and years. I used to play with Rachel and Sebastian. He always won but we said he cheated.'

'Let's have a game.' Will was clearing away the tea things. 'Look, here are the score cards.' Together they studied Mathilda's small precise writing; the two columns of figures headed M and I. 'She must have been quite a player,' he said, chuckling. 'Beat old Isobel nearly every time by the look of it.'

'There are more in the box.' Tessa picked them up. 'These columns are headed M and N. I wonder who N was?'

'Sounds like the old Catechism,' said Will cheerfully, setting out the board and the racks on the low table. '"What is your name? N or M?"'

Tessa fingered the yellowing paper thoughtfully. Will glanced up at her, surprised at her silence, and felt a sudden surge of affection for the small figure with the serious down-slanted face and its aureole of bright hair. Sensing the slight change of atmosphere, she looked at him and they smiled at each other with deep satisfaction and contentment.

'It'll be all right,' he told her confidently. 'Come on. You can draw first.'

Sunday morning. The chapel was full but the faint warmth from the heaters had not yet dispelled the chill of the frosty December morning. The boys' breath appeared in smoky puffs and they rubbed their hands together and blew out their cheeks, exaggerating the cold. Bea sat at the back of the chapel, trying not to feel superfluous. Her arrival back in the environs of the school had received a mixed response. At first her old friends had greeted her welcomingly and with affection but, when they realised that she was not just on a visit but had rented a flat in the town, their reactions altered. There was a certain raising of eyebrows which indicated surprise and, in some cases, faint disapproval. Bea hid her disappointment and anxiety and tried to make herself feel at home. The shopkeepers knew her and were friendly enough but, now that she was no longer officially attached to the school, there was a very real sense of exclusion.

As she tried to make her new flat comfortable she told herself that she was being oversensitive. After all, she'd lived close to the town for fifteen years and had as much right to retire here as anyone else. She looked critically at the indifferent furniture with which the flat was furnished and tried not to feel lonely. She had not been ready to deal with the impression that, to her ex-colleagues, she was already an outsider. On the odd occasions when she'd popped into the school for a chat there had been an undercurrent of suspicion; a 'What's *she* doing here?' atmosphere which had made her feel uncomfortable. The new matron, fresh from a school in the north, was openly hostile and even the headmaster, when he saw her chatting to the boys as they came off the playing fields, seemed reserved. Although he offered her tea he looked relieved when she refused, and hurried the boys away to the changing rooms.

Bea spent hours wandering round her three rooms, fiddling with the small personal possessions which gave the flat a less bleak look, and trying to decide how she could overcome this hurtful sense of hostility. The boys had been pleased to see her, waving when they saw her coming down the drive from the school so that she'd strolled over to watch the game. She'd stood with them on the sidelines whilst they cheered their team on and they'd talked easily and naturally with her, as though she were still part of their lives.

No one could have guessed what courage it took for her to make this appearance at the Sunday morning service. She sat just inside the door, dressed in her grey flannel suit and navy felt hat, and stared at the back of Tony Priest's head. She had seen him briefly and only at a distance. He had noticed her as she passed out through the hall from the secretary's office—

mercifully June was just as friendly as she'd ever been—and he had raised a long arm in greeting before turning back to the small boy who stared earnestly up at him. She'd paused, pretending to study some photographs pinned to the notice board, but pride had made it impossible to hover there indefinitely.

This morning his wife sat beside him, thin and elegant in soft lambswool, her fine fair hair cut in a short bob. Bea clasped her hands on her grey flannel lap and stared down at her ample, cotton-covered bosom. She had surprised a disapproving stare from Marian, the headmaster's wife, and a glare from the new matron and she felt as miserable and alone as any new boy. She knew now that Norah had been right but she simply could not go back to Winchester. She would rather stay here and risk the snubs . . .

The headmaster's voice, reading the lesson for the first Sunday in Advent, caught her attention. '" . . . *it is high time to awake out of sleep . . . The night is far spent, the day is at hand: let us therefore cast off the works of darkness, and put on the armour of light . . .*"'

Bea, moved as always by the Epistle for Advent, thought that this was probably the most exciting time of the whole school year. Christmas loomed ahead with the promise of the carol service and the Christmas party; the decoration of the tree that stood in the hall and the rehearsals for the nativity play which took

165

place in the chapel. The Advent hymns had always thrilled her with a sense of anticipation and there was an ongoing atmosphere of happy expectation. Surely they would not exclude her from all that lay ahead? There must be some part she could play; some area in which she could make herself useful?

As the organ played the opening bars of 'Lo he comes with clouds descending', Bea rose to her feet determined to make a very great effort to be integrated back into her old familiar world. She had yet to collect her few odds and ends from the headmaster's attic and, whilst doing it, she would talk to Marian and let them see that she was no threat. On reflection, she realised that she should have thought of this before. Perhaps the new matron felt that she might be undermined by Bea's presence; perhaps it had been a little thoughtless to turn up unannounced . . . Encouraged, Bea held her hymn book higher and, with her eyes on Tony Priest's broad shoulders, sang the well-known words with new-found confidence.

*       *       *

Giles stretched out his hand to the telephone, dithered and, folding his arms across his chest, tucked both fists into his armpits. His stepfather, seated at the kitchen table, maintained a tactful silence but Kate drew in her breath and closed her eyes in

166

frustration.

'Giles,' she said in a low dangerous voice, 'will you please pick up that telephone and talk to Tessa?'

Giles looked at her. 'The trouble is . . .' he began but stopped as Kate slapped both hands flat on the table and gave a cry of anguish. David courteously but silently drew back his newspaper and Kate glared at him briefly before returning her attention to Giles.

'And *don't* tell me what the trouble is,' she said warningly. 'You've already told me what the trouble is. Once on the phone from London. Again on your arrival yesterday lunchtime and all over again last night after supper. We know how you feel about it. We know that your photographic business might not be able to support a wife; we know you feel that you're not in a position to enter into an ongoing relationship; we know that Tessa has a crush on Sebastian Anderson. We decided, on the telephone and again when you arrived yesterday, and for the third time last evening— or rather at two o'clock this morning—that none of these things matter since you are merely going to invite her out to lunch.'

The word 'lunch' came out on a rather high note and Kate paused and cleared her throat. Giles and David watched her anxiously.

'The thing is, old chap,' said David after a moment of pregnant silence, 'that the girl probably won't give a hang about your job or your bank balance. You're not proposing marriage. Just lunch.'

'I don't believe this.' Kate sat down at the table and ran both hands through her hair. 'No wonder you're thirty years old and not married, Giles. Do you ever manage to ask any girl to go anywhere? I thought that young girls were free and independent and self-sufficient. Why the third degree?'

'Tessa's special,' said Giles simply.

Kate stared at him, her irritation evaporating. 'Oh, darling,' she said. 'I know. At least, I think you could say we suspected. Oh hell! Can't you see that's why we want you to phone her?'

Suppressing a desire to howl with frustration she fetched a bottle of wine and the corkscrew and put them down on the table in front of David.

'Sorry,' said Giles miserably. 'Only it means a lot and I'm afraid of cocking it up. I know she's very independent and all those things and I seem to be a bit old-fashioned where women are concerned and they don't care for it much . . . And then there's Sebastian.'

David and Kate exchanged a glance and David pushed a glass of wine across the table towards Giles where he stood, leaning against the dresser, hands now thrust deep in his trouser pockets.

'Giles,' said Kate carefully, 'please try to be sensible about this. It's one thing being

168

honourable and another being stupid.' David winced and looked quickly at Giles, who was staring into his wine glass. 'Tessa has had a schoolgirl crush on Sebastian for years and, because she rarely gets the opportunity to meet any other young men, she hasn't grown out of it. From what I've read between the lines he treats her like a little sister and has never given her a serious thought. If you're going to let that stand in your way then you're a twit. For heaven's sake, give her the chance to choose for herself.'

Giles stood his glass on the table and looked at the telephone.

'Got an idea.' David smiled at him. 'Why not use the extension in my study? More private.'

'I'll do that.' Giles picked up the address book, nodded at them and disappeared into the hall.

'And now I shan't hear what he says,' groaned Kate. 'I shan't be able to spur him on if he needs it. He looked just like he used to when I left him at school. It's ridiculous.'

David reached a hand across the table to her. 'As you said, my darling, he's thirty years old. Got to let go sometime.'

'I've been letting Giles go since he was eight and he went off to prep school,' said Kate wretchedly. 'I've hardly seen him for the last twenty-two years. Where did I go wrong? Perhaps I wasn't motherly enough.'

'I notice he still telephones when he's got a

problem,' said David. 'I think he looks upon you more as a friend than a mother. Nothing wrong with that. Stop fretting. This is the first time I've seen Giles like this in the four years that I've known him. It's love, that's what it is, poor chap.'

'He's been in love before.' Kate swallowed some wine. 'It was a girl he was at university with. Went on for years. Giles is very faithful and loyal and had great difficulty when he knew that it was over for him but that she was still keen. It was hell! For all of us!'

David began to laugh. 'Then why are you so hellbent in putting us all through it again?'

'Shh!' said Kate. 'He's coming . . .'

Giles came in, looking self-conscious. He paused, grinning at their expectant faces and then punched the air with both fists.

'No problem,' he said. 'Sounded very pleased. She's bringing Charlie Custard and we'll take him for a walk afterwards.'

Kate let out a gasp of relief. 'Thank God for that! Let joy be unconfined. Stop hogging the bottle, David. I need another drink!'


## CHAPTER FIFTEEN

Tessa replaced the telephone receiver and stroked Charlie Custard as he leaned heavily against her leg.

'That's nice, isn't it, Custard?' she said. 'We've got a lunch date for tomorrow at the Elephant's Nest. Giles is coming here first. We'll have to go in my car so that you can come too.'

She glanced at her watch and saw that it was nearly lunchtime. As she opened a tin of soup she thought about Giles, remembering how easy he had been to talk to, and how he'd made her feel rather special. If it hadn't been for Sebastian . . . Tessa switched on the heat under the saucepan and put two slices of bread in the toaster. Charlie Custard watched hopefully but Tessa was deep in thought, remembering her visit to the Andersons a few weekends before. It was Commander and Mrs Anderson's thirtieth wedding anniversary and Tessa had been invited to the party. It was lovely to see the twins and Rachel, who was now a hard-working lawyer in the City, and even more wonderful to see Sebastian, who was on leave from his ship. When she saw him in the flesh she wondered how on earth she had been so indifferent to his postcard. Not exactly indifferent, she told herself as he hugged her, but simply preoccupied with the house. He was delighted to see her, ready to listen to her news about the cove, and—when he'd had a few drinks—more than ready to kiss her while they were supposed to be looking for extra glasses in the kitchen.

By the time the weekend was drawing to its

close, she was convinced that this was the turning point she'd been hoping for; the moment when he saw her as a woman. Even Rachel noticed a difference in his attitude and teased them about it, embarrassing Tessa who feared it might frighten Sebastian away. He, however, merely laughed and took Tessa out for a walk and then into the pub, where they sat in a corner and he said the things to her that she'd always longed to hear. They arrived back in time for supper and there was no more opportunity then to be alone. Tessa was sharing a bedroom with Rachel, just like the old days, and they talked until the early hours and parted the next morning promising that they wouldn't let it be so long before they met again. Sebastian slept late and Tessa was obliged to leave for Wales before he appeared.

As Tessa poured the soup into a bowl and put the toast on a plate she relived the disappointment she'd felt when he telephoned later in the week to tell her that he wouldn't be driving to Wales to see her after all. His father needed the car, he'd said, and the train journey was too complicated, but when he was next on leave they must spend some time together . . . They'd talked for a while and Tessa had managed to joke and laugh with him and not let him guess how hurt she was. A naval wife needed to be strong and independent and he must see that she would be able to cope with separations. Since then there had been no word but the weekend remained like a warm glow in her heart.

Now she had lunch with Giles to look forward to as well as her very first Christmas at the cove. It was Isobel who had suggested that she should come across from Mrs Carrington's for Christmas Day. It was barely half an hour's drive and she could bring Romulus and Remus with her. Isobel and Will had tried to persuade her to come on Christmas Eve and stay over for Boxing Day but Tessa was firm. Part of her duties was to look after the house as well as the dogs and she felt that it would be wrong to leave it empty at night. They made no attempt to dissuade her from what she rightly saw as her responsibility but promised that the three of them should have the best Christmas Day ever.

Tessa broke a few crusts into her soup bowl and put it down for Charlie Custard to lick, remembering how he and she had spent last Christmas together. She thought of the presents Freddie had left under the little tree and how Kate had invited her to lunch. This year she would be spending most of Christmas Day in her own home. She repeated those last three magic words aloud to herself, hardly daring to believe them, and, unable to contain herself, wrapped her arms round the dog's great neck and gave him a hug of pure joy. She wondered what she'd do without all these long-suffering dogs to talk to and cuddle when she felt happy or miserable, and it struck her that she led a very strange life. Even when she went back to London, Cousin Pauline very rarely talked to her; she was much more interested in the latest television soap. She had shown a faint animation when Tessa told her about the cove but it had quickly faded. Refusing to allow a tinge of self-pity to depress her, Tessa pulled on her coat and, taking the rope halter which served as his lead, she and Charlie Custard went out into the raw winter afternoon.

\*     \*     \*

Isobel, too, was thinking about last Christmas. She remembered the humiliating scene with Simon and how he'd told her that he and Sally were going to the Lakes together. She had come rushing back to Mathilda and they had planned their trip to Oxford together. Isobel shook her head and swallowed hard. Only a year ago ... and now Mathilda was dead; even then she must have been dying. The bitter thing—the thing she could not come to terms with—was that Mathilda had not confided in her. Isobel had believed that they were friends and yet Mathilda had kept her illness a secret and had gone to her death as she had lived—alone. No matter what other people might say or think Isobel was convinced that Mathilda had taken the boat out that night intending to take her own life. She remembered quite clearly their conversation on euthanasia and Mathilda's words: *'If he is terminally ill and in his right mind I think that he should have as much right to choose the manner of his death just as he has chosen the manner in which he has lived.'*

She knew now that Mathilda had consulted her doctor and a few nights later had taken the boat out. How had she seen her end? Had she switched off the engine and let the boat be washed on to the rocks? If so, how would she have known that she would die? Isobel suspected that Mathilda had set out intending to slip over the side when she was too far out to be able to swim back. She guessed, too, that Mathilda had been unable to carry out the plan when the time came. *'This life is all we know,'* she had said. *'It is the human condition to cling to what we know.'* It was Isobel's private nightmare that, when Mathilda's courage had failed, the engine had failed with it and she had been swept helplessly to her death. Over and over she imagined her terror and her loneliness and blamed herself that Mathilda had been unable to confide in her. Worse, she blamed herself because she had not noticed that Mathilda was ill; that she had never suspected that she was dying. She had been too absorbed in her own problems and she writhed when she remembered her words to Mathilda; 'Go and drown yourself and see if I care!'

James was quite right in suspecting that

Isobel couldn't forgive Mathilda for leaving her but she couldn't forgive herself either for what she saw as her own failure. Because of her selfishness Mathilda had been denied the solace of unburdening herself or sharing her fear. If she had been able to talk to Isobel openly and frankly she might not have felt desperate enough to contemplate suicide.

On her worst days, Isobel saw herself as a complete failure; she had failed in her marriage to Simon, she had failed her daughter and, finally, she had failed Mathilda. Guilt lived and flourished in her like a malignant disease and, when it became too painful to bear, she let herself out of the cottage and went to find Will . . .

This morning he was clearing out the room across the passage from the kitchen; the room which had once been the dining room. She leaned in the doorway watching him and feeling comforted merely by the sight of him in his baggy cords and his shapeless old Guernsey.

'So what's all this in aid of?'

Will beamed at her, grey hair on end, flushed with exertion. He pulled a pile of boxes nearer to the door and sat down on the edge of a half-full tea-chest, wiping his brow with a large red handkerchief. Already he loved her so much that he could sense her deep unhappiness but he did not know yet how he could help her.

'It occurred to me that we would need an extra bedroom,' he told her. 'It could just be

176

that the three of us might be here together, d'you see? It would be best if the two girls had the bedrooms. This will do very nicely for me if I can get the rubbish out and give it a lick of paint.'

'You're certain then that you'll be able to stay here?'

'Oh, I think so. Bea has agreed to give us time to raise the money and my flat is up for sale. I've got a buyer.' Will had returned to Geneva for a few days to sort out his affairs and was going back again after the New Year to tie up loose ends. 'Can't give up now.'

'I was thinking.' Isobel wrapped her arms around her body; it was chilly in this unused room. 'If I were to vacate the cottage you could sell it. That would give you what you need, wouldn't it?'

'Absolute nonsense.' Will stood up and began to root in the box. 'You belong here as much as we do. More. You knew Mathilda. You're our link with her. Wouldn't want strangers in the cottage.'

Isobel blinked back her tears and tried to smile, accepting his gesture of friendship. 'Looks like you've got your work cut out. Want some help?'

'Now you're talking.' Will hid his relief—he dreaded the idea of Isobel leaving the cove—and straightened up again. 'I thought that I could pack all this away somewhere. In the garage, perhaps. There's acres of papers and

177

notebooks and all sorts of odds and ends. If we could store it away for the time being, we could have a chance to look at it later when the others are here and I could get on with decorating this room.'

'Won't you mind being down here?' Isobel glanced round the room. 'It looks damp to me.'

'I shall rather like it. Get some heating into it and regular airing and it'll be fine. And I shall have my freedom, d'you see? I'm a bit of a nocturnal animal and when young Tessa is here I'm afraid that I shall disturb her if I go wandering about in the middle of the night. It'll be handy being just across from the kitchen.'

Isobel remembered how she and Mathilda had stayed up late on stormy nights and how comforting it had been to tuck up with a hot-water bottle, knowing that Mathilda was pottering about or in the next bedroom. She wondered if Tessa felt the same about Will.

'You're very like Mathilda,' she said. 'It'll be nice for Tessa to have company. She must get so lonely, all on her own in strange people's houses with only dogs for company.' She watched him for a moment and then shook herself mentally. 'Look, I'll find the key and get the boathouse opened up. It would be better than the garage. It's got a huge loft room. We can pile all this stuff in and you can start painting.'

After her second trip across to the boathouse she went into the kitchen to push the kettle on to the hotplate. Presently Will came to join her. He had just finished washing his hands when the telephone rang. He dried his hands quickly and picked up the receiver. 'Rainbird.' Isobel sipped her coffee, her eyes on his face but mentally reviewing how much more was to be done in preparation for Christmas, now less than two weeks away. 'Of course. Of course you must come,' he said. 'We shall be delighted to see you.' Isobel came out of her reverie and looked at him with renewed interest. He grimaced at her. 'Come to Totnes,' he said, 'not Plymouth. That's right. Let us know and we'll be able to fetch you. No trouble at all. The more the merrier. Yes, we'll all be here. Look forward to hearing from you.'

'Who was that?' asked Isobel curiously as he replaced the receiver.

'It was Bea.' Will looked thoughtful. 'It seems that she'd like to spend Christmas in the cove.' He smiled at Isobel's amazed expression. 'Looks like it's going to be a real family Christmas.' He gulped at his coffee. 'I'd better get on. We're going to need that extra room sooner than we thought.'

'She could come over with me,' offered Isobel. 'I've got a spare room.'

Will stood, brooding. 'No.' He shook his head. 'I think the three of us must make shift together. Don't want anyone to think they don't belong in the house, d'you see? If Tessa or Bea suggest it that's different but to begin with we must share equally.'

'Well, it's there if anyone wants it.' Isobel hesitated. 'Will, I'm still not happy about living rent-free.'

'Look,' Will began to pat his pockets for his pipe, 'we talked that over with James. It was how it was arranged with Mathilda and until the estate is finally sorted out that's how it stays.'

'But I looked after Mathilda,' cried Isobel. 'Well.' Her face changed. 'I tried to.'

Will saw the bitter twist to her mouth but he held his tongue. Now was not the time to find out what was eating away at Isobel's peace of mind.

'And you're looking after us,' he said. 'You clean the house up after me and cook delicious meals. And you've worked like a slave getting things ready for Christmas. No more arguments. Please.'

'OK.' Isobel gave in gratefully. 'Let's make a start on your bedroom. You must be psychic, that's all I can say.'

'It has been said of me,' said Will modestly, hoping to make her smile, 'that I can see further through a brick wall than most.'

He was rewarded by her grin and later, when they set off happily together to buy paint and brushes, Isobel realised that her depression had dissipated and she could look forward more cheerfully and with a lighter heart.

180

# CHAPTER SIXTEEN

Once again, Bea was travelling west. She was grateful that she had managed to find a vacant seat next to the window; at least she wouldn't be obliged to make friendly noises at other travellers. The young man in the seat beside her sat with his eyes shut, plugged into his Walkman, oblivious to the noise around him. The train was full of people going home for Christmas and Bea tried to persuade herself that she was doing the same. Slowly and painfully during these past weeks the unpleasant fact had been borne in upon her consciousness; she had no home and no roots.

Her tired eyes looked out unseeingly on the muted colours of the winter countryside. The frosty grass was washed pale gold by a thin faint sunlight and the trees looked like iron against the lemon sky. The bright berries of a holly bush were a shock of colour in the quiet landscape. Bea was seeing none of the beauty that streamed by silently beyond the window. Superimposed over the shadowy reflection of her own face was that of Marian Goodbody— the headmaster's wife.

'. . . so Angus felt that it was only right that we should mention it. You know how fond of you we all are but we have to look to the future. Try to put yourself in Matron's place. She feels that you are undermining her position. The boys know you so well and she feels that it makes it much more difficult to relate to them whilst you are around . . .'

Bea sat on the stiff cretonne-covered chair in Marian's drawing room and watched Marian's mouth moving in her large pale face. Bea's belongings, fetched down from the attic, stood beside her on the carpet whilst Marian continued to render Bea's past valueless and her future bleak.

'. . . and I do feel that it is never wise to try to turn the clock back. It would be so difficult to live on the edge of a community, not quite part of it. Of course, we shall always be glad to see you. Good Heavens! You've been part of our lives for so long . . .'

How triumphant Norah would be, thought Bea observing the squareness of Marian's teeth, to know that she was right. How humiliating to have to tell her.

'. . . but I'm sure that you can sympathise with Matron's feelings. Put yourself in her shoes. Children are so fickle, aren't they? So ready to play one adult off against another. She's going to find your act *quite* difficult enough to follow as it is . . .'

Bea stared at Marian's mouth stretched wide, now, in an encouraging smile whilst her head nodded archly as she tossed Bea this sop to her pride.

'. . . so difficult for the staff. It's a question of

loyalty, isn't it? Of course, we all miss you but life goes on and we have to look forward not back . . .'

Bea stood abruptly. Marian stopped mid-speech, head flung back as she stared up at her.

'If you've finished, Marian. I'll be getting on. Thank you for your little talk. Very interesting. Have you ever thought of taking up counselling professionally?'

The headmaster's wife flushed a dull and unbecoming red. 'I'm sorry that you should take it like this, Bea.' Her mouth no longer smiled. 'I've tried to be tactful . . .'

'Have you?' Bea smiled a little. 'Well, no doubt it's difficult to tell someone that they're superfluous to requirements. Have you any objections to my remaining in the town or will that upset Matron's delicate sensibilities too? Perhaps we should ask *her* where I should be allowed to live? Perhaps it should be brought up at the next staff meeting?'

'That's a very insulting thing to say.' Marian got to her feet. She looked upset and Bea felt a twinge of remorse. 'I am merely doing what is best for everyone . . .'

'I think it is quite breath-taking that you should imagine you know what is best for everyone. Shall we take the rest as read?' They stared angrily at each other. 'I think that Pete is waiting to help me with my belongings. Shall we call him? Thank you for storing them for me.'

In silence Bea waited whilst Marian went to find the groundsman; in silence they carried the things out to his pick-up truck. When they were safely stowed, Bea turned to Marian and held out her hand.

'I shall be away for Christmas,' she told her. 'Thank you for everything.'

Marian took the proffered hand and held it briefly, her lips compressed, and turned back into the house without a word.

'What's eating her?' asked Pete curiously, as Bea climbed in beside him.

Bea felt guilty, they should not have allowed their feelings to show before the staff. A tiny voice reminded her that Marian had never been popular and a sense of wicked rebellion filled her. Why should she worry about Pete guessing that a row had been going on in the headmaster's drawing room? Such things—as had just been firmly pointed out—were no longer her problem. Momentarily, loyalty deserted her.

'She's been giving me the sack,' she said.

He gaped at her as they moved off down the drive. 'Sack? Thought you'd gone already.'

'So I have.' Bea pulled herself together and reassembled her ideas of duty and responsibility. 'Just a joke. Keep your eyes on the road.'

Bea shifted in her seat as the train drew in at Newton Abbot. She watched a young woman struggling along the platform. A baby lay against her chest in a sling, a toddler clung to one of her hands whilst, in the other, she carried a suitcase. A man and a woman broke free from a crowd of people and went to greet her. As Bea watched, the man swung the toddler into his arms and gave him a hearty kiss, the woman touched the baby's cheek, embraced her daughter and relieved her of the case. Moving as one unit, chattering all together, they moved towards the exit.

Bea found herself remembering Will's voice when she had telephoned to tell him at what time she would be arriving at Totnes. He had made her feel that nothing could have given him—or Tessa and Isobel—more pleasure than to know that she would be joining them for Christmas. Her sore heart had been warmed by his friendliness and she had spent the remaining days choosing presents for them in the town. She had warded off curious looks and questions, glad that she had somewhere to which she could escape. The thought of spending Christmas alone in her flat was a chilling one and there had been very few offers of hospitality.

During those lonely days after Marian's 'talk' she realised how important her job had been. It had given her status, a title and a position within the community. Now she was no-one; Matron no longer, nobody's mother or wife or child or aunt, just Bea. As she had stood, staring out of the flat window at the

185

shops opposite, a thought had slipped into her mind. She had cousins, now; cousins who wanted her to make a home with them and to share their inheritance and their lives. Bea stared thoughtfully out into the gathering darkness. Tony Priest issued from the bookshop across the road and raised his hand. For one golden moment she thought that he was summoning her. Almost she hurried down to meet him but, hesitating, she saw his wife emerge from somewhere below the window and cross the road to him. He made some laughing remark and she gave him a friendly push. Slipping an arm about her shoulders they vanished into the evening. After a moment or two, Bea turned back into the shadows of the darkening room and sat down. The next day she had telephoned to the house in the cove . . . and now here she was, collecting her belongings, stepping over the legs of the recumbent young man and going to meet Isobel and Will at Totnes station.

*　　　*　　　*

'I wonder why she's coming,' mused Isobel for the fiftieth time as she and Will drove through Harbertonford.

For the present, they were sharing the Morris. Will had managed to sell his own car whilst he was in Switzerland and was now looking around for something to replace it.

186

Isobel had suggested that, instead of spending money on a hired car, he should use the Morris until he found what he wanted. Will readily agreed. For one thing it meant that he and Isobel did so much more together. It was sensible to make joint journeys to go shopping or to the library and, on the days when Isobel was at the bookshop, Will was more than content to potter in the cove. Slowly he was pulling the house together, unobtrusively giving it a face lift, and, as he worked quietly and happily, he thought about Isobel. He was surprised at how strong his feelings were for her. He remembered that it had taken him quite a while to approach Bierta; not because of shyness but because he was cautious.

Will had inherited the Rainbird qualities of self-sufficiency and the ability to live alone, as well as a low physical drive. He, like Mathilda, was not cut out for passion or dramatic scenes; jealous rages and extravagant reconciliations were unknown to him. Bierta had charmed him but the qualities which he attributed to her had been, very largely, in his own imagination. Isobel was so different in almost every way to Bierta and he had loved her as soon as he had seen her on the beach. 'No fool like an old fool,' he told himself. This was very different from his love for Bierta and he had no intention of declaring it. For one thing he must be at least twenty years older than Isobel and for another he knew that she was unhappy.

Quite soon she had begun to tell him about her marriage and how she had left Simon and had an affair. Gradually she told him how it had come to nothing but that it had destroyed her marriage. Her husband had found another woman and was now seeking a divorce.

'I still love him, you see,' Isobel had said, staring away from him, looking out over the sea. 'That's the whole bloody irony of it. I threw it all away.'

Will had remained silent. Everything he thought of to say sounded trite or inadequate. Presently she had looked at him and shrugged.

'Do you think happiness is important?' she'd asked him.

There had been an earnestness in her voice and she had watched him eagerly while he thought about it. He felt ill-equipped to answer such a question and that odd tenseness about her made him nervous.

'I suppose it all depends on what you mean by happiness?' he'd said slowly at last and she'd given a great cry, covering her face with her hands. 'What is it?' he'd asked. 'What's the matter?' He felt almost angry with her, as though she was making him play a game without telling him the rules.

'Nothing,' she'd said, shaking her head, but she'd looked distressed. 'It's just that you're *so* like Mathilda. You even speak like she did. She always used to say that. "It all depends on what you mean..." That's how she always answered.'

'I'm sorry,' Will said helplessly. 'I don't think I'm being much use.'

'Yes, you are.' She'd jumped up and gone to the window. 'It's a lovely afternoon. Come on. I'll show you Bolberry Down. It'll be glorious up there. We'll watch the sunset.'

Her words struck a chord in Will's memory. He'd taken Bierta to watch the sunset on the lake once, early on in their relationship. Afterwards she'd been cool and evasive and years later he'd heard her say rather bitterly to a friend, 'Will's the kind of man who takes you to see the sunset and then actually expects you to sit and watch it!'

He'd realised that she'd thought his invitation was an excuse to get her alone in a romantic setting and he'd wondered how often he had failed her in that area of their lives together. Luckily, Isobel had expected him to watch the sunset and afterwards they stopped for a drink at the Cricket at Beesands and had come home to one of her delicious casseroles. She treated him with the ease and affection of a long-standing friend and he was grateful. He had no intention of rocking the boat with presumptuous declarations but he wished that Isobel had been his first love rather than his second.

When Bea telephoned, Will had sensed that all was not well with her and he hoped that she was not coming to tell them that she'd changed her mind and wanted to sell the house after all. If that was the case then he and Tessa would have to fall back on his plan to sell some of the furniture. James had confirmed his suspicions that some of it was very valuable and had agreed that, if Bea changed her mind, then it would be wise to sell some of the pieces and buy her out.

Now, as they drove through Harbertonford, Will shook his head at Isobel's question. He had not voiced his fears, no point in panicking unnecessarily. Anyway, Bea hardly needed to come for Christmas to tell them that she wasn't prepared to wait after all.

'I thought she was sharing a house with a friend,' he said. 'Perhaps they've fallen out.'

'Fatal. I should have thought.' Isobel pulled her scarf higher round her neck. The Morris's heater was extremely inefficient. 'Fraught with difficulties.'

'Don't say that.' Will glanced at his watch. 'Plenty of time. Like some coffee?'

'Oh, yes please. But why do you say "Don't say that," in that tone of foreboding?'

'Because,' he said, turning into Cistern Street and heading for the car park, 'it is what we are all attempting to do. Well, me and Tessa and probably Bea as well, by the sounds of it.'

'Well, it *will* be fraught with difficulties,' said Isobel frankly. 'No good pretending. Bound to be. You'll manage.'

He pulled into the Heath Nursery car park,

smiling at the confidence in her voice. 'You'll have to be referee,' he told her. 'Got any change for the meter? Just time for a quick cup of something hot in Rumour if we get a move on.'

*       *       *

They were waiting for her on the platform, taking her case, walking on each side of her, hurrying her out to the car. Isobel insisted that Bea sat in front and leaned over her shoulder so as to point out the old castle ruin as the Morris chugged up the hill on the Kingsbridge road.

Bea settled back in the seat and began to relax a little. Her fears that they might have been dreading her arrival, that she would be in the way, began to fade a little. Isobel explained that Tessa was coming for Christmas Day.

'It's such a pity she can't come for longer,' she said, 'but we must make the most of it. She's bringing Romulus and Remus.'

Bea turned to look into the face so close to her own. 'She's bringing *who*?'

They laughed at the expression on her face and explained as the Morris turned off into five-mile lane and wound its way down to the coast. The short winter day was drawing in and the sea looked like grey slate as they parked behind the house and drew her inside. They took her up to the sitting room where a

Christmas tree sparkled in the alcove with a pile of presents waiting temptingly beneath its boughs. Will made up the fire and Isobel drew the curtains and went to make tea. Bea sat looking at the tree with its tiny wooden carved figures. and at the shimmering glass balls and the tinsel, and then she looked about the room, cosy and welcoming in the firelight.

## CHAPTER SEVENTEEN

The young man who had bought Mrs Carrington's bureau sat in his car, parked unobtrusively in the quiet road, and watched Tessa pull in at the gate and stop her car in the drive. She climbed out, shut the gates and released the two labradors from the back. They flopped out heavily and went to drink at a large bowl by the back door. Tessa let herself in and the dogs lay down, panting stertorously, on the concrete apron in front of the garage. The young man had his eyes on his watch. Two minutes passed, three, four ... He imagined her kicking off her boots, hanging up her coat, going into the kitchen and filling the kettle ... He switched on the engine and drove along to the gate.

Romulus and Remus heaved themselves up and, with a bark or two as a token of their vigilance, came wagging to greet him. He touched their heads perfunctorily, his glance alert; no one seemed aware of his arrival. He went to the front door and rang the bell. After a moment Tessa opened the door. She was still wearing her woollen hat and on her feet were thick socks

'Sorry.' He managed to appear both slightly surprised and apologetic. 'I was hoping to have a word with Mrs Carrington. Is she about?'

'I'm afraid she's away. Back tomorrow.'

He bit his lip, frowning. 'Oh, that's a pity. I was hoping . . . Never mind. You look as if you were on your way out. I don't want to keep you.'

'On my way out? Oh . . .' Tessa swept off her hat and shook her head. 'I've just come in actually.' She hesitated, studying him. 'Don't I know you?'

'Amazing!' He laughed in his relief. 'You've made my day. I remember you, of course. Who wouldn't?' He made a gallant little bow. 'I came to collect Mrs Carrington's bureau last Easter.'

'Yes.' She grimaced ruefully at her forgetfulness. 'Sorry. I remember you now. Is there anything I can do?'

'Well . . .' He looked thoughtful, rubbing his chin as he stared past her into the hallway. 'Since I'm in the area . . . She suggested that I might come back and have a look at one or two things . . . Oh dear. Am I being indiscreet?'

'Of course not.' Tessa stepped back and

opened the door wider. 'I'm sure she won't mind if you have a look. Although I'd better stay with you, if you don't mind.' She shifted uncomfortably. 'You know how it is?'

He smiled at her as he preceded her into the hall. 'Don't give it a thought. I understand perfectly. You are responsible in her absence.'

'That's fine, then.' Tessa relaxed. 'Come on through. Where do you want to start?'

The young man looked about him. 'There were one or two things in here and a chest of drawers in her bedroom.' He sighed and shook his head. 'I have the horrid feeling that Mrs Carrington would really rather not part with her treasures. Sometimes my job is not a nice one.'

Tessa looked at him sympathetically, liking him for his compassion. She thought of all Mathilda's things, glad now that the fear of selling them had receded for the time being.

'Have you one of your leaflets?' she asked him. 'Or a card?' If an emergency cropped up and they were obliged to sell any of Mathilda's pieces, this young man would at least be sensitive about it.

He was digging in his pocket, staring at a small inlaid table which stood under the window. 'I hope *you* haven't got to part with some family heirloom.'

'Not yet.' She took his card and studied it. 'Are you Adrian Pearson?'

'I am.' He made her another little bow. 'And

you . . .?'

'I'm Tessa Rainbird.' They shook hands a little awkwardly. 'I look after people's dogs and houses.'

'Quite a responsibility. Especially in these lawless times.'

'I must admit that there are one or two places where I feel rather nervous.' Tessa perched on the arm of a chair and watched him examine the little table. 'Just a couple of the houses are fairly remote. I have to rely on the dogs to protect the stuff. And me.'

He laughed with her, dropping down to balance on his heels whilst he examined the table underneath. 'I think I'd better give you some of my leaflets to take round with you.'

'Well, I could I suppose.' Tessa sounded a little reluctant. She shrugged. 'Why not?'

He looked at her quickly as he straightened up. 'Well, I was joking actually but I suppose it's not a bad idea. You never know when people might need some ready cash. You'd get a commission, of course.'

She frowned and he saw that he might have looked too eager. 'Don't be offended. It would be only fair, if you think about it. You have access to places I could never hope to find. I wouldn't be happy if you weren't rewarded for your trouble.'

'Well, it's hardly a trouble to leave a few leaflets about but it's nice of you to offer.' She slipped off the chair. 'Finished?'

'I think so.' He was making notes in a little book. 'If I could just have another look at that chest?'

'Of course.' She led the way to the bedroom and stood at the door watching. 'It's pretty, isn't it?'

'Very.' He ran his hands gently over the polished rosewood of the little bow-fronted chest.

'We've got one like that.' She spoke without thinking. 'Well, it looks like that. I don't know anything about antiques.'

'That's at your home, is it?' He spoke absently, running the drawers in and out, examining them closely.

'Yes.' Tessa smiled to herself. 'It's at my home.'

Isobel and Will had given her Mathilda's bedroom and the little chest stood against the wall bearing a tiny bookcase of strange old books, so small that she could hardly read the writing. It was wonderful to go into that room and shut the door and feel that she belonged there ... Adrian was watching her curiously and she smiled quickly, defensively.

'Sorry. Just daydreaming. All done?'

'All done,' he agreed. He glanced at his watch. 'If you're quite serious about those leaflets ...?'

'Absolutely,' she assured him. 'It's no problem.'

'If you're certain.' He looked concerned. 'I

feel that I offended you over that commission business. I was clumsy . . .'

'No, honestly.' It was her turn to look distressed. 'Don't give it a thought.'

'If you say so.' He smiled at her. 'Look, I've had an idea. It's nearly lunchtime. Perhaps I could take you out and buy you a drink and you could give me a contact number and I'll give you the leaflets. Please,' he said pleadingly as she hesitated. 'Then I know you've really forgiven me.'

'Honestly . . . OK.' She gave in. 'But I mustn't be too long. We could go to the Pack Horse in South Brent and have a sandwich.'

'Wonderful.' He looked so pleased that she felt flattered. 'I'll wait in the car while you lock up.'

Tessa called the dogs inside and, dragging off her thick socks, slid her feet into her trainers. As she laced them up she found that she was thinking about Giles and their lunch together at the Elephant's Nest. He was so nice . . . She grimaced a little at the word. He had made her laugh about his job as a photographer and had listened in turn—and with a concentration she was unused to—as she recounted some of the more amusing moments of her work. She remembered how he'd listened to her at the Roundhouse and how, hardly knowing him, she'd talked to him so openly. She wondered if it might be because he was so much older, or because she felt she

197

already knew him through Kate. She had arranged to see him again when she was next in London ... Tessa dragged her thoughts away from Giles, locked the back door and hurried out to where Adrian waited patiently for her in his car.

\*     \*     \*

'The thing is . . .' said Giles. He paused and Kate braced herself, knowing that these words generally prefaced a confidence. 'The thing is—I didn't want to rush it.'

Kate and David studiously avoided meeting each other's eye. They had been having supper at the London house when Giles had arrived. He had sat with them, drinking wine while they ate and now, with supper cleared away, the moment for which Kate and David had been waiting had arrived. Even as a child it had taken Giles some time to come to the point. 'But he's more open than Guy,' Kate had once told David. 'Guy never tells me anything at all.' Giles thought things through carefully and rarely did anything on the spur of the moment. He was not over confident but he was kind and sensitive to the needs of others.

'Well.' David cleared his throat as the silence lengthened interminably. 'I wouldn't say that two meetings in three months is absolutely rushing it, old boy. No need to fear that.'

Kate who, in her anxiety had drunk too

198

much wine, knew an urge to giggle hysterically. She made a strange noise—a cross between a groan and a scream—and David glanced quellingly at her.

'That's true.' Giles swirled his glass of whisky thoughtfully. 'I was just wondering whether . . . I can't decide . . . If she's down there with Felix . . .'

'Giles!' said Kate sharply. 'Come to the point!'

'Sorry.' He looked guiltily at her. 'I was wondering if I might just pop down to see her. You know. Just for the day or something.'

'Wonderful idea,' said David easily. 'Poor girl must get terribly lonely with only old Felix to keep her company. I should go . . . if I were you.'

'Would you?' Giles looked at him eagerly. 'You don't think she'll wonder if I'm . . . well, pushing it a bit?'

Kate clutched her glass tightly and closed her eyes for a moment. She took several deep breaths lest she should scream with frustration. David smiled quickly at Giles.

'Shouldn't think so for a moment.' He pursed his lips and shook his head as though giving the matter serious thought. 'After all, it's your home, isn't it? No reason why you shouldn't be there.'

'It might be embarrassing for her. That's what I was wondering. There on her own. As if I'm hoping that . . .' He took a quick gulp at his

199

whisky. 'Well, you know what I mean.'

'Perhaps she might like it,' said Kate. Both men stared at her. She stared back at them. 'Don't look at me as if I'm some kind of pervert,' she said crossly. 'Do you know what I think, Giles? I think you should go down to Devon and tell Tessa exactly how you feel. Just do it! Stop pussy footing about! Stop trying to find the answers before she's even thought of the questions. Stop wondering, if she might be offended or shocked. Just go down and . . . and *do* it!'

Giles looked at her with an expression of such hope and excitement that Kate felt a great surge of love for him—followed by pang of guilt. Was it because of her unhappy marriage and subsequent divorce that her sons were both so chary of relationships with women? They seemed so afraid of committing themselves— but could she blame them? They'd witnessed at first-hand a disintegrating and unhappy situation; was it so surprising that they were unwilling to take the risk? She knew that it was the girl who had taken the initiative in Giles's first relationship and she had seen how he had been prepared to be miserable rather than break it up. She guessed that if he finally committed himself to Tessa, he would remain loyal whatever happened. No wonder that he wanted to be certain that it was absolutely right. He was unable to enjoy casual sex. In a rare moment of confidence he had once told her that for him sex, without love, was no good. She respected him for it and was relieved, too, in these dangerous days but she wished that he could find love and be loved in return. He had a good many friends of both sexes but she suspected that he was often lonely. Had her own mistakes put happiness out of court for him?

She smiled at him, wondering if it were possible to pass through life without feeling continually guilty. It corroded and destroyed and prevented her from seeing clearly; she overreacted in an attempt to compensate. She knew that her guilt would encourage her to sympathise with Giles; it made her afraid to be tough with him lest she spurred him on to actions which he would regret or which would hurt him—leaving her with more guilt. Deliberately she hardened her heart, remembering her instinctive reaction to the sight of Giles and Tessa together at the Roundhouse. She must not allow him to dither.

'Honestly, Giles,' she said quietly, 'I really think you should go. I think that you know in your own heart how you feel about her. Tessa may be young but she's grown up in a hard school. There's nothing precious or silly about her. She'll be honest with you, either way. You've got nothing to lose and everything to gain.'

He stared at her, impressed by her serious tone, feeling his fears sliding away. He knew

201

that he tried to cross too many bridges, to make certain that no one would be hurt, to legislate for every eventuality. Usually his relationships sank beneath all these anxieties before they ever got launched and usually it really didn't matter too much. He had been surprised—and rather frightened—at just how much Tessa mattered.

'You're right,' he said, with so much conviction that David looked at him in surprise and Kate felt her heart lift. 'Absolutely right. I'll go down first thing in the morning. Should I telephone first? Warn her?'

'No,' said Kate instinctively. 'Take her by surprise. Pretend you forgot we weren't there or something. Don't look so shocked! I know you hate telling even the whitest of lies but trust me. Honestly, I just know that this is right.'

\*     \*     \*

'And the frightening thing is,' she said to David when Giles had gone and they were washing up together, 'that he believes me. Like when I told him that he would love school or that he could get to university if he tried. The responsibility is frightening.'

'The trouble with bringing up children,' said David, who had a daughter of his own, 'is that by the time you know you got it wrong it's too late to do anything about it.'

Kate dried plates silently, fighting fear and guilt. Why had she been so confident? Supposing she was wrong and Giles was right to proceed cautiously? Why did she feel that she always knew best when she'd managed to make such mistakes in her own life?

'Oh, David,' she said miserably. 'Why did I open my big mouth?'

'Because he needed you to.' David dried his hands and took her into his arms. 'Don't fight it, my darling. It's impossible to get it right. Sins of omission or commission, we err either way. Just accept it.'

'But it's his life,' she cried against his chest. 'Oh, why do I always interfere?'

'He'll be fine. He's simply got to have a shot at it. Look how happy Guy is. If he can make it then so can Giles. Surely you've no regrets about Guy?'

'Oh no, of course not! But he and Gemma have known each other since they were babies and she's so good for him. Yes, Guy is happy. Perhaps you're right . . .'

'Of course I am,' said David comfortably, returning to his washing-up.

Kate went back into the sitting room and stood staring into the fire. She had felt so certain earlier but now she was eaten up with doubt. David had put his finger on the problem of parenthood; you saw the results of your mistakes when it was too late to rectify them and the anxieties continued long after the

203

children were grown up. She knew that she would be feeling just as worried if she had urged Giles to go cautiously. Kate sighed, put the guard round the fire and went upstairs to have her bath.

## CHAPTER EIGHTEEN

After the New Year a mild spell set in; there were violets growing in the lane and hazel catkins trembling in the hedge. Bea, stooping to look at an early primrose, was possessed of a desire to start afresh. The soft air, which presaged spring and new life, touched her cheeks and filled her with hope. She straightened up and breathing deeply and eagerly, walked on between the banks that sheltered the lane. The centuries had eroded this track long before it became a metalled lane; ground to dust each summer, scoured by winter rain, so the track had sunk until now, beneath the dry-stone walls, the very rock could be seen. Beech mast, acorn and seeds had rooted in the earth that covered the stones so that the hedges that flourished along the top of the walls grew high above the sunken lane. Their roots had pushed down through the soil, displacing stones, gaining a foothold. These thick gnarled roots were covered with lichen and moss and ferns, supporting small ecological worlds, sheltered from the west winds which roared above their heads.

Bea watched a company of long-tailed tits swinging in the bare branches of an oak tree above her head. They flitted busily, darting from branch to branch, until the whole party took wing and swooped away. She saw a tiny wren, fossicking amongst the drifts of beech leaves in the ditch, and felt a sense of satisfaction and gratitude. The holiday had been a great success. She had been both surprised at the warmth with which Tessa had greeted her and aware of the efforts Will had made to ensure that all three of them felt at home. He insisted that he was very happy in his room downstairs with its proximity to the kitchen. This morning Bea had woken, unusually early, to the smell of frying bacon and had thought herself, for one brief moment, back at school. She lay for a while, thinking; if she were to settle here in the cove then the pattern of life must be set from the beginning. It seemed that Tessa would rarely be with them for any length of time so it was important that she and Will should work out a plan for living compatibly. She hoped that, having spent most of her life living in an institution, she had a head start. Will had been married, so he was used to having females—or at least one female—about the place. It was clear that he and Tessa had very quickly established an easy relationship and Bea knew that it was up to her to maintain the family atmosphere.

Rising from her bed, she had pulled on her thick plaid dressing gown, pushed her feet into sheepskin slippers and descended to the kitchen. Over the Christmas holiday she had breakfasted late, fully dressed, having given Will plenty of time to have his own breakfast and finish his chores. Up until now she hadn't wanted to be in his way but this morning she had felt differently. If Will had been surprised to see her he gave no sign of it. There was a large pot of tea on the table and he took a cup and saucer from the dresser and put them beside her.

'I always like to stoke up for the day,' he'd told her. 'If you have a good breakfast then it doesn't matter too much what happens after that. Care to join me?'

'Who can resist the smell of frying bacon?' asked Bea, pouring herself a cup of tea. 'I certainly can't!'

'My wife could.' As Will dropped a few more rashers into the frying pan he looked uncomfortable; as though he felt that he had been disloyal. 'Had a delicate stomach, d'you see?' he said. 'Had to be careful what she ate.'

'How very tiresome,' said Bea bluntly. 'For her,' she added politely—but she had seen the small grin with which Will had accepted her gesture of understanding. 'Living with small boys tends to destroy one's sensibilities. I doubt I ever had any in the first place.'

Whilst they ate they had exchanged family backgrounds, trying to trace their ancestry back to Mathilda. Bea discovered that Will was two years the elder and that his father had been killed during the evacuation of Dunkirk; they had both lost their mothers fairly recently.

'I suppose,' said Bea, chasing a mushroom round her plate, 'that I always imagined that I'd look after my mother in her old age. I spent most of the school holidays with her. We were very poor. My father was not particularly strong. He was on convoy duty during the war and was torpedoed twice and I don't think that he ever fully recovered from it. I remember him as a quiet nervous man. He taught History but he was only fifty-two when he died. My mother was eighty. I was fully expecting to look after her for a few more years yet.'

'It must be difficult,' said Will thoughtfully, 'to retire from your kind of job. Must feel at a bit of a loose end, I should think. It's a way of life, isn't it? Not just a job.'

'Yes,' said Bea, after a minute or two. 'That describes it rather well. I stayed for a while with an old friend. She's newly widowed and rather lonely. We hoped that it might solve both our problems.'

Will remembered his conversation with Isobel in the car. 'Sounds fraught with difficulty,' he suggested.

'Why?' asked Bea sharply. 'Why should it be any more difficult than what we are contemplating here?'

'Because it's *her* home,' answered Will promptly, although he sounded much more confident than he felt. 'She would have to be a very generous sort of woman for you to be able to feel that you had as much right in it as she did. This is your home as much as mine. Quite different I would have thought.'

Bea was silent, mollified by his reply, rather surprised by her flash of aggression. It was evident that she was still feeling rather sensitive when it came to the question of belonging.

'It is different,' she admitted, watching him spread marmalade on his toast with a generous hand. 'But it's rather difficult to feel at home in a house you never saw before in your life.'

'And with two people you never saw before in your life?' He was smiling at her. 'Are we crazy to try it? Is that what you're thinking?'

'No.' She shook her head. 'It's just that I'm not particularly looking forward to telling Norah that I've finally made up my mind. She'll think I'm quite mad. And I have to go back to pick up my belongings from the flat. I hope the landlord can find someone to take it over.'

'Like me to come along?' Will made the suggestion lightly but his heart beat anxiously. He had no wish to patronise her.

'Come with me?'

'I wondered how much stuff you've got? Could you manage it on the train? We could drive up and pack it in the back of the Morris.

It's amazing how much she'll take if you drop the back seat.'

It occurred to Bea that it would be a great deal easier to cut the ties to her old life with Will's comforting presence in the background but she was not used to people sharing her burdens or shouldering her problems. It sounded rather tempting . . . Her independent spirit struggled against such weakness. She sat with her eyes on her empty plate, attempting to justify an acceptance of his offer. Will watched her.

'Difficult trying to struggle with it all on the train,' he pondered, hoping to ease her into seeing it as a sensible proposition whilst maintaining her pride. 'Of course you could hire a van but it seems a bit daft with the old Morris out there. Or maybe I'll get on with getting us a car. We'll need one, won't we? Or would you prefer that we had one each? I can understand that. Perhaps we could try sharing one for a start.' He beamed at her. 'It's going to be great fun. Don't you think? Lots to look forward to. Look, I'd be very glad to come with you. I'd like to see the school and where you worked for so long. Fills in the blank bits, d'you see? And it would be a bit of a jolly.'

She looked at him and discovered that she could accept his friendliness. 'Thank you, Will,' she'd said. 'That would be very kind.'

Now, as she walked in the lane she wondered what Norah would think of him . . .

*     *     *

'. . . and I think it's just too bad of you,' hissed Norah, when Will had excused himself and disappeared to have a pipe in the garden, 'to bring this cousin—or whatever he is—along with you. I'd have preferred to talk with you alone.'

'He is my cousin,' said Bea calmly. 'No whatever-he-is about it.'

'And furthermore,' continued Norah, discounting this observation, 'I have to say that I think it's quite mad. Going back to your old friends at school was foolish enough . . .' She looked at Bea sharply. 'Well, it was, wasn't it? I was right, wasn't I?'

'Yes, Norah,' sighed Bea. 'You were right.'

Norah nodded, smug self-satisfaction writ large upon her face. 'Of course I was. You can't go back. I warn you, it never works.'

'But I'm not going back,' said Bea. 'I'm going forward.'

Norah stared at her with a rather unpleasant look on her face; it had an avid, unhealthy kind of eagerness mingled with a measure of contempt.

'So you're going to live with this . . . cousin?'

'With Will. Yes.' Bea looked back at her and felt a sense of revulsion. 'For goodness' sake, Norah. Don't look so . . . so *prurient*. There's nothing like that about it at all. We are sharing

210

the house, the three of us. We have a young cousin called Tessa. I told you all about it in the letter. Please try to accept it. I hope you might come and visit me there. It will be lovely in the summer.'

Before Norah could reply, there was a light knock on the door and Will appeared. He smiled at them both.

'Sorry to break up the party but we ought to be getting on . . .'

'Of course.' Bea was on her feet, trying to hide her relief. 'Forgive me, Norah. I'll be in touch. Don't forget that invitation. Give my regards to Andrew.'

They kissed goodbye, though Norah's face was stony and she barely acknowledged Will's farewell . . .

'What invitation?' asked Will suspiciously after they had been driving for some miles in silence. Bea snorted and then she began to chuckle.

'I've invited her to stay,' she admitted, and burst out laughing at Will's horrified expression. 'Don't worry. She won't come.'

'I hope you're right,' said Will fervently. 'Please forgive me if this is tactless but how on earth did you imagine you could live with her?'

Bea felt a twinge of guilt mixed with relief. Norah was an old friend and it was disloyal to laugh about her. At the same time she was glad that Will saw the difficulties involved in living with her; it made her feel less guilty. She told

211

him so. He shook his head.

'It wouldn't have worked,' he said. 'Best to find out early before damage is done.'

Bea stared out through the windscreen and prepared herself for the meeting with Marian Goodbody, the headmaster's wife. She had decided not to collect her belongings and sneak away like a thief in the night. Instead she had telephoned Marian and arranged to have tea with her. After their last meeting Marian had been cool but Bea said that she had some news to tell her and Marian's curiosity had got the better of her pride, especially when Bea asked if she might bring a friend.

'A friend . . .?' Marian had hesitated and Bea had grinned to herself. 'Why, yes, I suppose so . . .'

'His name's Will Rainbird,' she had told her. 'See you at three o'clock then.'

As they drove into the quadrangle and parked outside the headmaster's house, Bea was overcome by a fit of nerves.

'I have the feeling that I am about to behave very badly,' she told Will. 'Marian and I have never hit it off.'

Will looked alert—Bea had reluctantly told him something of her last interview with the headmaster's wife—rather like someone preparing for a scrap.

'Nothing to lose,' he told her. 'Aha! Is this She Who Must Be Obeyed?'

Bea saw that Marian had appeared at the

212

front door and nudged him in the ribs. 'Yes,' she said. 'For heaven's sake, you're supposed to be helping, not encouraging me.'

From that moment, or so Will told Isobel afterwards, the meeting went downhill.

'How nice to see you, Bea,' Marian stood at the top of the steps, looking graciously aloof. 'And this is . . . your friend.' She took in his cavalry twills and tweed coat—Bea had bullied him into dressing for the occasion—and extended her hand. 'How nice . . .'

'Will Rainbird,' said Bea nonchalantly. 'This is Marian Goodbody, Will. She is the headmaster's wife.'

At this point Will seemed to lose his nerve. He took Marian's outstretched hand and kissed it. Marian coloured a little, smiled upon him, obviously affected by this courtly and unexpected gesture and led them inside. Behind her back Bea stared at Will outraged by this overfriendly, if not downright sycophantic, behaviour and Will gazed back helplessly; shoulders, hands, even eyebrows, raised, in abject apology.

'Sorry,' he whispered, 'Got carried away . . .'

Bea pushed him irritably ahead of her into the drawing room where tea was laid and Marian waited, her eyes on Will.

'Do sit down,' she said. 'This is very nice. I admit that I can't wait to hear your news, Bea.' She looked girlishly excited. 'Now you mustn't think I'm being inquisitive, Mr . . . er Rainbird

213

. . . what a delightfully unusual name, isn't it? But Bea and I are old friends, aren't we, Bea, dear?'

'Certainly old, anyway,' snapped Bea rudely—and tried desperately to control her uprush of anger. 'We've known each other for many years.'

With a look of patient resignation, Marian turned to the tea-tray. Her glance at Will said that, whatever kind of friend he was, he had her sympathy. Will tried to look non-committal. She began to deal with the tea.

'The thing is,' said Bea, sitting upright on the cretonne, 'I've really come to say goodbye.'

She paused whilst Marian continued to pour, head politely inclined, waiting for Bea to continue. Bea glanced at Will who sent her a tiny wink. Encouraged, she cast around for inspiration.

'I'm so glad,' said Marian fatally, 'that you saw the wisdom about not remaining in the town.' She smiled at Will 'Don't you agree, Mr er, Rainbird, that it is better to make a clean cut when certain parts of our lives come to an end? I'm sure you see the wisdom in Bea making a new life for herself. You can imagine how hard it would be for her to be on the edge of a community that she has served so faithfully.'

'Don't talk about me as if I'm deaf, Marian,' said Bea, irritation returning. 'Don't do that "Does she take sugar?" stuff.'

214

Marian passed her a cup, her lips tightening. Will absently patted his pocket for his pipe but, remembering where he was, took a cup of tea instead. She looked at him meaningly but he was afraid to smile back lest Bea should see and misinterpret his smile. He busied himself with the sugar bowl.

'I had no intention of upsetting you, Bea,' said Marian, maintaining her saintly air of tolerance. 'I have been very worried for you. Though you mayn't believe it, I have your welfare very much at heart.' She looked at Will. 'It will probably come as no surprise to you, Mr er Rainbird,' ('Oh, for goodness' sake call him Will,' said Bea, 'and have done!') 'that Bea has been a somewhat unconventional, if extremely popular, matron. If I may venture such a remark without being taken to task again.' She shot an unfriendly glance at Bea and smiled again upon Will. 'Naturally we are all concerned for her future.'

'I'm very gratified to hear it,' said Bea acidly, 'though I'm sure you'll understand when I say that it comes as a bit of a surprise. Anyway, there's no need to concern yourselves further. I'm delighted to tell you that I've inherited a considerable estate in Devon and I'm moving down there. In fact I have already moved. I'm sure, given your anxiety for my welfare, that you noticed that I wasn't about over Christmas or the New Year.'

Marian, who had come to attention at the

words 'considerable estate' ignored the jibe. She goggled at her. 'An estate? But who . . . I didn't realise that you had . . .' She stopped.

Bea grinned evilly. 'You didn't know that I had respectable relations? Landed gentry, even? No, neither did I. I am as surprised as you are, dear Marian. However, it solves the question of my future. I must be in Devon to oversee it.'

'I see.' Marian looked dumbstruck. 'And er, Will. Are you . . .?'

'Oh, I come with it, d'you see?' said Will easily, avoiding Bea's anxious eye. 'A kind of factor or land agent. She has to put up with me, too, I'm afraid.'

'I think she's extraordinarily fortunate to have you,' she answered crisply. 'So tell me.' She settled more cosily into her chair, trying to hide her envy, 'where exactly is this estate? How large is it?' She laughed a little, making big eyes at Will. 'We shall expect an invitation, you know. What fun! I don't know Devon too well.'

Will inhaled heavily through his nose and sent up a prayer of thanksgiving. 'It's on the south coast,' he said casually. 'Tucked right away by the sea. Difficult to find.'

'This is so exciting. A considerable estate, you said. Is the big house in good order? How much land . . .?'

'It's in very good order,' said Bea recklessly. 'Much too big for me, really. Will has a little

216

cottage in the grounds. And there's a dower house in the private cove with a cottage for staff and a boathouse . . .' She gulped at her tea.

'Well!' Marian closed her mouth which had been hanging open during these revelations. 'Well, I must say. We shall look forward to visiting you. Now where . . .?'

Will shot his cuff and looked at his watch. 'Sorry, Bea. We really ought to be on our way.'

Bea jumped to her feet. 'Absolutely. Look, we'll pop in later, Marian. We've got to collect my bits from the flat . . .'

\*  \*  \*

'Sorry,' she mumbled later to Will as they drove back to Devon. They had left a message for Marian saying that they'd had to rush away, lest she should demand an address or a telephone number. 'I warned you that I might behave badly.'

'I think you were splendid,' said Will. He pulled hastily into the inside lane as a Mercedes snarled past, its driver gesticulating rudely. 'Perfectly ghastly woman.'

'I don't know why you had to go kissing her hand,' grumbled Bea, staring out at Somerset.

'Neither do I,' admitted Will guiltily. 'It just came over me. She unnerved me, standing up there on the steps . . .'

Bea glanced sideways at him, his hair

217

rumpled, his slate-blue eyes fixed anxiously on the road, and was filled with remorse. 'You were terrific,' she said. 'I behaved shockingly. She always brings out the worst in me.'

'"Considerable estate",' quoted Will, beginning to grin. '"Dower house in the cove", "cottage for the staff".'

'Don't!' said Bea guiltily—and burst into hearty laughter. 'Her face,' she moaned. 'Her face when I was telling her!'

'And what's all this about being unconventional?' he asked, settling down to a steady fifty, which was all the Morris was capable of doing comfortably. 'We have an hour or so before us. New readers start here . . .'

## CHAPTER NINETEEN

Isobel watched the growing friendship between Bea and Will with interest. Occasionally Bea was seized with fits of independence and would fret at Will's refusal to be hurried or bullied. Will allowed these moments to wash over him and would carry on with the job in hand whilst Bea betook herself to the cliffs or the lane to walk off her irritation. The domestic decisions were generally taken, however, with very little difficulty or friction.

Having settled the sleeping quarters to

everyone's satisfaction the next question was one of a shower room for Will. It was Tessa who insisted that it was unfair that he should have to wait his turn for the women to use the bathroom and that it would be fairer all round if a shower unit could be put in beside the lavatory behind the kitchen. This was undeniably true and so it was costed out and the three of them voted that it should be done as soon as possible. Another problem was how the bills should be divided. It was obviously unfair that Tessa should pay as much as the other two but she wanted to pay her share on the upkeep of the house and on its improvements.

Isobel could understand that; it made Tessa feel that the house was truly hers and that she had a say in it. She came back to the cove between jobs as often as she could and fitted in as easily as if she had never been away. Isobel wondered if the reason why it all worked so well was because the three of them made no emotional demands on each other. It was like being aboard a small ship; each assigned his various tasks for the wellbeing of their small community but with no messy, emotional muddles.

'It's not the same as being married,' she told Will, as they walked on the beach one wild March evening. 'You can argue and discuss and do your own thing and no one gets uptight. Not in the same way that husbands and wives do, or

219

lovers. You know what I mean?'

'I think that's true,' he agreed. 'The problem within an emotional relationship is that both parties need to feel that they are put first. You get the "what about me?" syndrome.'

'That's so true,' sighed Isobel. 'But what's the answer?'

'The answer must be that each trusts the other to put him—or her—first.'

Isobel paused for a moment to watch the waves thundering in across the sand. They were both shouting to make themselves heard above the boom of the surf. Will thrust his hands deep into his pockets and looked far out where the white horses hid the horizon. A gust of wind buffeted them and they braced themselves against its force.

'It's all a question of trust,' said Will, as they turned towards the house. 'You need to feel safe. To be able to say, "I don't have to worry about myself because my partner is doing that for me. This leaves me free to look after her—or him," d'you see?'

'You must have had a pretty good marriage,' said Isobel, as they reached the warmth and silence of the kitchen. Bea and Will had invited her to supper and inviting smells issued from the aged Rayburn. She put her hands to her ears which still seemed to be ringing with the sound of the wind and the sea. 'That's a very idealistic approach to a relationship.'

'I didn't say that I had achieved it,' he said

220

cautiously as he followed her upstairs. 'I was answering your question about the "what about me?" syndrome. You don't have to worry about "me" if someone else is doing it for you.'

'Most marriages are the reverse.' Isobel, entering the sitting room, had to resist the urge to draw the curtains or put a log on the fire. So little had changed that she still half expected to see Mathilda sitting in her chair, reading. 'More like open warfare.'

'I think that married people do often regard their partner as an enemy. Someone to be outwitted. There is a kind of triumph if one wins a skirmish or dupes the other. A desire to win points or to use emotional blackmail. It seems to be a series of battles rather than a love affair.' He watched her thoughtfully, wondering if this was a moment for a confidence. It was at such times that he learned about her life. 'Was your marriage like that? A series of battles?'

'Oh no.' She came to sit on the low stool beside the fire, staring into the flames. 'We rarely quarrelled. Simon is very sweet-tempered and certainly put me first. The trouble was that I am a restless kind of person. I took him for granted.' She pulled up her knees and wrapped her arms around them. 'I'm the kind of person that likes to stir things up. If the water gets too peaceful I heave in a bloody great rock just to see what will happen.'

221

She glanced around and sighed with satisfaction. It was good to be here. The Scrabble board was in evidence on the small fireside table and, in the corner of the sitting room, a jigsaw puzzle was spread out on the gate-leg table. It was Bea who did the jigsaw puzzle. 'Bringing order out of chaos,' as James described it on his last visit to the cove. 'Just like being Matron. She needs something to organise.'

It was evident that she was delighted to see him; that his reference to her as 'Matron' brought back happy memories. They talked about the boys and recalled amusing incidents.

'Of course,' Bea had said thoughtfully, 'I should have guessed that James was destined to be a lawyer. From a small boy he liked things to be explained very clearly to him and he always abided by the letter of the law. The rule stated that on Sunday mornings each boy must put a clean handkerchief in his suit pocket Towards the end of term I noticed that James seemed to have lost most of his handkerchiefs. As I watched him in chapel one morning I saw that he was getting quite portly. He looked like a baby Michelin man. Afterwards I examined his suit. He had ten handkerchiefs crammed about his person, all quite clean and unused. He had obeyed the rule exactly.'

James had laughed with the rest and Isobel smiled as she remembered the story. She wondered where Bea was; probably in the study. It was she who had suggested that the study should be a 'quiet room'. It was impossible for each of them to have a private sitting room and, whilst they could go to their bedrooms if they wished to be private, it was agreed that the study should be a place where letters could be written or peace and quiet could be found. A notice bearing the words 'In Use' was made ready to be hung on the door handle at the appropriate times.

'We must hope,' Will had said to Isobel, 'that we don't all want to be quiet at once.'

Isobel listened to wind howling round the house. No longer did she tuck up in the spare room with a hot-water bottle on these wild nights. She felt quite certain that no one would have minded if she used Tessa's room but she would never have asked. In many ways she felt that she no longer belonged as she had when Mathilda was alive. After Bea's arrival she had continued to do a certain amount of work about the house but Bea was not happy at watching Isobel work whilst she looked on; nor did she need Isobel to shop for her. Isobel began to feel nervous that she would soon be redundant. She did not know that Will had intervened on her behalf. He had explained to Bea on what terms Isobel had the cottage; Bea looked thoughtful, frowning a little.

'I think that Mathilda would have wanted us to honour her agreement,' he added, looking unhappily at Bea's stern face. 'I don't think she can afford the rent, d'you see?'

'I understand that,' said Bea, 'but it goes against the grain to be idle while someone works round me. I'm not that old yet.'

'I know that,' said Will pacifically. 'But we have to think about Isobel's pride.'

'Do we?' asked Bea sharply. 'I don't quite see that Isobel's pride is my problem.'

Will felt the tiny frisson of anxiety that he always experienced when Bea's antagonism surfaced; there had been several moments when he had felt the need to tread warily.

'I think it might become our problem if she were to leave,' he said, 'and we had some stranger living in the cottage.'

'So what do you suggest?' Bea's voice was cool.

'I don't know.' He shook his head. 'She knows that she's not earning her keep, so to speak. She suggested leaving when we first arrived but I really do feel that in such a small community our neighbour is terribly important to us. And she was very good to Mathilda. We mustn't overlook that. I should hate to appear ungrateful.'

'I can't quite see why *you* need be grateful,' said Bea, shrugging a little. 'I think we should keep things in proportion. Isobel did a job for which she was paid, in kind. Mathilda left her the Morris as a sign of gratitude. If Mathilda had wished her to live rent-free in the cottage no doubt she would have left her that, too.'

224

'That's true.' Will tried to keep calm. He knew that his personal feelings for Isobel coloured the situation but he also knew that championing of her cause would only antagonise Bea further. 'Would you prefer to let the cottage to someone else who could afford to pay rent?'

'I agree with you that it is better to have someone we know and like at the cottage,' said Bea at last. 'What I can't understand is why Isobel should not try to find some other employment and so be able to pay her rent. It is clear that her arrangement with Mathilda no longer works with us. I see no reason why she should not work on the days when she is not at the bookshop. Even if she paid a nominal rent it would be better for her self-respect and better for us, too. Our pensions are not so enormous as to allow us to be foolishly philanthropic.'

'I think that's perfectly fair,' said Will after a moment's silence. 'In Isobel's defence I would merely say that I think she has been waiting to see how things worked out with us. If we don't require her help then I shall put it to her that she tries to find some other employment and that she pays a nominal rent until she can afford the full amount. I think she will do her best to do that. She doesn't want to be a parasite.'

'I have never thought that she did.' Bea coloured a little, feeling that he was accusing

225

her of being hard-hearted. 'But I really think that it would be the best solution. There must be something she can do. She's a bright intelligent woman.'

'I'll talk to her,' said Will. He had done so at the first opportunity.

Now, watching him as he filled his pipe, Isobel felt her heart warm towards him. How kind and tactful he had been to her on that occasion! She remembered how frightened she had felt. Here was change indeed. The house in the cove was no longer her second home; to wander about in, cook in, draw the curtains and make up the fire. With Bea's arrival there had been a subtle change. Although Will made it clear that Isobel's friendship was important, and he included her as much as he could, she missed those early days when it had been just her and Will in the cove. It had almost been like having Mathilda back. She liked Bea, however, and when Will told her how unkind Marian Goodbody had been Isobel, who knew how it felt to be rejected, had secretly sympathised with Bea's resentment and loneliness.

She could see, however, that things must change and she was grateful that they did not wish her to leave and were prepared to be very generous about the rent. She started once again to apply for the very few teaching posts that were advertised but, although she was once short-listed, she was never offered a post.

Eventually she managed to find a job working the lunchtime shift in one of the local pubs at the weekends and two days a week, and thus was able to squeeze a small amount of rent out of her earnings. Now, when she came to the house, she came as a guest and was careful not to wander in unannounced. She had invited Bea to the cottage for lunch and had found her an amusing, if forthright, companion and Isobel was determined not to rock any boats.

As she stared into the flames she wondered if, once she heard that Simon and Sally were married, she would feel some kind of change in her own life. It was as if she were afraid to leave the cove and the safety it represented—or was it because she still hoped that Simon might yet change his mind and that he and Helen would be restored to her . . .?

'Penny?' Will was watching her.

She smiled and shook her head. 'Not worth that much, I'm afraid.'

She wondered why she never found his questions intrusive; perhaps it was because she felt that he really cared about her. When Will listened she felt that he really *heard* what she was saying. He thought about it and genuinely entered into her fears and ideas. So many friends listened with half an ear, her problems merely striking a chord in their own breasts so that, when she'd finished, their response was invariably, 'Oh, I know *exactly* what you mean. When I was . . .' and she knew that they weren't

227

really interested in helping her but had been waiting for the opportunity to tell their own story. Or, 'I know *just* how you feel.' Whilst she was grateful at this attempt to sympathise she had an urge to scream, 'No you *don't*! How I feel is unique to me. Please respect it. Try to understand me.' Even worse was the flat, 'Tell me about it,' which Isobel always saw as a put down; as a 'I've been through all that and far worse than you could be suffering it. You can't tell me anything about pain . . . or loss . . . or loneliness . . . or being broke . . .' or whatever it was that she had been about to communicate. 'Tell me about it' always shut her up at once. She had a fear that her own problems had been brought about by her own selfishness and that she really had no right to sympathy. To have Will to talk to was a tremendous luxury.

The door opened and Bea put her head round. 'There you are,' she said cheerfully. 'I'm just going down to check on the supper. Drinks time, Will?'

As Will went with alacrity to fulfil his job as barman, Isobel felt a lifting of the heart. She was lucky to be here; to be just across the cove. She pushed away all thought of Sally and Simon and of Helen's continued coolness. With her usual optimism she told herself that, even yet, things might work out and, when Will brought a glass of wine across to her, she raised it to him with a smile.

# CHAPTER TWENTY

Indigo clouds towered above the high tors and rolled eastwards, swallowing the tender blue sky and spilling heavy drops of rain on the wide spaces of the moor. The crabbed and twisted thorn trees, their branches flushed soft green with new young leaves, bent lower beneath the wind's cold breath as it fled across the bleached rustling grass. The river, stained brown with peat and white-flecked, raced beneath the old stone bridge and the flooded bog-lands reflected back a brief bright glint of sunshine.

As Tessa turned right at Moorshop and plunged into the lanes behind Mary Tavy the rain descended suddenly, drumming on the car's roof and streaming down the windscreen. Even with the wipers at their speediest she could barely see out. She pulled into Freddie's drive and sat for some moments, waiting for the storm to abate. When it showed no sign of stopping she took her coat and, with it held over her head, made a dash for the back door. Freddie opened it as she reached it and she followed him in, shaking her jacket and pushing back her hair.

'What weather! So how are you?' He herded her before him into the kitchen where Charlie Custard was lounging gracefully in his favourite position on the old sofa. 'Look who's here,

Custard.'

The dog waved a languid tail and then heaved himself off the sofa and came to greet her.

'Good grief!' said Tessa. 'I feel very honoured. You didn't have to get up for me, Custard.'

'We're feeling very proud,' said Freddie, unable to hide his delight. 'Custard has passed his PAT test. He's got his badge to prove it.'

'Oh well done!' Tessa patted Custard's broad head. 'So how does it feel to be a fully paid-up Pet as Therapy? All those people patting you and telling you how wonderful you are.'

'He did very well when he went for his test,' said Freddie. 'A friendly gentle temperament is the great thing but they have to be immune to sudden noises. He didn't flinch when they dropped a tin tray behind him. It was as if he'd been doing it for years. Of course I've been training him intensively. He was brilliant, weren't you, old chap?'

Charlie Custard yawned deprecatingly and looked suitably modest. Having allowed Tessa to demonstrate her admiration and affection he returned to his position on the sofa and slumped down, exhausted by such an effort.

'Congratulations, Freddie.' Tessa beamed at him. 'So now you and Custard'll be round at the nursing home every minute, bringing down the blood pressure like mad.'

'We shall spread ourselves about,' said Freddie grandly. 'Custard's going to be a great hit and if anyone wants to stroke or cuddle me as well, I shall make myself available. Now then. I think everything's ready for you. I'm catching the three o'clock train so we've got plenty of time. Have you eaten?'

Tessa nodded. 'Stopped off at the Roundhouse,' she said. 'We'll take Custard with us and I'll give him a walk on the way back from the station. If it isn't raining . . .'

\* \* \*

As she drove home from Plymouth she felt the usual happiness at being back on the moor. The cove must be her first love, now, but the moor ran a very close second. The storm had passed. Huge gold and white clouds sailed majestically in the rain-rinsed sky and the full moon hung, serene and pale, in the east. The wind had dropped but the breeze was chill and Tessa huddled into her jacket as she and Custard walked on Gibbet Hill. She was glad that the nights were drawing out. The long winter evenings were nearly past and her job always seemed less lonely in the summer. Her brief returns to the cove had begun to show her how much she was missing in companionship. It had been such fun to draw the curtains against the dark and sit beside the fire playing Scrabble with Will whilst Bea pored over her

231

jigsaw and chuckled at Will's expostulations at Tessa's spelling. It was only after she had left and was back at work that it occurred to her that there had been no television at the house in the cove. Usually she would have been barely able to exist without the company of the television to while away the endless hours. It must be bliss, thought Tessa, to have company instead of being alone all the time. She thought of Giles. He had turned up quite unexpectedly in the middle of the morning at Whitchurch and her first exclamation had been one of distress.

'Kate isn't here,' she'd said, disappointed for him. 'Oh, what a shame. She's up in London.'

He had looked taken aback and she had hastened to make him as welcome as she could before she remembered that it was his own home and was promptly overcome by embarrassment. They had stood for a moment in silence, neither of them quite knowing what to say next, and then Giles had laughed.

'This is silly, isn't it? Sorry to take you by surprise. It's great to see you. How's life in the cove? Come and tell me all your news.'

They had sat in the kitchen together, talking and talking . . . or rather she had talked and Giles had listened. Later they had driven over to the Old Oak at Meavy and had a drink and some lunch and then taken Felix for a walk above Burrator Reservoir. As they looked down on the lake, set in the hills beneath

232

Sheepstor and surrounded by woodland, Giles began to tell her of his childhood. He recounted amusing tales of naval quarters but explained that they had lived mainly here on the moor. He showed her Dousland, below them in the trees, where Kate had rented a bungalow, and pointed out the roof of Meavy school which he and Guy had attended until they went to Mount House at eight years old. He told her about the break-up of his parents' marriage and how he had feared the later visits to his father. Tessa listened in silence, aware that this was no light thing for Giles. She guessed that he was not given to unburdening himself. She remembered how she had talked to him at the Roundhouse and suddenly felt very close to him.

They drove over the moor whilst he showed her his past; where he and Guy had played and picnicked and where they had walked Felix's forerunners, Megs and Honey. They looked across the playing fields to Mount House school and stopped to have a stroll at Bellever Bridge where the twins had paddled in other earlier summers. When they got back to Whitchurch he had lit the fire whilst Tessa made the supper and the evening had stretched ahead, relaxed and comfortable, until bedtime.

As Tessa called to Charlie Custard and strolled back to the car, she remembered how she had felt at that point. It seemed almost wrong to separate and go to bed in different

233

rooms. It would have been nice, she thought, to have continued in that feeling of closeness, to have wandered in and out of bathroom and bedroom, talking with that same sense of familiarity and easiness; to have shared the warmth and comfort of their bodies. She suspected that Giles felt the same but would have never suggested it, feeling that he was pressing home an unfair advantage. Afterwards she wished that she'd had the courage to suggest it—and then felt rather ashamed.

'It would have looked so pushy,' she told herself as she opened the tailgate so that Charlie Custard could jump into the back of the car. 'And what about Sebastian?'

She felt the usual sinking of the heart when she thought about Sebastian. She had received another card from him and a telephone call. There was definite progress but not enough to satisfy Tessa. Being a part-owner in the cove had given her a measure of confidence and she was beginning to find it difficult to be grateful for Sebastian's crumbs of affection; only beginning though. She had been in love with him for so long that he was a habit that she could not quite break—nor did she want to; he was still special.

The telephone was ringing as she opened the kitchen door and, leaving Charlie Custard to follow her in, she hastened to answer it.

'Hi!' said Sebastian. 'So how's my favourite girl?'

234

Tessa sank down on a kitchen chair and began to laugh. 'You must be psychic,' she told him. 'I was just thinking about you.'

'So I should hope.' He didn't sound surprised. 'Want to guess where I am?'

'Are you in Plymouth?' Her heart began to beat faster. 'Is the ship in?'

'It is indeed. I phoned up your people and got your number. Clever, aren't I?'

Tessa glowed at the casual phrase 'your people'. 'Was it Bea or Will?' she asked eagerly.

'It was a chap,' answered Sebastian. 'Gave me the third degree before he'd part up with the number, I can tell you.'

'Dear Will.' She smiled at Will's protectiveness. 'He's allowed to give it to one or two special people.'

'I see. And who else is special?' His bantering tone suggested that he was not overly anxious.

She decided to tease him a little. 'Oh, one or two girlfriends and Giles, of course . . .'

'Giles?' He sounded just the tiniest bit put out. 'Who's Giles?'

'A boyfriend,' she said lightly. 'Anyway. Are you in for long?'

'For a few days.' He still sounded faintly aggrieved. 'I was wondering if you might like to come down and meet me? That is if your social diary isn't overloaded.'

'Down where?' she asked. 'To the dockyard?'

'That's right. I shall need the registration number to get you through the gate. Are you on your own?'

For a moment she was puzzled by the question. 'Well, there's Charlie Custard,' she said.

'Charlie *who*?' His amazement made her laugh. 'Who *are* all these chaps?'

'He's a dog,' she told him. She glanced at Custard who was reclining indolently on his sofa. 'You wait till you see him.'

'So I can stay?'

'Stay?' She swallowed. 'You mean . . .?'

'I mean "stay" As in "the night". His voice, emphasising the words, was suddenly intimate and she remembered the things he had said in the pub when they'd last met and how he had kissed her. 'I've been really looking forward to seeing you again.'

Confused, she stared unseeingly at Freddie's curtains. Part of her was angry that he imagined that he could telephone out of the blue and expect her to sleep with him; part felt as though she were dissolving with the old treacherous longing.

'I don't know,' she said weakly. 'This isn't my place. It's a bit . . . a bit . . .'

'Nonsense,' he cut in robustly. 'These people can't expect you to live like a nun just because you're looking after their dogs. Look, give me the registration number of your car. It's a Peugeot, isn't it? I'll give you directions to the

Camel's Head Gate and they'll tell you what jetty we're on. I'll be looking out for you . . .'

Tessa replaced the receiver and stood for a moment, lost in thought. Charlie Custard watched from the sofa, hoping that she was thinking about his dinner. She shook her head, folded her arms across her chest, changed her mind and stuck her hands in her pockets. There was an air of anxiety and uncertainty about her whole demeanour and Charlie Custard began to feel uneasy. He had had a demanding and exhausting week. He had been patted and stroked and talked to by a number of strangers whilst other inconsiderate people dropped things and made sudden noises behind his back. He stretched out his back legs and rested his head against the top of the sofa, an ear cocked for the familiar words: 'What about dinner, then?'

'Come on then, old chap,' said Tessa. 'We're going out. Come on.'

Custard stared at her in disbelief. *Going out?* He'd only just come in after a tiring trip in the car and a quite unnecessary walk. Going out? Surely she meant 'What about dinner?'

'Get a move on.' She was collecting car keys and picking up the coat she'd dropped on a chair as she'd hurried into the house. 'Come *on*, Custard!'

There was a fraught note in her voice which he distrusted. Sighing heavily, he climbed down off the sofa and, with a meaning look at the cupboard which contained his dinner, he followed her out to the car. As the engine burst into life the telephone started ringing.

\* \* \*

Will hung up with a sigh. He brooded for a moment and then decided that it wasn't important. As he peeled some potatoes for supper he ran through the conversation again. It was obvious that the young man—what was he called?—knew Tessa fairly well and there could surely be no harm in his coming over. On second thoughts, however, it seemed that he didn't know her *that* well.

'Is that Mr Rainbird?' the voice had asked. 'You don't know me. I'm a friend of your daughter, Tessa. Is she about?'

'I'm afraid not.' Will did not correct his mistake. 'She's away for a few weeks. Who is this?'

'My name's Adrian Pearson. Away is she? Mmm . . . I'm sorry to miss her . . .'

Whilst the young man hesitated, Will had time to unhook the sheet containing a list of names which hung by the telephone. He peered at it; Adrian Pearson was not one of those to whom he was allowed to give Tessa's working telephone number.

'It's just that the last time I saw Tessa—we were having lunch together actually—she mentioned that you have some pieces of

238

furniture that you might want to sell. I'm an antique dealer. I should have mentioned that earlier. Sorry if I'm speaking out of turn. It's just that I'm in the area for a few days . . .'

There was another pause. Will thought quickly. Obviously Tessa had seen this young chap at the time when they were debating how they might raise some money to buy Bea out. He and Tessa had talked about the possibility of selling some of Mathilda's pieces and perhaps she had seen this Adrian fellow and mentioned it to him. It was a coincidence that Bea had raised this subject only that morning at breakfast. What with the few items of furniture which she had inherited from her mother and Will's personal bits and pieces, the house was rather overcrowded. They had talked about installing a modern stove and perhaps putting in some central heating and had wondered whether the sale of an item or two might not be a good idea. They both knew that Tessa felt strongly about Mathilda's things, nevertheless there were certain repairs to be done and they needed to keep warm . . .

All these thoughts ran through Will's mind whilst Adrian made tentative noises on the other end of the line. Will made a decision. There would be no harm in this young man coming to look at, and perhaps value, a few things. Obviously Tessa thought that he could be trusted.

'If you would like to check with the office,'

239

Adrian was saying, 'I can give you the number Or you could speak to Mrs Carrington at Ivybridge.'

'That's all right,' said Will, who remembered Tessa talking about Mrs Carrington and her bureau. 'Since you're in the area why not come and see us? Tomorrow morning? About eleven? Excellent. Now you'll need some directions . . .'

Will dropped the last potato into the saucepan. After all, no decisions need be taken at once and it would be interesting to see how accurate the young man would be in his valuations. Will tried to remember what had happened to the inventory which James had given to him; in Mathilda's bureau, perhaps? He decided that after supper he would hunt it out.


## CHAPTER TWENTY-ONE

Tessa lay watching the moonlight streaming through the window. Sebastian, curled beside her in the narrow bed, was heavily asleep. She wished that she, too, could fall into such deep oblivion. She was wide awake and as confused as she had been when Sebastian had telephoned the previous evening. On the journey into the dockyard—aware of Charlie Custard's reproachfulness emanating from the back of the car—she had tried to analyse her feelings. She knew that she must not let Sebastian take her over; that she must resist his attempts to override her own wishes.

'But what do I want?' she asked herself as she drove into Plymouth. She still had not answered this question when she reached the Camel's Head Gate. Sebastian had been waiting for her at the end of the jetty. He flung his grip on to the back seat, said, 'Good God! Did you know you had a bear in your car?' and guided her out of Devonport en route to the nearest off-licence. It was impossible to remain uninfected by his high spirits and witty remarks and, by the time they were back in Mary Tavy, she had relaxed and was enjoying his company.

He was unimpressed by Freddie's bungalow—and her plans for supper—and took her out instead to the Elephant's Nest, leaving Charlie Custard to enjoy his long-awaited dinner. It was strange to be sitting at the same table where she and Giles had had lunch together and she felt on odd qualm which disappeared when Sebastian took her hand and told her how he had missed her. As usual his physical presence undermined her doubts: he was Sebastian. So she laughed at his jokes— and wondered what would happen when they got back to Freddie's. Since she was driving she drank only one glass of wine but, once they were at home again, Sebastian opened the carrier bag from the off-licence and produced a

241

bottle of Chardonnay and some cans of beer.

They sat together in front of the fire, Charlie Custard snoring heavily on the hearth rug, and Tessa was soon aware that willpower was ebbing away and when he kissed her she responded readily.

Now, as she watched the shadows on the wall, she felt confused. There was something missing, she told herself, but what? Her inexperience was unable to supply the answer. She loved him and, even though she had remained uneasy about having him here for the night, she had enjoyed his lovemaking. Gently she eased her body away from his inert form and slid from the bed. She stood still, waiting, but Sebastian did not stir. Taking her dressing gown from the chair and picking up her slippers, she went quietly out and down the passage to the kitchen.

Charlie Custard, stretched on his sofa, opened an eye and felt a twinge of misgiving. He hoped that more patting and stroking would not be necessary. He decided that he was not cut out for social work after all and, groaning gently, he settled himself more comfortably. Tessa—clad now in dressing gown and slippers—stood staring out of the window whilst she waited for the kettle to boil. Moonlight stippled the grass with silver and the shadows lay long and black across the meadow. The lean form of a fox prowled in the shelter of the hedge, disturbing the small roosting birds in the bare branches above him. On an impulse Tessa opened the back door and wandered out, hunching her shoulders against the cool breeze. Charlie Custard raised his head to watch her. Now what? Curiosity hauled him from sleep and he padded out after her, sniffing at the air and following her down to the meadow. The fox slipped silently away and somewhere to the east a cock crowed.

In Tessa's bed Sebastian stirred and came suddenly awake. He lay quite still, reviewing the events of the past night and wondering where Tessa had gone. Needing a cigarette, he slid out of bed and went to feel in his trouser pocket. As he picked his trousers up from the chair his attention was caught by a movement outside and he paused, staring out of the window. Across the pale-washed grass of the meadow Tessa walked, slim and straight in her long dressing gown, the great dog at her heels. There was something almost medieval in the scene and Sebastian was moved beyond his usual desires and sensations. For the first time he saw Tessa as other men might see her; not as the adoring girl who could be picked up and put down as his whim took him—but as an intelligent, successful and desirable young woman. She had enterprise, property and a great deal of generous charm. As he stood watching her, he remembered the name she had mentioned earlier: Giles. She had spoken of him again in the pub. 'Giles brought me here,' she'd said.

Sebastian took his cigarettes and lighter from his pocket. He lit up thoughtfully, staring out at Tessa as she stopped, looking at something beyond his vision, her hand on the dog's head. His heart moved in his breast as he imagined a future with Tessa in the background; waiting for him when he came home from sea, gracing ladies' nights and parties, pouring out her love upon him. Turning abruptly away, he dragged on his shirt and trousers, crammed his bare feet uncomfortably into his shoes and went out through the kitchen and into the meadow.

She turned as he came through the gate, standing still, her hand still resting on the dog's head. She looked remote and unapproachable in the ghostly light and he knew a moment of fear. He came up to her, taking her by the elbows and staring down into her face.

'I love you,' he said. 'I've just realised it. Will you marry me?'

She stared at him in amazement, wondering if it might be some kind of joke. 'Marry you?'

'Yes.' He shook her slightly, frightened still further by her remoteness. Surely she loved him? 'I thought you loved me.'

'Yes,' she said slowly. 'Yes I do. But—'

'No.' He crushed her against him. 'No buts. It's right. I just know it. It is, isn't it?'

'Yes,' she said—but a kind of terror possessed her. Was it right? He began to kiss her and the terror ebbed and relief took its place. Of course it was right. This is what she had longed for; waited for all these years. 'Yes,' she repeated and began to tremble.

'Come back inside.' He was dragging her with him. 'You're shivering. Come in and we'll have some hot coffee. Oh, Tessa. I do love you.'

They went inside, forgetting Charlie Custard who wandered around for a while before pushing the back door open and padding into the kitchen. There was no sign of them but Tessa's dressing gown lay in a pile on the floor. He sniffed at it, climbed on to the sofa and settled himself to sleep.

\* \* \*

Adrian Pearson sat for some moments in his car at the head of the track. He was taking a tremendous chance. Supposing that Tessa's father had telephoned her to ask about this young antique dealer? She would say, no doubt, that she had never said that her family wished to sell any of their belongings. He knew he could bluff it; say that he'd muddled her with someone else or completely misunderstood something she'd said. He'd carry it off and, after all, the old bloke had asked him to come. Tessa had let out a few things over the sandwich in the Pack Horse; not much, but enough to get him started. She'd talked of the old house in the cove somewhere near Kingsbridge and he'd looked up the name of Rainbird in the telephone directory. There were very few of them . . .

It was always worth a chance. He'd discovered that. In these hard times, there was a good chance that someone—generally an old person, living alone—was in need of ready cash. It was easy to disarm them with his sympathetic approach and public school voice; and he never rushed or harassed them. He made it clear that there were other pieces around and that they should give it serious thought. The touch about phoning the office was a good one, especially as the 'office'—a small back room where his girlfriend manned the phone—was in London. Many people had telephoned it but, since his targets were always in the West Country, no one as yet had turned up on the doorstep.

'If anyone wants to come, make sure they make an appointment,' he'd told her. 'You can be well away. Otherwise keep the door locked. Don't worry. No one will bother.'

His cards and leaflets were very professional; his own local contact number was his mobile telephone. He had had one or two frights but he was making a very nice profit, selling the pieces on to a friend in Essex who fed them at discreet intervals to a London showroom. It was worth taking a few chances. A hunch had led him to the cove. He had a sixth sense which was invaluable to him. He spent a great deal of time getting to know each small area that he targeted. He would sit in cafés, watching lonely old women who talked to the waitress about how hard the times were and how they longed to see their grandchildren; he sat in pubs and listened to lonely old men who missed their wives and were struggling to manage on their pensions. He generally avoided the younger women, who might need cash for their student children, but were fairly well clued up on the value of old furniture. He did very well out of the old and vulnerable. Adrian glanced at his watch, started up the engine and swung the car into the track.

Will was filling the coal hod at the bunker by the back door. He straightened up and watched Adrian park, wishing that he could have had a word with Tessa. He had telephoned earlier but there was no reply.

'I hope she's all right,' he had said worriedly to Bea.

'Probably walking the dog,' she'd answered. 'Stop fussing.'

Will dusted his hands on his old cords and went to meet the smart young man who was climbing out of the car. They shook hands and exchanged banalities. Will led him inside, introduced him to Bea in the kitchen and took him upstairs to the drawing room. Adrian's eyes were making a quick inventory although his remarks were studiedly casual.

'What a place you've got here, sir!' He

strolled to the window trying not to show his excitement at the sight of the bureau in the alcove. Putting his hands in his pockets he stared out over the sea, wondering if they knew that they were using a valuable Georgian table in their kitchen or that the chest on the landing was probably Jacobean. 'Fantastic!'

'Pretty good, isn't it?' agreed Will genially. 'My cousin is making us some coffee. Sit down, won't you?'

Bea arrived, somewhat out of breath, with the tray. 'Never mind central heating,' she muttered to Will. 'What we need is a dumb waiter.'

He laughed and gave her a tiny private wink. 'Good for the waistline,' he said. 'I hope we haven't got you here on false pretences, Mr Pearson. I'm not certain what Tessa said . . .'

'Don't worry about that, sir—' Bea, pouring coffee, raised her eyebrows at the 'sir'—'I was hoping to see Tessa, actually. That's the real reason I telephoned. The other was of secondary importance but if there's anything I can do while I'm here . . .'

'Why not?' Will shrugged. 'It's always nice to know if one owns anything worth having. We've inherited a lot of this stuff. Haven't got a clue, have we?'

He smiled ruefully at Bea who shrugged noncommittally and retired with her coffee to a distant chair.

'Some of it looks like jumble sale to me,' she

said. 'That old table in the kitchen...' She shook her head and sipped at her coffee.

Adrian felt his excitement rising. 'It's often a disappointment to people,' he said, 'when I make them an offer for their treasures.'

'I believe you,' said Will. 'Never mind. Luckily we're not desperate yet, are we, Bea?'

'Aren't we?' she answered grimly. She snorted. 'If you say so.'

Will looked terribly embarrassed. He laughed a little, smoothed his hand over his hair and coughed awkwardly. 'I expect you're kept pretty busy, Mr Pearson...?'

'Please call me Adrian, sir.' His voice was earnest and kind. 'Try to see me as Tessa's friend who happens to have some knowledge of antiques.' He glanced at Bea. 'She's a delightful girl, if I may say so.'

'You may say what you please, young man,' said Bea. 'I am not responsible for her genetic brew nor did I bring her up.'

'Please, Bea,' murmured Will. He shot a distracted look at Adrian who gulped back his coffee and rose to his feet. 'Shall we...?'

'Where would you like me to begin, sir?'

'Let's start in the study,' suggested Will. 'Through here.'

Bea sat perfectly still in her chair, listening to their voices. Presently they reappeared. Adrian was making notes in a small book; Will was jotting figures on a piece of paper. He glanced at Bea, who swallowed the last of her

249

coffee and stood up.

Will smiled at her. 'If you'll excuse us for a moment, my dear?'

She stared at him for a moment then collected the cups and the tray and went out. Will shrugged and blew out his lips a little. Adrian smiled sympathetically, his eyes on the bureau.

'I've noticed,' he said tentatively, 'that the women seem more ready to part with their treasures than the men . . .'

'Well, there you have it,' said Will with a measure of relief. 'I'm reluctant to part with things, d'you see? Pure sentiment, according to my cousin, but there it is. And she's right. We need a new stove and central heating . . .' He sighed heavily. 'Never mind. You don't want to hear my problems. Let's get finished. By the way, not a word to her for the moment, if you don't mind.'

'I quite understand, sir,' said Adrian. 'And if you need to contact our office, just to put your mind at rest . . .'

'No need for that, my boy,' said Will. 'Now what about this bureau . . . ?'

\*      \*      \*

A piece of cake, thought Adrian as he drove away. The old biddy's got her claws into him, all right. He'll be back. No wonder he didn't want her to see my quotes. He's probably going to snaffle a bit on the way through. Good luck to him.

He turned on to the main road and began to make some very satisfying mental calculations.

*       *       *

'The man's a crook,' said Will softly, his eyes gleaming. 'I laid all the traps and he walked right in to them. You were splendid, Bea.'

Bea looked modest. 'Good thing we'd decided on a code. What made you suspect?'

Will shook his head. 'Some gut feeling. On the phone first, just a twinge, and then when I saw him. I don't know what it was . . . but I was right.'

'So what shall we do?'

'I'll phone the London office for a start. No.' He looked thoughtful. 'I'll try and get hold of Tessa first. See what she really said to him and how he got on to us. I'm sure she didn't give him our address.'

'But he had our number,' Bea pointed out.

'Could have got it from the book. He certainly knew her name and there aren't that many Rainbirds about. Hang on. Let me try Tessa again.'

Bea watched whilst he dialled and stood waiting. 'Hello. Tessa? Oh good. I was trying to get you earlier but there was no reply . . . Gone to what . . .? But who . . .? Well, of course I am. It's just rather sudden . . . Yes. Yes, I see. Well,

251

it's wonderful . . . For tea? Why not . . .? Yes, and Charlie Custard, too . . . See you then. 'Bye, my dear.'

'Will,' said Bea, infuriated, 'whatever are you talking about? Who is Charlie Custard and why didn't you ask her about Adrian Pearson?'

Will sat down suddenly at the kitchen table. 'I didn't feel I could,' he said. 'She's just got herself engaged to be married and she's bringing him over to tea.'

'She's got herself engaged to someone called *Charlie Custard*?' Bea shook him by the shoulder. 'Pull yourself together, Will. What's going on?'

Will sighed; he looked anxious. 'Some childhood sweetheart called Sebastian has turned up out of the blue and they've got engaged. They've been to Plymouth to buy the ring and she wants to bring him over to meet us. What could I say? It was hardly the time for talking about crooked antique dealers. The child is over the moon. She was hardly coherent.'

'So I gather,' said Bea grimly. 'And who is this Charlie Custard?'

'He's the dog,' said Will wearily. 'He's coming, too.'

'All I can say,' said Bea going to the larder, 'is that dogs these days have very silly names. What with Romulus and Remus . . . However. What are we going to do about Adrian Pearson?'

'I shall talk to James.' Will looked happier as this thought presented itself. 'See if he's got any advice.'

'Good idea.' Bea brought out the scales. 'I shall make a cake for tea and then I'll see if Isobel's around. If Tessa is going to get herself engaged I'm sure that Isobel will like to have a look at him, too.'

Will, finding James's office number, decided that he would never understand women. The relationship between Isobel and Bea was too complex for him. Bea was insistent that Isobel should pay her rent, yet was anxious that she should meet Tessa's young man. As for Tessa getting engaged . . . He put the problems of his womenfolk out of his head and dialled the offices of Murchison, Marriott.

## CHAPTER TWENTY-TWO

Two days after the announcement of Tessa's engagement, Isobel received a letter from Simon. She picked it up from the hall floor and turned it over in her hands, examining the handwriting and the postmark. At last it had come. Isobel had no real doubt that the letter contained the news of his marriage to Sally and, with its arrival, came the realisation that she had no desire to read the words that would destroy her last hope. She put the letter in her shirt pocket and wandered into her living room. The cottage had been furnished with saleroom pieces but Isobel had contrived to give it a character of its own and this was a cheerful room. The shabby armchair and the sofa were made bright with huge heavy cotton throws in old gold and bright scarlet. A cream Indian cotton bedspread covered the scratched table which stood under the window, and pine-framed reproduction posters hung on the cream-washed walls. Rag rugs hid the worst spots of the threadbare carpet and the kitchen chairs at the table had been rubbed down to their original pine and given padded cushions of scarlet. The patterned curtains in thick chenille seemed to embrace all these colours in a rich warm glow.

A second-hand wood-burning stove had been fitted in the wide stone fireplace, and Isobel kneeled on the hearth rug and opened the glass doors. The weather was still cold and she was keeping the fire in overnight so that there was a centre of warmth in the house. She put some wood into the stove and let it blaze up. Presently she took out the letter and tore open the envelope almost indifferently. She scanned the words quickly, then read them properly. Simon had been as tactful as was possible in the circumstances; the wedding had been a very quiet one at Sally's home in the Lake District and they were spending the Easter holidays there in a holiday cottage.

Helen would be staying with friends. He sent Isobel their best wishes and hoped she was well . . . She screwed up the paper and flung it into the flames. So that was finally it; no more pretending that he might come back to her. It was over. She had told herself this several times in the past but soon hope had come creeping back. For some reason Isobel found herself remembering Tessa's face when she had introduced Sebastian to them. She had looked happy but there had been something else as well; a kind of hopeful anxiousness . . .?

Isobel shook her head. She couldn't really pin down Tessa's expression but she had found herself praying that Tessa would be happy. Certainly Sebastian was a nice enough young man. His manners were excellent and he was extraordinarily good-looking. He had been charming to Bea, deferential to Will, sweet to Tessa . . .

'I know now that I'm really old,' Will had said afterwards. 'I've never been "sirred" so much in one day in my life. First Adrian Pearson and then Sebastian . . . Ah well.'

At the thought of Will a faint ray of comfort found its way to Isobel's unhappy heart. It became even more important now that she should be able to remain in the cove. She must redouble her efforts to get a worthwhile job and so be able to pay the proper rent. She knew that Will would not care about it but Bea was a different proposition and she realised that it was important to show that she was really trying to pull her weight.

Isobel drew up her knees and rested her forehead on them. She was well aware of Will's affection for her and for a brief moment she knew a temptation to trade on it; to rest against him and let him take the weight. What a relief it would be to pass all her problems over to Will. She knew that it would be easy to make him really love her and she wondered if she could love him enough to repay him for all that he would give her . . .

Suddenly, in one swift movement, she got to her feet—as though physically rejecting such ideas—and passed into the kitchen. It was shameful to think of Will in such cold-blooded terms she told herself as she began to wash up the breakfast things, along with last night's supper plates. She caught herself thinking of Tessa again. How would Sebastian fit into the cove? Would Tessa give up her job and move around with him, living in married quarters? Even if she did they would want to come home to the cove for leaves and weekends. What then? Would Sebastian share Tessa's room, next door to Bea; and what about when the babies came along?

Isobel stood staring out across the sea, her hands still in the soapy water. The obvious thing would be for Tessa and Sebastian to have the cottage—but where would she go then? She couldn't imagine herself sharing the house with Bea and Will. She thought of Helen and wondered how she liked sharing a house with Sally and Simon. The thought of Helen made her feel even more desperate as the knowledge of her loneliness and failure seized her and filled her with pain. As she emptied the bowl and dried her hands she saw Bea walking on the beach. She carried a bag into which she put her 'gleanings'. The sight made Isobel remember Mathilda and her loneliness became an intolerable weight. She simply could not bear to be on her own today.

She came out of her door and raised a hand to Bea. 'How are you?' she called in a remarkably steady voice. 'Have you recovered from your shock?'

She went to meet her and they strolled forward together, the early April sunshine pleasantly warm on their faces.

'Will has been talking to James,' Bea told her. 'It seems we can do nothing about this wretched young man.' For one mad moment Isobel thought she was talking about Sebastian. 'You see he is too clever to state his opinion of the worth of the items he purchases. He merely tells you what he is prepared to offer. According to James that is no crime. He doesn't force you to sell, you see. Will said he was very cunning in what he said. He didn't actually admit to anything although he unerringly picked the most valuable pieces.'

'How frustrating,' said Isobel. 'Surely there

must be something we can do?'

'We're thinking about it. Will would like to set a trap for him and expose him but it's rather complicated. As James says, no one is obliged to take his money.'

'Did you tell Tessa about it?'

Bea shook her head. 'We didn't feel that it was quite the right moment.'

'And what did you think of Sebastian?' asked Isobel, after a moment.

'He seemed a nice enough young man,' said Bea cautiously.

Isobel sighed. 'I hope she'll be happy.'

Bea looked at her sharply. 'You don't sound too sanguine.'

Isobel laughed. 'Don't take any notice of me,' she said lightly. 'I had a letter this morning from my ex-husband to say that he has just remarried. Not a day for too much optimism, I'm afraid.'

They stood at the edge of the cove, looking out over the calm sea in silence.

'I understand that there is a very good market in Totnes on Friday mornings,' said Bea at last. 'I do enjoy a market. Will's tied up this morning. No chance, I suppose, of us going together? I'm sure I could find my way alone but it would be very pleasant to have your company if you can spare the time.'

'I should love to,' cried Isobel. 'It's a wonderful idea. It's my day off and I must say it's not a good day to have too much time to think.'

'Perhaps you wouldn't mind driving the Morris?' suggested Bea, who felt that, in her present state, it would be better if Isobel were to be kept occupied. She had been looking forward to exploring Totnes alone; preferring to take her own time rather than be worried lest the person with her was bored or waiting at some pre-arranged spot, an eye on the time. On her own she could truly relax, although she enjoyed her jaunts with Will who was an unexacting companion. She suspected that Isobel would rush her from place to place, chattering and requiring regular stops for coffee. Nevertheless, it was clear that Isobel needed company and some task which would take her mind off her troubles. Bea had not been deceived by the brightness of Isobel's voice. 'We could go in the other car,' she said, 'and you could navigate but since you know these lanes so well I should prefer it if you would take charge.'

'No problem,' agreed Isobel promptly. 'We'll take the Morris. I shall really enjoy showing you round. It'll be fun. Market day is really busy.'

'In that case,' said Bea, 'perhaps we should make a start?'

Isobel looked at her gratefully, rather surprised by this gesture. Apart from the fortnightly stock-up at the supermarket and the visits to the library which she did with Will, Bea usually went off alone to do her private shopping. For some reason Isobel was reminded of Mathilda and their trip to Oxford. She did not wait to analyse these feelings but she felt a rush of affection for the older woman and, agreeing to meet her by the car in five minutes, went hurrying back to the cottage.

\*     \*     \*

Will waved them off and returned to scraping down the woodwork of the downstairs windows. There was much to be done but he was enjoying even the most laborious of tasks. As he scraped away the peeling paint, he thought about Mathilda. What inner resources she must have had to live in near isolation yet remain the person Isobel had described to him. Will had remarked that, under such circumstances, most people went a bit potty.

'Mathilda wasn't potty,' Isobel had said indignantly. 'She might forget to eat or not notice the fire going out but she was so clear-sighted. It was Mathilda who made me really think about things. There was something . . . something . . . Oh, how can I put it? She was always the same, never deviating from her real self. There was an absolute serenity deep down inside her. Oh, I can't explain it.'

'You were very fond of her.' It was a statement.

'Yes.' Isobel, who had been talking eagerly,

260

looked suddenly bleak. 'I loved her. We were friends but I let her down at the end.'

'How d'you mean?'

Isobel was silent for a long moment. 'I never knew she was ill,' she said at last. 'I was too busy with my own troubles to notice and she obviously didn't trust me enough to confide in me.'

Will felt a pang of anxiety. This was something which had gone very deep and was corroding Isobel's peace and despoiling her memories of Mathilda. 'I think you may have that round the wrong way,' he said gently.

She'd looked at him quickly. 'How d'you mean?'

'Put yourself in her place. Here is a woman who has lived alone, by choice no doubt, but nevertheless alone. She is someone who prefers her own company to that of the wrong people. You come along and she finds that with you she can talk and joke and play Scrabble. What a joy you must have been to her! What a bonus! You give her plenty of freedom and space but you care for her, keep her warm and well fed and allow her to live happily and do exactly as she pleases. One day she suspects that she's ill.' Will looked directly at Isobel. 'If she had confided in you can you imagine how your relationship would have changed? Gone would have been that ease and fun that you had together. You would have been watching her, worrying, waiting. She would have felt the

261

weight of your anxiety, reminded constantly of her illness, unable to forget it for a moment. I think that Mathilda chose to preserve the quality of her life right up to the end and that your ignorance of the truth enabled her to do it. She would have been relieved that she could hide her knowledge from you and I am quite certain that she never meant to hurt you by her silence nor imagined that you'd feel guilty in any way. From what I know of her and the relationship you shared, I suspect that she assumed that you'd understand.'

The silence seemed endless. Will thought that he'd never made such a long speech and he prayed that it was the right answer. Something told him that it was how Mathilda had felt. He slid a sideways look at Isobel.

'She talked about the quality of life,' she said slowly, 'but surely, if you love someone, you notice if they're not well?'

'Not if they're deliberately hiding it from you,' he answered promptly. 'I think Mathilda did that. She sounds like a woman with very great strength and courage. You are wronging her in dwelling on what you see as your shortcomings. You should be remembering what you had together and being happy and grateful for it. You are debasing the great friendship you shared.'

He heard her swallow at the harsh words and longed to throw his arms around her. Instead, he began to pat about his pockets for his pipe.

'She killed herself,' said Isobel in a small voice. So far she had kept this dreadful thing from Mathilda's relatives. They had been told that Mathilda died by accident, rendered helpless by the weakness caused by her illness and by the onset of hypothermia. 'I know she did. We talked once of euthanasia and she said that she would rather die than face the indignity of suffering. She felt very strongly about it. When she knew she had cancer I think she decided to take her own way out.'

'How wonderful then,' said Will calmly, 'that she had the courage of her convictions. Most of us talk but few of us act.'

'I don't think she did.' Isobel's eyes were dark with horror as she looked at him. 'I think she went out that night intending to drown herself.' She swallowed again, always remembering those fatal words of hers, and her lips trembled. 'I think she *did* lose courage. I think that she changed her mind but the engine wouldn't start. She hadn't bothered to get the boat overhauled. I think that when the storm got up it swept the boat into the rocks and she died of exhaustion and hypothermia. She took a flask with her but that's because I bullied her. I joked and said,' her voice trembled and Will braced himself, 'I said, "Go and drown yourself and see if I care!" But I went over later and made a flask of coffee for her and put it on the kitchen table beside her duffel bag. I knew she wouldn't bother or she'd forget to do it. The

263

flask was half empty when they brought it back. I think she lost her nerve when the time came and then she couldn't get back.' Isobel began to weep. 'I can't help thinking how frightened she must have been. Oh God. I did love her and if only I'd realised I might have saved her.'

'Saved her from what?' Will gave up and put his arm about her shaking shoulders, holding her close. 'Saved her from painful treatment and being a vegetable and dying a humiliatingly undignified death? Would you honestly have brought her back to that, given that you loved her? Can't you see what a blessing it was that fate took things out of her own hands? In the end she died peacefully and painlessly and at that moment of fear she had the warmth and comfort of the flask you made her. In those last moments you gave her what she needed; what you'd been giving her for the last years of her life. The tangible comfort of your love and caring for her.'

Isobel put her head in her hands and gave herself up to violent weeping but, when the storm had passed away, her guilt had been washed away with it. She looked at Will with swollen but clear eyes, the dark grief gone.

'I did love her,' she said shakily. 'She was . . . Mathilda.'

He smiled at her. 'Then give thanks for her and for your opportunity to love her,' he said. 'It is a great privilege to be able to love someone wholeheartedly. Don't throw it away

264

or debase it in grief and guilt and self-indulgent remorse.'

Now, as he felt the sun warm on his back, Will straightened up and watched a cloud of gulls screaming above a fishing boat as it plied its way towards Dartmouth. He remembered his own sense of guilt after he had talked so confidently to Isobel but the change in her convinced him that it had been the right thing to do. Thanking God that he had been given the means to help her, Will stretched and bent again to his scraping.

## CHAPTER TWENTY-THREE

The woods were full of birdsong. Tessa, hands in pockets, strolled slowly with Sidney pottering in the rear. A shower of upflung leaves and earth showed that Harry was far ahead, scratching busily at a hole deep in the roots of a tree, and quite unconscious of the squirrel who watched him slyly from a branch high above his head. A jay flashed between the trunks of two great oaks, disturbing a wood pigeon who rose with a clapper of wings and, with its odd curving flight, dipped into the meadow where lambs played at the edge of the wood. The pale gold of primroses gleamed from amongst beech mast and dead leaves, wood anemones glowed ghostly in the shadows beyond the path and the constant chuckle of water hinted at the presence of an unseen stream.

Tessa, who had hoped to spend Easter at the cove, was back in Wiltshire. The two families had once again united for a repeat trip to France and Tessa had been unable to refuse their pleas for help. She was not yet in such a position to be able to turn down work and she knew that these two women, struggling to make ends meet, had made great sacrifices to be able to take the children away on holiday for the week.

'It's rather a lot of driving,' Sidney's owner had admitted, 'but it's a wonderful break and the kids love it. Having you here is a great luxury but I couldn't put Sidney in kennels. He's much too neurotic. He was my husband's dog, you see, and when he went off it broke Sidney's heart, and his new woman wouldn't have him near her. He might slobber on the chair covers. Cow! So he stays with me. Poor old Sidney. He hasn't really got over it.'

It occurred to Tessa that he hadn't got over Harry, either. Despite a second week together, there was still a certain amount of tension on Sidney's part although his gentlemanly instincts obliged him to endure in silence. Harry, with all the insufferable confidence of the street urchin, never even noticed.

Tessa stood still and whistled. There was a scurrying as Harry appeared from nowhere and barged past them—he always had to be ahead—and, with Sidney fairly close to heel, she turned back towards the road where the car was parked. She yawned, feeling terribly tired, and realised that she had felt this weariness for some while. It was odd that, having achieved her heart's desire, she should feel such lethargy now that the first excitement was over. Her limbs were heavy and her brain was dull; unable to be stimulated to happiness, even by the thought of Sebastian or the sight of her engagement ring. As she walked she stretched out her hand so as to stare at the pretty hoop of sapphires, remembering how they had rushed in to Plymouth to choose it and then gone on to the cove so that Sebastian could meet Bea and Will.

Tessa had been swept along on a rising tide of excitement and happiness. Sebastian, having had his eyes opened at last, had behaved perfectly. For the few days that she was at Freddie's it was almost as if they were a couple in a film or an advertisement; he bought flowers and champagne, raced across beaches with her, sang as they drove along in the car, took her out to dinner. It had, she thought now, a sense of unreality about it: tremendous fun but quite unrelated to anything that had happened before or since. It was as if they were both playing parts in a brief moment of romance that had nothing to do with real life.

Tessa yawned again and felt irritable. Why

couldn't she be satisfied? For nearly ten years she had yearned after Sebastian and, now that she had him, all she felt was a dull exhaustion. Perhaps it was bound to be like this, she told herself as she let the dogs into the car. There was bound to be some sort of anticlimax after ten years of longing and hoping and waiting. She climbed in, switched on the engine and began to turn the car. Sidney whined miserably as she backed towards the hedge and she felt another surge of irritation.

'Shut up, Sid,' she said crossly. 'For goodness' sake! Nobody's hurting you!' She caught sight of his big domed head and sad eyes in the driving mirror and remembered what his owner had told her. 'Sorry,' she said, filled with compunction. 'Sorry, Sid. I'm being a cow!'

She drove along the lane, a now-familiar sense of confusion making her even more depressed. Deliberately she thought about Sebastian and how happy the Andersons had been when she and Sebastian had telephoned the news of their engagement. She thought of how sweet he had been to her and how he had made love to her—and her heart remained obstinately heavy.

'I'm tired,' she told herself. 'I need a holiday. A real one. Not just bits and pieces here and there. It's been a pretty exhausting year one way and another.'

Comforting herself with this reason for her

contrariness, she drove back to the cottage. Tomorrow she would leave Wiltshire. She had a few days to herself before her next job and she had planned to spend them at the cove; not as long as she would like but better than nothing. As she opened the door she could hear the telephone ringing and ran to answer it. It was a few moments before she realised who was at the other end.

'I've been ringing and ringing,' said Harry's owner, sounding near to tears. 'It's terrible. Poor Caroline's been taken really ill. We think it might be some seafood she had. She's in hospital. There's no way we can get back tomorrow. Can you hang on for a few days?'

Tessa shut her eyes for a moment, seeing her precious holiday disappearing. She tried to summon some sympathy for Caroline. 'I'm sorry,' she said. 'How awful for her. For all of you. I can stay three more days. I've got to be somewhere else after that.'

'She's really poorly.' The voice was trembling. 'The doctor says she might not recover. She's vomiting all the time. I don't know what to do . . .'

Tessa was shaken out of her lethargy and disappointment. 'How awful for you! Poor Caroline. Are the children all right?'

'We're all fine. Only she would have the mussels.' She began to cry. 'It's food-poisoning, you see. Her mum's coming over.'

'I'm so sorry.' Tessa felt inadequate. 'Look,

269

don't worry about the dogs. I can cope here until Tuesday. Stay in touch though, will you? I'm just . . . Well, I don't know what to say.'

'No. I know. I can hardly believe it myself. And I don't know what to say to the kids. I'll be glad when her mum arrives.'

'Of course you will. Try not to get too upset.'

'No. I'll phone again tomorrow, then. 'Bye.'

Tessa replaced the receiver. She felt frustrated and guilty for being more concerned about not being able to go to the cove than she was about the poor, sick Caroline.

'Shit!' she muttered. 'Damn! Blast!' She kicked off her boots whilst Sidney watched her anxiously. 'Sorry,' she said, automatically, seeing his distress. 'Sorry, Sid.' She stroked his silky head. 'How about a biscuit?'

As the day progressed, her frustration and depression settled back into a mild lethargy. Longing for some communication with the outside world she wrote a letter to Sebastian who was back in Portsmouth—a specially loving letter so as to assuage her guilt—and decided to ring Will and Bea to explain that she might be delayed. There was no reply and she spent some time trying to remember Isobel's surname and cursing herself for not having had the foresight to ask for her telephone number.

After lunch, worn out with so many negative emotions and the tiring boredom of having nothing to do, she fell asleep on the sofa in front of the television with Sidney stretched out on the floor beside her. Harry was patrolling the garden, a sharp eye out for the neighbour's cat with whom he had an ongoing sparring match. The telephone bell jerked Tessa out of a deep slumber and she hauled herself upright and stumbled out into the kitchen.

'Oh God!' said the voice of Harry's owner. 'It's awful. Caroline's dead. She's dead. Just like that. Isn't it terrible? I can't believe it.' She began to sob.

Tessa stood holding the receiver, trying to comprehend the horror of it. 'I'm so sorry,' she repeated meaninglessly. 'So sorry.'

'Thank God her mum arrived in time. It's awful here. Look, I'm coming back tomorrow morning. It's not fair on my kids to keep them here now. They're in a terrible state. Caroline's mum is coping with her two. They'll be staying here for a bit to arrange for . . . things.' She began to cry again.

'I simply don't know what to say,' said Tessa honestly. 'It's the most awful shock.'

'I know. It doesn't seem possible, does it? Alive one minute—and the next . . . nothing. I can't bear it.' She gave a kind of retching gasp. 'Look, I must go. The kids are waiting. See you tomorrow about three o'clock.'

Tessa filled the kettle and switched it on. The shocking news had penetrated the dullness of her spirits and she was filled with horror. The woman's words repeated themselves in her head. 'Alive one minute—and the next . . .

271

nothing.' So it had been with her parents and her brother. Her old companions of loneliness and isolation weighed upon her so terribly that she became desperate to speak to someone. The need to dispel the terrifying awareness of the transitory nature of man's existence was acute. She simply must smash through her fear and communicate with some warm, living, understanding human being. She found her address book and went back to the telephone. To whom should she speak? She found herself thinking of Giles but gave herself a mental shake. She could hardly phone him up out of the blue and weep down the telephone at him, especially now that she was engaged. Instead, she picked up the receiver and dialled the house in the cove . . .

Only much later did she remember that it had never occurred to her to try to contact Sebastian.

\*       \*       \*

Giles lay on the sofa-bed in his small studio, listening to some jazz and thinking about Tessa. He knew that his mother would have been disappointed at his lack of initiative but he was pleased with the way things were going. He and Tessa had spent two magic days together and, though nothing concrete had been said and he hadn't so much as kissed her, he was certain that progress had been made.

On his return to London he had been obliged to leave almost immediately for Ireland, to take photographs for a series of articles on Celtic Britain. Afterwards he had travelled on to Scotland and so he had been away for several weeks. He wished that it was not quite so difficult to contact Tessa. Because she was never in the same place for very long she had given him a contact number and, having arrived back and gathered up his confidence, he had dialled it. There was no reply. Later he had tried again . . . and again—but the number had been engaged for hours.

Giles settled himself more comfortably and closed his eyes. It was true that his upbringing had given him a wariness about entering into relationships, which reinforced his genetic inheritance. Until Tessa, he had never felt strongly enough to make the effort required to sustain such a relationship but, now that he felt as he did about her, he was determined that nothing should go wrong. He was frightened of hurrying her but afraid of losing her. He knew how she felt about Sebastian Anderson which, to begin with, had made it impossible to approach her. Now, he was more of his mother's persuasion; all was fair in love and war. The two days he had spent with her had convinced him that this, at last, was the real thing; now he was ready to fight for her.

He propped himself up a little and pressed the redial button on the telephone. Will answered the telephone so quickly that he took Giles by surprise.

'Hello,' he said. 'Mr Rainbird? My name's Giles Webster. Tessa gave me the number. I'd like to get in touch with her.'

'Ah, yes.' Will appeared to be dithering. Giles did not know that he was checking his list. 'Yes, of course. Giles Webster. The thing is, Giles, she's had a bit of a shock. I've just been speaking to her, as a matter of fact. The woman she's dog-sitting for died abroad yesterday and Tessa's just had to deal with the woman's friend and children collecting the other dog.'

'Died?'

'Shocking, isn't it? Food-poisoning apparently. Poor Tessa's a bit overwhelmed. She was supposed to be coming home today but she's stuck with the dead woman's dog, d'you see?'

'How terrible. Poor Tessa. And poor woman, whoever she was. I'm sorry.'

'Quite. Well, I'll give you her number but I warn you, she's a bit low.'

'I should think so. Thanks for the warning. Don't worry, I'll be as tactful as I can. Yes. I've got a pencil . . . Thanks.'

He dialled the number and waited. Tessa, when she answered, sounded tired and unhappy and Giles was filled with a new, strange tenderness.

'Tessa,' he said, 'it's Giles. I just phoned the

number you gave me and Mr Rainbird told me the sad news. I'm terribly sorry. What a shock for everyone. Are you OK?'

'Oh, Giles.' The caring note in his voice warmed her. 'Oh, isn't it awful? I've been talking to Will. I couldn't bear to be on my own, if you see what I mean. The terrible suddenness of it brought everything back.'

'Poor Tessa. Look.' He decided to take a chance. 'I'm just back from Scotland and Ireland before that. I've got a few days off. Would you like me to come and see you? Where are you?'

'I'm in Wiltshire. Oh, it would be lovely. I must admit I'm feeling silly and feeble. I shall probably cry all over you.'

'That's OK.' Giles felt full of protective love. 'Is there a pub I could put up in somewhere at hand?'

'Yes. I suppose ... It's a bit tricky ...' She sounded confused. 'Giles, I ought to tell you ... It's embarrassing because it sounds as if ... Oh shit! ...'

'What's the matter?' asked Giles, puzzled by the change in her voice. 'What have you been doing?'

Tessa gave a deep sigh. 'I hope this won't make you change your mind but I feel it's only right to tell you. Sebastian and I are engaged ...'

'I see. I hope you don't expect me to congratulate you.' He tried to keep his voice

275

light.

'Oh, Giles.' She was trying to laugh. 'I can't tell you how much I'd like to see you.'

'Then I'll be there,' he said calmly. 'But if the pub's shut you may have to find me a bed.'

'Come straight here,' she said recklessly. 'Please, Giles. There're plenty of beds and I'm sure it won't be a problem. If you really want to come . . .'

'I'll be with you in a couple of hours,' he said. 'Give me the address and the telephone number . . .'

When she'd rung off he sat staring at the telephone. To his surprise the news of her engagement had served to stiffen his resolve. He had been able to hide his anger and disappointment—he had no intention of antagonising her—but now his fists clenched involuntarily as he thought of Tessa and Sebastian together. 'Shit,' he muttered through clenched teeth. 'Shit, shit, shit!' As he packed a few things his mind was busy. It came as a revelation to him that he was not prepared to let her go. Usually he would have backed down at once, never dreaming of trying to come between an engaged couple, but not now. He knew that he was prepared to make a fight for Tessa but he would need to be careful. As he drove west, Giles laid his plans.

# CHAPTER TWENTY-FOUR

Bea strolled on the cliffs above the cove, her eyes fixed on the hazy horizon. It was a cold damp afternoon and the watery sun had disappeared behind a thin veil of cloud but she was unaware of any physical discomfort. Her brisk walk had warmed her and she was deep in thought. It seemed strange that she had settled so quickly here in this remote cove, far away from her friends and all that had been familiar. A few nights before, as she and Will played Scrabble before the fire, she had mentioned it to him. This, in itself, was surprising. She had come to the cove almost resentfully, simply because she did not know what else to do. To admit that it was working was tantamount to saying that there had been nothing in her previous life that was worth retaining. Normally she would not have allowed anyone to suspect such a thing but somehow Will was different. She could trust him to understand; she could expose weaknesses, put weapons into his hands, knowing that he would never use them against her.

'I feel the same,' he'd said at once. 'Odd, isn't it? All those years in Geneva and now it's as if they never happened. Not true, of course. We carry our experience and memories with us.

We're lucky, you and I, Bea. We had no ties to keep us from starting a whole new life.'

Bea fiddled with her tiles, thinking of Norah and of Tony. She knew that these friendships had been part of her school life and that it had been unrealistic to think that they would survive beyond it.

'It's sad though,' she'd said, thinking particularly of Norah. 'Rather selfish to pass people over when they no longer fit in to your life.'

'It all depends on what you mean by "passing people over",' remarked Will. 'If you're thinking of Norah then I think you'll find that she's just as happy, if not happier, without you. It wouldn't have worked, you know, and then you'd have fallen out. As it is, you're keeping in touch with her. She'll probably come down to see you in the summer and the friendship remains ready to be called upon in an emergency.'

Bea sighed and began to arrange tiles upon the board. 'You're probably right,' she said. 'Why does one feel guilty when the right thing just happens to be the thing that one wants? I can't help feeling selfish in knowing that what is right for Norah is exactly what I want.'

Will smiled. 'Poor Bea,' he said. 'What an uncomfortable companion a conscience is. Cheer up. When she comes down for a week you'll soon see it in perspective.'

'You're a cynic,' Bea had said—but she was

laughing. She knew that he was right. A day or two of Norah's self-righteous whining would bring all her own intolerance to the surface. 'But you've got a point. We're better apart.'

Will jotted down her score whilst Bea delved for some more tiles. 'Anyone else you're regretting?' he'd asked casually.

The silence had been a long one. 'Not really,' Bea had said at last. 'Just . . . just someone I rather cared for. Married, of course. Nothing to it except my own foolish imagination.'

'Very painful, that sort of attachment,' said Will thoughtfully. 'Best to get free of it, perhaps?'

He'd left the question hanging in the air and Bea had remained silent.

Now, as she walked on the cliff she thought about Tony Priest. She conjured up his image but, for some reason, it no longer had the power to disturb her. He seemed remote, unreal, and she wondered that she had ever allowed herself to become so romantically attached to him.

'Like a schoolgirl,' she muttered, 'with a crush on a film star.'

She took a deep breath, as though she would dispel all such negative and humiliating thoughts, and looked about her. So immersed in thought had she been that she had not noticed that the mist was rolling in from the sea. The sun had completely disappeared and the soft grey clouds were now pouring across

279

the cliffs, shrouding tree and rock and obliterating the familiar landmarks. Bea knew a moment of real anxiety. Trying to be calm, she stood quite still and listened. If she could hear the sea then at least she could keep well away from the edge of the cliff. She could work her way back to the field and make her way along the hedge.

She strained her ears but was unable to hear any noise. The mist, clothing her now in moisture, had the effect of deadening all sound. Bea pushed down a tendency to panic. She had been walking back to the path that led down to the beach, therefore the sea was on her left; but which was her left? She had stopped to look about her and now she couldn't decide which way she had been facing. Bea felt utterly disorientated; afraid to go either forward or back. Tentatively she took a few steps in what she hoped was the right direction. She stepped into a hole, stumbled, and fell to her knees amongst some gorse, crying out with pain as her hands plunged down amongst the spines and prickles. Kneeling there she gave a dry little sob, raising her head and straining to hear some sound that might guide her forward. Silence. The mist flowed over and around her, thick and wet, chilling her. She cried out, her voice thin and insubstantial. Scrambling to her feet she shouted again but the clouds seemed to bear her voice downwards, drowning and muffling it. As she stood helplessly, near to

280

tears, she heard a noise. Straining every muscle and nerve, she peered about her. 'Help!' she screamed again. 'Help! Please!' Something appeared suddenly out of the mist beside her and she stifled a scream. The collie from the neighbouring farm, gave a brief wag of the tail and hurried on. He had been rabbiting on the cliff but he knew it was time to start for home.

'Wait!' cried Bea. 'Stay! Sit! Come back. Please.'

The dog paused, looking back enquiringly and already barely visible as the mist washed over him, and Bea ran to him and grasped his collar. Holding on to it tightly she stroked his head with her free hand, feeling a measure of comfort at the feel of his warm hairy body against her leg.

'Good boy,' she said. 'Now then, go slowly. Good boy, then.'

The dog was puzzled but his tail wagged once or twice as he watched her with bright intelligent eyes.

'Come on then,' she encouraged him. 'Good boy. Come on.'

He set off again, Bea almost running at his side, but he did not keep to the short turf or the well-worn path. He was heading for the farm and he took her across country; her feet stumbling into shallow holes, her ankles scratched by gorse and heather. By now the mist was all-enveloping and she could see nothing. The dog, however, trotted confidently forward and she clutched at his collar, grateful for his presence. Suddenly he paused and braced himself. Bea, grasping even more tightly at his collar, sensed that he was about to jump. 'Wait!' she cried. 'Wait a minute.'

She thrust her hand forward and cracked her knuckles on the wooden bar of a farm gate. Pulling him with her she felt for the bolt, praying that it wasn't lashed up with binder twine as was so often the case. Her fingers encountered the smooth clammy iron of a thick hook and she lifted it up and pushed the gate open, shutting it carefully after they had passed through. On they went, across the cropped grass of a field laid down to permanent pasture. The going was easier now but Bea was panting as she hurried along with him. The next gate stood open and Bea found herself splashing through mud and water where the cattle had poached the path into the farmyard.

She caught back a cry of alarm as a tractor loomed from the mist beside her and she shook her head at her fear. She saw the shapes of the farm-buildings and knew that she was safely at the farm in the lane. The track down to the cove was a few hundred yards away. The dog had stopped politely, clearly anxious to find warmth and food. Bea patted him as she released him, flexing her stiff fingers.

'Thanks,' she said. 'Good boy.'

He disappeared towards the outbuildings and Bea picked her way carefully out into the lane, watching for the entrance to the track. She turned into it, her heart beating fast with relief, her feet slithering on the loose stones. She realised that she was trembling, and tried to pull herself together. Near the bottom of the path she heard voices calling to her. She recognised Will's deeper voice chiming with Isobel's anxious one and, with an answering cry, she went to meet them.

*  *  *

Will and Isobel had been in the kitchen when the mist rolled in. Tessa had just telephoned and Will was discussing this call with Isobel.

'I'm a bit confused,' he admitted. 'Apparently Giles is staying with her. Do you know this Giles?'

Isobel, perched on a kitchen chair, feet on the rung, shook her head. 'Sure it's not Sebastian?'

'Quite sure.' Will sat in Mathilda's chair by the Rayburn, frowning. 'He phoned us for her number, d'you see? This Giles. He's on the list she gave me so I could give it to him. It seems he went straight down to her when he heard the terrible news.'

'It's awful.' Isobel shivered. 'Poor Tessa.'

'Quite. So this Giles goes haring down. Nice chap, by the sound of it.' He glanced at Isobel. 'What did you think of Sebastian?'

She pursed her lips and wrinkled her nose. 'OK,' she said. 'He's nice. Good-looking. It's just . . . I felt he wasn't quite right for her. And she was . . . nervous. Or something.' She shook her head. 'I don't know. What did you think?'

'It's difficult,' said Will. 'I'm not sure I can judge. I'm so fond of her that I'm afraid I might feel that no one was quite good enough for her. Anyway, they're coming home together. With Sidney.'

'Sidney? Who's Sidney?'

Will sighed. 'He's the dog. The other woman turned up to collect her dog, d'you see, and she told Tessa that it will be some time before anyone will be thinking about what to do with Sidney. The mother lives in a flat in London and the children will be going to their father.'

'Can't he have the dog?' asked Isobel, faintly confused. 'What's the problem? Surely Sidney would be a comfort if they've just lost their mother?'

'Tessa explained it to me,' said Will, 'but it was all the least bit confusing. The father has remarried and his new wife won't have Sidney in the house. I told Tessa to bring him here for the time being.'

Their eyes met; Will's guilty, Isobel's alarmed.

'What will Bea say?' asked Isobel. 'She's not too keen on dogs, is she? Oh hell!'

'I know,' said Will miserably. 'But what could I do? Poor Tessa is in a frightful state.'

'Perhaps it'll be OK. I could have him in the cottage. Where *is* Bea? Is she still out? There's a mist rolling in.'

They both glanced involuntarily at the window. 'Heavens!' said Will. 'It's come down a bit, hasn't it?' He stood up and went to the back door.

'Is she up on the cliff?' Isobel followed him. 'God! It's really thick! She'll be frightened. Oh, Will! I hope she's OK. Let's go and meet her.'

She was pulling on her coat, awful visions of Bea alone on the cliff, and worse. Will was already out of the door, much the same thoughts in his head.

'She might have gone up the track,' he said. 'She often walks in the lane.'

'Shall we separate?' asked Isobel anxiously. 'I'll go up the cliff path. You go up the track.'

'Certainly not,' said Will sharply. 'Then I'd have both of you lost up there.'

'Oh, Will.' Isobel sounded frightened. 'People fall off the cliff sometimes and the coastguard gets called out. Well, it's usually dogs, actually, or people cut off by the tide. Should we telephone the coastguard?'

'Wait,' said Will. 'Just wait a minute before we get panicky. We'll go a little way up the track and, if there's no sign of her, we'll try the cliffs.'

'But if she's on the track she'll be OK,' argued Isobel. 'It's the cliffs I'm worried about.'

'I see that,' said Will, more calmly than he

285

felt, 'but if she's on her way home it's pointless for us to go crashing about on the cliffs. Let's just check.'

Isobel took his arm, thinking about Mathilda and imagining Bea stuck on a ledge—or . . .

Will squeezed her arm beneath his own. 'Let's shout,' he suggested. 'Ready?'

Their voices sounded reedy and Isobel shivered. 'Bea!' she shouted again, with more energy, and Will joined in with her. They stopped abruptly, each clutching the other, as an answering hail came from the mist ahead.

'Oh, Will!' cried Isobel, nearly weeping in her relief. 'It's her. She's on the track. Oh, thank God!'

\*     \*     \*

When they drew the shivering Bea into the warmth of the kitchen, they both exclaimed at the state of her hands and feet.

'What's happened to you, Bea?' asked Isobel. 'All those cuts on your hands—and it looks as if you've been paddling in mud. Your trousers are soaked.'

'It's nothing serious,' said Bea, kicking off her shoes, and finding that she was still trembling uncontrollably. 'Honestly. Please don't fuss.'

'Tea,' said Will, getting busy, 'and then a hot bath and clean warm clothes. You'll soon be right.'

'Were you worrying?' asked Bea, with an attempt at lightness.

'We were when we saw that the mist had come down,' said Isobel. 'Before that we were engrossed in Tessa's problems.'

'What's happened now?' Bea was glad to have the attention taken away from her own plight. She was not quite ready yet to admit to her fear or that she hadn't been keeping an eye on the weather.

'Well,' began Isobel—and paused as Will shot her a warning glance. 'Well, someone called Giles telephoned for her number and when he heard about this terrible tragedy he went rushing down from London to see her.'

Bea frowned a little. 'Giles?' she repeated. 'I thought his name was Sebastian?'

'Another chap,' said Will succinctly. 'Old friend. Nice chap. Tessa's on her way home and he's coming with her. They're driving in tandem. Tessa's a bit overwrought so he's coming along to keep an eye, as it were.'

Bea raised her eyebrows as she accepted a large mug of hot tea. 'Thank you, Will. It sounds a very philanthropic gesture to me. Old friend or not.'

'That's what we thought,' said Isobel eagerly. 'Why isn't Sebastian there?'

'Be fair,' said Will. 'Can't just jump ship like that. The Navy have responsibilities. There would be chaos if every sailor thought he could dash off each time some drama occurred on the home front.'

Isobel looked sceptical; Bea sipped her tea thoughtfully. Will passed a mug of tea to Isobel, wondering how to approach the next part of the story.

'She's got a bit of a problem,' he began carefully. 'Woman dead, two children to worry about, not to mention the dog. Woman's mother still out in France. Terrible thing! Tessa's bringing Sidney with her, just until things are sorted out, d'you see?'

'Sidney?' Bea looked at him enquiringly. 'Sidney? Is he one of the children? How are we going to cope with a child here?'

Will sighed. He had a sense of *déjà vu*. 'Sidney's the dog,' he explained. 'He's a clumber spaniel. Tessa can't just leave him alone in the house until they all come back from France. I said she could bring him but I know that I should have checked with you first. Trouble was, it was all a bit sudden, d'you see? You weren't here and Tessa was naturally very upset . . .'

He stopped, aware that he was gabbling. He and Isobel watched her anxiously, waiting for her usual criticism on the unsuitability of names given to the modern dog. Bea sat quietly sipping her tea, remembering the collie's patient intelligence and bright eye; the feel of his soft hair under her hand; the comfort of his warm body against her cold legs; the way he had unerringly led her to safety. She smiled a little, catching the worried glance that slipped between the two of them.

'I'm sure that we can manage,' she said serenely. 'He'll find it strange in a new place. I hope Tessa's remembered to bring his bed.' She finished her tea and stood up, a little shakily. 'I'll go and have that bath,' she said, 'and then we must think about what to give Tessa and Giles for supper.'

## CHAPTER TWENTY-FIVE

Giles drove carefully along the A303, his eyes on the tailgate of Tessa's car. From the back window Sidney watched him mournfully, cocking his head occasionally when Tessa spoke to him but turning back again to watch Giles in the car behind. He had made a great hit with Sidney. Giles felt a tiny surge of triumph and elation as he remembered Tessa's greeting. She had been waiting for him, the front door open the moment he pulled in outside the gate, hurrying down the path with Sidney at her heels. She had hesitated momentarily and then flung herself into his arms.

'Oh, Giles, I can't tell you how good it is to see you.'

He had held her without fuss, taking no advantage of this warm greeting, merely comforting her.

'It's a beastly thing to have happened,' he said. Still holding her in one arm, he bent to pat Sidney who was sniffing cautiously at his jeans.

'That's Sidney.' Tessa released herself, ashamed of her outburst. 'He's feeling it a bit. He's one of these dogs who can't cope with a bad atmosphere. The other family came and took Harry and there was a bit of drama, obviously. The poor woman is completely gob-smacked by it all.'

By this time they were inside the cottage. Tessa took him into the kitchen and began to heat some soup, already prepared and waiting in a saucepan on the electric cooker. Giles looked about him and sat down by the table. Immediately Sidney came to sit beside him, head on Giles's knee.

'He slobbers a lot,' warned Tessa.

She sounded more cheerful now and Giles looked at her, taking in her leggings and big sweatshirt and rumpled hair. She'd smiled at him and his heart had crashed about in his breast making him feel breathless. He bent down to stroke Sidney's head, hiding his expression. He was determined to abide by his plan.

'I don't mind a bit of slobber, do I, old chap?' he'd asked. 'Used to that with Felix, aren't I?'

'He's even worse,' said Tessa, taking relief in light chatter. 'His mouth is so loose and soft.

290

But he's a sweetie, if somewhat neurotic.'

'So tell me all about it.' Giles rested an elbow on the table, his feelings for her under control. 'Mr Rainbird told me a bit about it but I'm not exactly sure what's happened.'

Whilst she explained, serving up the soup and taking hot rolls out of the oven, he watched her intently and presently they sat down together to eat their supper.

Now, as he drove behind her, he marvelled at the strangeness of his feelings. All his life he had been diffident, cautious of change, wary of any alteration to the status quo. He knew that it was a fault in him, to be so unwilling to commit himself, and it worried him as much as it worried his mother. He knew that Kate suffered on his behalf; encouraging and pushing him, yet fearful lest she should be misjudging him. He also knew that she blamed herself for the problems that he had inherited from her unhappy marriage.

He had told her that, from his point of view, the divorce was far from being responsible for his dilatory and unconfident character; on the contrary, he had been relieved when his parents had parted and especially when his father, Mark Webster, had emigrated to Canada when he had not gained his promotion in the Navy. From his earliest days his father's inconsistent approach—now indifferent, now stern and bitingly sarcastic—had unsettled Giles and he was always much happier when

291

Mark returned to sea. Guy, his twin, had been able to cope better and had tried to protect Giles from tongue-lashings and other subtle psychological forms of cruelty when they had visited their father after the divorce. Guy had been more successful in his dealings with Mark and had done his best to stand between his father and his twin.

Giles wondered how he would have coped without the steady kindness of his uncle Chris, his mother's brother, and, later, David Porteous. Seeing David with Kate had restored some of Giles's confidence in the married state but the thought of committing himself to a long-term relationship still filled him with anxiety. He had seen, both with his parents and with his friends, how extraordinarily fragile these structures were. He thought of the responsibility involved and felt a faintness of heart. This, he told himself, was nothing to do with his dilatoriness. It was simply a fear that he would be unable to sustain what was required when the time came.

He was old enough to realise that, once you became a husband or a father, expectations followed close behind. Your wife and children made demands, had requirements, and how were you suddenly to know the right answers? Being a husband or a father did not automatically invest you with knowledge, patience, understanding. Supposing you were unable to supply these quite reasonable demands? If you could not, then you let down your wife and children—and what then?

When his father was Giles's present age, he and Guy had been seven years old. Giles shuddered at the thought. Would he be able to deal with a seven-year-old son? He wondered whether his father's behaviour had been a mask for his own inadequacies; his weakness and fear had taken the form of verbal bullying and psychological arm-twisting. Might not he—his father's son and the recipient of his genes—react in the same way with his own children? He had read that abused children often became abusers and he felt horrified at the idea of being cruel in his turn to a vulnerable child.

He had been amazed when Guy—more like Mark and less social than Giles—had married Gemma Wivenhoe. That Guy, who found most women a bore, should marry the light-hearted Gemma—who was, moreover, nearly nine years younger—had come as a shock.

'What happened?' he'd asked his twin bluntly. 'Gemma's a sweet kid but you've known her all your life. Why suddenly?'

'Probably because I've known her all my life,' replied Guy honestly. 'I feel safe with her. We know each other. Or, more to the point, she knows me. She knows how to deal with me.'

It was typical that he hadn't mentioned the word 'love'. Giles could see, however, that Gemma adored his brother.

'How does she do it?' he'd asked Kate later. 'She teases him and makes fun of him and simply won't let him bark and bite. What's even more amazing, I don't think he wants to!'

Kate had laughed, shaking her head. 'She's just like her mum,' she'd answered. 'Cass is so good-natured that it's almost impossible to be grumpy when you're with her. You forgive her anything. Gemma's just the same. Guy is very lucky but, thank God, he knows it and he's working at it, too. He'll need to. He's very like Mark. So like him that sometimes I feel ill with terror. I couldn't bear it if he were to hurt Gemma.'

It was then that Giles had told her how he felt about himself and marriage; that his indecisiveness was something apart from a natural fear of committing himself to another human being. She had remained silent for some time.

'I think it *is* part of the same thing,' she'd said at last. 'Sorry, Giles, but you can't separate them. They're part of the same instinctive anxiety. Your natural urge to dither merely underlines your fear of letting people down. I understand and I sympathise but you must try to overcome it. Your reluctance to commit yourself is a really negative trait. You'll miss out on so much. OK, so you'll get things wrong. So do we all. You will hurt and be hurt. It's life. It can be painful but it's better than never living at all.'

294

'But you say *you* feel guilty because you got it wrong,' he'd argued. 'It's you who say that your mistakes have affected our lives, too. Supposing I turn out like Dad and repeat the pattern all over again?'

'Oh, Giles, I know.' She had looked at him with compassion and remorse. 'It's just that you're not much like Mark and, more importantly, you're aware of your weaknesses and attempt to overcome them. I just hope that when the moment comes it'll sweep you along and you'll forget all these misgivings.'

Giles put a Gerry Mulligan cassette in the car tape deck and listened to the mellow notes of the saxophone. Kate had been right. When Tessa had told him of her engagement to Sebastian all his doubt and caution had been swept away. He knew quite surely that he loved her and that he was going to make a fight for her. He knew, too, that this must be a calm, quiet, determined fight—but he had a strange conviction that he was going to win it.

\*       \*       \*

Tessa, peering in her mirror, checked to see that Giles was still behind her. His quiet strength had been exactly what she needed and she felt grateful.

'I'll drive behind you,' he'd said firmly, 'then you can set the pace and stop when you want to have a cup of coffee or if you feel tired. Don't worry. You won't lose me.'

Nor had she. Every time she overtook a vehicle or a car pulled out directly behind her, she would glance anxiously in the mirror until she saw Giles's little hatchback closing up behind her. Sidney watched, too. He had been drawn to Giles's calm approach, a pleasant change after the tension of the previous few days, and he wanted to keep him in sight.

'He's nice, isn't he, Sid?' said Tessa. Sidney's ears cocked at the sound of her voice but he continued to stare out of the back window. 'I really like him,' said Tessa thoughtfully. 'I feel like I've known him for ever but there's something about him ...'

Her voice tailed away. She was remembering with faint embarrassment how she had rushed into his arms. He had taken it all very naturally—and she had been able to regain her composure quite quickly—but she was surprised at the strange conflict of emotion which she had felt in that moment when he had held her closely. The old confusion was back. Why had she not thought of telephoning Sebastian? Because, said an inner voice, he wouldn't have really wanted to be bothered with it all. Tessa felt the need to come to Sebastian's defence. He had been brought up in a service family and was used to seeing his mother cope with all kinds of disasters. The Navy couldn't let its men go on leave each time there was some small domestic crisis or there would be no fighting force left. She knew that she must learn to manage alone and that it was not Sebastian's fault that he could not be on hand every time she felt emotional.

She brooded on this, her respect for naval wives increasing. What a lonely life it must be. Suddenly she remembered something Kate had said to her when she was talking about her divorce from Mark Webster.

'The Navy taught me to live without my husband,' she'd said, 'and then I found I could. It's like giving something up for Lent and then discovering that you don't need it any more.'

Tessa could understand that and, after all, it was no lonelier a life than the one she was leading. She felt an affinity with Mathilda who had lived so contentedly by herself in the cove. No doubt she had known loneliness but she had learned at some point that it was better to be alone than to live with the wrong person. Tessa felt a deep satisfaction at the knowledge that Mathilda, Will, Bea and she, Tessa, shared the same great-great-grandfather. No doubt they also shared similar character traits. Bea had managed quite happily, unmarried, and Will seemed quite ready to move to the relative isolation of the cove. All three of them recognised something familiar in the others; they were family.

Tessa slowed a little to allow Giles to catch up. She tried to see Sebastian fitting in at the cove once they were married and frowned. He had been very polite to Will and Bea but there had been something missing.

'Nice old things,' he'd said, as they drove away up the track with Will waving goodbye on the beach. 'And Isobel's OK. Let's hope she moves on soon and then we can have the cottage when I'm on leave. Can't imagine us bouncing about in bed with that old biddy in the next room. You can tell she was a matron. She's got all the hallmarks. I'd probably be impatient at the mere thought!'

Tessa had tried to laugh with him but she'd felt hurt and upset. Bea and Will were her people and she hated it when he laughed at them. On the other hand, it was exactly as he talked about his own parents. Perhaps, because it was so long since she'd had a family of her own, she was being oversensitive. Tessa felt the now-familiar confusion. She knew that he was right and that it would be quite impossible to make love with Bea in the next room; but she had never contemplated such a thing taking place until they were married, any more than she would have considered sharing Sebastian's bedroom at the Andersons'. She tried to be reasonable but simply remained confused. This was what she had longed for and dreamed about for so many years but there was something not quite right somewhere.

She glanced at her mirror. Giles was driving easily, arms relaxed, head on one side. He looked as though he might be listening to music. She knew instinctively that he would not mock Will or Bea, nor suggest that he and she make love in the house in the cove. She felt quite hot at the thought of making love with Giles and experienced a sudden sinking sensation in the pit of her stomach. At that moment she feared that she had got things terribly muddled.

'Surely,' she said aloud—and Sidney turned to look at her—'surely I'm just being silly and over emotional? Oh God! Don't let me have got it wrong.'

She bit her lip, driving a little slower now as she tried to sort things out. Could her childhood passion for Sebastian have blinded her? Had she been so infatuated with him that she had never bothered to consider whether they were truly suited? She realised that she was slowing right down and looked quickly in her mirror. Giles flashed his headlights at her and gave her a little wave. She waved back, knowing a desire to burst into tears. His friendly caring gesture confirmed her terrors. She had got herself engaged to the wrong man. She remembered how delighted Mrs Anderson had been, how she'd hugged Tessa and said how thrilled she was to have her as a proper daughter at last. She thought of how Rachel, her oldest friend, had shrieked her joy down the telephone. She recalled the kindnesses of all the Andersons over the last ten years when she had been so lonely and unhappy. Tessa stared miserably at the road before her. She had become engaged to the wrong man and there was absolutely nothing she could do about it. She could never hurt the Andersons after all that they had done for her; without them she would not even have her job.

She was aware that Giles was flashing his headlights at her and pointing ahead where the bright and cheerful sign of a Happy Eater café glowed. Tessa understood what he was trying to tell her and pressed her indicator. She guessed that he had read her slowing down as a sign of weariness and was suggesting that it was time for a break. Gratefully she pulled into the car park and began to reverse into a space by some grass. Sidney whined anxiously.

'Shut up, Sid,' she said automatically. 'Don't fuss. I'm just about to give you a run.'

Somehow the familiar action of opening the tailgate and freeing Sidney had the effect of calming her and she was able to greet Giles with a smile.

'Good idea,' she said. 'I was getting a bit tired.'

'I thought you might be,' he said as they strolled behind Sidney. 'You must be exhausted after all the traumas. Shall I go and order some coffee?'

'I suppose . . .' she began reluctantly, not wanting him to go, willing him to remain with her. 'If you . . . Yes, why not?'

'It'll save a bit of time,' he said, pretending

not to notice her hesitation. 'Don't want to hurry Sidney. See you in a moment.'

He disappeared through the swing door and Tessa felt a moment of despair. She longed for him to put his arms round her, kiss her, tell her he loved her. Instead he was behaving as though he were a very nice elder brother. 'What else can he do?' she asked herself drearily. 'Oh shit, hell, damn.'

Giles watched her from the window, longing to rush out and seize her but knowing that he must hold back: his moment had not yet come. He pulled the cups closer and began to pour coffee for them both.


## CHAPTER TWENTY-SIX


Adrian Pearson, his car parked in a lay-by in a quiet lane, was making calculations on a small pad. He raised his head, his brain busy, and stared unseeingly at a cow in a neighbouring field. He was doing very well indeed. Mentally he reviewed his list of victims and wondered which of them he should next approach. Mrs Carrington had nothing else of value but there were one or two others in this area . . . Adrian tapped his pen thoughtfully against his teeth. The Rainbirds had not yet contacted him. He frowned, turning the pages in the pad until he came to the inventory he'd made at the house in the cove. As he read it through, excitement began to mount; he couldn't possibly let this one pass. He remembered the desperation which the old buffer had not quite been able to hide and wondered if he were still trying to overcome his scruples or his sentimentality for the pieces. The old bat had been ready to sell, he'd swear to it.

Adrian gave a sigh of pure irritation and snapped his notebook shut. Maybe the time had come for a tiny nudge, a gentle reminder . . . He wondered what the old couple had said to Tessa—and did it matter? After all, they clearly needed to raise money and selling some family heirlooms was the obvious way to do it. He shrugged, flicked the book open again and picked up his mobile telephone. The woman answered almost immediately.

'Ah.' Adrian was caught slightly off balance. For some reason he had expected Mr Rainbird. 'Hello. Miss Rainbird? It's Adrian Pearson here.'

'She's not here,' said the woman. 'Who did you say it was?'

Adrian was puzzled. 'It's Adrian Pearson. The antique dealer. I think we met when I came down to the cove.'

'Ah, yes,' said the woman. 'Of course. Well, Tessa's not here. Shall I take a message?'

'Oh, I see.' He laughed in a conciliatory way. 'I do apologise. I thought that you were Miss Rainbird too, you see.'

302

'My name is Beatrice Holmes,' she said flatly.

'Yes,' he said awkwardly into the silence and cursing her lack of friendliness. 'Well, I seem doomed to miss Tessa, don't I? Uh ... any other thoughts about the conversation we had? Any movement there? I'm in the area again for a day or two. I'd be very happy to pop over.'

'I'm sure you know my feeling in the matter, Mr ... er. My cousin, however, is full of the finer feelings and is having difficulty in bringing himself to the point. It's only a matter of time.'

'I see.' Adrian's spirits began to rise again. She might be an old cow but she was much easier to deal with than these dithering old idiots who wanted to hang on to their relics. He chuckled, trying to introduce a more friendly note into the proceedings. 'Is he there? Would you like me to have a little chat with him? You know? Encourage him a bit?'

The conspiratorial note seemed to soften her a little. 'We-ell, it's not a bad notion, I suppose. He has to be pushed into every decision he takes. Quite exhausting! I'm afraid he isn't here at the moment. Perhaps you could try again later. Have we your telephone number?'

'It's on the card,' said Adrian quickly. 'The London office and my mobile. There's no point in giving you any other number. I move around such a lot. Have you still got my card?'

There was a pause whilst paper was shuffled

about at the other end of the line. Presently her voice read out the number of his mobile telephone.

'That's it!' he said cheerfully. 'Excellent. Well, I'll give you a bell later this afternoon, shall I? Meanwhile you can get hold of me on that number unless I'm with a client.'

He switched off and stared out through the windscreen. It looked as if all would be well. 'It's only a matter of time,' she'd said—and there had been no mention of Tessa. Adrian took a deep breath and beat the steering wheel lightly with a triumphant fist. He glanced at his watch. He had one other call to make and then he would be free. The old chap might be back by then and he could give him a nice gentle going-over; a hint that he might not be able to place the pieces if he didn't have them soon; an indication that he might have to drop his offer because of other pieces he'd seen of greater value . . .

Adrian put his notes into his briefcase, shifted in his seat and fastened his seat belt. With luck he might have the whole thing sewn up by this time tomorrow.

\*       \*       \*

'I gather that it was my name that you were taking in vain?' asked Will, placidly turning the page of the *Kingsbridge Gazette* at the kitchen table. 'Was it our nice friendly crook?'

'It was.' Bea sat down opposite. 'What are we going to do about him?'

Will crossed his arms and brought his mind to bear on Adrian Pearson. 'According to James, there's nothing we *can* do,' he said regretfully.

'Nothing legal, perhaps,' said Bea. 'I know we can't get him locked up but perhaps we could give him a good fright.'

Will looked interested. 'Got any ideas?'

'Not yet,' she admitted. 'All this business with Tessa has put him out of my mind but surely if he knew that we know he's a crook . . .?'

Will ran his hand through his hair and gazed into the middle-distance; Bea watched him with well-concealed affection. She tried to analyse these new sensations and decided that they were summed up in the word 'contentment'. Her life with Will was without passion but it was deeply satisfying. He was companionable, but left her room to breathe, and his cheerful kindness made him an ideal person with whom to share her home and her life. It was hardly odd that she was barely able to contemplate a different existence.

Bea looked about her. The French windows stood open to the balcony and the room was filled with bright trembling light. Sidney lay stretched out in the May sunshine and she realised that his presence was fast becoming as familiar as the gentle, persistent whisper of the sea. The cries of the gulls could be heard above the sound of the Morris jolting down the track. Isobel was home.

Will, too, had heard the engine and straightened a little in his chair. He could not prevent the upward leaping of his heart at the thought of seeing her; dark, tall, eager. He hated to think of her being unhappy; longed to shoulder her burdens and surround her with his love. Sometimes he imagined her accepting that love, marrying him; would he ever have the courage to ask her? Sometimes, when her loneliness brought her across to the house to sit and talk or play Scrabble, he thought that he might. He knew that he had helped her with her grief and guilt about Mathilda but he was sure that she still loved Simon and that his marriage had hurt her deeply. So, too, had the continuing indifference of her daughter. Like Mathilda before him, Will knew that Isobel was happiest when she was needed.

Sidney raised his head. He, too, had heard Isobel's approach and his tail began to thump. He was happier than he had ever been, since his master's defection, here in the cove and he padded in through the French windows so that when Isobel opened the kitchen door they were all waiting for her.

Her hair was constrained by a twisted silk scarf and she wore a cherry-coloured T-shirt tucked into a long swirling skirt of navy and red, her waist clasped by a wide leather belt.

306

She was carrying a bunch of narcissi in one hand and a bottle of claret in the other and she looked radiant. Will clamped himself to his chair with both hands, lest he should leap up and embrace her, and it was left to Bea to say: 'How summery you look. Goodness! Are they for me?' as Isobel deposited the flowers beside her and held out the wine to Will.

He freed his hands and took it, smiling at her. Something wonderful had happened to her, he could see that at once, and he wondered what could possibly make her look like a young girl in love. He was filled with a horrid foreboding. Perhaps Simon had come to his senses at last and wanted her back. Will stood up quickly so that she should not see the anxiety he was, for the moment, unable to hide and he was grateful for Bea's calm voice asking Isobel what good fortune had blessed her.

'Oh, it's the most fantastic, unbelievable thing,' she was crying as she sank down at the table and hugged Sidney. 'You'll never believe it. *I* can't. I've waited so long.'

Will kept his back to the table, pretending to fiddle at the draining board so that they should not see the sudden tremor of his hands.

'Don't keep us in suspense,' Bea was saying. 'We don't know whether to offer you coffee or champagne. Not that we've got any. So what is this fantastic and unbelievable thing?'

'I've been into Kingsbridge,' she said, trying in vain to control the joy in her voice, 'and I popped into the shop, just to give a message to Pat, and she had a letter for me. Oh, it's just so amazing! I didn't recognise the writing to begin with—well, it's been so long—and I thought it might be a customer. Just occasionally they write to thank you for getting a book or something, so I just shoved it in my bag and went over to Somerfields. And when I'd done my shopping I was just sitting in the car getting my keys out and I saw the letter and opened it.' She took a great breath, half laughing, half sobbing. 'Oh, you'll never guess. It's from Helen. She couldn't remember my address, you see, so she sent it to the shop. She's written from Durham and she's asked if we could meet. Oh, can you believe it? I feel that I might just burst into tears,' said Isobel—and did so.

She stretched her arms out on the table, buried her face in them and wept. Sidney watched her anxiously and moved closer to Will who, weak with relief, turned round at last to look at her. Bea grimaced comically at him and patted Isobel on the shoulder.

'It is certainly wonderful news, my dear. Definitely bottle-worthy. How about that wine you've got there, Will?'

'Absolutely.' Will pulled himself together. 'Or perhaps something a little lighter. I've got a rather pleasant Chardonnay, haven't I, Sidney old chap . . .?' He talked to himself and Sidney, attempting to reassure Sidney and bring himself under control. For one terrible moment it had seemed that he might be going to lose Isobel. 'Glasses,' he murmured. 'Corkscrew . . .' He touched Isobel briefly on passing and she gripped his hand, still sobbing. He held on tightly, swallowing a little, and smiled at Bea, who watched tolerantly. She had no idea of Will's real feelings for Isobel but saw that he was moved by her happiness.

'I thought I'd never see her again, you see,' explained Isobel, mopping her cheeks. 'Sorry. I'm just completely over the top.'

'And why not?' asked Will. 'I am so happy for you. Does she suggest a time for this meeting?'

'Well, she's just about to do her finals.' Isobel fished the letter out of her bag. 'And it seems that she's been offered a research job at Bristol University.' She glanced down the page. 'She's coming down at the end of June and has asked if we could meet then. She doesn't say much else.'

'It must have been a rather difficult letter to write,' remarked Bea thoughtfully. 'After all this time.'

'It is a bit tentative,' agreed Isobel, 'but it's a start. I shall write back at once. No reproaches or recriminations. I shall say that I can't wait to see her.'

Will smiled at this eager generosity. 'Good for you,' he said. 'Where will it take place?'

'Here,' said Isobel at last. 'At the cottage. I know it's on my ground but she has no place down here and I can hardly go to Modbury. I don't want to meet in a pub or some public place.'

'Well, here's to a new beginning.' Will distributed glasses. 'May the meeting be crowned with success . . .'

\*       \*       \*

It was after lunch, when Isobel had disappeared to the cottage to write her letter to Helen, that the subject of Adrian Pearson resurfaced. Will dialled the London number and spoke to a young woman who confirmed that Adrian Pearson was one of their agents. She told him that the items purchased were distributed to various showrooms throughout the country. The agents were given a list of pieces that were required so that they were usually placed very quickly, often to a waiting customer, which was why the agents were able to pay cash at once.

'No joy there,' reported Will to Bea, 'although I should like to have a look at that office. Pity London is so far away. They count on that, I expect.'

Bea stared at him. 'Giles!' she said, as one inspired. 'Giles could go and check it out.'

'Brilliant!' said Will softly. 'So he could. That would be a start.'

'Once we know what's going on that end,' said Bea, 'we might have some idea as to how to lay a trap for him. Meanwhile, perhaps we should let him visit us again. Just to keep him on the hook.'

'I'll phone Tessa for Giles's number and then I'll phone Mr Pearson,' said Will. 'I must say I rather liked that boy.'

'Giles?' Bea began to stack the washing-up on the wooden draining board. 'Mmm. I think he's in love with her.'

'It sounds silly,' said Will, picking up the tea cloth and standing by, 'but I felt that he was more right with her than Sebastian, if you know what I mean.'

'Well, he's older, of course, less bumptious,' Bea plunged her hands into the soapy water.

'I hope she's not making a mistake,' said Will worriedly.

'What an old mother hen you are,' said Bea affectionately. 'First Isobel. Now Tessa. Perhaps it's as well that you had no children to worry about.'

Will began to put away the plates, glad that Bea assumed that his feelings for Isobel were purely paternal. There was no need yet to rock the boat. He knew that Bea would not like the idea of him and Isobel getting together, although they need not be far away; he could move over to the cottage, leaving the house for Bea. And Tessa and Sebastian? Of course, the boathouse could be converted . . .

'Come on.' Bea was hustling him. 'Make that phone call. I feel just in the right mood for a bit of a run-in with our Mr Pearson.'

Will abandoned his musings with relief. It was rather complicated working out the logistics of fitting everyone into the cove but he had no doubt that, given time, it could be done. Drying his hands he went to find Adrian's card.

*       *       *

Adrian switched off his mobile with relief. It was so much more satisfactory to have the clients ring rather than having to chase them up. Looking too keen was a very bad mistake. The old chap had invited him to tea. Adrian grinned to himself; very couth. Mr Rainbird had been trying not to sound too anxious but that might simply be because the old bat was breathing down his neck.

He laughed a little, the usual exhilaration sending the adrenalin flowing through his veins. How he enjoyed the chase and the kill! He turned off the A38 and headed towards Kingsbridge, planning his campaign. He'd start by being less confident, this time; notice a few flaws he'd ignored on that first visit; show a little anxiety as to where he might place the stuff. He'd get them on the run all right and tie the whole thing up. He thrust his foot down on the accelerator and overtook a tractor dangerously and at speed. Those lovely pieces were as good as his.

# CHAPTER TWENTY-SEVEN

Isobel lay on her face on the beach, the sun hot on her back. Will and Bea had taken a picnic up on to the moor and she had the cove to herself. The heat seemed to press upon her, relaxing her but sapping her energy. The excitement of the last few weeks had exhausted her. She had written a long letter to Helen and then lived in terror lest she had overdone it. She worried as to whether she had been too eager, too gushing, and feared this might frighten Helen away. She was like her father, calm and quiet, and, on reflection, a gentle approach would have been more sensible. Her relief, when another letter arrived from Helen a week later, was overwhelming. The content of this letter had been more relaxed and Helen wrote that she was revising like mad and feeling very nervous about her exams. She agreed to come to the cove, when she arrived back from university, with the proviso that there should be no one else present but she and Isobel.

Isobel guessed that this was because she had written enthusiastically about Bea and Will—not to mention Sidney—and Helen feared that a reception committee might be waiting for her. There was no danger of that. Isobel wanted her daughter absolutely to herself. There was so much catching up to do; nearly five years of lost time. As she thought about this, Isobel became increasingly nervous. It would be like meeting a stranger. When she left Simon, Helen had been a child still; now she was an adult. Isobel stretched her arms out and dug her fingers into the sand at the edge of the rug. How, she asked herself for the thousandth time, could she have abandoned her husband and daughter for a man like Mike? How could she have flung away all that she had for a moment of madness? She wondered how many other women, on the brink of middle age, lost all that was precious and dear to them, all that they'd worked for and achieved, because of a brief descent into boredom and restlessness. Her misfortune had been to have a Mike ready to distract and charm her; to alleviate that boredom and soothe the restlessness with placebos that brought only temporary relief. She had seen her life with Simon as dreary and uneventful; a domestic desert, especially now that Helen was growing up. Mike had offered excitement and fun which she had believed to be happiness.

'*But how do you define happiness*?' she heard Mathilda asking. '*Do you mean joy? Or do you mean contentment? If you mean some kind of ephemeral excitement bound up with physical gratification, then I must reject your values.*'

How well she summed it up, thought Isobel, rolling over and crossing her arms across her eyes. Ephemeral excitement bound up with physical gratification expressed it very neatly

314

but it certainly did not add up to happiness.

'I was mad,' she said aloud. 'Quite mad. And I've paid for it.'

Now, however, the dark clouds had drawn back a little and the sunshine was breaking through. Helen was coming to see her. The familiar mixture of joy and terror gripped Isobel's stomach. It simply had to work between them; there must be no more misunderstandings. Again she wondered what had made Helen write the letter. Why this change of heart? Was it simply that she was growing up at last and could approach the whole subject with more tolerance? Perhaps she herself had experienced an unhappy love affair? Perhaps it was simply that she missed Isobel? She was, after all, her mother and, however wonderful Sally might be, there was no blood tie. It might be that Simon was more preoccupied with Sally now that they were married and had less time for his daughter. Was that why Helen had not asked him for her address but had sent the letter to the bookshop?

Isobel stretched lazily. Speculation was useless. It might be any number of things but, in the end, it really didn't matter. Helen was coming to see her. She started up violently as Sidney thrust his cold nose into her neck. It was rather hot for him in the car and, since the moor offered very little shade, it had been decided that Sidney should remain at home.

Isobel had agreed to look after him and he had been left in the kitchen until the car had disappeared up the track, lest he tried to follow them. He preferred to have Will within sight or sound but Isobel made a fairly satisfactory substitute. As soon as the car was gone, Isobel let Sidney out so that he could stretch full length on the slate path in the shade behind the house.

Now he was in need of company and Isobel sat up and slipped an arm around his neck. He licked her nose briefly and sat staring out to sea, his silky white coat glistening in the sun.

'How about a little walk?' she whispered into his long ear, which twitched slightly as she blew on it. 'It'll be a bit cooler up on the cliff and you might see a rabbit.'

Sidney's tail moved slightly at the word. Since he'd come to live at the cove he knew all about rabbits. Not that he'd ever caught one but he lived in hope. Isobel stood up and wrapped a cotton skirt about her waist, thinking about Sidney's family; the poor dead mother and the two children. Tessa had told her the story and Isobel wondered how much the children missed Sidney; how they were coping with a new stepmother who hated dogs and who had refused to have Sidney in the house. Isobel wondered, too, how this dog-hater had taken to the two children and why the father had left them and their mother in the first place. Perhaps the man, like herself, had been seeking after the elusive bluebird of happiness. As she strolled towards the cliff path, Sidney trotting expectantly before her, Isobel remembered Mathilda's question and her own answer.

'*And did you find happiness?*'

'*No. But it was worth trying for, surely?*'

Isobel looked out over the dazzling brilliance of the sea, hearing Mathilda's voice in reply.

'*That rather depends on what you lost in the attempt.*'

Until now the answer to that had been, simply, 'everything'. Now it was different. Helen was coming to see her.

\*       \*       \*

Giles emerged from his dark room and went into his tiny galley kitchen to make himself some supper. His work derived mainly from catalogue and fashion photography but he was being used now by the tourists boards and glossy magazines which dealt with country pursuits. His reputation was at last beginning to build and he was able to convince himself that he could make a fairly good living from his work. As to whether or not it was good enough to support a wife, he could not yet be certain. As he stir-fried his vegetables he thought of Tessa. He had enjoyed his trip to the cove and had taken immediately to Will and Bea. He fully understood how Tessa felt about this new family of hers and was moved by their evident affection for her. To be sure, Bea's keen glance had given him cause to wonder if he needed a haircut and made him wish that he'd cleaned his shoes but the feeling soon passed. Will had been interested in his work and he'd been surprised at how readily he'd opened up to him, telling him of the pitfalls and the disappointments of his career.

It was rare for the reticent Giles to be so forthcoming but Will was easy to talk to and genuinely interested. In the end they had persuaded him to stay the night. The woman from the cottage, Isobel Stangate, had offered her spare room and Giles had readily accepted. It had given him an opportunity to spend more time with Tessa and to become more familiar with the place she now knew as home. He had fallen in love with the cove and the cliffs above it and had taken some photographs—Giles never travelled without his photographic equipment—which he was hoping to use in conjunction with the South Hams Tourist Board.

Giles tipped the food on to a plate and took it into his living room. It was a studio flat and this room doubled as his bedroom, the sofa opening out into a bed. It was the darkroom that had persuaded him to look at a flat in such an expensive area; that and the fact that his mother had inherited some property and money from a friend who had died in rather tragic circumstances. Kate, at a loss as to what to do with such unexpected wealth, had insisted that Giles accepted some help from her. Guy had recently made the trip to Canada to see his father, and had returned with enough money to set up his chandlery business in Dartmouth, but Giles could not bring himself to visit the man who had caused his mother and himself such unhappiness. Naturally, therefore, no money was forthcoming from his father for Giles's career and, in the end, he had accepted his mother's assistance with gratitude.

He wondered now, as he ate his supper, whether it was the manifestation of their father's unsociable genes which had pushed him and Guy into careers which relied on no one but themselves to operate. Obviously both of them relied on clients but these remained on the periphery of their lives. Giles felt his old anxiety returning and quickly fixed his mind on Tessa. He must not weaken. Each time he saw Tessa he was confirmed in his certainty that he could be a marriageable viability. Although the least conceited of men, he felt sure that she loved him. There was a rightness that gave him confidence. He was well aware of her difficulty and this was the thing that exercised his mind a great deal. He knew how much she owed the Andersons and how much it would upset her to break the engagement. Her loyalty would be called into question and the friendship threatened.

As he sat with his long legs stretched out in front of him, his dark head bent over his plate, Giles racked his brains for some painless way of extracting Tessa from the engagement. He wondered if Sebastian truly loved her or whether it had been some momentary madness. After all, it had taken him long enough to get round to it. Giles forked up the last mouthful and set the plate on the cushion beside him. On his return to London, he had telephoned Kate and told her the whole story. She had listened in silence until he had announced his decision to fight for Tessa.

'Great,' she'd said briefly. 'Go for it.'

He'd laughed—and then hesitated; a shadow of his former fear looming. 'You don't think . . . .?'

'No,' said Kate. 'I don't. I know Sebastian and I'm quite certain he isn't right for Tessa. And her infatuation for him is just part of all that tragedy of losing her family. It's her need to love and be loved. It just happened that he was there at the vital moment. Don't dither! Go for it.'

'I just don't know how she'd cope with breaking the engagement. She owes the Andersons so much.'

'That's true,' said Kate thoughtfully, 'but there's no need to immolate herself as a sacrifice on the altar of friendship. No good to anyone. But I take your point. And then again she must feel an awful twit, poor girl.'

'Why?' asked Giles, indignant at even the least slight on Tessa.

'Come on,' said Kate scornfully. 'Think about it. She's been mad about him for years and suddenly he asks her to marry him just when she falls in love with someone else. Poor old Tessa! She must be kicking herself.'

'Of course we don't know that she's . . . you know . . . fallen in love with me.' He felt rather embarrassed at saying the words but at the same time, filled with exultation.

'Yes we do,' said Kate. He could hear the smile in her voice. '*You* do.'

'How d'you mean?'

'Why do you think you're suddenly behaving like Attila the Hun and his boys?' she teased. 'Ah, 'tis love, 'tis love . . .'

'Shut up!' he'd said—but he was laughing too. 'OK. But keep your fingers crossed.'

'And everything else,' she promised. 'David and I will try to think of some way of getting her out of this mess.'

'Are you going to tell him?' he'd asked, rather disconcerted, his usual reticence up in arms.

'Only David,' she'd said wheedlingly. 'No one else, I promise. But I must share it with him. He won't say a word, honestly.'

Giles stood up and took his plate into the kitchen and rooted in the freezer compartment of the fridge for some ice cream. It would be hard to share one's thoughts and fears with another person; to allow them in to all those secret places of the mind and heart. He took his pudding back to the sofa and had just taken an icy mouthful when the telephone rang. It was Will. Giles hastily swallowed and felt the coldness run down inside his chest.

'How are you?' he asked. 'Are you all well? Thanks again for a wonderful time the other week. I really love your cove.'

As Will's voice quacked busily, Giles sat listening, his ice cream melting in the dish.

'OK,' he said at last when Will had related the whole Adrian Pearson saga. 'Let me get a pencil and I'll telephone them and ask where they are. No, I take your point. I won't let them know I'm in London but I shall need the address, shan't I? No, I'll try not to frighten them off. Hang on.'

When Will had finally hung up, Giles looked with distaste at his plate and, taking it into the kitchen, dumped it in the sink and ran water on it. As he stood watching the ice cream disappear the telephone rang again. This time it was Tessa.

'Has Will phoned?' she asked. 'Did he tell you about this awful man who's going round robbing people?'

'He did.' His heart was pounding and he could hardly keep from smiling as she talked indignantly into his ear. 'I'm going to check out the office.'

'Bea's trying to think of a way of giving him a fright, since he can't be stopped legally. Isn't it infuriating? Oh, when I think of poor Mrs Carrington . . .'

'How are you?' he asked at last when she'd talked herself breathless.

'OK.' Suddenly she sounded shy. 'It was fun, wasn't it? Our trip to the cove with Sidney. He's settled in wonderfully which is just as well since they won't have him back. Apparently he's very happy in the cove.'

'I'm not surprised,' said Giles lightly. 'I could be very happy in the cove myself.'

'Yes,' she said—and there was a long silence.

'Tessa,' said Giles gently, when the silence had really said it all, 'this may not be fair or gentlemanly or whatever—but I have to say it. I love you.'

'I think I guessed,' she said faintly. 'Oh, Giles . . .'

'Don't worry about it,' he told her. 'Just think about it sometimes.'

'I think about it all the time,' she said almost inaudibly, 'but there's nothing I can do about it. I *can't* let the Andersons down.'

'I understand how you feel,' he said calmly. 'Try not to worry. I just want to be sure you know. It's important, although I don't want to make things difficult.'

'Of course it makes things difficult,' she cried almost angrily. 'But I don't want you to stop,' she added, suddenly forlorn.

'I shan't stop,' he assured her.

She hung up abruptly and he sat for some time, staring at nothing. He knew that, whilst her engagement stood, Tessa would find it impossible to tell him that she loved him but Giles was in no doubt of it; he felt moved and elated by the exchange. Presently he stopped thinking about Tessa and concentrated on Adrian Pearson. Slowly but gradually an idea began to take form.

## CHAPTER TWENTY-EIGHT

Tessa drove slowly up the lane and parked the car on the wide grassy space at the top. Here she could look up at the high hills of the moor to the west and away across the misty valleys to the thin line of sparkling sea to the south. Already it was hot although it was barely half-past seven. Tessa released Romulus and Remus and wandered down the lane towards the field where the grass had recently been cut for silage. It was good to get the two old dogs out on to cool grass before the sun's heat became unbearable. She sniffed, luxuriating in the warm-scented summer smells, and smiled to see the two labradors going down the field at a gallop in pursuit of a rabbit. She pulled on her old denim sunhat and followed them slowly.

In the stillness of the morning a lark rose up somewhere close at hand, the cadence of his song falling back to earth in clear flutelike notes. Small brown moths fluttered lightly in the tall feathery grasses below the hedge; above them a bee, droning heavily, lumbered amongst the delicate flowers of the convolvulus. A rabbit raced across the grass, white scut bobbing, and vanished into a hole almost hidden in the twisted roots of a great beech tree. Strolling down the field, Tessa wondered why her problems seemed so much easier to handle when she was out in the open air. Here it became possible to confront Sebastian and tell him that she had made a terrible mistake; simple to explain the situation to Mrs Anderson and Rachel. In these sunny spaces, with the green springing turf beneath her feet and the blue sky arching into eternity, everything was possible ... Everything was possible until she saw Sebastian in the flesh or heard Mrs Anderson's voice on the telephone asking if they had made any plans for the date of the wedding.

Fortunately Sebastian had refused to be pinned down to this. There was talk of a staff job in Washington which he was keen to pursue though not, it seemed, as a married man. He had been rather cagey about it when he telephoned Tessa, reluctant to tell her too much, anxious to indicate that it would be difficult to arrange the wedding before he took up the post. Mrs Anderson had been plainly embarrassed by his reluctance and was quick to talk about career structures and dedication to the service, lest Tessa should be hurt. There had been some kind of personality clash, apparently, and Sebastian was in the right place at the right time to be hurried out as a replacement.

For the first time for several weeks Tessa saw a ray of hope. She told Mrs Anderson that she quite understood the position and, gathering all her courage together, suggested that perhaps she and Sebastian should rethink the whole thing; perhaps they'd rushed into it . . .? Before she could finish Sue Anderson was protesting strongly: . . . never heard so much rubbish in her life . . . break Sebastian's heart . . . simply a question of patience . . . Tessa must go out to Washington to stay . . . such fun . . . By the end of the conversation Tessa had felt convinced that she would never have the courage to tell the Andersons the truth.

Later, Sebastian had rung again. He was charming and persuasive and Tessa guessed that his mother had been talking to him. She suspected that Sebastian knew that Washington would be more fun if he were single and his mother had taken him to task over it. Tessa decided to test him a little and, heart in mouth, had asked if it wouldn't be possible to have a simple ceremony before he flew out or perhaps on his first leave? Instantly he became

326

defensive and even a little sulky; he didn't want any hole-and-corner business, he said, and his mother and Rachel would be so disappointed if they were denied all the panoply of a proper wedding. Moreover, it was absolutely essential that he gave all his time and energy to this important job which would almost certainly lead to promotion if he played his cards right.

Now, as she watched Romulus and Remus panting towards her, Tessa wished that she'd had the courage to be honest with him. Then had been the moment in which she could have pointed out that she wasn't prepared to wait two years for him. Perhaps she had hesitated because Sue Anderson's voice was still too clear in her ears. She suspected that, should she really make a stand, the Andersons would bring pressure to bear on Sebastian and she would find herself married to him after all and flying out to Washington with him.

She bent to stroke the two golden heads and turned back to the gate. As one dog they panted their way to the corner where, for most of the year, there was a standing puddle. The hot spell, however, had dried it to a hard mud bed at which they sniffed, puzzled. Tessa lifted the tailgate and produced a big plastic bowl and a container. She stood the bowl on the grass and filled it with water for them and they stood side by side, lapping gratefully. As she waited for them to drink their fill she thought about Mrs Carrington and how difficult it had been to see her again knowing, as she now did, about Adrian Pearson. Anger rose within her. It was one thing unwittingly to find a bargain or make a reasonable profit but to set out deliberately to cheat the weak and vulnerable made her speechless with fury. She decided to say nothing to Mrs Carrington; better that she remained in ignorance than to know that she had been duped.

'In you get, boys,' she said. Already the brief courage she had experienced in the field was deserting her. How could she reject Sebastian without hurting his family or losing their love and respect? Guilt settled back like a cloud, obscuring the bright morning. Reversing the car, she headed off back down the lane.

\*       \*       \*

Far out at the edge of the cove, Will swam in the cold sparkling water. Despite it being past midsummer and hot into the bargain, the water of this coast remained breathtakingly icy. Nevertheless, Will swam as often as the weather allowed. As he pushed through the gentle swell he finally made up his mind. As soon as Isobel had seen Helen and sorted things out with her daughter, he intended to ask her to marry him. Just as he had wondered if he should exploit Isobel's loneliness by offering her love and support, so now was he tempted to take advantage of her happiness.

She was so warm, so affectionate; a hundred times he had been on the brink of proposing marriage to her but always, at the last moment, he had held back. He knew in his heart that it was unfair to her; that he should wait until she had come to terms with what might lie ahead before she should be asked to take such a decision.

Will rolled over on to his back and floated, allowing the tide to take him. Part of him still recoiled at offering himself to her. He was so much older; his muscles flabby, his hair thinning. She seemed unaware of these things. They swam together, lay in the sun and talked, walked on the cliffs. She had never by glance or word showed that she found him repulsive. A summer in the cove had made him hardy. He had trimmed off any surplus weight and was deeply tanned and looked better than he had for years. As her affection and friendliness grew, so did his confidence. The one thing that remained a real problem was the effect of this—should Isobel accept him—on Bea. He could not decide how much she relied on him. He spent even more time with Bea than he did with Isobel and they had developed a relaxed easy companionship which was important to both of them. If he moved across the cove, how would Bea fare alone? Of course she would hardly be alone with he and Isobel so close at hand but he had the intelligence to realise that three single people do not add up to the same sum as two married people and one single person. He wondered if she would be as contented as Mathilda had been; after all, Tessa would be coming home often. Of course, once Tessa was married it might become a little more complicated . . .

He pulled up his knees sharply, disappeared briefly beneath the surface and then began to swim back strongly to the shore. Sidney, watching anxiously from the beach, wagged his tail with relief as Will waded out, wiping the wetness from his eyes, water streaming on to the hot sand. He picked up his towel and gave Sidney a pat. Bea had gone into Kingsbridge early to the library and Isobel was at the bookshop. He was at liberty to spend the morning how he chose. Before he could decide exactly how he should employ his time, he heard a car's engine in the track. Tying his towel around his waist he waited to see who his visitor might be.

He smiled to see Tessa's old Peugeot bump into sight and park behind the house. He and Sidney went to greet her.

'No dogs?' He bent to peer in at the back.

'Too hot,' she said, hugging him. 'I've left them in a nice cool kitchen. Anyway, it's not fair to Sid. This is his territory now. How are things, Sid? You're looking good.'

'Which is more than can be said for you,' said Will bluntly. 'You've lost weight.'

'You sound like Bea.' Tessa laughed a little

330

but she was grateful that he cared enough to notice. 'I couldn't resist hopping over to see you all. How are things?'

'Not bad at all. Look, let me get dressed and then we'll have a nice cold drink and exchange all the gossip. Yes?'

'Sounds wonderful. I'll stay out here if that's OK.' She looked about her, breathing deeply and visibly relaxing. 'It's lovely to be back.'

'Shan't be a moment.'

He hurried indoors, leaving her in possession of the beach, but reappeared in record time, a rug over his arm and carrying a tray.

'Been talking to Giles,' he told her, placing the tray with its burden of two glasses and a jug of fresh lemonade in the shade beside a rock. He spread the rug on the sand. 'Bright lad, that. We've thought up a pretty good plan for Mr Adrian Pearson.'

Tessa, whose heart had bumped erratically at the mention of Giles's name, sank down on the rug. 'Tell me,' she said. 'I'd do anything to frighten the wits out of that little toad.'

'I'm glad to hear you say that,' said Will, filling her glass and passing Sidney a Bonio. 'You may have to. I have to say that Giles and I are counting on you.'

He grinned at her surprise and, whilst she sat in the shade of the cliff and sipped her cold lemonade, he explained the scheme that he and Giles had planned so carefully together.

Sue Anderson cursed as the telephone rang for the fourth time in ten minutes, dumped the laundry basket on the step and hurried back into the house.

'Yes?' she cried impatiently. 'Oh, sorry, darling. It's been one of those mornings. How are you? Still in the dockyard?'

'Yes. Still here. Sorry to spring this on you, Mother, but I've got to talk to you.'

'Talk to me about what?' Sue's heart sank at his serious tone. 'What's the problem? Not *another* enormous mess bill? Oh, Sebastian, you promised me you'd make an effort—'

'It's nothing to do with my mess bill,' he interrupted impatiently. 'It's just that I've been thinking about this posting to Washington and, honestly, Mother, I think it's wrong to ask Tessa to wait until I come back before we get married.'

'Well,' Sue perched on the chair beside the telephone and pushed the hair off her face, thinking furiously. 'It would be the most awful rush but we could probably get something sorted out before you go. After all, Tessa's got hardly any family to worry about so that side would be quite simple. We've agreed that she's got nobody to arrange a wedding for her. She feels that it would be a bit much for her elderly cousin. Do you want me to start organising?'

'I think so. What I feel is, that if we don't do it now then it will never happen. I've got the most terrible attack of cold feet. I know it's unforgivable but I think that I got carried away and now I'm scared to death I've got it wrong.'

'Oh, darling.' Sue clutched the receiver. 'Oh hell. Look, most people get terrified at some point or other, you know. It's a big step but you know Tessa so well and she absolutely adores you.'

'I know that.' He sounded irritable and her heart sank even lower. 'You and Rachel have been telling me that for the last five years. So now we're engaged. If you don't mind the rush then we'll soon be married. Everyone will be happy.'

'Are you saying that you don't love her?' asked Sue sharply, frightened by the heavily sarcastic tone of his voice.

'I tell you I don't know *what* I feel any more,' he cried. 'She's a sweet kid. I'm very fond of her but I don't know about love. What does it mean? All I'm saying is that if we don't get married before I go then it won't happen at all. I know that much.'

'Oh, Sebastian. I . . . I don't know what to say. If you don't love her then you shouldn't marry her.'

'I don't know whether I love her or not.' There was a long pause and when he spoke again the aggression had vanished from his voice. 'How do you think she'll react if I back out?'

'I don't know,' said Sue slowly, remembering her conversation with Tessa and how she'd suggested that she and Sebastian should rethink the situation. Sue had put it down to hurt pride because Sebastian was unwilling to set a date for the wedding but there might just be the faint chance that Tessa herself was having second thoughts. 'Damn!' she said, recalling her own remarks about how such a thing would break Sebastian's heart. 'What a muddle.'

'Can I assume from this that you would not be suicidal if we were to call it off?' he asked her. 'I don't understand women. You and Rachel were so excited.'

'My dear boy,' it was Sue's turn to sound exasperated, 'I love you and Tessa far too much to want either of you to be unhappy. I certainly don't want you to marry Tessa because she's been like one of the family. On the other hand . . .'

'Quite,' said Sebastian, correctly interpreting the pause, 'if she does want the wedding to go ahead we've got problems. I don't want to hurt her.'

'You'll hurt her more in the long run,' said Sue, 'if you don't love her.'

'I've told you,' he said wearily, 'I simply don't know.'

'Have you . . . you know . . . slept with her?'

'Of course I have, Mother,' he said crossly.

'For heaven's sake! She enjoyed it as much as I did. And yes, I took precautions. It was good but then it's been good with other girls.'

'Oh, Sebastian,' she said. 'I'm sorry. I know it's not my business. I was just thinking that if you hadn't ... with Tessa, then it might be quite sensible. Probably get your feelings sorted out more clearly. But since you have ...'

'Then it's not going to help us either way,' he finished.

'You know the old test?' she said at last. '"Do you want to touch her; do you want to see her; do you want to hear her"? I might have that the wrong way round but you get the sense of it. Do you?'

'Not often,' he said frankly. 'Sometimes. Honestly, Mother, I can't answer the only necessary question. So what do I do?'

'You must go and see her,' said Sue at last. 'Go and talk to her and tell her what you feel.'

'Shit!' he muttered. 'What if she ... Oh Christ!'

'I know. But you've got to,' she said. 'It's the only way. I can't help you except that we'll try to back you up without abandoning Tessa.'

'Thanks.' He gave a short laugh. 'Sorry about all this.'

'Don't give it a thought. I just want you both to be happy. When can you see her?'

'We're going down to Devonport next week for sea trials. She's in Devon, too. I'll see her then. No chance before. She's up in Wales

335

somewhere. If we do decide to go ahead would you be able to cope?'

'Of course I could. Don't worry about that but . . . Oh, Sebastian, I don't know what to say. Stay in touch.'

'I will. Thanks. 'Bye.'

The line went dead and with a heavy heart Sue went to hang the washing out in the hot sunshine.


# CHAPTER TWENTY-NINE

On an overcast morning in July, Helen arrived at the cove. Since first light Isobel had been wandering about her cottage; tidying, smoothing, puffing up cushions, rearranging the roses in the living room, straightening pictures. Her fingers shook a little and she drank numerous cups of coffee and wished that she'd never given up smoking. Just before ten o'clock she saw Will and Bea emerge. She had taken Bea aside some days before and asked if it would be possible to have the cove to herself just for that particular morning.

'I know it's pushy,' she said, 'but I'm afraid that Will might be overanxious. Helen's such a strange girl and I'm terrified of anything going wrong. I know it sounds melodramatic . . .'

'I quite understand,' Bea had said. 'You'll be able to relax better. Don't worry. I want to have another look at Tavistock. Pray for a cool day so that we can take Sidney.'

'I can cope with Sidney if necessary,' Isobel said, relieved that Bea wasn't offended. 'It's just that I'm so uptight about this. Bless you for understanding, Bea.'

Now she watched Bea encourage Sidney into the back of the hatchback whilst Will stowed the hamper on the back seat. Presently the sound of the engine died away and there was silence.

Except, thought Isobel, as she drifted back into the living room and stood staring aimlessly out of the open window, that it's never silent when you live this close to the sea.

The tide was running out, the wet sand gleaming under the grey sky. The dark, opaque surface of the sea was splashed with pools of dazzling silver which showered down through breaks in the thick blanket of cloud. A seagull balanced on a newly exposed rock, one yellow leg drawn up as he watched the waters receding. The soothing, rhythmical shushing of waves calmed Isobel and she turned back into the room, feeling relaxed and able now to prepare herself for the coming meeting.

It was just after eleven when she saw the car—Simon's car—emerge from the track and hesitate. Controlling an impulse to run out, Isobel waited. She saw the car pull in beside the Morris and presently Helen climbed out and stood looking about her.

She looks like I did at her age, thought Isobel, watching from the kitchen window. She took note of the dark hair cut in a short shining bob, the slim square shoulders beneath the baggy cotton shirt, the long legs in faded denim. She recognised the quick nervous gesture as Helen pushed back her hair and came on long, easy strides towards the cottage. With a deep breath Isobel went to meet her.

'Hi.' She stood looking down at her daughter who had paused at the bottom of the steps. 'This is . . . wonderful. Come on in.'

With the same anxious gesture, Helen ran her hand through her hair and climbed the steps.

'What a terrific place.' Nervousness sent her voice up the scale a little. 'That's some view.'

'Pretty good, isn't it?' Isobel was determined that no hysteria should creep in. 'It's the light that gets me. Like living at the bottom of the sea. Although it's a bit dull today . . . Coffee?'

'Thanks. Got any decaff?'

'I have.' Isobel gave silent thanks for her foresight. 'Milk? Sugar?'

'No thanks. Just black.' Helen looked around the kitchen. 'Oh, you've still got the picture of Soot.'

'Of course.' Helen had drawn the sketch of the family cat when she was just fifteen but it was a very accurate and charming portrayal and Isobel had had it framed. It hung on the wall beside the dresser. Isobel made coffee, sensing that Helen was examining the photographs on the shelves beside the plates; photographs of Helen as a little girl, posed alone and with Simon. The silence lengthened but Isobel refused to blunder in with foolish observations. 'Here.' She passed Helen her mug. 'Let's go into the living room.'

She led the way, sitting down at the table under the window and gesturing to Helen to sit opposite. She slid on to the chair, staring about the room, taking it all in. It gave Isobel the opportunity to study her more closely; to see the drawn look and the tiny frown between the dark level brows. Helen's gaze came round to meet her own and they looked at each other for a long moment.

'So,' said Isobel lightly. 'Where shall we start?'

She had resolved that there should be no more apologies and explanations; that Helen must try to accept what had happened and be prepared to move forward. It was a pointless exercise to dig up the old bones of their relationship and chew on past grievances and recriminations. Nevertheless, she was not nearly so calm as she appeared and she sipped quickly at her coffee.

'It's difficult.' Helen glanced away, out of the window. 'I'm not sure I know where to start.'

'That makes two of us.' Relieved that the old antagonism was absent, Isobel relaxed a little. 'You've changed so much. Grown up.' She laughed a little. 'Stupid thing to say. Of course you have.' She became serious. 'It really is very good to see you, Helen. Thank you for coming.'

'I wanted to.' She continued to stare out of the window. 'I know that I behaved like a prig. I wanted to say sorry. I understand better now.'

Isobel swallowed, crushing down a longing to explain all over again; justify her feelings, explain her actions. 'I'm . . . glad,' she said. 'At least . . . I'm glad if it means we can be friends. Not so glad if you understand as a result of some problem of your own.'

Helen looked at her, studying Isobel's face, the frown more in evidence as she concentrated. Isobel met the scrutiny steadily, wondering if Helen would be candid with her. Suddenly the meeting had moved on to a much deeper plane and Isobel felt the stirrings of panic. Helen pushed her hair behind her ears and picked up her mug in both hands.

'I couldn't understand, you see,' she said—and took a tiny sip of the black liquid. 'It was terrible to have to believe that you loved that man more than you loved me. That you could leave me for him.'

Isobel's heart sank. So the bones were to be disinterred yet again; she prepared herself for battle. 'I tried to explain—' she began—but Helen shook her head.

'I know you did. But it wasn't that simple. Not then. I think it was something I had to experience for myself. I understand now what

340

you meant when you said it was like an illness. It sort of possesses you and when it goes you can't think what came over you.'

'Yes,' said Isobel sadly. 'That's about it. And then it was too late. For me, that is. Not, I hope, for you.'

'I'm sorry,' said Helen again. 'Really sorry. About Dad and . . . Sally.'

'Yes.' Isobel bit her lip. 'It was a shock. Are they . . . happy?'

Helen nodded, watching her, and Isobel nodded back and tried to smile.

'Do you still love him?' she asked compassionately.

'Oh, yes.' Isobel tried to sound matter-of-fact. 'I always did. The other was just a kind of madness. A very cruel and expensive madness. So. How about you? It's all over now, is it? Was he at university?'

Helen nodded, staring at the Indian cloth. In the silence Isobel wondered how far she should go. She dreaded to pry or open old wounds but how could she help if she did not know the facts? Helen had said that it was finished; that she did not know what had come over her. If she no longer loved whoever-he-was then it shouldn't be painful, unless . . .

'Is he married?'

Another nod; the frown deepened.

'Well,' said Isobel comfortingly, 'being married never made anyone immune. Does his wife know?'

A shake of the head; the lips were pressed tightly together. Isobel was puzzled. So what could be the problem? She guessed the answer at exactly the moment that Helen told her.

'I'm pregnant,' she said—and began to weep.

Instinctively Isobel pressed her hand to her lips; the next moment she was kneeling beside Helen, her arm around her. 'I'm sorry, so sorry.' She murmured the words over and over whilst Helen wept, her head buried in her arms. When she straightened up, Isobel hesitated for a moment and then went back to her chair. She felt she must leave Helen her space and her dignity.

'I want to keep the baby,' said Helen rapidly. 'I can't bear the thought of an abortion or adoption.'

'No,' said Isobel. 'No . . . I see. Does he . . . the father know?'

'No,' she answered fiercely. 'I don't want him to know. It's *my* baby. He has children. I don't want to get rid of it.'

She stared desperately at Isobel whose brain, behind her deceptively calm expression, was desperately seeking some kind of solution.

'But your job?' she said. 'Your job in Bristol? How will you manage? Oh, if only I could help you.'

'Oh, Mum.' The old familiar word slipped out and Isobel's heart lurched with tenderness. 'Would you help?'

'But of course I will,' said Isobel. 'It's just I

don't see quite how. I have to work myself, you know. I could try to help out with the baby.' She frowned, wondering how this could be achieved. 'Does Daddy know?' she asked suddenly.

'No.' Helen looked defiant. 'I don't want them to know yet. I can only handle telling you at the moment.'

Isobel experienced another stab of tenderness but it was mixed with a less generous emotion. She felt a triumphant sense of pride that Helen had turned to her rather than to Simon and Sally. Helen was watching her anxiously and she smiled at her.

'Let's not panic,' she said. 'When is the baby due?'

'December. At Christmas. I've been thinking about it,' said Helen, 'and I've thought of a way through. It's an awful lot to ask, especially after . . . after what's happened. I feel very badly but I don't know what else to do. I don't expect you to agree to it.'

'Tell me,' suggested Isobel, wondering if she was going to ask if she and the baby could come to the cove. How would they manage? She felt anxious and even frightened. 'Tell me what your plan is?'

Helen began to speak very quickly, her fingers pleating and repleating the cloth, her eyes on the sea. 'When I knew for certain, I panicked a bit but after a while I began to think it all through. I spoke to the research

343

department at Bristol University and they agreed to give me time off to have the baby, providing that I go back afterwards full time with no problems. There are all sorts of crèches and baby-minding agencies so I told them that I'd got it all fixed. There were a couple of small flats that go with some of the university posts so I've taken one. It's quite nice and it's cheap . . .'

'So what's the problem?' asked Isobel gently, when Helen fell silent. 'It sounds as if you've got it all sewn up. Do you want to come here to have the baby?'

'No. No, I don't want to stay round here with all my friends nudging each other and Dad and Sally fussing.' Helen looked at her mother. 'I'm moving in to the flat next month and I want you to be with me when I have the baby and to look after him when I start work. I don't want to shove him into a crèche or with some baby-minder. How can I bear to leave my brand-new baby with strangers?' Her eyes filled with tears. 'I wouldn't mind if you were with him.'

'But . . . but how could I?' Isobel sounded dazed. 'I'd have to give up my job and . . .' she looked around her as if seeing it for the first time, 'and my home.'

'I know.' Helen wiped her tears on the back of her hand. 'That's why it's such a lot to ask. It's just that I'm not sure that I can cope with it all. A baby and a new job. I know that it's all my fault and I have no right to ask anyone for help but I feel so terribly alone.'

'Oh, darling.' Isobel stretched her hand across the table and Helen took it and gripped it tightly. 'Of course I'll help. I'll do everything I can. It's just . . . It's just such a shock.'

'I know,' said Helen miserably. 'It's been awful, trying to concentrate on exams with all this hanging over me. But it was my fault, you see. I pestered him and wouldn't let him alone. I was sure I could make him happy. I had all these silly fantasies. And then one night we were both at a party. He was on his own. We drank a bit and then we . . . You know.' She frowned, smoothing out the cloth. 'I can't explain but after that I felt differently. It was all gone. All the excitement and the feverishness. I didn't even like him much. And then when I realised . . .' She shook her head and lifted her hands in despair.

'I'm sorry,' said Isobel inadequately. 'I understand as far as anyone can understand another person's predicament.'

'I knew you would.' Helen pushed the cold coffee aside with a sigh. 'And I know how selfish I'm being. I'm asking you to give everything up for my stupidity. Other people manage alone in these situations, why shouldn't I?'

'I don't want you to manage alone,' Isobel told her, but her heart was heavy. 'We must think it through carefully. Don't worry. You won't be alone. I'm going to make us some more coffee.'

Leaving Helen sitting slumped at the table, she went into the kitchen and rinsed the mugs. As the kettle boiled, she stood staring out at the familiar and much-loved view. Her heart ached for her daughter but a small corner of her mind was rebelling. How could she bear to uproot herself from the cove and go to Bristol to live in a small flat with Helen and a baby and how would they survive financially? Would she ever be free again to take up the threads of her old life; would they still be there, waiting for her? Isobel felt a sickening panic as she stood, gripping the edge of the sink, her eyes on the water. She could not bear to leave Will and Bea; to give up her job in the bookshop; part with her cottage. Why should she? Helen had refused to see her for five years. She had ignored her and hurt her and now expected her mother to sacrifice herself for her own mistakes. Her resentment faded and guilt seized Isobel's heart. If she had not abandoned Helen when she met Mike it was possible that none of this might have happened. Was it the shock of seeing her father absorbed with Sally that had turned Helen's love towards an older man? It was impossible to know the truth but Isobel had a cold feeling that it was time to try to make amends for her own selfish actions.

As she turned away from the window, Isobel heard a muffled sound. She paused, her hand on the kettle's handle. It was the despairing sound of Helen weeping. Isobel took a deep breath, imagining her daughter's unhappiness and her loneliness. What a terrible way to start her young life! Bleakly Isobel recognised the fact that there were no choices here; she could not abandon Helen a second time. If she wished to rebuild the love and friendship between them then, somehow, they must manage this together. Isobel made the coffee and, summoning every ounce of courage and optimism, she picked up the mugs and went back to her daughter.

## CHAPTER THIRTY

Sebastian stood at the bar of the Skylark at Clearbrook buying drinks. He'd managed to wangle a few hours' leave from the ship but his time was limited and he'd hardly been five minutes at Kate's house at Whitchurch before he'd suggested that he and Tessa should go out for a drink. Sebastian hunched his shoulders and jingled the coins in his pockets as he watched the beer frothing up the glass. Tessa had not realised that this invitation was because, at the sight of her standing at the door, he had completely lost his nerve. As he'd driven out towards Tavistock he had made up his mind to be absolutely honest with her but, when he saw her small figure waiting for him, his courage had deserted him. How could he let her down? He remembered the tragic events which surrounded her younger life and the brave way that she had taken opportunities and carved out a life for herself. He also remembered her unwavering devotion to him and the occasions when he had taken advantage of it.

She'd smiled as he climbed out of the car and approached her but there was an odd expression in her eyes, almost as if she had guessed his cowardly intentions. Desperately he tried to resurrect the feelings he'd had when he'd seen her wandering ethereally in Freddie's meadow but all he could see was the old, familiar Tessa in jeans and sweatshirt, a younger sister of whom he was very fond. He knew from past experience that, when he'd had a beer or two, a certain amount of the magic would return, after all she was a very attractive girl, but being permanently inebriated was not quite how he wished to spend his married life.

Well, it was rather too late to think of that now. The damage was done. Sebastian took a pull at his beer as he waited for his change. He knew now that he was not capable of dealing the blow that would break the engagement. He comforted himself with the knowledge that it could be a great deal worse; she was pretty and very sweet and she loved him. It would simply have to be enough.

From her table in the corner Tessa watched him with a sense of despair. Each time she saw him she was reminded of the past; of all those weekends and holidays when the Andersons had taken pity on her and welcomed her into their home. She remembered how she had first seen him and fallen in love with him and, from that moment, had idealised him. She knew now that the real Sebastian was far removed from those fantasies but how could she possibly explain that to him? His voice on the telephone had been almost curt and, for one glorious moment, she had hoped that he might be coming to tell her that he'd changed his mind. When he arrived, however, he had hugged her in the old friendly way and since then had been chatting perfectly normally. Certainly the new passion he had shown on that night at Freddie's was not apparent, he was much more like his old self, but this was a flying visit and he was probably preoccupied with the ship and her coming sea trials.

Whilst she'd waited for him to drive out from Plymouth she had steeled herself to tell him the truth. She rehearsed what she would say to him, how she would explain her feelings, but, the moment she saw his tall figure, she was swept back into the past with all its memories and obligations and she knew that she would never be able to hurt him or his family. She told herself that he would be away a great deal and that he was kind and good-looking but, when she thought about Giles, she felt as though her heart were being squeezed to death. Her only hope was that, whilst Sebastian was in America, be might meet someone else or change his mind.

She smiled as he set the drinks down and tried to think of something to say. 'Thanks. Well, this is a nice surprise. Here's to the trials.'

'I'll drink to that.' He drank deeply. 'I've got something to suggest, actually. It's a bit sudden but I'm sure you'll understand.'

She looked at him quickly and once again he saw that odd look in her eyes. Could she possibly have guessed at his real feelings? If she had, then at least what he had to say would put her mind at rest.

'I've been thinking.' He put down his glass and reached for her hand. 'You know I think I was wrong to say that we should wait to get married until after Washington.' She stiffened a little and he held her hand more tightly, knowing that she had been hurt at his refusal to go along with her idea of a quiet ceremony before he took up his post. 'I've changed my mind. What about fixing the wedding as soon as possible. Mother's perfectly happy to organise it. What d'you say?'

'Have you spoken to your mother about it?' She was staring at their joined hands; at the winking of the stones in her engagement ring.

He thought quickly. 'Well, I have. Don't be cross with me. I had to clear it with her. To make sure she could cope before I asked you. It'll be a bit of a rush and you did say that you felt your cousin couldn't be expected to deal with it.'

'I know I did. Don't worry. I wasn't accusing you of anything. What did your mother say?'

'She said that it could be done. It would be a bit hectic but that she's perfectly happy to take it on.'

'I see.' So that was that. Her escape route was closed.

'You don't look too certain about it?'

He was watching her with a strange expression in his eyes and she was distressed lest he should be hurt by her lack of enthusiasm.

'Sorry.' She made a tremendous effort and smiled at him as brightly as she could. 'It's come as a bit of a shock. I'd ... well, I'd resigned myself to waiting. In fact,' she made one last try, 'I had a tiny suspicion that you might be changing your mind.'

She was staring at him so desperately that he felt a stab of guilt followed by a rush of tenderness for her. 'What rubbish!' he said and leaned over to kiss her. 'Just too much on my mind, that's all. So what about it?'

'Wonderful.' She raised her glass. 'Here's to us.'

For moment he thought that she had tears in her eyes and he sighed inwardly. How could be possibly have imagined that he could hurt her?

'Here's to us,' he said.

Bea ordered coffee and went back to the table in the corner where Sidney, waiting obediently by her chair, wagged his tail and lay down with a sigh. Bea sighed too as she looked about her and settled herself more comfortably in her chair. Isobel had brought her to the Bedford Hotel, several months before, and she had been struck by the quiet comfortable bar where locals and residents alike sat talking over pots of tea or coffee or reading the newspapers. Well-behaved dogs were welcomed and Bea felt content to sit here in this peaceful atmosphere and wait for Will. She glanced down at Sidney who was attracting attention from a couple at a neighbouring table. Clumber spaniels were by no means a common sight and his square sturdy body and big domed head drew much praise. Strangers approached crying, 'Oh, isn't he beautiful. But what is he?' and Sidney stood patiently as they stroked his silky coat and gently pulled his long ears.

Bea stretched out a foot and patted him with her toe, smiling at the couple. She was secretly enjoying the vicarious admiration which he attracted and was becoming resigned to white hair on the carpet and slobber marks on her skirt. This surprised her but she knew that there was always a price to pay if life was to be lived fully; the mess a cat or dog made; the ash and dust from a wood fire; the clearing up after the preparation of a delicious meal. It was tempting—and Bea knew that living alone she might easily have been so tempted—to simplify life, to pare it to the bone, cutting out anything that made unnecessary work. The trouble was that this nihilistic attitude could lead to boredom and emptiness. Bea was grateful that Will saved her from this temptation. Will lived with great enthusiasm and Bea was very happy to be taken along with him.

The coffee arrived and Bea shuffled forward on her seat so as to pour herself a cupful. She was reaching for the sugar when the sound of her name, uttered with great surprise, arrested her action. Hand outstretched she stared up at Tony Priest.

'It *is* you,' he said with the lazy smile that had caused her such flutterings in the past. 'Well, well.' His eyes took in the casual shirt and sailcloth skirt, her tanned skin and well-cut cropped hair. 'I must say you're looking extraordinarily fit. Being a landowner obviously suits you.'

Bea swallowed and dropped a lump of brown sugar into her coffee. 'It ... has its moments,' she said, wondering whether Will was likely to arrive and unwittingly show her up. She remembered her mother saying. 'Oh, what a tangled web we weave, when first we practise to deceive,' and took a deep breath. 'How are you, Tony? How's everyone?'

'Fine.' He glanced down at the slumbering

Sidney and, to Bea's dismay, sank into the chair opposite. 'Missing you, of course.'

He smiled at her again and she remembered how he had enjoyed making her a little confused, delighting in her silent admiration. Bea looked away from him—outraged that she had ever been fool enough to have given him such satisfaction—and saw Will come in and look about him. The expression on her face caused Tony to glance round, giving Bea just long enough to make a warning face at Will. He came across, smiling at Bea and noticing the wariness with which she greeted him.

'This is Tony Priest,' she said. 'The History master at my old school. This is Will Rainbird,' she told Tony. 'My land agent. He met Marian when we came to collect my things.'

'So I heard.' Tony had risen and was shaking Will's hand, looking at him appraisingly. 'She was very impressed . . . with the whole thing, of course.' His implication that Marian had been taken with Will was left hanging in the air and there was a moment of awkwardness. Bea remembered how he had loved to create these little frissons, often very amusing ones, and how he liked to stand back and watch the effect. Generally—and flatteringly—he had invited Bea to be a fellow spectator. This time she refused to play his game.

'Oh, Marian was all over him like a rash,' she said dismissively. 'Poor Will. Very embarrassing wasn't it, darling?'

Tony's eyes opened wide and he looked sharply at Will, who was patting himself all over, his face expressionless.

'Dreadful woman,' he said, producing his pipe. 'Terribly obvious. What an afternoon! Now then, my darling, are you ready or do you want more coffee?' He took her hand and held it for a second and then turned back to Tony, who watched this by-play with amazement on his face. 'Sorry. Am I butting in? Are you staying in the hotel?'

'We are.' Tony took a grip on himself. 'Nicola will be along in a moment. Why don't you stay to see her?'

Bea, who was dithering between fleeing whilst there was time and a desire to brazen it out, looked at Will. It was clear that, having given her the opportunity to escape, he was leaving the next move to her. She remembered that he'd had no coffee and that Sidney would probably not be welcome in any of the other cafés. Moreover, she had not yet drunk her own coffee.

'Good idea,' she said easily. 'You need some coffee, Will, after the drive over. Why not order some. Tony?'

'No, none for me,' he said quickly. 'I had plenty at breakfast. So, Bea.' He sat down, looking at her intently as Will went to the bar, the old teasing smile willing her to share her secrets. 'What a dark horse you are.'

She refused to be drawn or flattered. 'Oh,

not particularly,' she said, meeting his eye provocatively. 'I just take advantage of what life sends. Don't we all?'

'We do indeed. Ah!' He got to his feet. 'Nicola. Over here. Look who's here?'

Bea looked at the slim, smart, pretty woman and realised that she no longer felt inadequate, nor clumsy and plain. She smiled, raising her eyebrows at Nicola's surprise.

'What fun,' she said calmly. 'How are you, Nicola?'

'I'm well thanks, Bea. And you, I hear, have become a wealthy landowner.'

Her sharp eyes examined Bea coldly: Bea laughed.

'Old Marian does like to be first with the news, doesn't she?' she asked admiringly. 'I expect the whole school knows. Probably the town, as well. Did she tell you about Will, too?'

'Will?' Nicola looked faintly discomfited. 'Well, I'm not absolutely certain . . .' She looked at Tony, who was obviously enjoying the encounter enormously.

'No need to be prissy, Nicola,' said Bea impatiently. 'I'm sure she did. And here he is. Will, darling, this is Nicola, Tony's wife. This is Will Rainbird, my land agent.'

'How d'you do?' Will shook her hand warmly. 'Perhaps I should have ordered more coffee.' He sat down beside Bea, leaving the other two standing, and stroked Sidney who groaned and rolled over on to his side.

'Did he come with the estate, too?' asked Tony, still looking amused.

'He comes from a broken home,' said Will blandly. 'He's learning to trust again. We're a very happy little community, aren't we, my darling?'

He beamed at Bea, who smiled at him with genuine affection. 'We certainly are,' she agreed. She looked up at Tony and Nicola. 'Do sit down,' she said, a testy note creeping into her voice. 'Are you sure you won't have some coffee?'

'Perfectly sure.' Nicola stared disbelievingly as Bea laid her hand upon Will's and their fingers intertwined. 'We must go. So nice to see you, Bea. Come on, Tony. We shall be late.'

Tony looked down at Bea with a little smile as Nicola turned away. 'I have a feeling,' he said softly, 'that I underestimated you. What a pity.'

Bea raised her cup to him. 'Good luck,' she said. 'Don't forget to give our love to Marian. Off you go. Nicola's waiting.'

When they'd gone she sat back in her seat with a gasp of relief. Presently she began to laugh. Will's coffee arrived and he began to pour, smiling at Bea's reaction.

'We shall have to be careful,' he said. 'Who knows who else may pop out of the woodwork?'

'She'll go rushing back to Marian with the

news,' said Bea with enormous satisfaction. 'Her eyes were like organ stops. Talk about Lady Chatterley!'

They laughed immoderately and drank their coffee companionably, temporarily forgetting about Isobel and her meeting with Helen at the cove. It was pleasant to be at leisure together and presently they fastened Sidney's lead to his collar and wandered out into the town. The weather was brighter and they pottered slowly. Since Isobel had asked them to give her plenty of time with Helen they had the whole day before them. Bea, delighted with her routing of Nicola, took Will's arm.

'Just in case,' she told him demurely, 'they're still about.'

'Quite right,' he said, giving it a squeeze. 'And if I see them approaching we'll go into a clinch and pray that Sidney can cope with a sudden display of unbridled passion.'

'I wish I'd thought of that,' said Bea wistfully. 'That would have really given them something to think about.'

'There's still time,' said Will cheerfully. 'They're staying at the hotel. We'll go back for lunch and give 'em a treat.'

Chuckling together, arms linked, they strolled across the road and disappeared into the market.

# CHAPTER THIRTY-ONE

Sebastian put down the telephone receiver, glanced at his watch and shrugged at his oppo, Rob Walters.

'She's not there,' he said. 'I've left a message on the ansaphone.'

'So you'll come anyway?'

Sebastian nodded. 'Why not? She's probably only walking the dog. It's a pity to waste time and if you really don't mind me coming on with you if she's not there . . .?'

'Not a bit. Barbara will be pleased to see you again. She was rather miffed that as soon as we bought a house down here I got posted to Pompey. She's settling in but she'll be pleased to see a friendly face. She's thrilled that we've got more problems and the ship'll be stuck alongside for a day or two. Let's get going then.'

'You can spare a minute to see Tessa, I hope,' said Sebastian, as they went down the gangplank together. 'Seeing that you're going to be best man.'

'Can't wait to meet her again,' said Rob, feeling for the car keys. 'We must all get together while the ship's in.'

'Good idea,' said Sebastian—but he sighed as he waited for Rob to unlock the door. He was determined to be positive but it was not quite as easy as he'd hoped.

Adrian Pearson drove slowly past the church looking for the house which Tessa had described to him. He had been wary when he'd first heard her voice on his mobile. How was she going to react to his visits to the cove? His second visit had been unproductive. The old boy had checked the figures over again and indicated the one or two pieces he might be prepared to sell. One of these was an elegant, if simple, Regency writing table and, although the sabre legs had been repaired with brackets and the leather top was scored and marked, it would easily bring five and a half thousand pounds. The old buffer had been delighted at an offer of four hundred pounds for 'that old table', as the old aunt or whatever-she-was had called it, and had promised a final decision soon.

Adrian, peering through the windscreen, had been quickly reassured by Tessa's call. She had been friendly, apologised for not getting in touch before and explained that she had some rather interesting pieces to show him. He felt the familiar excitement begin to build. Should he, he'd asked, give the owner a bell? Tessa answered that the owner was away but that she, Tessa, had permission to show him a few pieces with a view to selling. Could he come over to Tavistock? she'd asked. He could.

So here he was, turning in through the gate

of a Victorian house set well back from the road, and there was Tessa opening the front door. She led him straight through to the kitchen and invited him to sit down while she made coffee. He glanced about him; nothing particularly exciting here but that was often the way. It was surprising how many people had just one or two really valuable things, inherited over the years and regarded with the contempt that familiarity brings. These were the kind of customers he wanted; not those whose homes were stuffed with goodies and who knew their value down to the tiniest silver thimble. He looked at Tessa and smiled to himself. Perhaps he hadn't misjudged her after all. She could lead him to all sorts of treasures but he must make certain that she was on his side.

'How are things?' he asked, bringing his charm to bear on her. She was not really his type—but business is business. 'I tracked you down to the cove, you know, but you weren't there. I've been hoping that I would see you again.'

She smiled at him and he realised that there was none of that early caution he remembered. She leaned against the sink and looked at him appraisingly.

'I've been thinking about you, too,' she said.

Her smile was a peculiarly intimate one and he raised his eyebrows, smiling a little in return. He was surprised—and a faint excitement stirred which had nothing to do with profit-

361

making.

'I'm flattered,' he said lightly. 'You shouldn't be so elusive. Those relations of yours are very efficient guard dogs.'

She laughed and shook her head. 'What a pair of old dinosaurs they are. I inherited the property with them, you know, so we all have to rub along together.'

He grimaced sympathetically. 'Not too easy, I should think. The old . . . um, Mr Rainbird seems a nice enough chap but your aunt is a bit fearsome, isn't she?'

'She's my cousin.' Tessa turned away to make the coffee. 'She's been a matron in a boys' school all her life.'

'I should have guessed.'

He studied her, wondering how far this might lead. She was wearing a denim mini-skirt and a T-shirt and, as he watched her moving about, the excitement increased.

'So.' She turned round so suddenly that she caught his eyes on her legs and once again she smiled that intimate knowing smile. 'Making a valuation?' she asked provocatively.

He burst out laughing, throwing his hands up to signify that she'd scored a hit. 'I admit it. Should I apologise?'

She shrugged, pushing his coffee towards him. 'That depends on the valuation.'

'Out of my league.' He pretended despondency. 'I've known it all along really.' He sighed. 'But you can't blame me for trying.'

'Oh, I don't.' She leaned her elbows on the table, mug in her hands and stared at him. 'I'm wondering how truthful I can be with you.'

He pulled down the corners of his mouth. 'That sounds very serious. Totally, I hope.' He conjured up the sympathetic interest he reserved for the Mrs Carringtons. 'Got a problem?'

'Uh-huh.' She nodded. 'Between you and me—and not a word to my old dinosaurs—I have quite a serious financial problem. I ... Well, the truth is, I was led to believe that the house in the cove was going to be left entirely to me and I borrowed against my expectations. I won't go into why, for the moment, but you can imagine my horror when the two old fossils turned up on the doorstep.'

'Sure.' He watched her, fascinated. 'So ...' He hesitated. 'So how can I help?'

'Do you want to help?'

'Certainly,' he said swiftly. His heart knocked against his breast. 'Do you have any suggestions?'

'It's already occurred to you that I go to many places where there are odd items of furniture that are up for grabs. You offered me commission ...?'

'Certainly,' he said again. 'That would be only right and proper. But I thought that you were rather upset the last time I mentioned it.'

'I wasn't on the ball that day,' she admitted. 'I'd just got engaged and it seemed that my

363

problems were over. Well.' She shrugged. 'He's changed his mind.'

'Must be mad,' said Adrian softly. He let her see how much she attracted him. 'Not looking for a replacement, are you?'

'Why not?' The old provocative look was back. 'I'm a firm believer in mixing business with pleasure.'

He laughed. 'I should like to apply for the post. Where do we start?'

'I'm afraid,' she said, 'that we start with the business. This commission . . .'

'Well.' He thought quickly about the least he could afford commensurate with keeping her on the hook. 'Shall we say a percentage of the profit? Ten percent?'

'You mean the real profit?'

He stared at her. 'Well, of course.'

'You see,' said Tessa, smiling, 'I could sell those pieces at the cove myself, couldn't I? I have to be sure that it's going to be worth going in with you, don't I? If I sell the things at the cove I have to split three ways. Of course, they trust me . . .'

'I'm not quite with you.' He frowned a little. 'I can understand that you may want to dispense with me as middle man but you'd have to get rid of the pieces somehow.' He hid his panic at the thought of losing the profit. 'You see what I'm getting at? Whoever sells it for you will have to take a cut.'

'True.' She nodded. 'But then *they* might

offer us the real value.'

Her eyes smiled coolly into his and he felt a lurching sensation in his stomach. 'I don't . . . quite understand.'

'Don't you?' Her eyebrows lifted. 'Let me be clearer. I could sell those pieces at the cove without telling the old ducks their real value. I could give them a bit but they won't have any idea of the profit I should make. But that cuts you out and if we're going to be partners I'd want to start fair.'

He decided to bluff it out. 'I'm still not with you.'

'Pity.' She pushed her mug aside and stretched back in her chair. 'I really thought you might be up to playing it straight for a moment. You see I'm not just thinking short term. I know a lot of people we could . . . help.'

Adrian was silent. If only he could be certain that she really knew the truth; if he could trust her. The golden eyes watched him coldly; presently she began to chuckle.

'You've disappointed me,' she said. 'I thought you were in a different class.'

For some reason this stung him. 'I'm not saying I'm not prepared to deal,' he said slowly, 'but it's a big step.'

'It certainly is.' She was still smiling. 'Who wants to share a profit of five thousand pounds?'

'Five thousand . . .?'

She pursed her lips. 'Give or take. Isn't that

what you stand to make on the Regency writing table you've offered my cousin four hundred pounds for? And that nice eighteenth-century stick-back armchair? Fifty quid, was it?' She was laughing openly now. 'How much did you get for Mrs Carrington's bureau? And that little Georgian chest? Come on.' She leaned across the table and touched his hand. 'I know lots of Mrs Carringtons. You should see the Queen Anne walnut tallboy upstairs. Don't look so worried. I shan't be greedy. After all, *you* have to get rid of the stuff.'

He was still too badly shaken to respond easily and she squeezed his hand encouragingly. 'I . . . may have misjudged a few items,' he began. 'Oh, for goodness' sake,' she said impatiently. 'Look, let's forget it. I'll arrange to get rid of the pieces from home. Now you've so kindly valued them Will and Bea won't expect much. I shall make a good profit and it will go a long way to sorting me out. It just seems a bit short-sighted, that's all, but I don't blame you. And you've got your girl in your London office to square, haven't you? Myra, isn't it?' She shook her head at him. 'Who else knows that it's a dingy little room, up four flights in a back street? All that knitting she gets through! Is it your baby she's expecting?'

'OK.' He stood up, frightened but fighting to stay in control. 'So you've checked it all out, have you?'

She smiled at him. 'What did you expect? I don't go into things blind. Myra had no idea she was being checked. She thought that I was looking for a friend who was supposedly living in the building. Look,' suddenly she was serious again. 'Let's just forget it, Adrian. I understand how you feel but I hoped we might be able to get together, in more ways than one.'

He looked down at her and she shrugged and crossed her legs. He began to smile a little, beginning to feel that he might trust her after all.

'Perhaps,' he said slowly. 'Perhaps you've got an idea.'

'Oh, I've got plenty of ideas,' she said suggestively—and hesitated, looking up at him. 'Is it your baby?' she asked.

The change of tone, some note of—what was it? Could it be jealousy?—gave him a much-needed surge of power. His confidence came back and he grinned at her. 'Not as far as I'm concerned,' he said. 'So. Where do we start this new partnership.' His eyes moved over her. 'What about this tallboy upstairs?'

She laughed at him. 'First things first. Let's talk about ways and means. I'm not as experienced as you are—' he raised his eyebrows—'in *antiques*. Tell me how we go about it.'

He perched on the end of the table. 'You look over the things and get the lie of the land. Go for the oldies. Find out if there's a cash shortage. If there is, you bring me in when you're on your own so that I can have a good scout round. Even with the *Antiques Roadshow* on TV every Sunday it's amazing how gullible people are. I suggest that we use the ploy of the leaflet through the door so that no one suspects the connection. You leave one behind. I can cover my tracks. Not so easy for you. But don't worry. I stay well within the letter of the law.'

She stared thoughtfully at the table. 'Sounds OK. How do I know you won't cheat on me? I can't check every piece thoroughly.'

'I won't cheat. Why should I?' He hauled her to her feet. 'Why should I risk the goose who lays the golden eggs. And talking of lays . . .'

He bent to kiss her but she held him off. 'Sure it's not your baby? She spoke of you with great affection.'

'That's her problem.' He strained her towards him.

'Hang on!' He swung round sharply at the sound of the voice behind him and blinked into the flash. 'Thanks.' Giles quickly took another photograph as Adrian gaped at him and smiled as he lowered his camera. 'Nice one,' he said and frowned. 'Good God,' he said slowly. 'Andy Petersen.'

'Andy . . .?' Tessa moved away from Adrian and folded her arms across her breast. 'Who did you say?'

'His name's Andy Petersen,' said Giles. 'We were at university together. He had a nice little line in crime going even then. Same principle. Preying on the weak and vulnerable.'

After one exclamation, Adrian Pearson stood still and watchful. 'Giles Webster,' he said scornfully. 'Always so upright and boring. You've got nothing on me. Everyone has free choice, remember. I've never made anyone do anything against their will. I suggest things; they respond. I don't force them. I never make a valuation, I offer what I think I can get for something. They don't have to accept.'

'How can you?' asked Tessa. She looked tense and distressed. 'How can you deliberately cheat people like Mrs Carrington? Or Will and Bea? You pretended to be so kind and sympathetic.'

'You put on a pretty good act yourself,' he reminded her. 'Quite the little tart, weren't you? So what are you going to do with the photographs? Send them to *Crimewatch* and make even bigger fools of yourselves.'

'No, no.' Giles set his camera on the table. 'I'm going to write an article about you and send it with the photograph to every paper that will carry it. Plus interviews and photographs of Mrs Carrington and Bea and Will. Good human interest. I can even write up one or two little memories of our university days. Remember Johnny Staines? Did you see that he hanged himself, he was so badly in debt? Well, I think it might be worth recording. What do you think?'

'I think you're the prig you always were. You honestly think anyone will print such rubbish?'

'Oh yes,' said Giles quietly. 'And so do you. You'll have to be careful when you knock on the next door, won't you? . . . Watch out!'

His warning was too late. Adrian pushed Tessa out of his path and made a grab for the camera. Their hands reached it together and knocked it to the floor. As Giles bent to retrieve it, Adrian seized a chair and brought it down on the back of his head. Giles gave a grunt and toppled forward, cracking his forehead on the dresser and slumping to the floor. Adrian kneeled above him, pulling the camera from Giles's slack hands whilst Tessa tried to drag him away.

'You bastard!' she shouted at him. 'You absolute bastard. You've hurt him.'

'Get off, you silly bitch,' he muttered, thrusting her violently away from him.

Caught off balance she fell heavily and Adrian made a leap for the back door and, wrenching at the handle, disappeared.

\*       \*       \*

'Just here,' said Sebastian. 'Oh. Looks like she's got visitors. Never mind. I can see her car up by the garage. Come on in and say hello.'

Rob pulled in just beyond the gate and they climbed out and strolled up the drive together.

'Nice spot,' said Rob appreciatively. 'Just on

370

the edge of the moor here and handy for the town ... Hello!' His voice changed. 'What the ...? Grab him, Seb!'

The man, who had come racing round from the back of the house, hesitated and swerved away but Rob, sprinting after him across the lawn, brought him down in a rugby tackle. Sebastian bent to pick up the camera which had shot from his grasp and hauled the man to his feet.

'Inside,' he said. 'Quick. Hang on to him, Rob. I want to check that Tessa's OK.'

They frogmarched him round to the back door at a run and pushed him inside.

'Christ!' Sebastian let go of the man's arm and dropped the camera on the table. 'What the hell's going on?'

Tessa stared up at him and her gaze went beyond him to Rob who had Adrian held in a half-nelson. 'You caught him,' she cried. 'Don't let him go. He hit Giles with a chair. I think ...' her voice wavered, 'I think he's dead.'

'Have you called an ambulance?' Sebastian was on his knees beside Giles, reaching for his heart, his eyes on the gash across his forehead. He took the tea towel with which Tessa had been attempting to staunch the flow of blood. 'For God's sake, Tessa, stop wailing and call a bloody ambulance! And then get on to the police.'

As Tessa disappeared into the hall, Adrian struggled violently, swearing at Rob, who

371

forced him down into a chair and grappled his arms behind him. 'Got something to tie him with?' he asked breathlessly.

'Here.' Sebastian grabbed Felix's lead and together they secured Adrian firmly.

Tessa came back. 'They're on their way,' she said and went back to crouch beside Giles.

'He's not dead,' said Sebastian. 'What the hell's been happening?'

'He's a con man,' said Tessa, her eyes fixed on Giles's pale face. 'He's been cheating old people. He tried it on Will and Bea and we decided to set him up to frighten him. He admitted it to me and then Giles appeared and took a photograph of him so that he could send it to all the papers as a warning. He tried to get the camera and when Giles bent to pick it up he hit him with the chair.' She swallowed. 'He hit his head on the dresser as he went down. And then Adrian . . . Andy knocked me over and made a run for it.'

'What did you call him?' asked Rob curiously.

'He calls himself Adrian Pearson but Giles recognised him from university. His name's Andy Petersen.'

'Perhaps we should have taken him down to the hospital ourselves,' said Sebastian, watching Giles. 'How long will they be?'

'I don't know. The hospital's not far away.' Tessa stared up at him, her eyes full of tears. 'Do you think he'll . . .? Oh God. It was all my

372

fault, you see. I couldn't bear to see him getting away with it. Conning these old people like Mrs Carrington. It was my idea to set him up. Oh, Giles.' Her lips shook and holding his limp hand tightly she pressed it to her cheek and burst into tears.

Sebastian stared down at her thoughtfully and then glanced at Rob who looked uncomfortable. Adrian, his jaw set, stared at the table and tried surreptitiously to free his hands. There was silence except for Tessa's sobbing. The peal of the front doorbell made them all jump and Tessa looked quickly at Sebastian as Rob went out into the hall.

'I'm going with him to Derriford,' she said. 'You'll deal with . . . him, won't you?'

'The police will want a statement from you,' he told her. 'You'll have to tell them what happened.'

'I know. But they'll have to wait. I'm staying with Giles.'

'Yes,' he said gently. 'Yes, love. I can see that. Don't worry. I'll sort everything out.'

She continued to look up at him, Giles's hand still clutched in her own. 'Sorry,' she said. 'I'm sorry, Sebastian.'

He smiled reassuringly at her and touched her lightly on the cheek. 'Forget it,' he said. 'Don't worry. Everything will be OK, kiddo. Just trust your Uncle Seb.'

# CHAPTER THIRTY-TWO

Isobel put an empty cardboard box on the kitchen table and began to fill it with carefully wrapped plates. The cottage was being gradually stripped of Isobel's character and warmth. It was beginning to look now as it had looked four years ago when she had come to see it and Mathilda had shown her round. Thanks to Will she could remember Mathilda now with love and gratitude; the guilt was gone. Isobel wandered to the window and stared out at the sea which pounded across the beach, creaming over the sand, and sending spray high over the rocks. The autumn was here and the equinoctial storms would soon be upon them. She knew how terribly she would miss this view and the cove but she had made up her mind and nothing would detract her. Through a friend with whom Helen worked, they had heard that there was a part-time vacancy for an assistant at the local crèche and Isobel had immediately made an appointment to be interviewed for the post. She had been honest about her situation hoping that, once Helen's baby was born, the child could accompany her to work and, to her delight and surprise, she had been offered the job on those terms. She was much happier now that she had something of her own to look forward to, and the money would be useful, but it would be a wrench to leave all that she had come to love, here in the cove.

Isobel glanced at her watch. She had arranged to meet Pat with the other two assistants, Laura and Louise, for a farewell lunch and, abandoning the packing, she collected her bag and hurried out. As she drove through the familiar lanes to Kingsbridge she remembered how Bea and Will had reacted to her news. She knew that Bea thought her quite mad to give up her work and her home for her daughter. She was shocked that Helen had asked it of her and had been unconvinced by Isobel's attempts to reconcile her to a different point of view. To begin with, Isobel had found it difficult to come to terms with the idea of sacrificing her own life for Helen's and, at first, it was almost wholly guilt which had persuaded her that she must support her daughter. Later she thought about it more carefully. It was no more selfish of Helen to make such a request than it had been of Isobel to leave husband and daughter to pursue her own idea of happiness.

'Like mother, like daughter,' she had muttered disconsolately to herself. 'Except that I was forty-two and Helen is only twenty-one.'

Bea's reaction had made it much more difficult to be confident about her decision and even Will, whom she had counted on for comfort and support, had been strangely reticent. She remembered that afternoon clearly. Helen had gone back to Modbury when

Will and Bea arrived home from their day in Tavistock. She had given them time to get indoors and, unable to keep it to herself any longer, had gone hurrying over.

'But it's madness, my dear.' Bea had stared at her in consternation across the Georgian breakfast table. 'You can't be expected to give up everything. There are excellent crèches and nurseries now for working mothers.'

'But she needs me!' Isobel had cried. 'Can't you see that if I let her down now I shall never have a relationship with her? This is my chance to make up for abandoning her. And be fair, Bea! Surely it must be better for a baby to be with its grandmother than with strangers. It's a bit different when it's three or four years old but a new baby . . .?'

'I should have thought a new baby would find it easier than a three-year-old,' Bea had said stubbornly. 'It knows nothing at that stage. It should be able to adapt to anything.'

Isobel had looked helplessly at Will. Even now, three months on, she remembered the look of shock on his face. She had been surprised; surely Will was too broad-minded to be so deeply affected by Helen's lapse.

'Will?' she'd said pleadingly. 'What do you think? Am I mad? She's frightened, you see. She's got no one to turn to. She *needs* me.'

'Yes,' he'd answered quietly. 'I quite understand that. It was you that I was thinking of . . .'

376

'I know.' She'd smiled at him gratefully. 'But I wouldn't be able to live with myself if I refuse her. I let her down badly when I went off with Mike and, now that Simon's got Sally, I think that Helen really feels that she's on her own.'

'It must be very frightening for her,' he'd said quietly.

He had sighed heavily as he turned away to feed Sidney and she'd suddenly realised that he would miss her. She had been so taken up with Helen's news and the shock of it all that, for a moment, she had completely failed to understand his sadness.

'I shan't be far away,' she'd said consolingly. 'Bristol's not far. I shall come and see you. I'll bring the baby.'

'When will you go?' asked Bea. 'As soon as the baby is born? When is it due?'

'At Christmas,' said Isobel, her eyes still on Will's back. 'But I shall go before then. She'll get dreadfully tired, working full time. I can help her then.'

'But what if the baby should . . .' Bea hesitated.

'If she loses the baby or there's a problem, she'll need me more than ever,' Isobel had said firmly. 'I've got no choice,' she'd cried at Will's back. 'Please try to understand. I don't *want* to do this. Please help me.'

He'd turned round at that, putting Sidney's bowl on the floor and smiling at her. 'Of course we understand,' he said. 'We just don't want to lose you. And I think that Bea is simply trying to make sure you've thought it all through. That's all.'

'I haven't had time to take it all in properly,' admitted Isobel. 'But I feel quite sure that I must help her.'

A few days later, Tessa had telephoned to say that their plan for unmasking Adrian Pearson had gone badly wrong and that Giles was in hospital with a split head and concussion but at least Adrian had been detained by the police and his scheme exposed. The anxiety that followed this had, to some extent, taken Isobel out of the spotlight. Bea and Will had hurried off to see Tessa and visit Giles in Derriford Hospital and, when they returned, told her that Tessa had broken her engagement with Sebastian and was now engaged to Giles. Confusion reigned for a few days and Isobel had almost welcomed the opportunity to suspend her own anxieties in lieu of Tessa's. Giles recovered, Adrian was charged with assault and serenity was restored to the cove.

Meanwhile, Isobel carefully considered her own situation and finally came to the conclusion that her first decision was the right one. Through the following months she never changed her mind and, as the days passed, a sense of excitement had grown in her. She began to look forward to the change in her life and went to Bristol to see Helen in the flat. Isobel had taken one look at Helen's tired, anxious face and set out to cheer and amuse her; she made plans for the future and rearranged the flat and presently Helen had been able to join in, becoming more positive and even excited. Encouraged, Isobel had made light of the lack of space and money, making it all seem like a delightful adventure. By the time she left she was confident that she was doing the right thing for both of them. Her own old feelings of futility were gone; she felt needed, useful, happy. The expression on Helen's face, when she told her that she'd been offered the job and would be moving to Bristol as soon as she could, was all that she needed as a reward.

The farewell lunch at Orchard's in Fore Street was a heart-wrenching business. She knew that she would miss her hours in the bookshop. Her friends were full of sympathy and encouragement but as she drove out along the embankment, slowing down on Bowcombe Bridge to stare out over the estuary, she knew a moment of terror. The boats rocked gently at their moorings and the golden light of late afternoon washed the quiet scene with a soft hazy glow. Two swans glided silently on the rippling water and, on the foreshore, someone had lit a bonfire. The sharp scent of smoke drifted in the autumn air and Isobel felt nostalgia tug at her heartstrings. How could she bear to leave this place for a small flat in a busy city?

She drove on slowly, bumping down the track, and parking as usual behind the house. She stood for some time, watching the tide sweeping in, listening to the mournful crying of a gull, remembering Mathilda. For some reason she began to feel soothed. Her fear gradually diminished and hope took its place. In her mind's eye she saw the slight figure, with her gleanings bag on her arm; remembered the keen look of the slate-blue eyes; heard the clear precise voice.

'*And did you find happiness?*'

'Oh, Mathilda,' said Isobel aloud. 'I think that this time I might just be in with a chance.'

\*      \*      \*

Tessa and Giles said goodbye to the Perrymans, who had been admiring her ring whilst she and Giles drank their coffee, left the Roundhouse and drove up on to the moor. Charlie Custard lounged in the back of Tessa's car, wondering if he might be allowed a walk. He was bored by the comings and goings of Giles at Freddie's. He preferred to have Tessa's attention all to himself and none of this hugging and carrying-on generally. He sighed deeply and leaned heavily against the side window.

'Nearly there, Custard,' said Tessa cheerfully and swung into a narrow lane made brilliant by the glowing colours of the beech leaves now in

380

full autumn splendour. The red rays of the sun slanted low through the woods and the cold wind scattered the fallen leaves across the lane. Tessa parked and she and Giles climbed out, pulling on coats. They released Charlie Custard, who jumped out and ran to sniff about. Giles held out a hand to Tessa who took it, grinning up at him. He shook his head.

'I'm still getting over it,' he said 'If it hadn't been for Andy you'd be married to Sebastian now and far away in Washington.'

'Don't talk about it.' She shivered and held his hand tighter. 'And he was so fantastic about it, saying that he'd got cold feet himself. It's worked out so well. The Andersons have been so kind and understanding. Oh, Giles. Aren't we lucky? Look! There's a leaf falling. Quick. Catch it. It's a year's good luck if you catch a falling leaf. Damn!'

The leaf twirled gently away, eluding her frantic snatches at it. Giles laughed and began to run after her as the wind sent an eddy of leaves whirling across the lane. Charlie Custard, surprised at such behaviour, began to bark. He danced about, getting in the way, and Tessa, breathless with laughter, reached up for a leaf and fell over his back. They stumbled together, falling on to the verge, and Charlie Custard scrambled up and shook himself, shocked at such disrespect. Giles hauled Tessa to her feet and kissed her.

'I've got a ready-made family,' she told him

happily. 'Kate and David, Guy and Gemma. Not to mention dear old Bea and Will. And now that Isobel's off to Bristol, we can have the cottage. I shall miss her but she's promised to come back often. I think it's a brilliant idea to convert the top of the boathouse into a darkroom for you. It's going to be such fun.'

'We'll be like Mum and David,' he said, putting an arm about her as they strolled after Charlie Custard. 'Divided between Devon and London.'

'It'll be fun,' she said again. 'I shall keep my favourites, though. Mrs Carrington and Freddie. And Kate, of course.'

He held her closer, too happy to speak, and she fell silent, remembering her terror when she thought she'd lost him for ever. Another gust of wind shuddered through the trees and she reached up towards the leaves.

'OK,' he said, resigned. 'One each and one for Custard. Come on.'

They began to run, their shouts echoing in the lane, their hands stretched upwards towards the leaves which floated down from the branches above them.

\*       \*       \*

The Morris, with Isobel's hand waving madly from the window, disappeared up the track. Bea and Will stood for a moment looking after her and then glanced at each other. There was a faint feeling of constraint.

'Well,' said Bea. 'I'm sure we shall be seeing her often.'

'Yes,' said Will. He bent to pat Sidney's head and then straightened his shoulders. 'Cold wind. Think I'll go and check the fire.'

'Good idea.'

They went inside together and Will went upstairs, followed by the faithful Sidney. Bea stood silently beside the sink, aware of Will's unhappiness and wondering how to help him. She had realised, quite quickly after the meeting with Helen, that Will's feeling for Isobel was, after all, more than a paternal affection. It had come as a shock but very soon she had been able to feel compassion for him. Occasionally a burst of irritation might sweep over her at the thought of it but she was too fond of him by now to be very sharp-tongued. She knew that Isobel had never viewed Will in that light and this private certainty increased her compassion and made her kind.

She was sure that Will would come to terms with Isobel's absence; he was too positive, too cheerful a man, to allow himself to become bitter. There was something ridiculous in an elderly man falling in love with a much younger woman, and Bea knew that Will was aware of this and that the knowledge helped him to hide any emotions which might damage his self-respect. Sighing to herself, she began to assemble some tea. Toast by the fire and a

383

game of Scrabble might help to console him.
'No fool like an old fool,' she told herself.
'But it doesn't mean that it hurts less.'

*       *       *

Will, standing on the balcony, staring out
over the sea, would have agreed with her. He
had tried to conceal his disappointment from
both Isobel and Bea but he suspected that he
had not done too well. The shock had been too
great and the thought of losing Isobel filled him
with unhappiness. It had been a relief to
concentrate on Tessa and Giles and the court
case against Adrian Pearson but the pain had
been there, gnawing away in the background.
He knew now that she would never have
married him, that it had been a moment of
Indian summer madness on his part, but the
knowledge that she was gone from the cove,
that he would never hear her voice calling from
the kitchen or see her wandering on the beach,
was hard to bear.

For Bea's sake he tried to pull himself
together. There was still so much to be grateful
for and Bea's companionship was very
important to him. He wondered if it were the
genes they had inherited from old John
Rainbird which were responsible for the ease
they found together. He thought of Mathilda,
living peacefully here in the cove, and
wondered if she had known love. For some

reason the knowledge of her life here, the use of her belongings, a sense of her presence, brought him comfort and he took a deeper breath and raised his head. She, too, had stood here, holding this balustrade, listening to the boom of the surf against the shelving sand . . .

When Bea came into the room behind him, carrying the tray, he was able to come in from the balcony and smile at her with real happiness. He looked with pleasure around the room, at the two chairs pulled up to the hearth, the Scrabble board on the low table between them, and at the blue and yellow flames that danced over the bone-white salty wood. He took comfort from Mathilda's books on the bookshelves and her bureau in the alcove and the security of the house all about him. He saw that Bea was watching him and laughed a little.

'Ever feel that she's here?' he asked her. 'Old Mathilda? I get the feeling of her sometimes, d'you see? It's . . . comforting.' He chuckled at the expression on Bea's face. 'Crazy? Is that what you think?'

'Possibly.' Bea went to fasten the window and draw the curtains, concealing her delight at the genuine expression of contentment on his face. 'Probably. But for someone bordering on senile dementia you play a mean game of Scrabble. Best out of three games and the loser does the washing-up. Have you seen the toasting fork . . .?'

Evening advanced across the darkening water. The moon rose above a ragged wrack of black cloud, pouring its cold brilliance down upon the cove where the waves rushed in over the sand and the only sound was the eternal murmurings of the restless sea.

We hope you have enjoyed this Large Print book. Other Chivers Press or Thorndike Press Large Print books are available at your library or directly from the publishers.

For more information about current and forthcoming titles, please call or write, without obligation, to:

Chivers Press Limited
Windsor Bridge Road
Bath BA2 3AX
England
Tel. (01225) 335336

OR

Thorndike Press
P.O. Box 159
Thorndike, Maine 04986
USA
Tel. (800) 223-2336

All our Large Print titles are designed for easy reading, and all our books are made to last.